Praise for Ca

'Genuinely unputdownable books are rare in
my experience. This is one. A brilliant,
original comedy'
Daily Mail

'A joyously wicked read that will cheer you up no end.
A genuine tonic. So clever, so funny and so refreshingly
different. I loved it'
Ruth Jones, co-creator of *Gavin & Stacey*

'I have a feeling Caroline Hulse might be a genius, this
book is so brilliant. Funny, clever and original'
Lucy Vine, author of *Hot Mess*

'Razor-sharp comedy'
Sunday Mirror

'Witty, whip-smart and wincingly observant, pure
entertainment from start to finish. A Caroline Hulse
book is a reading highlight of my year'
Cathy Bramley, author of *The Lemon Tree Café*

'I loved *The Adults*! Funny, dry and beautifully observed.
Highly recommended'
Gill

Caroline Hulse lives in Manchester with her husband and a small controlling dog. Her books have been published in fourteen languages and optioned for television.

All the Fun of the Fair is her third novel.

By Caroline Hulse

The Adults
Like A House On Fire
All the Fun of the Fair

All the Fun of the Fair

Caroline Hulse

ORION

An Orion paperback
First published in Great Britain in 2021 by Orion Fiction,
an imprint of The Orion Publishing Group Ltd.,
Carmelite House, 50 Victoria Embankment
London EC4Y 0DZ

An Hachette UK Company

1 3 5 7 9 10 8 6 4 2

A CIP catalogue record for this book is
available from the British Library.

ISBN (Mass Market Paperback) 978 1 4091 9725 6
ISBN (eBook) 978 1 4091 9726 3

Typeset by Input Data Services Ltd, Somerset

Printed and bound in Great Britain by Clays Ltd, Elcograf S.p.A.

MIX
Paper from
responsible sources
FSC® C104740

www.orionbooks.co.uk

All the Fun of the Fair

PROLOGUE

Every year at primary school, the teachers held a special lesson when the fair came to town.

When I was six, we drew the fair.

Hunched over my section of the art table, I scratched out stick figures and shapes, mashing the coloured pencils across my sugar paper with a hard fist. I zigzagged across the page, showing the blur of a busy crowd.

'Great work!' Mrs Finnegan said. 'Now get your names on your pictures so we can put them on the wall.'

Mrs Finnegan must have taught little kids for so long, she'd forgotten what good pictures looked like.

Six-year-olds' drawings. On the *wall*.

When I was seven, we painted it.

I outlined a smash of candyfloss and people and lights. I circled my brush through purples and yellows in a whirling merry-go-round, stopping before the colours turned brown. I painted shapes round the edges, filling the paper.

I felt I was doing OK – until Martha leaned over the art table. 'Is that a *chicken*?'

I dropped my paintbrush. I shot my arms straight by my sides, hands pointing down like a soldier's. 'No.'

'It's got a beak, though.'

Green paint glooped from my brush onto the picture.

'You do know what the fair is, *Fi–on–a*? You're not getting confused with pets' corner?'

'I *did* paint a chicken, I remember now.' I gripped my seat with both hands. 'One of the farmers brought his best chicken to the fair with him. As a treat.'

Martha looked round the table at the others and held her mouth open in a silent laugh. A string of spit hung between her top and bottom sets of teeth.

I knocked my paintbrush onto my skirt, making a green splat, which worked because Mrs Leyland came over and made a fuss. But then I went home and Mum made that revving noise in her throat, and went on about *being careful* and *is that washable? Please tell me it's washable,* and *Jonathan, have a look at this mess,* and *you're lucky we won't make you go to school in your pants tomorrow, Fiona.*

Which I knew wasn't true, even then.

And now I'm eleven, I *know* it's not true. (Because of paedos.)

Still, I was in trouble.

When I was eight, school had just broken up for the summer when the fair came to town.

That was a good year.

When I was nine, we wrote haikus.

> *The fair is so loud*
> *The rides spin and people scream*
> *And so do my ears.*

I knew how the fair sounded. I'd hung out of my bedroom window like Rapunzel – except a crap Rapunzel who has nothing to dangle out, whose hair only reaches her shoulders because her mum says it's easier to manage that way.

I leaned out of the window and I heard the screams and the fast, fuzzy music. I watched the glow of the dancing lights, bouncing back from the metal shutters of the garage over the road.

The rides are so fun
That the people inside feel
The joy of a king.

When I was ten, Mum had a word with my teacher, and there wasn't a special lesson.

But kids brought their winning toys in anyway, a fluffy turquoise army of stuffed owls, all propped up fatly up at the side of the room against their owners' lunchboxes. *This is what you could have had.*

'Where's your owl, Fiona?' Martha asked, though she knew the answer.

'Didn't get one.' I held my voice light. 'Don't like owls.'

That evening, I stopped with Mum and Grandma at a service station, and spotted a claw machine magically full of the same stuffed owls, all wedged inside, edge-to-edge, in a turquoise, big-eyed sea.

When Mum and Grandma went into the toilet cubicles, I nipped back out to the machine with the pound coins Grandma had just given me.

I put the first pound in the slot and concentrated on the buttons.

Steer steer steer stop. Steer steer steer stop. Drop.

A wing! Yesss, hold on tight! It's going up but what's that, don't slip, no no no, please don't, please don't – no!

I put the next pound in.

3

I hooked an eye. The pincer looked firmly lodged behind the plastic and lifted the owl confidently, straight up, with only the tiniest sway, but – *hang on, what are you doing? You were gripping! KEEP GRIPPING, please don't – no!*

I put the coins in, one after another, pushing desperately at the buttons. Watching the claw pinch my chosen owl and lift it for a few magical seconds. Watching in slow motion as the claw dropped the owl, sending it rotating slowly through the air, bumping back into the fluffy turquoise sea.

Mum and Grandma found me there, in tears.

'You spent it all?' Grandma's T-shirt said *Don't Worry, Be Happy*. 'But why, darling?'

Mum made a line with her lips. 'You just snuck out of the toilets without asking? And thought it was OK?'

'All the kids have owls. They got them at the fair.'

Grandma turned to Mum. 'Gail,' she said softly.

Mum made hard eyes at Grandma. 'What were you thinking of, Mum, giving a kid ten pounds for no reason?'

'Hey now.' Grandma stood up straighter. 'I can give my granddaughter treats when I can afford it.'

Mum shook her head. 'If you'd asked me, I'd have told you she wouldn't spend it on anything useful.' Mum made a jerky gesture at me. 'And now she's all upset.'

I cried some more. 'Can you give me more money, Grandma?'

Grandma glanced at Mum and gave me a flat smile of *no*. And it wasn't mentioned again, though Grandma did post me a stuffed owl toy when she was back in Glasgow at the weekend. I said *thank you*, like I meant it, and didn't tell her the owl was the wrong size and colour, with long skinny woven legs rather than a ball of fluff. I didn't tell her it was the wrong owl, and a week too late.

4

*

Mr Lincoln might not have mentioned the fair in class that year – the year I went double digits, not as life-changing as I was expecting – but it was all anyone talked about in the playground.

'If you're a group of girls, you get pushed by the fit boy on the Waltzers.' Martha cradled her owl like a baby, supporting its head. 'How old do you think the boy is, Fiona?'

I swallowed a crisp. It spiked my throat from the inside. 'Eighteen?'

'Hmm.' Martha looked at Amy and back. 'Did anyone see Fiona at the fair?'

The other girls shook their heads with their whole bodies, the action reflecting sunlight from the big owl eyes they all had sticking out of the tops of their rucksacks.

I swallowed hard but the crisp stayed lodged. 'Probably no one saw me because I went at night. On Thursday.' I put my hands to my throat. 'At eleven o'clock. My parents say I'm mature so I'm fine to stay up.'

Martha nodded. 'What was your favourite ride?'

I thumped my throat with my fists to make the crisp move. 'Ghost Train.'

Martha looked at the others and back. 'The Ghost Train was out of order on Thursday.' She spoke in a voice that was so kind, it did a whole circle back to not being kind at all.

'It *was* out of order.' I didn't notice the stuck crisp anymore. 'But my dad fixed it.'

Martha looked at the others and back at me.

'He used to fix things,' I said. 'He was an engineer before he was a postman. That's actually true.'

I know now that if you say *that's actually true*, it doesn't help.

5

Martha shook her head at me. 'The Ghost Train wasn't broken on Thursday. It was a test.'

I pretended to see something fascinating in the nature area.

'You failed the test,' Martha said.

I narrowed my eyes at the imaginary thing. 'Hang on, is that . . .'

I moved across the playground, as if pulled by the beam of a UFO. Past Mr Crane, who was shouting, 'Stop bunching!' at the footballing boys moving in one zigzagging clump.

I stood by the nature area, studying a bit of soil. I pretended I didn't notice what the girls were saying behind me. Even though the words were being said specially for me.

That might have been the same day I cut off Martha's plait.

In fact – I'm pretty sure it was.

But because school scissors are rubbish, I didn't get the whole way through. I was still sawing at the plait when Mr Lincoln ran over and grabbed me. Still, I was happy with all the hair on the floor by the time he managed to pull me away.

Turns out kids like me are the reason they give you blunt scissors in primary school.

That night, alone in my bedroom *to think about what I had done*, I sat with my book of lists.

Next Year

1) I'll be eleven
2) It'll be 1996
3) I'll have started high school
4) I'll finally be in the same school as Lewis Harris from swimming club

5) I'll have *other* friends too – proper ones. Girls, even. Definitely not Martha.

6) I won't do weird stuff anymore

7) I'll be <u>normal</u>

Normal. No more of the bad stuff, the *Fiona* stuff – like the plait-cutting, or that thing with the monkey bars. The kind of stuff I didn't know why it happened, except it just did because I was STUPID STUPID FIONA.

Not next year. If anyone asked about me next year, people would say, *Fiona Larson? Oh, she's the normal one. Really normal.*

I added the most important line.

8) I'll GO TO THE FAIR

I snapped my book shut.
Next year. It was happening.
Next year.

I

One year later

A good spy stays alert to changes in his surroundings.
The Junior Spy's Secret Handbook™

Thirty-nine days to the fair
I found the secret bag on the way to school, on the first day back after half-term.

I'd been walking through the park, looking up at the blackening sky, wondering when summer would feel, well, *summery*, like in the adverts, when I spotted a white shape between the leaves of the park's second-biggest bush.

I dropped my rucksack on the grass, hitched up my skirt, and crawled into the bush's open den-space. I pulled the white shape – a plastic bag – from the leaves, my heart beating fast. I took a breath and opened the bag.

Magazines. Nine magazines – all with girls on the front.
So many girls.

Girls in underwear, girls in bikinis. Naked girls with their arms covering their bits.

It's a long time since I've believed in hidden treasure, but still.

I flicked through the first magazine.

Inside – girls, *everywhere*. Naked girls, *without* arms over

9

their bits. Girls in the shower, lying-down girls. Girls on all fours, sleepy girls, confused-looking girls. Girls with no clothes on, but still in shoes. Girls who looked both old and young at the same time, who didn't look anything like the girls I knew. Or the mums. I didn't think even Selina Baker and the sixth-formers would look like *this* naked.

After looking at so many pages, my brain was swimming with bellybuttons and legs and boobs, so I took a break by reading an article: *My Favourite Things, by Kelly, 18, 36–24–36, from Winchester.*

Turned out Kelly liked spending cosy evenings in with a nice fella, watching the soaps, and taking long rosy-cheeked walks with her dog in the New Forest.

I turned the page and Kelly and her friends were gone, replaced by new, shiny girls in underwear. I closed the magazine and looked up at the trees.

All in all, it was a lot to take in. I wasn't sure I actually liked the magazines, though they were clearly treasure, so the best thing that had ever happened to me.

But I couldn't be late for registration or I'd get done, so I slotted Kelly from Winchester back in with the others and pushed the bag back between the branches.

I crawled out of the bush and hurried into school.

I'm not meant to walk into school on my own, even though I'm nearly twelve. The hours either side of the school day are the best hours – *my* time. I don't have to hurry home from school or tell my parents what I'm doing, not as long as I'm with a friend.

I was only on my own on the way in that day because, for some reason, Lewis wasn't there to meet me at the lamppost, and you can't always rely on Sean.

It's fair enough that Sean doesn't always want to walk in with us. He might have been good friends with Lewis back when they were both at Beech Avenue Primary, but there are two hundred kids in our year at high school. There are a lot more kids for Sean to choose from now.

Lewis is my best friend – has been since I lent him 10p for a cup of Ribena in the leisure centre café after swimming club, when we were seven. But Lewis isn't as good as other boys, and it's not his fault, exactly. It's just Lewis doesn't like football. And he doesn't have a good coat and rucksack, and everyone knows, if you go to his house, the glasses taste of dishwasher. But Sean *does* have a good coat and rucksack, and he *does* like football, so Sean can make friends with better boys – maybe not the lads from the blue estate, not all the time, but better boys than Lewis. And *actual* boys, so better than me.

These are the facts of our school so, once you get your head round them, you can't mind.

I was desperate to tell Lewis about the secret, but he's not in my registration class.

Dr Sharma, who is my form tutor as well as my science teacher, watched me hurry into the room just as the bell was ringing. She sat at her high lab bench with the locked fridge behind her, the fridge that kids say holds bleeding animal hearts.

Dr Sharma marked me off in her book. 'Fiona. I was just asking who needs the day off for the farm show tomorrow, but I don't need to ask you, do I?'

I tried to hold Dr Sharma's gaze. I ended up looking at the bleeding-heart fridge.

'The *day off for the farm show* rule only applies to farming families, as you well know,' Dr Sharma said. 'Are you saying you're from a farming family now?'

I gave a tiny nod.

'Fiona, your mum's car is always outside school and it says *Gail Larson, Driving Instructor* right there on the side.'

That got a laugh from the other kids. And a round of *'(cough)-Gail!*'s.

Mum's job causes me loads of problems. If you wanted to design a job to make your kid look stupid, it would be one where you wait outside the school gates in a car with your kid's surname on it. Mum doesn't understand why *'(cough)-Gail!'* is a problem. But she also doesn't understand Lewis's parents shouldn't have taken him to France at Easter – that no one had thought how easy to chant *'Lewis Harris went to Paris'* would be.

Dr Sharma was still talking.

'And I know your dad's a postman, Fiona, because he delivers to my house. We talk about the seasonal visitors at my bird table.'

I shuffled to an empty lab bench and pulled out a stool.

Dr Sharma gave me a long look. 'So I don't appreciate being treated like I was born yesterday.'

I sat down. 'I'm not asking for a day off for the farm show.'

Dr Sharma moved on to taking the register while I unpacked my pencil case.

The bell rang and I stayed where I was for science. Some kids left the room and others came in. The high lab tables were all made for two stools, and every table except mine had two people on it, but that was fine. It meant I had a spare stool for my bag and I could get my books out without leaning down. On experiment days, I even got the Bunsen burner to myself, and didn't have to take turns with another kid.

It was better this way. I would have chosen it this way.

Today was a day to work on our summer projects. There was clattering and unzipping all around, and I watched the other kids get their project books out. Most of their projects had pictures of leaves and trees on the front – probably because we'd just been taught photosynthesis. And because kids could fill lots of pages by gluing in leaves.

I pulled my own project book from my bag. *Blood, by Fiona Larson, 7E.* I'd written the title in postbox-red bubble letters and drawn the letters dripping down the cover, into a pool of blood at the bottom.

I've always liked blood. I've even said to Lewis we should swap blood, prick our fingers and mash them together to show we're proper friends. But he didn't like that idea.

I smoothed down the next blank page and started copying sentences from the textbook.

Blood is a bodily fluid. It has four main parts. They are plasma, red blood cells, white blood cells and platelets.

I kept copying for a bit longer until I remembered the secret bag, and then the excitement and daydreaming took over.

When the bell rang for break, I thought I'd finally get to tell Lewis about my secret, but I couldn't find him anywhere. And he wasn't in my English class, either. So there was nothing to do but listen to Mr Kellett bang on, while I imagined Lewis's face when I told him what I'd found.

This would *blow his mind.*

Sean *was* in my English class, but when I turned around to look at him, he didn't say *hi*, so I just turned back. It's fine, Sean's still my friend – it's not his fault he can't talk to me with other kids there. He's not the one who made the rules of school.

Mr Kellett was late, of course. He hurried in, his tie skew-whiff. As well as teaching English, he teaches PE. And when he moves from one type of class to the other, he has to get changed.

He turned to write *paradox* on the board. 'A paradox is a seemingly absurd or contradictory statement that, on reflection, may prove to make sense after all.'

Mr Kellett talked some more and I sort-of listened.

He didn't used to get changed between lessons. He used to do our English classes in his PE kit, his whistle round his neck, the hair on his legs just there, like a coat of fur. But that changed when our school got the New Head. These days, instead of a whistle round Mr Kellett's neck, there's a tie.

'So how can something,' he asked, 'mean two things at once?'

Things I Know About the New Head

1) She's called Mrs Shackleton
2) She makes Mr Kellett change out of his PE kit to teach English
3) She always wears an animal badge on her blouse
4) She likes things Just So – *Dr Sharma**
5) She makes it so you can't do anything right – *Miss Jarvis, RE**
6) She's an iron fist in a velvet glove – *Mr Carter, IT**
7) She's got gumption, I'll say that about her – *Mr Kellett**
8) She just doesn't understand about the relevance of RE, that it's about so much more than just organised religion, it's about society – *Miss Jarvis, again**

9) She's as bad as bloody Thatcher – *still Miss Jarvis**
10) She wants to get rid of us all and bring in her own teachers, and then where will we all be? – *Miss Jarvis talks a lot**

*I use spying techniques from The Junior Spy's Secret Handbook™ to listen in on people. Grandma got me the handbook as a Christmas present. Mum wishes she hadn't.**
** Grandma also taught me about asterisks

Mr Kellett went on a bit longer. He talked about what's true and what's not, and different perceptions, and two things being true at once, and it was all a bit complicated for someone whose mind was on important bag-related things.

He cleared his throat. 'Now write a paradox of your own.'

After finding those magazines, I didn't even have to think. I picked up my pen straight away.

The best secrets can be hidden in plain sight.

Mr Kellett leaned over my pad. 'Perfect. And also intriguing, Miss Larson!'

I held my breath because he was so close, though his smell wasn't as bad as some teachers'. Mr Kellett did loads of sport, but his smell was wet towel mixed with broken twigs, whereas Mr Matheson in Music did *no* sport and smelled of *actual* BO. He was always lifting up his arms to conduct us on our triangles and recorders, shaking the smell up and wafting it over.

Mr Kellett smiled at me. 'And what are the best secrets, I wonder?'

I gave my head a tiny shake and took a gulpy breath. *Wet towel broken twigs.*

From the back of the room, Liam leaned back in his chair.

'Sir, how about people saying Leeds United are a quality football team – is that one?' Which I don't think counted, and Liam only said it because Mr Kellett supports Leeds. But everyone burst into laughter and Mr Kellett smiled. And Sean caught my eye while he was laughing and then looked quickly away.

I found Lewis in the computer room that lunchtime.

'You should have walked in with me.' I threw my rucksack down onto the floor and dropped into the chair next to him. The chair rolled backwards on its wheels. 'You'll wish you had.'

Lewis kept tapping the keyboard, like I wasn't there. His rhino on the screen leapt up platforms.

I got my sandwich box from my rucksack. 'I found a bag. Of secrets.'

Lewis paused his tapping. A baddie walked into his rhino and the screen flashed red, black and white. *Game Over.*

He wanted to ask, I know he did. But he was being stubborn.

I opened my sandwich box. 'Why didn't you meet me at the lamppost? And where were you at break?'

He inched his chair round, finally looking at me. 'You wouldn't let me show you my magic trick at the weekend.'

'But we were outside the newsagent's. There were *people* around.'

Yes, I'd stopped Lewis doing a magic trick. But he knew the rules.

How to be Normal

1) Don't eat any weird food for packed lunches. And no eggs.
2) Don't talk to yourself when you're on your own
3) Push your socks down
4) Have a school jumper exactly the right shade of green. Don't let your mum buy one from the market.
5) If you're wearing sports clothes, make sure they always have exactly three stripes
6) Don't get angry if you're being picked on, just pretend you don't notice
7) Don't do any old-Fiona stuff, like the thing with the monkey bars
8) Definitely no magic tricks where anyone can see you (LEWIS)
9) Be allowed to go to the fair

This list is not exhaustive. That's what it said at the bottom of the new school rules Mrs Shackleton brought in.

Anyway, number eight, right there, in ballpoint pen. *No magic tricks.*

Even though Lewis is the only person allowed to look in my book of lists, he doesn't always seem pleased.

'Anyway,' Lewis couldn't wait any longer, 'tell me about this bag of secrets.'

After lunch, we had drama. It was the only class I had with Lewis and we sat together in the circle of kids in the school hall.

He'd forgiven me, of course. How could he not? I had a *secret bag*.

'All right, everyone.' Mrs Vernal clapped her hands and the circle of kids went quiet. 'What does drama mean to you? Really?'

Mrs Vernal was new. The old drama teacher left to have a baby and this one took up just as much space as the pregnant teacher in the corridors. Mrs Vernal was made up of lots of layers, and always had a bit of scarf flapping about her.

'Drama's about acting,' Katie Russell said.

'Not *just* acting,' Mrs Vernal said. 'It's bigger than that.'

Mrs Vernal made eye contact wth me, but there was no way I was answering. Nothing good ever comes from answering questions at school.

'Drama' – Mrs Vernal made sure we all felt her looking into our eyes, one by one – 'is about self-development. It's about *life*.' Pause. 'It's about getting to the *emotional truth* within.'

We all nodded.

'Do you all understand what I mean by *emotional truth*?'

We all nodded again. Nodded just hard enough for her not to say it again. Not so hard that she asked us to explain.

No, I don't answer questions in class. There was a kid once, about ten years ago, who said 'orgasm' in science when he meant to say 'organism'. Simon Rutherson, that was his name. He's a scaffolder now. Whenever kids in Monkford see scaffolding, we stand underneath and shout up *'Orgasm!'* – just in case he's there.

Mrs Vernal clapped. 'Everyone get up!'

We dotted ourselves around the school hall. I stood in front of a long curtain, looking at the layer of dust across it like a lace sheet. Hundreds of dust speckles. Millions.

Numbers too big make me feel weird and dizzy, so I made myself stop thinking.

Mrs Vernal weaved between us, her heels like tap shoes on the polished floor, the noise echoing up to the hall's high ceiling.

'I don't want you to act. I want you to *feel*.' *Tap, tap, tap*. 'I want you to think about a time you were really excited.' *Tap, tap, tap*. 'How does it feel in your toes? In your fingertips?' Mrs Vernal tapped over to the other side of the hall. 'I want you to hear what you heard and smell what you smelled. *Go!*'

I heard thumping sounds behind. Flashes of movement reflected in the windows as kids fist-thrusted the air and jumped up and down.

I closed my eyes and remembered how it felt to wait for the special sundae in the American diner on my last birthday. But it was hard to get *that* worked up, ten months later.

Mrs Vernal circled the room. Making little comments, adjusting people. *Tap, tap, tap*.

I noticed a lot of kids were showing excitement by scoring goals. England had drawn with Switzerland the week before in their first game of Euro '96, which meant there was even more football talk at school than usual.

It also meant Nino – the shy Year Eight Swiss kid whose dad came over here to work at the medical plant – wasn't having a brilliant time of it.

'Now,' Mrs Vernal said, 'let that feeling go. Shake yourselves.'

I stared at the dust on the curtain, listening to the rustling and jangling of bracelets against watches. The sound of thirty kids flapping limp arms round their bodies.

I've always tried to like football. It's a boy thing, so a good thing, and liking it would be really useful. I mean to keep trying it till I like it. You have to put the effort in with a lot of the best things – cigarettes too, I hear. You can't stop trying just because they're awful at first, or you'll *never* learn to smoke.

'Let's do a different emotion.' *Tap, tap, tap.* 'Think about a time you were sad.'

I felt a hand on my shoulder.

'Don't do the sad exercise, Fiona. Join in for the next one.' Mrs Vernal patted me twice and was gone.

Twenty minutes later, we were doing *thoughtful* (lots of frowning and fingers on lips) when the bell rang.

'That's it.' Mrs Vernal clapped her hands. 'Enjoy your evenings.'

I turned to get my rucksack.

'Fiona.' She caught my arm. 'Stay with me.'

I waved Lewis to go on ahead.

Mrs Vernal waited until the last kid had left. 'I just wanted you to know, I'll look out for you in this class, Fiona. Drama can be a purpose, a saviour – but also a risk.'

I felt my forehead bunch.

'It might get hard for you, the more we zero in on the emotional truth within.'

I nodded.

'Fiona?' Mrs Vernal made her voice a special soft. 'I heard that your sister died.'

I felt my forehead unbunch. *Ah.*

'You will have more powerful feelings than most kids your age. You're in control of those feelings and it's up to you whether you use them. This class should be a safe place for you.'

'OK,' I said.

'If things ever get too much, I'm always here.'

'Right.'

Mrs Vernal seemed to be waiting for something. 'Always here. For you to talk to.'

'OK,' I said. 'Thanks. Bye.'

I hurried out of the school hall. Lewis was waiting with our coats.

He handed mine over. 'What did you do?'

'Nothing.' I took the coat and put it on. 'She wanted to talk about Danielle.'

Lewis shook his head. *People.*

2

The best secrets can be hidden in plain sight.

(paradox)

Thirty-nine days to the fair

Lewis and I headed straight for the park after school, down pavements damp and black from the recent rain shower. Water droplets glistened on bushes as we passed, and that smoky just-rained smell filled the air.

Despite the rain, when we got to our bush, the den-space inside was dry.

The two of us sat cross-legged inside, pulling magazines out of the plastic bag and sliding them back in.

'It *is*. I didn't believe it could happen, but it *is*.' Lewis looked up from leafing. 'It's hidden treasure.'

'I don't know how Finders Keepers works in a park situation.' I picked up a magazine. 'Are these ours now?'

I held the magazine up to look at the cover.

This girl stood in a bra and tiny shorts. She pulled her shorts down at one side so you could see how flat her tummy was. Her body was wet but her face was thick with make-up, like she'd had a shower but kept her face out of the water. She looked sleepy.

'Do you like her?' I asked.

Lewis kept looking at the girl. 'She's fit.'

He glanced at me.

'Fit,' he said again. He looked away.

I nodded and pretended it didn't sound wrong coming from Lewis. We've all got to practise this stuff, and it's better to do it in front of friends.

He turned the page. *My Favourite Things, by Kelly, 18, 36–24–36, from Winchester.*

'I know she's scowling in the picture,' I said. 'But she's friendly in the article. See, she's given out her phone number.'

'She can't want loads of calls though – she's only given the short number.' Lewis tapped *36–24–36.* 'You'd have to look up the area code if you weren't local.'

He closed the magazine and handed it back.

I slid it back into the plastic bag. 'I don't like leaving these here. It's not safe.'

'Who do you think they belong to?' Lewis had to ruin it.

We both went quiet.

I pictured a huge, scary man, shaking with anger – a massive snarling face on a wall of man-rock. Arm muscles veiny and bulging like Popeye's.

'Let's leave them here for now, and make a decision tomorrow,' I said.

'Let's not tell anyone. Or they'll all want a look.'

'Does this mean you've forgiven me?'

'Almost,' Lewis said.

I pushed the bag between the branches. 'Sweet.'

On the way home, I saw our next-door neighbour, Mrs Carpenter, across the street, walking her Papillon. She was wearing a baseball cap, even though she was nearly as old as Grandma.

We waved.

I like Mrs Carpenter, even though I'd preferred Mr Carpenter when he was around. He always offered me Polos and, if we had shopping bags, he'd make a point of coming over and asking if we'd bought tomatoes or courgettes and how much we'd paid for them, because *the supermarkets see you coming* and it's *so much cheaper to grow them yourself*!

He'd tell us this every time, even though we'd heard it before. Even the times we hadn't bought any tomatoes or courgettes.

But he moved out last year and moved in with his brother's wife, and I'm not meant to ask about him.

His brother's wife was *welcome to him*. I found that out from Mrs Carpenter, in one of those spying missions that left me understanding less, not more.

The bad side of finding things out by spying is that you can't ask people to explain.

Later, I sat with Mum and Dad on the stools round the peninsula, eating Dad's homemade pizza.

That's what we call the bit of kitchen surface that sticks out: *the peninsula*. It sticks out of the wall under the diagonal bit where the stairs are, and I sit in the stool that fits under the stairs. It's fine, I just have to remember not to jerk my head around while I eat.

'I'm just wondering. If you found some special things in a public place'– I picked a piece of sweetcorn off my pizza – 'would it be stealing to sell the things?'

Dad looked at Mum. He'd finished work for the day, but was still wearing his postman's uniform.

'What valuable things have you found?' Dad asked.

'I haven't found anything, I'm just wondering how Finders Keepers works, exactly.'

He stared at me and I looked down.

Dad is too good at reading faces. He was born *significantly hearing-impaired*, but he says *deaf*. I forget most of the time, until something happens, like Dad needs me to make a phone call. He usually asks Mum to make his calls, but he always asks me if he wants to phone a premium rate line for a TV quiz show because *it's just less hassle this way, darling*.

Dad being deaf doesn't affect things much, except that he can't use the phone, and sometimes he needs something he's missed explaining. The good bit about it is he's always able to lipread what a footballer on telly is swearing. The bad bit is that our overhead lights flash when someone rings the doorbell. I've asked Mum and Dad if we can stop that, because it's embarrassing when kids come over, but Mum's face went hard and she said I *need to think about my priorities*.

So I just don't invite people over now. I love Dad – I wouldn't swap him. I wouldn't even swap Mum, most of the time. It's just sensible not to hand kids bullets about how your family's different from other people's.

Mum peered across the peninsula at me, eyes made into slits. 'Why are you asking about valuable things and Finders Keepers? Is this about the car boot sale?'

'It's nothing to do with the car boot sale.'

She wiped her fingers and adjusted the clip in her hair. She wore clips like two claws, that bounced back when stretched too far open. 'You wouldn't lie to me, Fiona? I really hope not.'

'Mrs Vernal mentioned Danielle today, out of nowhere,' I said quickly. 'Mrs Vernal. She's the new drama teacher.'

Mum reached for a slice of pizza. Pieces of her grey-blonde hair fell out of the clip again. She glanced at Dad and back to me. 'What did she say?'

'She just really, *really* wanted to talk about Danielle.'

Mum put the pizza slice down. 'What did she say *specifically*?'

'She said that I could use having a dead sister to get better at drama. She talked about *emotional truth*. She held me back at the end of class and told me she was *here for me*.'

Mum looked at Dad. '*Mrs Vernal*, you say?'

Dad put his pizza slice down. He put his hand on Mum's leg.

'Some people,' Mum adjusted her hair clip jerkily, not even wiping her fingers this time, 'like to insert themselves into other people's business.'

She pushed her plate across the peninsula, even though she hadn't finished her food, and the force of the push made hair fall out of her clip again. But my catalyst had worked because there was no more talk of Finders Keepers and the car boot sale.

Dr Sharma taught us about catalysts in science. I use Danielle as a catalyst to change conversations.

Thing is, when you're not quite twelve in a town that's thirty miles from the nearest city – where there's meant to be a retail park coming, with a cinema and megabowl but they've *still* not been built – where the most exciting events are kids putting bangers in cow pats, or farm boys riding into school on tractors on their sixteenth birthdays, and by *riding* I mean *trundling in slowly*, it sounds better than it is – well. Being a kid and being able to change a conversation is like a superpower.

My big sister died.

Some people head-tilt and go quiet. Some people ask questions.

Mrs Vernal is one of those who tell me how sad I am. She *wants* me to be sad, though she either doesn't know the full story or she hasn't thought it through. Because you don't get sad about someone you never met. Except if you're told there was this girl who used to live in your house, who *still* has a better bedroom than you, who laid the table without being asked and was a *good eater*.

So maybe I *am* sad. Maybe I'm sad I can't go back fourteen years and grab Danielle's arm and say *fine, you're going to die and I'm sorry, but could you say you don't like eggs? In fourteen years' time I'm going to have to eat sweetcorn because of you.*

Sometimes, when Mum talks about Danielle, it's like she forgets we were never all here at the same time. She talks like our family once had the right number for Hungry Hippos. Like we were once a family who once needed the fourth peninsula stool, rather than keeping it in the cupboard under the stairs.

And sometimes I wonder whether I should stop pointing out that I'm the replacement. Whether I should forget what the truth is, and try to believe Mum's instead.

Mum especially forgets me and Danielle weren't around at the same time when it comes to summer holidays.

She was looking at Cornwall hotels in the kitchen with Dad later that night, while I worked on a jigsaw in the lounge. I could hear what she was doing without needing to spy at all.

'SHIT THE BED!' There was a furious tapping – Mum

stabbing at a brochure with an angry finger. 'Jonathan, look at the single supplement for this one!'

Things That Make My Mum Angry

1) Single supplements
2) Me *not thinking about my priorities*
3) Me, generally
4) People cutting her up at roundabouts, especially if they're driving BMWs
5) People who walk *too* slowly in front of her, on the street or in a supermarket
6) Me telling another adult that she wanted to know how much money they had*
7) People who say they knew Danielle really well when they didn't
8) Snails on the step that don't move out of the way because *it's their fault if they go and get stepped on* and *they can't come crying to me*
9) Grandma buying unsuitable presents
10) The women from work who treated Danielle's funeral like an outing because they stopped at M&S on the way back
11) The timing sheets system at Parents' Evening
12) Me asking to go to the fair
13) Mrs Vernal (new)

I only did this once.
This list is definitely – definitely – not exhaustive.

Mum was still with Dad in the kitchen – 'LOOK! JONATHAN! What are the single beds made of, actual diamonds?' – when I heard a thud at the lounge window.

I pushed my jigsaw away. I ran to the window and looked out.

A sparrow lay on the paving stone below the window, its legs sticking into the air, cartoon-upright.

I let myself out of the front door. I picked the bird up carefully and rested it on my hand.

It was warm. I felt a flutter of movement inside it.

I rested the sparrow on top of the hedge so the estate cats couldn't get it. I looked back at the window, at the round greasy mark, whirling like a massive fingerprint.

When I checked the bird a few minutes later, it had gone. But the bird-head-fingerprint mark was still there. Below the mark was the back of a photo frame.

I sniffed. I bet I knew why that bird got distracted and flew into the glass. I knew what it was thinking.

Another one, I can't believe it. Another *photo of that dead kid on a windowsill.*

3

If you tell a kid not to do something, you might give them
the idea in the first place.

(paradox)

Thirty-eight days to the fair

I met Lewis at our lamppost on George Street the next
morning. He walked towards me, his anorak hood up, even
though it was hardly raining.

We nodded at each other and fell into step, crossing the
road when we reached the postbox.

'Wait for me!' Sean hurried to catch us.

I looked at Sean's feet. 'You're only allowed to wear black
socks with the uniform, You're going to get done.'

Sean pushed his hand through his hair. 'So, I get done, so
what?'

That's when I knew we were meant to notice his white
socks, but he was pretending we weren't.

These things might sound complicated if you're not at
our school, but they make sense once you've been there a
while.

*

The three of us walked through the park and Lewis and I glanced at each other. We knew what the other was thinking. We wanted to check the bag of magazines was still there, but we didn't want to tell Sean.

Sean's not as good at keeping secrets as us.

Or not as good with *our* secrets anyway. Sean told everyone Lewis was rubbish at the high jump after we held an Olympics in Lewis's back garden. Sean told everyone I was trying on a new accent – and really, there was nothing wrong with that, loads of people who only ever lived on cul-de-sacs in Monkford talk like the brothers from Oasis.

So I got nervous as we approached the second-biggest bush because Lewis is a panicker. Causes me loads of problems.

I thought quickly. 'You know when I turn twelve in August, I'll overtake Danielle. She was eleven when she died.'

Sean and Lewis both looked away.

'Our second-biggest bedroom is still kept for Danielle. But *I'll* be the oldest when I turn twelve.' I could make out a hint of white plastic through the branches. '*And* I'm alive. Do you think Mum and Dad will give me the second bedroom on my birthday?'

'No.' Lewis was looking at gravel path in front of him. 'And I definitely don't think you should ask your mum.'

Lewis is scared of my mum, more than any other adult. He's not used to a shouty mum because his is the quiet type.

Anyway, my catalyst worked, because we were now past the second-biggest bush and nearly at the playground.

Lewis and I glanced at each other. I gave a small nod.

A day, that bag of magazines had been there now. A whole day – at least. And no one had come to collect it yet.

*

After registration, we had a year-group assembly in the sports hall. We sat cross-legged on gym mats, low-level conversation all around as we waited for the assembly to start.

It was meant to be one of those *talent* assemblies, with kids with hobbies showing off, all hoping to wow the crowd. Kids who'd been told skills impressed people and won friends.

Kids who hadn't thought through what would happen when they left the sports hall. Who'd spend all lunchtime begging bigger kids for their juggling balls back.

Mrs Vernal stood at the front of the sports hall, waiting. Something felt different today. Dr Sharma and the other Year Seven form teachers looked more serious than usual.

I felt the waft of the door opening and shutting behind me. At the back of the room, the chattering stopped. The kids at the side of the hall, the ones with their jazz shoes and flutes, stood straighter. Even *the teachers* stood straighter.

I felt her before I saw her. The New Head.

Across the aisle, Liam hadn't noticed the air change. 'And his stereo has got two CD players and—'

The New Head padded up to him. She waited, looking at the floor, doing an impression of someone shy. The eyes of a cheetah brooch glinted out from her neat turquoise jumper.

Finally, Liam glanced up.

He shrank – instantly. *Liam.* One of the best kids in our year.

The New Head stood there a moment longer, letting Liam's fear properly soak in.

She walked to the front of the room and turned to face us. 'I've been contacted by the head at Radcliffe High School.'

Just the sound of her voice made my stomach squish. It was so calm and quiet, in the room that was otherwise silent.

'A group of his Year Tens were playing *chicken* on the railway track, and a child has been seriously injured by an oncoming train. He is in hospital. He will never be the same again.'

Not a whisper.

'I wanted you all to hear me say, personally, that playing *chicken* is the stupidest thing a child can do. And if any of you – *any of you*' – she looked into as many eyes as possible – 'risk the safety of yourselves or your fellow children in that way, you will feel the full force of my wrath.'

The New Head nodded to Mrs Vernal and walked out of the room. The only sound was the brush of the door as it came to a close, behind her.

Mrs Vernal took a step forward. 'That must be such upsetting news for you all.' Her eyes were shiny, but not crying-shiny. 'Awful.'

No one said anything.

'You need to take this as a learning opportunity. You're going to learn how not to follow the herd. You're going to learn about real life at this school – especially in drama.'

Did Dr Sharma exchange a look with Miss Jarvis?

'Resilience, not just the syllabus. You're going to *grow*.' Mrs Vernal pulled at her scarf like it was too tight. 'Does anyone have anything they want to share with the group?'

Everyone looked at the floor.

'These can be difficult years.' Mrs Vernal paced in front of the sports ladders at the front of the room. 'Remember – you are the star of your own life. You flower for yourselves, not for anyone else.' She turned and paced in the other direction. 'Being a teenager is hard.'

Teenager. *If only.* I wasn't even twelve till after the school year ended.

If I could change one thing in my life, I'd have been born in September, not August.

And being allowed to go to the fair, obviously.

And Danielle not being such a good eater.

And Mum realising dead people don't need bedrooms.

Still – *chicken*. And a *train*. There was a kid in hospital right now, who would never be the same again.

Maybe, today, being Fiona Larson right now wasn't completely awful, after all.

Lewis and I hurried straight to the park after school.

We passed a bunch of kids gathered around the big wasps' nest, taking turns to go up close, practically touching the nest, before jerking away again, and indicating to the next kid to do the same. Playing *chicken*.

I shook my head. 'The assembly must have given them the idea.'

Lewis shuddered – at the wasps, or the thought of disobeying the New Head, or both.

We checked the kids weren't watching us and walked up to the second-biggest bush, as though it was any other bush in the park. We climbed into the den space and – *sweet!* The magazines were still there!

We spread them out and went through them again.

We learned how to keep a girl happy in bed (*foreplay* and the *clitoris*). We learned about *premature ejaculation* and how to *keep the wolf from the door* by thinking about snooker and *Gardeners' World*. We learned to always flick past *Readers' Wives*, which raised more questions than answers and made Lewis, especially, feel like he needed a little break.

One of the magazines was different from all the others, and only showed the girls in underwear, not naked. It broke up all the girl pictures with other things – an interview with an actor, a page giving star ratings to different shaving foams, and a small section on films. We wouldn't get as much money for this magazine, but it was our favourite.

I stared at the picture from a film's car chase scene. 'When I'm a spy, I'm going to be the clever one who gets to drive, not the girl one who's the passenger.' I turned a page. 'And there's no way I'd let myself get kidnapped.'

With all our attention, some of the magazine pages were starting to look a bit ruffled. The cover with the sleepy wet/dry girl had got creased where Lewis had accidentally sat on it.

'The owner will be able to tell we've read his magazines.' I pushed the cover with my fist, straightening it. 'He's going to be furious now whatever, so I might as well take them. Finders Keepers rules says two days is fine.' And before I could think too much about it, I slid the magazines into the plastic bag and into my rucksack. I hurried out of the bush before I could think about what I'd done.

Lewis rushed after me, trying to put a rucksack on at the same time. 'I can't believe you did that!'

'We can sit on the swings and watch the bush. *Surveillance*, my spy book calls it. If the owner comes back, we can give him the magazines and say it was a joke.'

We sat on the swings. Out of the corner of my eye, I saw Lewis inch a pack of cards out of his pocket.

'Lewis! Not now!'

He pushed his cards back in.

I started swinging, even though I never swing anymore, not even when no one can see, on the swing in our garden. Only little kids swing. I just swung that day because we were there, doing surveillance.

I swung high enough for the chains to jolt, pointing my legs upwards, and made sure not to look at the sky. It's something about how big and empty space is – how the planets are just floating there and nothing's strapped in and there's so much *nothing*. It makes me dizzy.

Looking down, from this height, I could see the whole park. And there was no angry man going into the second-biggest bush to look for his treasure.

I'd done it. I'd taken the magazines and it was Finders Keepers, fair and square.

I was safe.

But I didn't have long to celebrate.

I'd said goodbye to Lewis and was heading back home, thinking how pleasingly full my rucksack felt, when I saw it.

I stopped and stared. I wrapped my arms around my body.

Opposite the petrol station, where there had been an advert for cat food that morning, there was now a new billboard.

Monkford Fair. Festival Field. Fri 19–Mon 22 July.

A clown face loomed out of the picture, the clown's smile so wide it looked mean. A cartoon picture of a Waltzer car whirled so fast that the people inside were just a blur.

I kept staring.

It's time.

My heart got fuller. My breath tighter.

I had to get this right this year. I had to *think*.

I had thirty-eight days to work out how to get to the fair.

4

In some families, the well-behaved kid is the bad one.

(paradox)

Thirty-eight days to the fair

Mum was in the kitchen when I got home, putting her home-made cover over the sewing machine. Next to the machine, a pair of curtains with horrible big flowers lay flopped over the peninsula. I could tell she'd finished making the curtains because she'd wrapped them in clear plastic.

Mum makes curtains for people around the village. She says she likes it, and it makes her extra money. It's really annoying.

'Hi.' I decided to work my way up to the billboard. 'Some kids from Radcliffe High were playing chicken on the railway and a kid got hit by a train.'

'What?' Mum stopped moving. 'Is the kid OK?'

I shrugged.

'How old was the child?'

I shrugged again.

Mum's eyebrows hunched up in the middle. 'That's really upsetting.'

With her face all screwed up with sadness, Mum looked old. Of course, she *was* old – fifty-two – she and Dad were so much older than other kids' parents. But she looked older still when she was upset.

'Mrs Vernal gave the assembly,' I said. 'She said being a teenager is hard.'

Mum shook her head. She started packing up the sewing machine again.

'She said kids should be the stars of their own lives.'

Mum slid the heavy machine under the peninsula. 'What does that *even mean*?'

I took a breath. 'I sometimes feel like I'm not the star of my own life.' I bunched up my hands. 'Mrs Vernal said I need to be my own flower and grow for myself. Or something.'

Mum gave me a look. 'I'm thinking I might need a little chat with this *Mrs Vernal*.' She looked younger again now she'd found a reason to be annoyed rather than sad.

I watched Mum reach for the plastic-covered curtains. She started folding them carefully, like she was handling a baby.

Don't say it.

But the words came out anyway. 'Mum, I've seen a billboard.'

Mum's movements slowed. 'No.' Her voice was calm.

'Everyone else gets to go.' My voice wasn't calm. It went wavy and uphill.

'When you're an adult, living an adult life, you can choose to go to the fair yourself.'

'But everyone else gets to go!'

Mum stared at the curtains, not folding anymore. 'You know why we don't want you to go? *You know why*, Fiona!'

'Just because Danielle died there doesn't mean I'll die!'

'Of course you're not going to die, that's not the point of the—'

'And I don't care about Danielle!' I screamed.

*

It's not my fault I do things like that. Every family has a good one and a bad one – fact. It just isn't always obvious because sometimes it's complicated.

Take Lewis's family.

Lewis *should* be the good one. He does his homework and picks up crisp packets in the street. But his dad likes Lewis's brother better, even though his brother doesn't pick up crisp packets and sometimes blocks us with his massive body when we try to get on the bus.

But it's simpler with my family. Danielle did loads of stuff that made my parents happy. She helped Dad put the toppings on his pizzas. She laid the table without asking and always cleaned her plate. She had a dance routine with Mum to songs on the radio and they danced round the kitchen together.

It's fair enough that I'm the bad one.

I'm the odd one out in my family. I'm the only one who's left-handed. You can tell we're related because I have the same small nose and big chin as Danielle, but my parents are tall and fair and so was Danielle – the *tallest girl in her class,* Mum never gets bored of saying, like Danielle managed it on purpose. I'm one of the shortest, and my hair's dark and heavy and stays where it is. It never falls out of a clip like Mum's.

If my family were *The Lion King* family, they would all be Simbas and I'd be Scar.

I don't want to be the Scar. But when you're the Scar, you don't get to choose.

Bad Scar Things I've Done – Countdown

6. <u>Cut Off Martha's Plait</u>

Everyone else thinks this was bad, but this was the least bad. Because Martha deserved it.

5. <u>Put Grandma's Money in the Claw Machine</u>

This wasn't really bad either. But it made Grandma sad and disappointed, and nothing feels worse than that. So it's on the list.

4. <u>Scratched My Special Shape Everywhere. The Shape Made from *F for Fiona*-s</u>

This one definitely wasn't my fault. And now I know what a swastika is, I don't want it to be my special shape anymore.

3. <u>Asked Candy's Mum How Much Money They Had</u>

Candy lived in the big house at the end of the road last summer, because her mum was working at the medical plant *on secondment*, which means you live somewhere new where you have no friends.

And, I admit, I got this one wrong. But Mum kept asking me questions – *'they went on a skiing holiday in January and now they're going to Rome?'* and *'a taxi to take her from school to the dentist, how much would that even cost?'* – and I honestly thought she wanted to know.

2. <u>Stole Candy's Pencil Topper</u>

I wanted Candy's Easter egg collection, all lined up on the shelf, even though Easter was *ages* ago. I even wanted Candy's mum instead of mine sometimes, like when she made us pancakes even though it wasn't pancake day.

But most of all, I wanted Candy's pencil topper. It was a perfect pale purple and shaped like a house, with a little fence and a cat in the garden.

Even though I'm not into stationery, I wanted it so much, it burned inside me. On one visit, I took that pencil topper and put it in my cardigan pocket.

When I went home, I put the pencil topper in my bottom drawer and said to Mum, 'I don't want to play with Candy anymore.'

And Mum looked really upset and said *you have to be open if you're going to have friends* and *not everyone's perfect* and she got angry then and said *beggars can't be choosers*. And then got upset again, and started apologising, even though it was fine – she wasn't lying.

I don't like to think about Candy.

I was happy when she moved away.

1. The Monkey Bars

This is the worst one. And everyone knows about it.

In the last year of primary school, the year I turned double-digits, we went to church services with the vicar once a month. And Mum got sad there because it was where they held Danielle's funeral.

One time, the vicar put his hand on Mum's shoulder and said, 'God takes the best of us and keeps them to himself.' And I thought and thought about that. About how God took Danielle, but let my parents keep me.

The next day at school, I hung upside down from the playground's monkey bars so my skirt flipped over my chest, showing my pants. Everyone pointed and shouted. Even when teachers shouted *'COME DOWN NOW!'* – even when the headteacher came out – I stayed on.

Two teachers had to pull me off the monkey bars, bruising my legs. I clung to that metal pole till it hurt. Then there were letters and doctors and people asking questions quietly, and I had to say that I'd bruised my own legs. That it was all my fault.

Which I had. And it was.

Proving I was the bad one. Proving it, once and for all. Just in case people weren't sure.

To Go to the Fair I Need:

1) Money for the rides
2) Girl friends, so the boy from the Waltzers will push my car
3) Mum and Dad to let me go

Sometimes the shortest lists can be the longest ones. Paradox.

5

**For surveillance, a good spy moves his eyes but not his
head to throw his adversary off the scent.**
The Junior Spy's Secret Handbook™

Thirty-seven days to the fair
The next morning, I waited with Lewis as we watched Sean
slow-walk towards our lamppost, kicking puddles as he went.
White socks – again – peeked out from between his trousers
and his shoes.

The New Head was going to kill him if she saw those
socks. Sean was *playing with fire*, but I guessed that was the
point. Still, after seeing the New Head's face in the chicken
assembly, how she shut down Liam with just a look, I would
have shivered pulling those socks on that morning.

Sean arrived at the lamppost. 'All right.'

We walked for a moment. Lewis turned to cross the road
towards school.

I followed Lewis, but Sean just watched us. 'Why do you
two always cross the road at this postbox?'

Lewis stopped in the road. I stopped so I didn't walk into
the back of him.

'Every day,' Sean said, 'you always cross exactly here.'

Lewis and I looked at each other.

We shuffled back onto the pavement, facing Sean.

'We just do,' Lewis said. 'Habit.'

'And on the way home, you two always cross *there*. At the big tree.'

I turned to Lewis and we blinked at each other. Sean was right.

It was funny he knew stuff about us that we didn't.

Lewis turned to me. 'I cross here because you do.'

I frowned. 'I thought I crossed here because *you* do.'

'Maybe it just feels like the best place,' Lewis said.

I thought about this. 'Maybe it *is* me. Mum always crosses here too.'

Sean pointed at a house. 'It means, in both directions, you never walk in front of that one.'

I looked at the house. 'Huh.'

His point made, Sean finally set off walking, talking about the weekend's England game. I took one last look back at the house, then Lewis and I followed.

In the park, Lewis turned to me. 'Shall we go into the bush then?'

I made big eyes at him. *Shush.*

'Oh,' Lewis gave a little laugh. 'I forgot you'd taken them already.'

I made my eyes bigger still.

That's when Lewis started to panic. He staggered to the left. 'I – I –'

Sean looked from one to the other. 'Taken what?'

I glared at Lewis.

I don't know exactly what it looks like when an eleven-year-old has a heart attack, but I bet it was something like this.

I looked back at Sean. 'Don't tell anyone. But I found some magazines, and they're mine now.'

Sean looked at the bush and back. 'What kind of magazines?'

I looked at Lewis and back. 'You promise you won't tell?'

'On my dog's life.' Sean made round eyes. 'And you know how much I love Alfie.'

I nodded. I looked at Lewis and took a breath. 'They were sexy magazines. With girls in.'

'Not only *girls*,' Lewis said. 'Old ladies. Remember *Readers' Wiv*—'

'*I told you to stop talking about* Readers' Wives!' *My mum* is a wife. *Lewis's mum* is a wife. *Mrs Vernal.*

I turned back to Sean. 'I took the magazines home because Finders Keepers. I'm going to sell them at the car boot sale to make money for the fair. For when I get to go. Because I *will* get to go.'

Lewis shook his head and kicked a stone in his path.

'Of course you will.' Sean nodded like I was the wisest person in the world. 'Can I, erm, see these magazines?'

'No.'

Sean leaned over when I was in English later. *Spoke to me,* in front of other people.

'How many magazines? And how much do you want for them?'

'Why do you want to know?'

'People are asking.'

'How do people know about the magazines?' I glanced round but Mr Kellett was on the other side of the room. '*Have you told people about them, Sean?*'

He shook his head.

*

Things were going topsy-turvy.

Sean was speaking to me in English and yet Richard Plant, the popular kid who moved here from Edinburgh and trains for Stoke City's youth team, walked through corridors alone. Everyone stuck their legs out extra-long to trip him in corridors now. Nino the Swiss kid was off the hook because England played Scotland in three days.

Now, when Richard Plant walked down the corridor, people wrinkled their noses and said, 'Can you smell Haggis?' or put their hands to their ears – 'Is that bagpipes?' Or, from the kids who couldn't be bothered with the effort of thinking, he got a shove in the back and 'Your team's shit, *aaah!*'

When Lewis and I walked out of the school gates that afternoon, Mum was waiting at the roundabout, leaning against the *Gail Larson, Driving Instructor* car.

I felt someone lean closer to my ear. A pretend cough. *'Gail!'*

I wished my mum wasn't a driving instructor. I wished that it wasn't seventeen-year-olds who learned to drive. I wished our school didn't have a sixth form.

That's a lot of wishes – but just one of those things would make my life better.

I usually pretend I haven't seen Mum. It's not great to admit to having a mum at the best of times, and it's worse when your mum's so much older than everyone else's.

But Selina Baker, the best girl in sixth form, was the one hurrying up to Mum's car today, so I decided to own my mum, for once.

I wandered over but Lewis hung back. Like I said, he's terrified of my mum.

'Hi.' Mum smiled at me, like she couldn't remember me screaming at her the night before. She was always happy to own me as her daughter – even though, in our school, that wasn't a good look for her. 'Selina, do you know my daughter, Fiona?'

'Hi, Fiona!' Selina was *beautiful*, close up. As beautiful as Kelly from Winchester. 'Nice to meet you. I love your mum. I've been *so* nervous about learning to drive since I got my provisional licence, but Gail is so patient!'

I looked at Mum. She kept smiling.

'My parents can't teach me at all,' Selina said, 'they get really frustrated. But your mum is so calm and so nice, and she never even raises her voice.'

Mum caught my eye. She kept smiling.

On the other side of the road, Lewis frowned.

I couldn't believe this. 'What about people who cut her up at roundabouts? People in BMWs? Does she not even shout at *them?*'

Mum's smile cracked. 'I'm very patient in a professional capacity.'

'We all love your mum,' Selina said. 'And she's funny. You're so lucky, Fiona.'

'Right.' I felt dazed. 'Bye.'

I headed over to Lewis.

'That conversation just got weirder and weirder,' he said.

I nodded.

I could hear Selina talking as we walked away. 'Oh. I can do the appointment next Saturday after all, Gail, if you've still got it? Shopping with my boyfriend's cancelled because all the lads from school want to go to some lame car boot sale all of a sudden.'

*

That made up my mind. I was never going to get a chance to get money for the fair like this again. This was my one shot. So on the way home, for research, I made Lewis go with me into Paper Rack, the newsagent's in the precinct.

When I say *precinct* I mean the bad, British kind – the square shopping area off the high street lined with shops. It has an off-licence, a Chinese takeaway and a tiny Co-op where everyone buys the things they forgot at the big shop. I don't mean *precinct*, like in an American cop show. No one here *ever* rolls over car bonnets with guns, shouting *freeze, punk!*, not here, outside our Co-op. We don't get that kind of good stuff in Monkford.

I walked past the pile of kids' bikes, piled up outside Paper Rack, and pushed open the door, Lewis following.

A bell rang above my head. I strode up to the counter and queued behind a bigger kid – one who'd taken off his jumper and tie, but was still, clearly, in school uniform. 'Two singles and a pack of Euro '96 please.'

The bald man in the stretched polo shirt didn't say anything. He reached behind the counter and got two cigarettes out of an open pack. He handed them over with a pack of stickers, and the kid pushed a fiver at him and hurried out of the shop.

I glanced at the magazines on the top shelf. They were all tucked behind each other, so you could only see a little bit of the title, a *Fi-* or *Ra-*. No boobs, just a tiny sliver of thigh or arm.

'They're so high,' I whispered, but Lewis wasn't looking. He was making serious faces, holding up two Euro '96 annuals, like he was deciding between them.

The bald man behind the counter peered at me. 'Yes?'

I panicked. 'I'll have' – I picked up a local paper – 'this, please.'

The man folded over a paper and gave it to me. I handed him the last of my change, furious with myself for panicking like Lewis. I was doing this research because I needed *more* money, not *less*.

'Something else?'

'I'm just looking.'

The man followed my gaze to the shelf with the magazines. He looked back at me.

'At my gentlemen's recreational magazines?'

'No. Though, now you mention them, what age' – I trailed my hand along the counter – 'do you have to be to buy those magazines?'

He stared at me. 'Eighteen.'

'And anyone can buy them? Boys and girls?'

'Yes,' he said finally.

'Great!' I gave a beaming smile. 'Thanks.' I waved my newspaper in goodbye and trotted out of the shop, Lewis slotting his annuals back hurriedly in the rack.

On the way out, he knocked a pack of crisps off the shelf with his rucksack. He put the pack back with hands as slippery as a squid in a bath.

Lewis and I stayed in the park for a while. When I got home, Mum was already back from her driving lesson. She was at the peninsula with the sewing machine out, making *another* pair of curtains.

'Good day?' Mum asked through the pins in her mouth.

I threw the newspaper I'd bought down next to her. 'Sweet.'

'Sweet?' Mum took the pins out of her mouth. 'Is that a new school saying?'

'No, I've always said it.' I felt my face going red. *Sweet* was a new school saying.

She looked at the paper. 'Was that put through the door?'

'No, I bought it.'

Mum gave me a funny look. She watched me as I got five digestives from the biscuit barrel *to keep the wolf from the door*.

'It's fine. I'm not on a diet yet,' I said, leaving the room.

After a moment, Mum shouted, 'Yet?'

I was nearly at the top of the stairs, so I didn't reply. I didn't know how to, anyway. I wasn't sure of the rules when girls have to go on diets – whether it's something you get to decide yourself or if you get instructions at school. Or a letter through the post. *Skimmed milk. It's time.*

I sat on my bed, eating, realising I was making crumbs. I was about to shake the duvet off but I got distracted. By a brilliant idea.

Yesterday, Mum said *When you're an adult, living an adult life, you can choose to go to the fair yourself.*

And today, when I threw that accidentally bought newspaper down, she looked at me like I'd confused her. Like she saw me in a different light.

So maybe there *was* something I could do to change Mum's mind about the fair, after all?

At the idea, the tips of my fingers and toes went light and fizzy. I put the last biscuit in my mouth in one go, and reached for my book of lists.

Things I Can Do to Make Mum and Dad Think I'm More Grown Up

1. Let them see me reading the newspaper
2. Put my dirty clothes in the washing basket every time

3. Use more long words
4. Get new friends. Better friends, older ones.
5. Take drugs
6. Get some condoms and leave them round my room
7. Get flashed at
8. Ask to listen to the news in the car
9. Change a lightbulb without being asked
10. Wear my glasses all the time, not just for distance stuff
11. Ask to watch a foreign film, with subtitles
12. Get a new name
13. Get pregnant
14. Get a job. Not a paper round. A grown-up job, like a police person or nurse
15. Act interested in *Gardeners' World* – and snooker

6

**A good spy always carries a notebook, in case he needs
to pass on a secret message.**
The Junior Spy's Secret Handbook™

Thirty-six days till the fair
School news!

Mademoiselle Brun, the student language teacher that all
the lads fancy – her real name's Miss Brown – brought in a
special French meal for her Year Ten class. Baguettes, smelly
cheese, tablecloths. And there was a massive food fight!

Massive. Brie in hair and shredded baguettes down jumpers. Quiche on the walls! By the end, the carpet was covered
in bits, like the bottom of a hamster cage.

Mrs Parton, the stern old lady French teacher, came in to
see what the trouble was, and Mademoiselle Brun told her
in a wavy voice that she had the situation all under control.
Behind her, a clump of pâté fell down a 3D display of the
Eiffel Tower.

Mrs Parton shouted at everyone and dragged three cheese-
covered kids to the New Head. Then the bell rang and all
the kids ran out, leaving Mademoiselle Brun to clean up the
mess.

And when someone saw Mademoiselle Brun in the corridor later, she'd been *crying*.

And there was more school news! School news about *me*!

Kids stopped and whispered now as I walked down the corridors. Normally, I jumped over the feet of the bigger kids who lined the benches at the side of the corridors and tried to trip people. But no one stuck their legs out as I walked past. Not that breaktime.

One older boy with an undercut stopped me. 'Fiona Larson?'

'Yes?' I said carefully.

'I'll give you a fiver for the lot.'

'If you want them, be at the car boot sale.' I might have tossed my hair. 'A week on Saturday, Festival field, two p.m. Look for the blue car that says *Gail Larson, Driving Instructor*. You know the one.'

And I walked away.

I'll be honest – I hadn't wanted to tell Sean about the magazines. But now I had, it felt pretty good.

I was feeling so good that I didn't even tell Sean off for blabbing when he sat with us in the computer room that lunchtime.

We sat in a line in front of the computers, playing Ninja Combat (Sean), Rhino Rampage (Lewis) and Park Ranger (me), but I wasn't concentrating.

'I've decided.' I spun my chair round to face the boys. 'I need Mum and Dad to think I'm more grown up. Then they'll let me go to the fair.'

Lewis pushed his chair away from his game. He pulled a can of drink out of his bag. 'Your parents know how old you are though.'

He opened the ring pull and drink splattered on him.

Sean and I both laughed. Lewis shook his shirt out, sending drips onto the floor.

'Jizzed on yourself,' Sean said.

'So childish. And it's called *premature ejaculation*.' I took my book of lists to the other side of the computer room and opened the book to look at my list from the night before.

'What are you doing? Homework?'

'No, Sean!'

He ripped the book off me anyway.

Lewis let his rhino die and peered over Sean's shoulder, both reading.

I felt my face flush. 'Not all the ideas are good ones. It's an early list.'

'Get new friends,' Lewis said. 'You mean rather than us?'

'Not *rather* than you,' I said. '*As well* as you.'

'Get pregnant?' Sean said. 'Who's going to want to get you pregnant?'

I snatched my book back. 'I knew I shouldn't let you see this. I knew you weren't mature enough.'

'Your parents are never going to think you're older,' Lewis said quietly. 'Whether you're wearing your glasses or not.'

I scratched the back of my neck and looked at my list again.

I underlined *14. Get a job. Not a paper round. A grown-up job, like a police person or nurse*. Then I underlined *12. Get a new name*.

I turned to Lewis and Sean. 'From now on, you have to call me *Fi*.' I paused. 'That's what other people call me. People from other schools.'

I waited for them to catch me out, but Lewis just shrugged. Sean said, 'OK.'

Lewis was watching me.

'What?'

'Are you going to put your glasses on now or later?'

After school, Mum made me go to the Co-op but, for once, I didn't mind. The Co-op had a pinboard for lost cats and step classes – and adverts for grown-up jobs.

I walked with Mum and her big shopping bag down the road.

'You've got your inhaler?' Mum asked.

'Yep. I should really have stayed at home. All this is going to change when I'm twelve.' I waved my arms to show *all this*.

'When you're twelve, you're allowed to be home alone.'

'We'll talk about it then.'

We reached the precinct. I got a trolley from the nest and pushed it through the Co-op doorway. I waited till Mum was in the fresh food aisle, choosing vegetables, then snuck over to the pinboard.

I glanced past the cards for coffee mornings and lost cats.

Babysitting Opportunity. *Two evenings per week. Two well-behaved primary-age children and one small dog. Requires . . .*

Kid's job.

Paper Rounds *available for motivated, responsible teenagers. Enquire at Paper Rack. Applicants need to be early risers, reliable . . .*

Kid's job. And with the Paper Rack man? *No way.*

I looked up, to check I was safe. Mum was heading over to a kid in a Co-op uniform, stacking baskets of oranges. I recognised the kid from school.

'Excuse me,' Mum said.

I glanced at the next advert.

Hairdressing Assistant required. *Must be presentable with good customer service skills and . . .*

A girls' job, but it couldn't be helped.

I got out my spy notebook and wrote down the details. I hurried back to Mum and grabbed the trolley handle again, like I'd never been gone.

'Like I said, we do *usually* have cherries.' The kid stacking oranges noticed me and blinked. 'Are you Fiona Larson from Year Seven?' He glanced at Mum and back. 'Have you got a sec?'

I gave the boy *not now* eyes. I turned hurriedly to Mum. 'Shall I tell you about my day? Do you know blood makes up seven per cent of the weight of the human body?'

But, out of nowhere, Mum jammed her hands on the trolley and swerved into the fridge aisle.

I skittered along after her, still holding the trolley. *Surely she couldn't have worked out about the magazines from . . .*

Mum leaned down. She kept her face there, too close to mine. 'So what did you learn at school today?'

'I was just telling you. Seven per cent of the human body weight is blood.'

'Seven per cent? Wow! So heavy! And what's in blood, is it plasma? Tell me about—'

'Hi, Gail.'

Mum raised herself to an upright position.

A man with a ponytail stood in her path, a half-smile on his face.

'Hi.' Mum got her house keys out of her bag. 'We're in a bit of a hurry, I'm afraid.'

The man's basket held a four-pack of lager and some chewing gum. 'It's been a long time.'

She gave a tiny nod. 'I thought you'd moved to Bristol.'

'My mother died a couple of weeks ago.'

The hard line of Mum's mouth didn't change.

'I'm not back properly, just living in the house while I sell it.'

'Right.' Mum put her hand on my shoulder. 'We need to go. I think I've left the iron on.'

A piece of hair fell out of her clip and into her mouth. She pulled the hair away roughly as she turned to me. 'Just leave the trolley.'

We hurried out of the shop.

'You were rude to that ponytail man, Mum,' I said. 'You didn't say you were sorry his mother died.'

'I just didn't feel like talking.'

I looked behind me. The man was outside the shop now, smoking a cigarette. He smoked quickly, barely finishing one puff before starting the next.

'Don't you like him?'

Mum adjusted her clip. 'Not really.'

I looked behind again, but the man had gone. 'Why, what's he done?'

'Nothing.' She took a deep breath. 'He's strange. That's all. Now, tell me again – what was that you were saying about blood?'

Mum asked about my blood project all the way home.

And it turned out she hadn't left the iron on – it was still in the cupboard! When I pointed that out, she hit herself on the forehead and said, 'Aren't I the prize numpty?' and we both laughed at her silliness.

Adult Sayings

1) Keep the wolf from the door
2) SHIT THE BED!
3) Nobody expects the Spanish Inquisition
4) Single supplements
5) A preposition shows relation, like on the bridge or at the station*

*I saw this saying on a wall at school, but no kid would ever say this, so I'm calling it an adult saying.

Adult Words

1) Paradox
2) Catalyst
3) Provisional
4) Antidisestablishmentarianism
5) Secondment
6) Foreplay
7) Clitoris
8) Premature
9) Ejaculation
10) Asterisk

7

The Scottish kids should hope England beat Scotland tomorrow.
(paradox)

Thirty-five days till the fair
I waved to Lewis and Sean as I walked towards the lamp-post, bouncing a little as I walked. It was getting warmer so I didn't have a coat with me, which made everything feel lighter. I actually had a plan to get to the fair now, a sweet, *sweet* plan – and now the sky had decided to cheer up too and stop raining.

We all turned to walk towards school. Lewis stepped to cross the road and—

'See, you're doing it again!' Sean's face was bright, like he'd caught us out. 'Crossing in the same place! Like robots!'

I looked at Lewis. We gave each other little *oops* smiles.

'And look,' Sean said, pointing. 'There's a man in the house you never walk past.'

I turned towards the house, 56 George Street. There was usually an old lady behind the net curtains, sitting on the sofa at all times of day, but she wasn't there now. Instead, there was a shape right behind the netting. A man, looking out.

'Do you think he's looking at us?' I asked.

'Definitely,' Sean said.

'Maybe because we're staring at his house?' Lewis said.

The man hadn't moved from the window. It was like a Mexican stand-off, but with no guns.

I felt a shiver of something both good and bad up my spine. 'Do you think he's a flasher?'

Lewis snorted. 'You and your flashers.'

'And you have your mercenaries. We all have our things, Lewis.'

It's not that I *want* to be flashed, exactly – it's just something that happens to the older girls. It happened to Selina Baker in the cut-through down the side of the newsagent's. Selina had to cancel her driving lesson so she could look at photos of flashers at the police station, on what sounded like the best day ever.

'I wonder if it's *him* back?' Sean spoke thoughtfully, like he was holding a conversation with himself, but I knew it was an act. His words were definitely for us. 'I know why your mum doesn't walk in front of that house, Fi – I remembered. My dad told me once what happened at number fifty-six.'

Lewis and I glanced at each other. We both knew something big was coming.

Sean put his hands on his hips. 'That's the axeman's house. A man went mad there and cut all his brothers' heads off once. On Halloween.'

My neck went colder. 'That can't be true.'

'You wouldn't have only just remembered that now,' Lewis said.

'The man must be due out of prison around now. He'll be back to get revenge on the village for grassing him up.'

I stared at the man in the window. 'Shut up.'

'How many brothers' heads?' Lewis asked.

'After the man cut off their heads, he cut up their bodies in the shed. He buried bits of his brothers all around the village.'

'That's not true,' I said.

'My uncle Neil found a foot in the fresh food aisle at the Co-op.'

'Now that's *definitely* not true,' I said.

'The foot was in with the bananas,' Sean said. 'Still wearing a flipflop.'

The three of us stood there, staring.

'Shall we go and ring the doorbell?' Sean said.

'NO!' Lewis had never sounded surer. 'You're so stupid, Sean!'

Lewis started walking towards school, his arms pumping. After taking one last look at the house, Sean and I followed.

Thing is, you can know something isn't true and still be a little bit scared.

I was starting to wish we met at a different lamppost.

I forgot about Sean's axeman story as the day went on. The school corridors were buzzing with football talk, and things were getting worse for the Scottish kids. Even Lewis, who usually piped up 'I'm one-eighth Scottish' whenever he could, was very quiet now about his great-granddad from Aberdeen.

It made me worry about my grandma up in Glasgow. An English person, all alone.

Grandma moved to Glasgow before I was born, to live with Kenneth, her old boyfriend from school. She hadn't seen him in forty years, but he sent her a letter after Grandpa John died. And now she's married to Kenneth. And that's fine because the first time Grandma was with Kenneth, she hadn't met Granddad John. And the second time, Grandad John was dead.

So no one minded. It was all fine.

I just hoped Grandma was OK in Glasgow.

The next day was Saturday and I spent the morning on my bed, working on my letter.

Dear British Hairways,

    I am Fiona Larson and I would like the job of Hairdressing Assistant you advertised. Please. I am young and quite small but mature for my age. I am. . .

I looked at my scribbled notes.

    presentable with good customer service skills. I—

'*Gail!*' Dad shouted from the lounge. 'There's been a bomb! In Manchester!'

'Oh my God!' Mum's footsteps thundered down the stairs. I grabbed my glasses and hurried after her.

On the TV, a reporter with a microphone stood in front of a row of police vans, lights flashing. Mum, Dad and I sat in a line on the sofa and stared.

'*The nearest estimates are several hundred injured. The number of dead and seriously injured yet to be confirmed, but sources expect it to be in double figures.*'

Behind the reporter, I could see an empty city street with blackened buildings. Police tape shivered in the wind. Dad had the teletext subtitles on.

'Are the bombers still around?' I asked.

'They will have left quick-smart,' Mum said quickly.

'The device was believed to be in a lorry parked on Corporation Street, outside Marks and Spencer's.'

Mum clucked her tongue against her teeth. 'Marks and Spencer's.'

'A warning with an IRA code word was phoned in to Granada Studios ninety minutes before. A hundred thousand were evacuated.'

'Why send a warning?' I asked. 'If they wanted to hurt people?'

Mum did a flapping thing, like a pigeon about to take off. 'Please.' She dropped her hands into her lap. 'I can't believe it's happened. *Here.* I want to cry.'

I looked at the clock. It was only two hours till England versus Scotland.

I shook Dad's arm so he was looking at me. 'Is the football going to be cancelled?'

At first, neither of my parents reacted.

Mum sat up straighter. 'Is it?'

Dad grabbed the remote.

Mum hunched forward to the front of the sofa. 'I mean, they don't think anyone's been *killed.*'

Dad booted up Teletext and jabbed numbers into the remote.

Mum flapped her hands at Dad, all pigeon again. 'Hurry up!'

'Page four of seven, Gail, *page four of seven!*'

Mum tried to grab the remote but Dad lurched his hand away.

'And we've just received notification from the FA that the match at three p.m. is still going ahead. I'll repeat that,

England versus Scotland at Wembley is still going ahead.'

The subtitles on the screen flashed up, *'ENGLAND SCOTLAND FOOTBALL STILL ON'.*

Mum sat back. 'I mean, it would have been fine if they'd cancelled it, of course.'

Dad nodded. 'Of course.'

We watched some more news. We even ate our lunch in front of the telly, listening to the presenter in the studio.

'And England v Scotland is still on. I will say that again for anyone who missed it: the football is still on.'

I adjusted my glasses. It was strange to be able to see this well. 'When will the police solve the mystery? They'll catch the criminals, right?'

'Oh.' Mum looked at Dad. 'Probably soon, Fiona. Don't be scared. As soon as we know what's happened and the bad people are caught, it will all be OK.'

We watched the news until the football came on. The news never changed, it was just the same reporters in front of the same wrecked black buildings and wind-rippled police tape; the same reporters saying the same thing, again and again.

I'd shown I was interested in the news, but it was wasted. It didn't make me look grown up at all. Every kid, everywhere, would be watching the news that day.

And the whole time, neither of my parents said anything about my glasses.

An hour later, still on the sofa, I watched the footballers run and spit.

I fidgeted. Who knew a day of telly could be this long?

The commentator kept his voice at all one level. *'Gary*

Neville there, protecting his keeper with a run from right-back position.'

'*Position.'* I sat up straighter. 'Like *preposition.'*

Mum glanced over and back at the telly.

I took a deep breath. 'A preposition shows relation, like on the bridge or at the station.'

'Nice block,' Dad said.

Mum nodded.

'*Neville jogging back there, he knows he's done his job and done it well.'*

I made my voice louder. 'A preposition shows relation, like on the bridge or at the station.'

Mum turned slowly to face me.

'What did she say?' Dad asked.

There was a pause.

'I'm not exactly sure.'

On screen, a whistle blew.

Mum yanked her head to look.

I pushed my lips together and glanced at the screen. A Scotland player jerked his hands angrily, shouting at one of the England players.

Mum and I both turned to look at Dad. Waiting.

Dad made a big drama of rolling his eyes. 'He said *you're an effing diving effing cheating mother-effer.'*

But even *that* didn't cheer me up. 'I'm going upstairs.'

Mum bounced forward on the sofa. 'Have fun.'

I walked upstairs slowly, trailing my hand along the wall. I bumped it over each door frame, one by one.

I stopped at the closed door where there used to be a tile sign with a yellow flower under the words *Danielle's room.* Dad chiselled the sign off when I was in primary school.

I stared at the closed door for a second. I hurried back to my own room and sat on the bed.

The shouts from downstairs were getting louder. There was a muffled banging of hands on sofa arms.

'YES, SHEARER, YES!' Mum.

'GET IN, MY SON!' Dad.

I was thinking hard.

Mum had said, *as soon as we know what's happened and the bad people are caught, it will all be OK.*

She wasn't talking about the fair, of course. She was talking about the bomb. But still . . .

I took my glasses off and folded in the arms.

The idea was *perfect.*

As well as showing my parents I was grown up enough to be trusted, I could prove that what happened to Danielle at the fair would never happen to me.

And that meant – *solving the mystery!*

I looked at my bookshelf, past Grandma's long-legged wrong owl.

I tapped *The Junior Spy's Secret Handbook™* gently, like I was saying *good girl* to a pet, then reached past it to my book of lists.

How to Investigate How Danielle Died

1) Ask the police
2) Ask *Crimewatch*
3) Ask the local paper
4) Ask Mum and Dad*
5) Ask someone else to ask Mum and Dad**
6) Ask Grandma
7) Ask Mrs Carpenter next door
8) Ask anyone and everyone else
9) Eavesdrop on people
10) Look for clues in Danielle's bedroom.

carefully
**better*

8

Dead people still have bedrooms.
(paradox)

Thirty-three days to the fair
The next morning, I wrote a letter.

> Dear Monkford and District Advertiser,
>   Please can you send me a copy of your newspaper that
> covers the night of 24 July 1982.
>   I can pay.
>   If you can't send me a newspaper, can you tell me the
> name and address of the reporter who covered news and
> fairs in 1982.
>   Thank you,
>   Fiona Larson

I'd only been to Danielle's grave once, before Mum and
Dad decided *it wasn't helpful.* But I remembered her death
day, because it was carved in gold on the sticking-up
stone. Right above *God takes the best of us and keeps them to
himself.*

I took two envelopes and stamps from the Cupboard of

Office Things. I enveloped up the letter, along with the letter I'd written to British Hairways.

And I ran to the postbox, as fast as I could. I pushed the letters into the slot and felt a fizzle up my spine.

No going back now.

My investigations had started.

And now I knew I'd *definitely* need money for the fair, I decided the next thing to do was to start planning for the car boot sale. I ripped out a page from a plain notebook and wrote in my best handwriting:

Available Magazines

Mayfair, *June 1996*
Razzle, *May 1996*
Fiesta, *June 1996...*

I didn't put any prices on. I didn't know what to write.

I wrote the same list out nine more times in my best handwriting, ready to hand out to customers at the car boot sale. When I'd finished writing, I put my leaflets and magazines in a cardboard box, and dug out old ponies and bears from my wardrobe. I threw them on top of the magazines, as decoys.

In the back of my wardrobe, I saw Sprinkles. I paused. She was my old favourite pony – from back when I thought it was OK to have a favourite pony.

I picked her up and turned her over in my hand. Remembering how I used to make her canter over the lawn while I whispered what a good horse she was. How Dad peeled carrots for me to leave for her on the bedside table.

How weird I felt about that now. How the thought made me want to kick Sprinkles down the stairs.

I shoved Sprinkles in the box, under the other toys, so I couldn't see her anymore.

Later, I read the Sunday paper at the peninsula. Mum sat next to me, sewing curtains on her machine. Across the kitchen, Dad chopped vegetables for tea.

I turned the pages as loudly as I could.

It took ages. Turns out there's *a lot* of news in a newspaper. And it takes even longer to read if you're making notes.

Grown-up Topics

1. The Manchester bomb
2. The IRA
3. How Paul Gascoigne is a mercurial player
4. The new constitution in Ukraine
5. The elections in Turkey
6. The situation in Bosnia
7. Bin collections
8. The chancellor Kenneth Clarke's upcoming Rolls Royce budget and the predicted economic growth of 2.5 per cent in 1996

Look Up

1. Tremble Trigger
2. Ammonium Nitrate
3. Criminal Injuries Compensation Authority
4. Republican
5. Masonry

6. Callous
7. Mercurial
8. Constitution
9. Chancellor

After what felt like *hours*, I closed my list book and turned the newspaper back to the front page.

People read that *every week*? Every *day*?

'The bomb's a lot to take in.' Dad glanced at Mum and back. 'Maybe best not to look in so much detail?'

Maybe I'd have better luck with Danielle's bedroom. 'I'm going upstairs.'

But then Dad came upstairs too and stood sorting out washing, so it wasn't safe to look. Then Mum said she wanted us all to have a nice tea and watch an old film that she thought I'd like. She wanted us to spend the evening together, as Dad was staying at Uncle Jim's the next night, for *a pool and pub and talking the hind legs off a donkey* session.

So I didn't get to sneak into Danielle's room that night. But the film was called *Caddyshack* and it turned out Mum was right. It had a dancing gopher in it, and it was actually pretty funny.

On Monday morning, I was up early before school. *Perfect.* I woke up at the sound of the door banging, as Dad went to do the post.

I went 0–60, just like that. Sleep. *Bam.* Wide awake.

Before I could get scared or think too much about what I was doing, I slipped into Danielle's room.

They've never said I'm not allowed to go in there. It's just I've never wanted to.

*

I put my arms around myself in a safety hug.

Danielle's room was so much bigger than mine. And so *pink*. As pink as a stationery set for girls.

Big, pink – and *cold*. And not because Danielle's ghost was haunting it. Mum had been really clear after I went in that one time – that the room was always cold because the radiator hadn't been switched on for fourteen years. Nothing to do with ghosts.

The room was faded. Even Danielle's few colour posters had the brightness sucked out, so they looked like posters from another century.

I felt a slow shiver trickle up my back.

Ghost or no ghost, it was like going into a cold pink time machine.

I'd better touch something soon, or I'd be too scared to do it, so I stepped across the room and made myself put my hands flat on Danielle's dressing table.

The table had old nail varnishes on it, the bottles dried up. Faded photos of Danielle and her friends lined the mirror, with thin scarves hanging down, scarves that – I knew from photographs – Danielle used to tie in her hair.

I caught my reflection in the mirror. I looked scared.

I shouldn't be in here.

On the shelf next to Danielle's bed sat a record player, a stack of records propped up against it. I leafed through the records.

Turned out Danielle *really* loved ABBA.

I opened Danielle's wardrobe and pulled out a *thing* on a hanger. An all in one shirt-thing, the trousers connected to the top.

No wonder Mum liked Danielle so much. That kid was so nice she even let Mum *make her clothes.*

I held the *thing* up against me, and the bottom of the legs draped on the floor.

I pushed it back into the wardrobe roughly. A bunch of unused hangers fell to the floor – a clattering of metal on wood.

NO!

There was a noise from across the landing. A rush of feet, and Mum burst into the room.

She stopped in the doorway, hand still on the door knob. She shut her eyes. 'Fiona.'

'I'm sorry.'

Mum put her thumb and first finger on her eyelids.

'I'm sorry,' I said again.

'Love.' Mum let her hand drop and opened her eyes. 'What are you doing in here?'

I thought I saw a dog run in.

I wanted to borrow a pen.

'I wanted to see if there was anything to sell for the car boot sale. I'm sorry, Mum. Don't be cross.'

Mum sank slowly onto the bed next to me. 'I'm not cross.'

'You are,' I mumbled.

'Danielle's stuff is really important to me.'

'I'll go, I'm sorry. I don't need anything to sell.'

Mum gave a big sigh. 'I know I'm being silly. It's just a room. Just – stuff.'

She patted the space next to her. I didn't want to, but I sat down on the heart-covered duvet. The bed creaked. *Dead girl's bed.*

'I'll have a think. Whether there's any of this stuff we don't need. I know your dad thinks . . .' She stopped talking and pushed hair out of her eyes. 'I'll look out for some stuff for you today.'

'You don't need to.'

'No.' Mum stared at the fluffy rug. 'I'll look today.'

And I didn't want to leave her there, but she made a shooing gesture. 'Close the door after you.'

9

**The good spy practises to improve his craft, as the
gifted musician practises with his instrument.**
The Junior Spy's Secret Handbook™

Thirty-two days to the fair
I tried to distract myself from my new levels of Scar badness
by telling Lewis my plans at the lamppost, and showing him
The Junior Spy's Secret Handbook™.

Lewis took the handbook from me and I followed his gaze
to the cover – to the picture of a man in a hat and long coat,
peering at fingerprints through a magnifying glass.

'The book only has pictures of men and always says "he",'
I said, 'but it doesn't say anywhere that I definitely *can't* be a
spy. I promise I won't get kidnapped.'

'I'll do the practising bit.' Lewis handed the book back.
'I'll make invisible ink out of lemons and practise crawls
with you, that's fine. I'll even sew a secret pocket. But
spying on your parents or investigating how Danielle died?
No *way*.'

I put *The Junior Spy's Secret Handbook™* away. 'But the
whole point of practising is so you can be better at the *actual
spying*!'

He made that stubborn face he does when I know he's going to ruin everything.

'OK,' I lied. 'We'll just do the spy practising.' I decided not to show him my latest list, after all.

How Did Danielle Die?

1) Fell off the big wheel
2) Fell out of a chair swing
3) Choked on candyfloss
4) Had a heart attack on the Waltzers
5) Got hit on the head with a whack-a-mole hammer – accidentally
6) Got hit on the head with a whack-a-mole hammer – deliberately
7) Fell through a funhouse mirror
8) Took a drug overdose
9) Got killed by a flasher
10) Got killed by a paedo
11) Got killed by a zombie
12) Got killed by someone who wasn't a flasher, a paedo, or a zombie

I know about paedos. They're the adults who tell you to sit on their knees when it's your birthday. They offer to tie your shoelaces and act interested in your day when – let's face it – adults have cars and go to nightclubs and can buy whatever they want – they're not *really* interested in kids' days. The only people who are really interested in kids' days are your mum and dad or grandma, the people who *have* to be interested – it's their *job*.

I put *drug overdose* on my list just to make Danielle seem

more interesting, but it definitely wouldn't be that. And I was pretty sure she wasn't killed by a zombie, either.

If there'd ever been a zombie at Monkford Fair, I'd have definitely heard.

Sean came round the corner and I rushed to zip up *The Junior Spy's Secret Handbook™* safely in my bag.

He bumped his shoulder into Lewis's in a friendly hello. He looked from me to Lewis. 'Did you see McAllister's face when he missed that penalty?' Sean put a hand to his forehead and made the *tosser* sign. 'Wanker!'

Me and Lewis both nodded hard.

'*What* a wanker,' Lewis said.

'Complete wanker,' I agreed. 'His face!'

I wondered whether to add *Gascoigne is such a mercurial player*, but thought – *not now.*

Sean had been hanging around us a lot more since everyone had heard about the magazines. At breaktime in the main corridor, a crush of kids came up to me and he made himself into a barrier. 'Come on, people.' He held his hands up like a lollipop lady. 'Let the girl through.'

And the crowd parted like I was . . . well, like I was Kelly from Winchester herself.

There was no real school news that day, probably because there was so much news from outside of school. Liam said his dad knew the policeman who stopped the bomb (not true – the bomb *went off*) and Sean said his dad was one of the people who scooped up the arms, legs and heads and put them all in a big paramedic bucket (and because I'm a good friend to Sean, I didn't say his dad drives an ambulance in Stoke, not Manchester. Or point out – *heads? Nobody died*).

I don't think anyone talked about anything but the magazines, the bomb and football all day. Not even the teachers.

Though the teachers didn't talk about the magazines, of course. Which was a good thing.

Oh – and Richard Plant, the kid from Edinburgh, was off sick. Bad tummy, his mum said.

I don't think anyone, kids or teachers, was surprised.

Mr Kellett was late for our English lesson, of course.

'Quiet!' He ran in, his face a little red, his tie skew-whiff. 'Today, we've got a very important lesson. Settle down.'

He started writing on the board. As his shirt stretched, you could see a line of sweat down his back.

There were some mutterings from the class, bored already. Mr Kellett made his face into a rock. 'I said *settle down*.'

He turned to write more. His back's big, with lots of muscles, because Mr Kellett does lots of boxing and used to be a semi-pro footballer and played for Altrincham Town. He's the one in our school who everyone knows would win if there was a teacher fight.

Dr Sharma would win if it was girls-only. Mr Kellett would win the overall.

'OK.' Mr Kellett stopped writing. 'Get your exercise books out. Today we're going to talk about...'

He stepped back and pointed at the board.

Gascoigne's genius volley, Seaman saving that penalty, and how England are DEFINITELY DEFINITELY GOING TO WIN EURO '96!

The class went wild. *Wild.* Kids jumped up, banged their desks, hooted like weird monkeys – and Mr Kellett just smiled.

It's things like this, why everyone likes him so much. Things like this, and how good he is at sports and fighting.

Sean ran across the room – 'He leaps like a salmon and . . .' He did an impression of a footballer heading the ball, and Mr Kellett didn't even stop *that*.

Even I was enjoying the class a little bit.

At least, I was enjoying it until Mr Kellett said, '*And* are we going to annihilate the Netherlands tomorrow night?'

Everyone roared and Mr Kellett said, 'Now, who can tell me the meaning of *annihilate*?'

Kids started shouting words – '*destroy*', '*take down*', '*murder*', '*crush*'.

But not me.

Tomorrow night? Again?

I supposed it was good for Richard Plant, at least. And I didn't think we had any kids from the Netherlands in our school – though if we did, I'd soon find out.

And I supposed it gave me more time for spying round the house. It was useful to know one time I could be pretty sure that my upstairs-downstairs, jack-in-the-box parents wouldn't be getting up from the sofa.

The bell rang and everyone rushed out.

I went up to Mr Kellett with my book of lists, a finger wedged inside to mark the right page. 'Mr Kellett?'

'Fiona.' He beamed. 'Not your kind of lesson, eh?'

'No, I love football,' I said quickly. 'Did you see McAllister's face when he missed that penalty?'

'Ouch.' Mr Kellett smiled. 'Poor man. Must have smarted.'

'I was wondering, as you're good at words' – I opened my book to show him – 'if you could tell me about these?'

He looked at my list.

He glanced up. 'Mercurial?'

'Gascoigne,' I said.

'Constitution?'

'Of Ukraine.'

He seemed to be waiting, so I added, 'I've been reading the paper this weekend.'

Mr Kellett laughed like I'd said *I went on a spaceship*.

'OK' – he pulled up the chair next to me – 'well, far be it from me to discourage *that*. Let's concentrate on *mercurial* and *constitution* for now, and maybe leave *ammonium nitrate* and *tremble triggers* for another time.'

Mrs Vernal didn't want to talk about football, of course. *Two hundred hurt* was more her kind of thing.

'Shocking. And less than thirty miles from here!' Mrs Vernal put her hand on the scarf at her neck. 'You kids. I don't know how you can even take something like this in at your age. The *futility*.'

It's things like this that make me want to like football. I feel I'd fit better on Mr Kellett's team than Mrs Vernal's.

She shook her head slowly. There was a long pause. Around our drama circle, kids shifted in their seats.

'Should we talk about the footy instead?' Greeney asked.

'Hard as it is,' Mrs Vernal said, 'we need to acknowledge these things. In my classes, what matters is authenticity. Real life. And all the horrors that come with it. Because that is how we flower and grow.' Mrs Vernal looked around the circle of chairs. 'Does anyone have anything they want to share with the group?'

No one answered.

'Surely some of you have some feelings about what has happened?'

The room was quiet. Even the *hands-up, me-me-me-miss* kids weren't going to talk about a bomb. However much Mrs Vernal wanted us to.

Mrs Vernal could try to make us talk about it till she'd run out of voice ... but even the smart-arse kids couldn't know where to start with knowing what the right answer was about *a bomb*, could they?

School distracted me from thinking about Mum and how Scar-bad I'd been, going in Danielle's room that morning.

After school, I was in a good mood in the park, as Lewis and I practised different spy crawls from the handbook.

I watched Lewis attempt feline crawl, using the broken bit of fence round the tennis courts for cover.

'The book says don't drag your feet,' I said. 'And it's important you keep your head low. Stop bobbing.'

'I'm not bobbing.'

'You're bobbing *all the time*. It's like you've got a chicken's head.'

He got up and dusted his hands off. 'You try.'

I threw the handbook down. 'Seal crawl.' I made sure my whole body was on the ground and just moved my arms.

Pretty quickly, I got out of puff. 'It's all very well for the book to say *pull with your arms and use your toes and push down to move forward*,' I said, my hot breath coming back from the grass in my face, 'but they don't have skinny arms like me, do they? *And* my toes hurt.'

'I think you're doing fine,' Lewis said. 'You've moved a few metres now.'

I stretched over to grab *The Junior Spy's Secret Handbook™*, which still felt closer to me than it should. 'I'm going to practise flat feline crawl instead. You try too.' I looked at the handbook and threw it on the ground. 'You have to stay down, and crawl with one leg straight. *Always*.'

And Lewis and I stopped talking and concentrated on pulling one dead foot behind us, like soldiers in a war film.

Crawling a distance in a proper, professional crawl is harder than it looks. Like doing doggy paddle, but without water. Lewis and I were so busy trying to stop our heads bobbing, we nearly flat-feline-crawled right into each other.

'Ow!' When Lewis lifted his head, he had light in his eyes. 'Look at us! It's like Spy versus Spy!'

We burst into giggles and rolled over onto our backs. We laughed into the sun. My laugh was still a bit breathy from being puffed out.

'You got your inhaler?' Lewis asked.

'Always.' I rolled back over onto my front to get my breath back. 'But I'm fine.'

'This is enough fun, just practising,' Lewis said. 'We don't need to investigate Danielle. See?'

I nodded. It *was* fun. Maybe Lewis was right. I didn't need to do any actual spying.

I thought how sad Mum had looked when she found me in Danielle's room that morning.

'OK,' I said. 'We'll just practise.'

'You mean it?'

I got down on the ground and made front crawl arms. I lifted my head. 'I mean it.' I tried to seal crawl again, the bumpy grass pressing against my tummy. 'And I'm not even lying this time.'

*

When I let myself in through the back door afterwards, the house was silent.

Nearly silent. I could hear the soft sound of music upstairs.

I remembered Dad saying he was staying at Uncle Jim's tonight. 'Mum?'

No answer.

The music got louder as I moved through the kitchen into the lounge. A woman sang in a high, sad voice about a winner who was taking it all. And a loser who was somewhere, standing small.

I dropped my rucksack. I moved to the bottom of the stairs and leaned against the wall.

Invisible creepy crawlies marched across my neck.

The song faded out.

I was about to walk up the stairs when the piano started up again. *The same song.*

I stood there, uncertain, as the sad woman sang. About victory and destiny. About gods throwing dice and people playing aces and building fences. The woman's voice was pretty, but strange. She sang *loo-serr* rather than *loser.*

I looked down at my feet, the creepy crawlies back on my neck again.

Suddenly, I felt hot. Boiling, *boiling* hot.

I stamped upstairs. 'MUM!'

I burst into Danielle's bedroom.

Mum sat on the floor next to the record player, her legs tucked to the side. The room was a mess – books off shelves, records out of sleeves. There were clothes all over the bed. Mum even had one of Danielle's scarves tied in a bow on top of her head.

The sad woman was reaching the long bit of the chorus.

'the winner takes it a–ll–ll–ll'

Mum slowly raised her head to look at me. Lots of hair had fallen out of the scarf, into her face. She didn't even try to adjust it.

We stared at each other.

I looked at the glass next to Mum. At the big bottle that said Bells on it, next to the glass.

The room smelt of pub. 'Have you been here all day?'

Mum looked at the bottle and glass, like she'd only just noticed they were there. She looked back up at me, her eyes filling with tears. 'Fiona, I'm so sorry.'

I folded my arms. 'Are you drunk?'

The song finished again.

Mum lifted the lid of the record player. She moved the arm so that it was back on the start of the record.

She dropped the lid and the piano music started up. The sad woman sang about how she didn't want to talk.

I just stood there. Frozen. Shivery.

Mum jerked her head up. 'I'm sorry. I'm sorry, I'm sorry, I'm sorry. Don't tell your dad, Fiona. I'm so sorry.'

I couldn't look at her screwed-up, pleading eyes.

I looked away. 'Did you find anything for me, then?' My voice sounded tighter, stretched like an elastic band.

'Any what, darling?'

'You were in here to look for stuff for me. For the car boot sale.'

Mum reached up and out with her arms, like a baby wanting a hug.

I ran out of the room.

I stood in the hallway as the song finished. The piano of the song started up again.

I stood there for a second, wavering. Then I made a decision, hard.

Never mind what I'd decided earlier. I'd changed my mind – I would investigate Danielle's death after all. I'd go to the police station, first thing tomorrow.

And with Mum out of the way, there was something else I could do.

I took a pair of scissors to the peninsula and cut a slice from Mum's curtain fabric. I took the slice upstairs with a needle and thread, and went to work on my coat, making a secret pocket.

If Mum ever left Danielle's room, I was going to steal that record and sell it at the fair.

So Mum could never *ever* play it again.

10

People always say Monkford is a great place for kids to
grow up – but it's only ever adults who say it.
(paradox)

Thirty-one days to the fair
I didn't see Mum the next morning.

I didn't even try to speak to her when I got up. I just
got in my school uniform and went straight to the police
station.

I threw my rucksack on the floor and put my hands on the
counter. 'I'd like some information, please.'

The man in glasses behind the counter blinked.

When he didn't ask, I said, 'About a murder in 1982.' I
looked at my feet. 'Well. *Maybe* a murder, it's not clear. I'm
not sure how she died. That's part of the problem.'

The man looked at his colleague and back to me. 'How old
are you, darling?'

'Nearly twelve.'

He leaned forward and put his elbows on the counter.
'We're quite busy catching adult criminals here. Probably
best you head into school, eh, love?'

I shifted my weight from one foot to the other. I swallowed.

'You've not left yet, little one?' The man looked at his colleague again and back at me. 'There something else?'

I made myself say it. 'Have you got any jobs?'

When he just started laughing, I picked up my rucksack and hurried to school.

I wouldn't be correcting anyone if they called police *the filth* later.

And I wouldn't want a job with *the filth* anyway.

School news!

Turns out we do have a kid from the Netherlands; we just didn't realise for a while because her name's Zoe Peters and that doesn't sound very Dutch. But all the kids did loads of looking until we found one.

So that's good.

Except maybe for Zoe Peters.

And those people who say Monkford is a great place for kids to grow up? They've never been in the girls' toilets at our high school.

It was my mistake. I shouldn't have bought that can of Sprite at the shop next to the police station. And I shouldn't have sung to myself in the toilets, especially not the song the Little Mermaid sings as she brushes her hair with a fork. I don't even watch kids' films anymore – haven't for ages. I must have heard someone else singing that song, and if I knew who that was, I'd be *furious*.

Bang bang bang on my toilet door. 'Who's that singing?'

I stayed completely still.

'If you don't come out, we'll batter you.'

I peeked through the slit at the side of the cubicle. Three older girls stood around, all arms and boobs and hair. Bigger than me in every way. If I was the Little Mermaid, they were all Ursula the Sea Witch.

I unlocked the door. I burst through the cubicle door as quickly as I could, a tough cowboy in a saloon bar.

'I was singing by accident.' I put my hands on my hips and stared the tallest one in the eyes. 'No big deal.'

'You're the girl who has the magazines.'

I looked up at her without blinking. 'Yep.'

She stared back. 'And you're also the kid who shows her pants.'

'I'm *the kid with the magazines*,' I said.

'Ew, monkey bars. That's so dirty,' another sea witch said.

You do something *once*, for a reason you don't even remember, and it stays with you for ever, like it's been written on all your school jumpers in permanent marker.

I made my voice strong. 'That was ages ago. In primary school.'

'Once a pants girl, always a pants girl.'

I strode towards the door. The three sea witches blocked me.

I folded my arms. 'Like I said, now I'm the girl with the magazines. Do you want me to tell my friends in Year Ten that you're picking on me? Do you want me to tell *Craig Parsons*?'

Craig Parsons was probably tall enough to buy his own magazines but, at the mention of the hardest kid in Year Eleven, the sea witches looked at each other.

I took that second to rush between them and out into the corridor.

'And they just let me go!' I said triumphantly to Lewis. 'I didn't get a Chinese burn or my head flushed or anything.'

We sat on the grass after school outside the second-biggest bush in the park, hunched over, concentrating. We were making spy kits out of matchboxes, our foreheads going sweaty in the sun.

'Everything's changed now.' I unfolded my matchbox's end sections. 'We're popular! If there was a school trip now, we could probably sit near the back of the bus. Three rows from the back, even.' I wrote *code flap* on each of the unfolded end sections in tiny writing. 'This is a bit fiddly.'

'At least you're not the one about to cut your fingers off.' Lewis sawed wobbily at two pushed-together pencils with his penknife. His job was making a short pencil for each of our spy boxes.

He stopped sawing and looked up, sunlight in his eyes. 'Did you see the section in the spy manual on teamwork? We can learn secret codes and write each other letters that only we would understand? In case they get intercepted.'

That was hope in his eyes, not sunlight. 'No way. That sounds more like mnemonics than spying to me.' I picked up a tiny piece of paper and wound it round a matchstick. 'So, are you going to help me sell the magazines at the car boot?'

'I'm not sure.' Lewis's penknife skittered off the pencils. He glanced up. 'Is . . . is your mum going to be there?'

I sniffed with laughter. But then I thought of my mum, on the floor, drunk and listening to that song, reaching up to me like a baby. I stopped sniffing.

I watched Lewis saw at the pencils. I picked up a piece of paper to wind round my matchstick. It seemed to make the paper take up *more* space, not less – but I supposed the people at *The Junior Spy's Secret Handbook™* knew what they were doing. 'I know they say matchboxes are great because they're a common household item.' I wound the paper some more. 'But I still think there are going to be questions asked if people see kids carrying round matchboxes.'

'We'll keep them in our secret pockets though,' Lewis said. 'So it'll be OK.'

'And the problem with the secret pockets,' I said, 'is it's only been a day, and already five people have said, "*Aren't you hot in that coat, Fiona?*"'

Lewis didn't answer.

I looked up. 'What's wrong?'

'It's the football tonight.' Lewis sawed at the pencils. 'I just can't wait for this stupid championship to be over.'

I made *sad fish mouth* at Lewis. Lewis's dad would be getting him to watch the football, trying to make him like it. And Lewis would keep having to jump up and celebrate and say stuff like *Did you see McAllister's face when he missed that penalty? Aaah,* or his dad would give him little punches on the arm and say *Buck up, son, don't be such a girl.*

Lewis concentrated. 'I think ... nearly there ...'

There was a crunching as the pencils broke. We whooped. Lewis's penknife skidded into his leg, but it was fine, it stopped at his trousers.

Lewis helped me with winding paper onto matchsticks, and I thought some more about Lewis's dad.

There are some days I'd prefer other kids' parents. Like Sean's mum, who lets him stay up to watch *Crimewatch*. Or Candy's parents, who let her have a telly in her bedroom and have pancakes when it wasn't pancake day. Or even Greeney's parents, who – I hear – let you eat sweets right before your tea *and* have a ride-on lawn mower.

And Lewis's mum is OK, though she only buys brown bread and won't buy biscuits with chocolate on. But I *definitely* wouldn't want Lewis's dad. My parents might have flashing doorbell lights, drive a car with our name down the side and keep our house's second-biggest bedroom for a dead girl – but they never *made* me watch the football or punched me on the arm all day and called it a joke and said I acted *like a little girl*.

I picked up *The Junior Spy's Secret Handbook™*. 'We need to find hollow twigs next. For putting secret messages in.'

Lewis waved at someone. I looked up.

Sean wandered towards us, his hands in his pockets, kicking every stone he could see as he walked.

He stood over us and looked at our equipment, all laid out. 'What are you doing?'

'Making spy kits,' I said. 'To keep in our secret pockets.'

Sean bumped down onto the grass and stuck his legs out. 'Secret pockets?'

I flapped open my coat to show him.

Sean looked at Lewis. 'Show me yours.'

'I haven't made mine yet,' Lewis said.

'It's a great idea, though.' Sean lay down and folded one foot over the other. 'Hey, Fi, you can keep all your money from the car boot sale in that pocket, can't you? You're going to be loaded.'

I watched Sean jiggle his body on the grass, making himself comfortable, and smiled. Never mind Mum. Life was *good*.

Sean blew his fringe out of his eyes and closed them. 'So this is where you two go when I'm not around, hey? It's a good spot.'

I glanced at Lewis nervously. We hadn't told anyone where we'd found the magazines. We thought it was safer that way. In case the owner with his angry face and veiny Popeye arms came back.

'Now.' I stood up and dusted my skirt off. 'There have to be hollow twigs round here somewhere.'

I came back from school to find Mum at the kettle.

I threw my rucksack down. 'Hi.'

Mum gave me a big smile. 'Do you want a cup of tea?'

I shook my head. I never want a cup of tea, and she knows that.

'Your father's back from seeing Uncle Jim.' She turned back to the kettle. Her movements were jerky as she stirred the teabag. 'They had a good time drinking and whatnot. Dad has a sore head today. He's out at the shops now.'

I didn't say anything.

She put the spoon on the counter with a *ching*. 'I'm sorry about yesterday. I wasn't myself.' She made her voice lighter. 'But don't tell your father, hey? We don't want to ruin the nice night he had with Uncle Jim. Or ruin the match. He's really looking forward to watching England on telly tonight.'

I still didn't say anything.

She kept her back to me, still facing the kettle. 'I'm really sorry, Fiona.' So quiet, I could hardly hear. 'It won't happen again.'

She put her hands flat on the countertop and waited.

'OK.' I slid off the stool. 'I'm going upstairs.'

I walked into the lounge, trying to work out if this was a good kind of secret to have or the bad kind. Either way, if Dad was out and Mum was in the kitchen, it was a good time to steal another stamp and envelope from the Cupboard of Office Things.

So I peeled off the last stamp in the book and carried it upstairs carefully on my finger. I sat on my bed and wrote a letter to the police asking about Danielle, making sure I used my best grown-up writing.

And hoping – really hoping – that if it was the man with the glasses who opened the post at the police station, he wouldn't be able to tell that the letter was from me.

II

**While you're shadowing your quarry, remember –
enemy spies might be shadowing you too! A good
spy stays vigilant, and has tricks up their sleeve
to shake off a tail.**
The Junior Spy's Secret Handbook™

Twenty-seven days to the fair

Summer was starting to feel like proper summer now. It was shiny-pavement hot. Ice-lollies-not-just-as-a-pudding hot. No one was wearing their jumpers to school anymore, and some kids even wore short-sleeved shirts. Not the good kids though, I don't know why – but I noticed, so I made sure I didn't wear short sleeves either.

England beat the Netherlands 4–1, so there was no decent school news because that was all anyone talked about. England had made the quarter finals and the next game was on Saturday, against Spain.

Another game.

I really hoped England started losing soon.

Speaking of losing – Richard Plant came back in, three days after the England–Scotland game. I saw him walking round the playing fields at lunchtime on his own, so things weren't back to normal for him yet.

And not for me, either. I walked through the corridors, my head held higher than it had ever been, and older kids spoke to me.

'All right, Fiona.'

'Great to see you, Fi.'

'Nice coat. Good toggles.'

And I'd answer with a smile.

'Hi!'

'Thank you.'

'Looking good yourself.'

It wasn't quite so good for Lewis, as no one knew his name. But, still, he got to walk next to me, so no one tried to trip him up in the corridors all week.

It was official. The magazines had changed my life – for ever.

Finally, the day was here.

Dad parked up on Festival Field, the place alive with cars and boxes, and the buzz of conversations and laughter. Camping tables were piled high with cooking dishes and ashtrays, alarm clocks and electric whisks. There were people *everywhere*.

I must have been really distracted because when Dad reached for two folding camping tables in the boot, he said. 'You're thoughtful today.'

I unfolded the legs of the other table.

'Aren't you hot in that coat?'

'I'm fine.'

Neither me nor Mum had told him about Mum playing records in Danielle's room when he was at Uncle Jim's. But then, Dad had asked me to phone a premium rate number to apply for a quiz show earlier that week. And neither of us told Mum.

I think that's just how families work.

I placed my cardboard box on the camping table and opened it. Under the toys, I could just make out a bit of blonde hair and the *e* of *Razzle*.

My heart beat loud in my ears. I was really going to do this.

I started pulling out the ponies and bears from my box, sitting the bears upright. I made their bodies lean forward and their feet stick out, like fat babies.

Dad opened his box to reveal plates and napkins from my other dead grandma's old house. I spotted our old kitchen lampshade. Mum's sewing patterns.

'You can have that other table for your stuff,' Dad said.

'Good,' I said.

'Let me know if you need any help with pricing. Or closing a deal.'

I nodded and laid my things out. The ponies. The bears. I felt my face going red that I'd ever played with this kids' stuff. I reached for Sprinkles and held her for a second, before making myself put her on the table with the others.

I pulled out the leaflets I'd made, listing all the magazines. I tucked the lists under a bear and left the magazines in the box. I folded the box's flaps in and slid it under my table.

'I'm gonna teach you to sell, Fiona. Watch and learn.' Dad puffed himself up as he looked out over the field. 'We don't put the price on the items in writing, so we can start high and adjust with the market.' He waved his hand over his table. 'We don't want to let the good stuff go too soon, too cheap. We listen to offers, and we set a good price.'

A woman came over. 'How much for the knitting patterns?'

Dad looked at her for a moment. 'Fifty pence each, or three for one pound twenty.'

The woman looked through the patterns and bought three.

Dad put the coins into his bumbag and zipped it up. He winked at me. 'How good's your dad at selling?'

'You are.'

'A proper barrow boy!'

I didn't know what that meant, except that Dad was proud of himself.

I thought I saw Dr Sharma walking down between the cars on the next aisle.

'Dr Sharma!' I did a big wave, windmilling both my arms. '*Dr Sharma!*'

But it couldn't have been Dr Sharma because the woman turned straight round and walked in the other direction.

Dad started chatting to the man at the table next to him. The man was dusting off a beige electric fan that was so old, it must have been from the war or something.

A woman pointed at my bears. She had a young kid trailing off her arm. 'How much for these?'

I leaned on my homemade leaflets, covering them with my hand. 'Fifty pence each,' I said. 'Or three for a pound.'

I looked up to share a secret smile, but Dad was still chatting to the beige fan man, his hands shoved in his jeans pockets like he was Del Boy, his thumbs fluttering against the denim.

The woman scooped up two bears – *and Sprinkles.*

I didn't have time to think about kids' stuff now, not with magazines to sell. So I let her drop the pound coin into my hand and put it carefully into my secret pocket. I watched the woman walked away. Trying not to feel anything.

It was fine. It was all fine.

Dad took a few steps away from our camping table, still talking to the fan man. 'What kind of auction?'

'*General household goods auctions*, they're called.' The man folded his arms. 'Dead people's stuff. I guarantee, you get the best gardening tools at dead house auctions.'

'Really?' Dad picked up a pair of secateurs and started squeezing them, testing the spring.

Now.

I grabbed my magazines from the box. I put them at the end of my table, furthest from Dad's. I arranged bears and ponies and jigsaws over them hurriedly.

Dad put the secateurs down. 'Well, I've learned something today.' He turned away from the fan man, smiling.

I looked around. Some boys from school were starting to gather at nearby stalls, looking carefully at plates and coat hangers.

A Year Ten kid came up to my table, his centre-parted hair sticking in two directions like a washing-up brush. 'Hi, Fi.'

I checked Dad was looking in the other direction. I snuck him a leaflet.

Dean Prince, who plays for Port Vale under sixteens, trailed his finger across my camping table. 'All right, Fi-oh.'

He swiped a leaflet and was gone.

One kid with baggy skater clothes picked up a pony and turned it over, like he was studying the quality. 'How are you doing, Fi?'

Dad looked over at that point. I waited until he was looking the other way, before nodding to the boy to take a leaflet.

'You need to share those leaflets,' I said, so all the boys could hear. 'I'm selling each *pony or jigsaw* at 1 p.m. Though I will listen to offers before then.'

The boys at the table melted back into groups, huddled and muttering. The boy with the washing-up hair had his arms round some other boys, talking and focused, like they were a sports team before a big match.

'I didn't think you knew so many people!' Dad turned to me. 'But Fi, don't get your hopes up. I know I said we should aim high, and listen to offers, but I don't think you should expect to get too much for your ponies.'

I nodded. I kept my gaze on the buzzing crowd.

Dad tapped me on the back. 'Mind the stall while I check out the competition.'

He walked up the aisle, looking at other people's tables as he went.

Dean Prince rushed up to the table. 'Fifteen quid for *Mayfair*.'

'Twenty-five and it's yours right now.'

Dean nodded. In seconds, we'd swapped the magazine for the money.

I rearranged my bears and ponies over the remaining mags and slipped the money into my secret pocket.

The skater kid came up. 'A tenner for *Fiesta*.'

I shook my head.

The kid looked like he was going to say something else, but I jerked my head. Dad was coming.

'Some advice.' Dad joined me at the table. 'Don't be buying anything from the last two stalls on the left.' He spoke to both me and the skater kid, who was now closely studying sewing patterns. 'A lot of things there off the back of a lorry.'

The kid picked a package of shiny fabric off Dad's table. He looked at it closely. 'Right you are.'

'That's an ironing board cover,' Dad said.

'OK.'

Another baggily dressed kid came up. He took the iron-ing board cover off Skater Kid thoughtfully, like they were a team, considering buying it together. 'There's more where that came from,' Dad said. 'My wife makes them. Fit all standard sizes.'

I saw a familiar bobbing walk in the distance. 'LEWIS!'

He waved. His mum waved, too.

I shouted, 'Aren't you coming over?'

He jiggled up and down like he needed a wee. 'Is your mum there?'

I narrowed my eyes. 'No.'

Lewis came scurrying up, his mum following.

'Hi, Mrs Harris,' I said.

'Hi, Fiona. Aren't you hot in that coat?'

'I'm fine.'

'I hear you're coming to visit after tea tonight.' She gave me a big smile. 'What lovely ponies. I—'

'Don't touch them!' I barked.

Mrs Harris stopped reaching for a pony.

'Sorry,' I said. 'I mean, I've laid them out carefully. In the best selling positions. Sorry.'

Dad leaned towards Mrs Harris. 'Fiona is taking her sell-ing very seriously today.'

Mrs Harris nodded. 'Right you are.' Dad and Mrs Harris chatted to each other, something about the bomb – '*so awful*', '*so pointless*' – but I stopped listening.

A lad with bright chin rash stepped up. He stood so close, I could smell Skittle breath. 'Twenty-five quid for *Razzle*.'

Lewis's eyes went wide. He glanced at his mum, but she was still talking to Dad.

'Sold. But' – I glanced at Dad and back – 'You can pick it up when the coast is clear.'

Chin Rash Skittle Breath nodded and handed me two notes.

Dad looked at the money. He looked at the boy.

Chin Rash Skittle Breath picked up a bear and walked on. Dad watched after him, looking dazed.

I dropped the money into my secret pocket. I moved my fingers around in there so I could touch all the notes and coins at once. Fifty-one pounds already. And I still had seven magazines to go.

I could feel the fair now. It was getting closer. I could practically *smell* the candyfloss.

I was going to be so popular at school after this.

To Go to the Fair I Need:

1) ~~Money for the rides~~ √
2) Girl friends, so the boy from the Waltzers will push my car
3) Mum and Dad to let me go

12

Sometimes, I'd prefer it if people didn't listen to me.
(paradox)

Twenty-seven days to the fair

I didn't get twenty-five quid for *all* the magazines. I only got the cover price for the film magazine, and only a fiver for *Readers' Wives*. I reckon if the boy who'd bought it had been able to see inside, I wouldn't have got that.

But – one hundred and twelve pounds. That was more money than I'd ever had in my life. That was fifty-six goes on the Waltzers.

Fifty-two goes, if you threw in popcorn and candyfloss. Which I definitely would, thank you very much. When I finally got to the fair, I would be doing it *in style*.

While Mum and Dad watched the England–Spain game downstairs, I opened the jewellery box where I keep my hair bobbles. The ballerina turned, the plink-plonk music played, and I tucked my money in the pouch at the back. I shut the box with a snap.

I ignored all Mum and Dad's shouts to come downstairs, even Mum's, 'Penalties! Fi, *surely* you want to come down for the penalties?'

There were roars from downstairs and I could guess the result, even before Dad shouted up, 'Semi-finals, Fi! We're in the *semi-finals!*'

I came downstairs to find out who'd scored what, and Dad and Mum had their arms round each other. They danced around the lounge to 'We Are the Champions' like they were dancing round Blackpool Tower ballroom, and I knew school was going to be *awful* all week, again.

While our teatime baked potatoes were in the oven, Mum and Dad decided to *use the time usefully*, so their good moods were over pretty quickly.

I eavesdropped on my *quarry* at the garage door. Just practising really. I didn't expect to hear anything good.

And I didn't.

Mum and Dad had been meaning to paint the hallway for as long as I can remember. *This* was as far as they got – occasionally checking if the paint in the garage has gone hard. And, for some reason, because they hate painting so much, that means they *both* had do it, which doesn't make sense, but that's my mum and dad for you.

'What, really?' Mum's voice went high. 'Fiona *made more money* than you?'

'Don't start, Gail.'

'I'm not starting. I just knew I should have gone. Did you sell *any* ironing board covers?'

'She seemed really popular with the older boys, Gail.' I heard the sound of shuffling feet and clanging tins. 'We don't need to be worried, do we?'

The clanging stopped.

'Of course not,' Mum said eventually. 'She's eleven, Jonathan. We're not *there* yet.'

I wondered where *there* was.

Didn't matter. I wanted to go *now*.

More shuffling and clanging.

'Do you think that one's OK?' Mum said. 'Poke it. No, harder. Break the crust.'

There was a crispy noise, like slicing through burnt toast.

'I reckon it'll do,' Dad said. 'So long as we give it a good stir.'

I heard the sound of the lid going back on the tin.

'OK, so that's paint sorted.' Mum said it like she'd run a marathon. 'Now, where on God's earth did we put the Polyfilla?'

Half an hour later, the three of us sat eating jacket potatoes at the peninsula.

Dad sliced into his potato. 'I've been hearing you get good stuff to sell on at dead people's auctions. So maybe I'll do that for the next car boot sale.'

'Sounds like you need to.'

'Don't start, Gail.'

'I'm not *starting*, just *saying*.'

I watched Dad chase a baked bean round his plate sadly. I was almost pleased it was the football the next day.

It didn't help that when he finished eating before us, he went to the Cupboard of Office Things.

'Bloody hell, Gail, why are we always, *always*, out of stamps?'

And then Mum and Dad had a big back-and-forth about why each other would have taken the last stamp without saying something, and I cut a big piece of potato and shoved it in my mouth and made myself eat it, even though it was way too hot.

*

After tea, Mum and I were in the car, on the way to the big out-of-town shopping centre to get new school shoes. So I was surprised when she pulled up at the precinct.

'Why are we here?' I asked.

'While I remember. To shut your father up.'

I followed her till I saw where we were going – Paper Rack – and slowed. 'I'll wait outside.'

'Don't be silly. And you can dawdle on your own time, Fiona.'

I zigzagged across the car park after her. 'Dawdle on your own time, *Fi*,' I muttered.

I passed some older kids gathered round a car with its doors open, rave music pumping. Two of the kids were swapping tapes, but I wasn't as impressed by older kids these days – not since I realised some of them *couldn't even get their own porn.*

And – *tapes.* Not even CDs.

Being older was wasted on some of these kids.

I followed Mum into Paper Rack and she went right up to the bald man at the counter.

'One book of six first and one of six second-class stamps, please. And I'll pay the paper bill while I'm here.'

The newsagent looked down at me.

I shuffled a little under his gaze.

'Larson, fourteen Archer's Way,' Mum added.

The newsagent jerked his head at me. 'This one yours?'

'For my sins.'

The man looked at me for a bit longer.

I stood up straight and did my best smile.

Mum looked at me and back at the man, her smile bright.

'That'll be twenty pounds forty,' he said finally.

Mum did a giggly laugh, being friendly enough for two.

'Now, my purse.' She started getting things out of her hand-bag and clanging them onto the counter – hairbrush, car keys, spotty umbrella. 'Hang on – sorry.' Mum always made up for strangers' rudeness by being overly, fussily nice. Unless she gets angry and decides to eyeball them back – you never quite know what you're getting with my mum. That's why she's so hard to live with.

When we hurried out of the shop, Mum put the stamps in her purse. 'I'm not sure I like that man.'

I walked quickly past the car with rave tunes. 'I don't think I do, either.'

We got back in the car and set off for the shopping centre.

'Can I listen to the news?' I said. 'I want to find out the latest in Bosnia.'

'Too depressing.' Mum flicked an indicator. 'So, Fi, you sold more than your father at the car boot today.'

I nodded.

'Your father's too nice, that's his problem. How much did you make?'

'Eighteen pounds,' I lied quickly. 'But I'm saving it.'

'Wow!' Mum looked genuinely proud. I felt a stab of something, knowing I'd have to write this on another Scar list someday.

Sometimes I really wish I didn't have such a good memory for the bad stuff I've done.

Mum shoved the middle of the steering wheel. The horn screeched.

'Oh, COME ON!' Mum threw her hand up. 'Yes, you *may well* wave. *Apology not accepted.*'

Mum sighed. She moved her head from one side to an-other, like she was stretching her neck, and kept driving.

*

We pulled up at the big out-of-town shopping centre and Mum bought my new shoes. She let me carry the bag and I banged it against my leg as we walked back to the car.

I saw a man who looked familiar, in the walkway by one of those stalls with a big awning. Those stalls that sell soft cookies and ice cream. The good stalls.

Was that Mr Kellett?

But the man stepped to the side and I realised it couldn't be Mr Kellett after all because he was holding hands with another man.

But then the Mr Kellett man dropped the other man's hand and turned so he was fully facing me – and it was *definitely* Mr Kellett. And he'd been smiling and chatting to the other man before, but now he wasn't. He was staring at me, and standing completely still.

The other man turned around with two cookies, and he handed one to Mr Kellett.

Mr Kellett took it without saying *thank you*.

And then I smiled, realising what I'd seen. The men weren't *holding hands*. What I'd seen was Mr Kellett giving the other man money to buy him a cookie.

I waved.

After a second, Mr Kellett waved back. His friend looked from him to me, then turned to look at something in a shop window.

'Dawdling again, my little sales pro?' Mum said.

'Just thinking.' I tugged on the sleeve of Mum's coat. 'Can I have one of those big cookies?'

'No.'

I followed Mum towards the exit. And I was so busy thinking about how much I wanted one of those cookies, and how big and soft and melty they looked, I forgot to even mention I'd seen Mr Kellett.

'How about next time?' I said in the car, nearly home.

'We'll see next time,' Mum said.

'It's just they're really soft.'

'I don't want to talk about cookies anymore, Fiona.'

We took a left down George Street. I pointed out of the window. 'That's our lamppost. Where I meet Lewis and Sean to walk to school.'

Mum didn't say anything.

I pointed at the postbox. 'We always cross the street *here*. And on the way back, we cross *there*.' I looked at the house in between. 'Did an axeman live at that house, Mum?' I pointed. 'The one back there. Fifty-six George Street.'

Mum didn't answer for a few moments. 'An axeman? What do you mean?'

'A man with an axe. Sean said a man lived there who cut off his brothers' heads and arms and legs and ...' I stopped before saying *and they found a foot with a flipflop in with the bananas at the Co-op.*

Mum stared straight ahead. 'What a ridiculous thing to say.'

'If there was an axeman there, you would have heard, wouldn't you?'

She looked at me, finally. '*Of course* we would have heard.'

'But we don't walk in front of that house, we always cross the street before it. I think I don't because you don't and—'

'But I do walk in front of that house.'

I blinked. 'You don't.'

'I walk in front of it *exactly* as much as any other house. You kids! Making up stories, based on silly little things like where people cross the road! With your imaginations, you could drive people crazy, you know?' Mum shook her head and turned to face me. '*Of course* it won't be true about the man with an axe. You think something like that could have happened, here, in Monkford, and the only person who knows about it is a twelve-year-old kid called Sean?'

She gave me a tight smile and turned back to face the road.

We reached our road and Mum parked up in the drive. I thought the conversation was over, but she said, 'There's been no axe killings in Monkford and I don't give any of this a second thought. We don't want you having nightmares.'

She patted me on the shoulder and got out of the car.

I unclipped my seatbelt and got out of the car slowly. I followed Mum into the house, questions popping like fireworks.

Because Mum *didn't* walk in front of that house. And how was I meant to forget *that*?

I know Mum wants me to be like her. She doesn't notice things if she doesn't want to notice. If she gets a scab, she puts a plaster over it straight away.

But if I get a scab, I pick it off and roll it up and wait for the skin to scab up again. Then I pick it again, and pick deeper.

Even if the area keeps bleeding. Even if my skin hurts.

13

When I try to make myself look older, it does the opposite.
(paradox)

Twenty-seven days to the fair

'I don't want to talk about it anymore.' Lewis gave himself a hug. 'I don't want to think about the axeman. It's not true, and it's horrible. So let's talk about something else. About how we're going to be so popular now you've sold all those magazines. The best kids in school.'

I smiled at him. I'd never dared even *dream* of us being the best kids at school. But that was before. Before the car boot sale.

The two of us sat on his bed that evening, the Scrabble board between us. Scrabble wasn't my first choice for a Saturday night, particularly a Saturday night when I'd made *a hundred and twelve pounds* – but I'd left *The Junior Spy's Secret Handbook™* at home, and I *really* didn't want Lewis to get out his book of magic tricks.

I looked at my tiles. *XJYAPCB*. 'Have you made your secret spy pocket yet?'

He moved one tile to a different place on the rack. He shook his head.

I put X down on a triple letter score in front of the letter I. Lewis stared at me.

'Xi's a word.' I pronounced it 'chee' like Grandma did.

'Xi?'

'Xi.'

'It's not a word.'

'It is! Go and get your Scrabble dictionary, I'll prove it.'

'We don't have a Scrabble dictionary.'

'I promise, I've seen it in the Scrabble dictionary with my own eyes.'

'What does it mean then?'

I jumped up. 'Let's ask your parents.'

I ran down the stairs, Lewis following. Lewis's parents were sitting, one on each sofa, watching telly.

'Mrs Harris, will you tell Lewis *xi* is a real word for Scrabble?'

'Chi? Short for cheese? I don't know.' She gave a little laugh. 'You kids know more than me.'

'Your mother's rubbish with word things,' Lewis's dad said, reaching for the remote control. 'No point asking her.'

Lewis's mum laughed again, like she always did when he was being mean about her. Sometimes she didn't even need Lewis's dad to be mean, she did it to herself. *What a mess I look today! Oh, this old thing? Oh, I'm sorry it's a little overdone, I'm a hopeless cook.*

I turned to Lewis's dad. 'Do you know *xi* then? If you're better at words?'

'It's not a real word. And you need to be careful with that cheek.' He turned back to the telly.

'Can we phone my grandma, then? She'll tell you.'

'Give it up, little girl.' Lewis's dad switched the volume up. 'Quit when you're behind.'

I looked at Lewis. He begged me with his eyes not to say any more, so I walked upstairs.

'Leave that bedroom door open,' Lewis's mum said.

'No harm if the boy's feeling red-blooded, Lisa.'

I shut the door and sat on the bed again.

Lewis looked at the letters on his rack. 'You shouldn't be cheeky to him.'

'Your dad doesn't know *anything*, so I don't know why he always calls your mum stupid. I would never let anyone call me stupid like that.'

I left a gap. Lewis was always letting his dad say that about him.

'I don't believe *xi*'s a word,' Lewis said quietly. 'Dad says it isn't.'

'I *promise* it's in the Scrabble dictionary. I'll bring it in to school with me on Monday.'

I counted up the score in both directions, including the triple letter score, and wrote *38* on the score sheet.

I picked out a new letter from the bag. *T.*

I shook my head at how unlucky I was and put it on my letter rack. 'Why does your mum want us to keep the door open? She thinks we're going to be kissing? Or having sex? She's crazy.'

Lewis punched me lightly on the arm. 'I don't want to kiss you.'

'I know.' I shook my head. 'Maybe your dad's right after all.' I moved my letters around. 'Maybe your mum *is* stupid.'

The next day was Sunday and Mum and Dad were both around, so I used the time first thing in the morning to write letters. And the good thing was, we had stamps again.

I applied for a job at the dog rescue centre, one at the

laundrette and one at the chicken farm, though I almost hoped I didn't get that one. The advert said you needed a *strong stomach,* and I thought I did – but I really didn't want to have to find out.

Later, I helped Mum and Dad do the gardening. Dad was trimming the bushes with his big clippers while Mum weeded the flower beds.

My job was deadheading the roses. I quite liked it, as jobs went. Walk along the flowerbed, check out each flower. If it's dead – *snip.* Head tumbles like Anne Boleyn's. Pick up the head and put it in my basket.

Maybe I should be an executioner when I grow up. 'I've been thinking of watching *Gardeners' World.'*

They both kept weeding. Even though Mum, at least, would *definitely* have heard.

I snipped the head off another rose. 'You won't believe this. Lewis's parents don't have a Scrabble dictionary.'

'That's not an *actual* crime,' Mum said.

Dad stopped clipping to watch the conversation.

'And they don't know *xi* is a word.'

Mum dug her trowel into the soil. 'I think that's fair enough, Fiona.'

I snipped the dead head off another rose and looked at the next rose along. It wasn't properly dead.

They all would be soon though. *Snip.* 'Lewis's mum says we shouldn't shut the bedroom door after us. Though his dad says it's fine if Lewis is feeling red-blooded.'

Dad snorted.

I picked the deadish head off the grass and put it in my executioner's basket. 'What?'

Mum lifted her knees and adjusted the position of her knee protector. She twisted and gave Dad a look.

I stared at Dad. 'What?'

'Nothing.'

'Shall I ask Lewis's dad?'

Mum gave Dad another look. She kneeled down again and put her trowel on the grass. 'Geoff wants Lewis to be normal. People find it easier for their kids to be normal.'

'Lewis *is* normal.' Even as I said it, I knew it wasn't true. He was Lewis-y, and being Lewis-y was something you carried about with you. Kids can smell these things from the other end of the playground.

'*Of course* he's normal,' Mum said. 'Your dad means that we want our kids to take the easy path in life. That's what Geoff will be thinking with this red-blooded stuff.' She hunched her eyebrows. 'Don't ever – *ever* – tell Geoff I said this.'

'But *normal*. Mum, what—'

Mum moved round on her knees so she was looking at Dad. 'Jonathan, you started this conversation.' She dug at the soil with her trowel. 'You can have the pleasure of finishing it.'

Dad put his clippers on the grass and sat down at the bench. He patted the seat.

I placed my secateurs and basket on the ground and sat next to him.

'Lewis is a sensitive boy.' Dad smiled. 'Sometimes sensitive boys can take different paths from the herd. Not necessarily. But sometimes.'

I folded my arms at this. 'Can girls take different paths too? Or is it another thing that's just for boys?'

Mum put down her trowel. She and Dad looked at each other.

'Do you think that you're on a different path?' Dad asked.

They were both looking at me closely.

Mum shook her head at Dad. 'We're confusing her.'

'But if—'

Mum cut me off. 'Another time.'

Frustrated, I snipped off two not-completely-dead heads and tipped the content of the basket onto the compost heap.

And maybe it's because I was frustrated. Maybe that's why I chose that day to ask.

I'd got money for the fair now, but I was still no closer to getting Mum and Dad to let me go. I needed to do some *concrete investigating*.

And that meant asking about Danielle.

I wasn't stupid. I knew, by asking, my parents probably wouldn't tell me about her death. But they probably wouldn't be able to help giving me something, would they? Give me some clues to work with?

And while Lewis had said it would be a bad idea to ask Mum and Dad how Danielle died, he didn't know how much chattier my parents got when they were talking about England winning the football and besides – as had been proven many times – Lewis Harris didn't know everything.

I waited till we were all eating Dad's spaghetti bolognese that night.

'Thing is,' Mum said twirling spaghetti on her fork, 'we've had penalty practice now. So that stands us in good stead.'

I ate a mouthful and swallowed. 'Can I ask something about Danielle?'

Mum stopped chewing for a second. 'This had better not be about bedrooms.'

'You know when Danielle died . . .'

I said it casually, but it didn't matter.

Dad put his knife and fork down on the peninsula, so quietly they didn't make a noise.

Mum stopped chewing, properly now.

I looked down at my plate. I made swirls with my fork, leaving parallel tracks on the plate, like four ice skaters had made trails through the sauce.

'I hope it was quick,' I said. 'For her sake.'

Mum took a deep breath. She looked at Dad again. 'Fiona.'

'I like Fi now.'

'Fi.' Still looking at Dad. 'We talk about how your sister lived. Not how she died.'

I crunched my toes up in my shoes.

'People want to talk about how she died all the time,' Mum said. 'And she was so much more than a tragic story. She was a wonderful, wonderful little girl. And I will tell you *anything* you want to know about her. I will talk about her all day, if you want. And I will talk about anything, except how she . . .'

When Mum tailed off, Dad squeezed her arm.

I swung one foot out and kicked the metal leg of the peninsula. *Clang*.

Hurt charged through my toes.

Frustration bubbled up in my chest.

I took a deep breath. 'OK.' A different angle. 'Was she fun? What did she do for fun?'

Mum looked at her plate. 'She was *so* much fun.'

And Mum looked up and told me the story about the routine they had when they danced round the kitchen to a song about a highwayman. I didn't listen. The whole point of these stories is they never actually changed. They were as dead as my sister.

Though I will say, I feel embarrassed for Danielle when Mum tells these stories to Danielle's mates, when they come to see Mum and Dad on her birthday. Dead or not, Danielle wouldn't want her mates hearing that, would she?

Not unless high school was a really different place in 1982.

'She was our miracle baby, you know. We didn't think we could have children, and then she came along.' Mum looked at Dad softly. 'Everyone said she was special.'

'Special,' I kicked the peninsula leg again. *Clang*. Toe-pain. *Don't say it.*

'She lit up a room,' Mum said. 'She was just one of those people. So special.'

'Special.' I kicked it again. *Clang*.

Don't say it.

'The world wasn't made for people that special,' Mum said.

Don't say it. No, don't –

'Special?' The words just rushed out on their own. 'Like the kids at St Joseph's?'

Mum dropped her knife and fork.

'GO TO YOUR ROOM! NOW!'

Her voice was the shakiest I've ever heard.

And Dad spent ages in my bedroom that night, explaining that Mum just needed some time, and that I probably didn't understand what I was saying – that I was being mean to both Danielle *and* to the kids from St Joseph's, and those kids don't find life as easy as I do. And I can't have meant it, because making fun of both Danielle and those kids was the worst thing I could ever do – and *surely* I wasn't the kind of kid who meant to say things like that?

I listened. Thinking I didn't know how in seven words I'd managed to deeply offend both Danielle and the kids in the special class, and that was quite *special* in itself.

But that was me. Scar-bad again.

<u>The Bad Scar Things I've Done</u>
<u>1996 Summer Term Update</u>

1) Called Danielle special, which made fun of her and the kids from St Joseph's
2) Cut up Mum's curtain fabric to make a secret pocket
3) Tried to sell stuff from Danielle's room
4) Sold jazz mags to underage boys

I haven't put these in order because I don't know what order they're in.
And I don't want to think about it anymore.

14

Tiny arteries and veins serve the individual muscles and skin on your head, so it can bleed a lot if you get a head injury. For example, if you were hit on the head with a whack-a-mole hammer.

Fiona Larson, 7E's Blood Project

Twenty-five days to the fair

On Monday morning, in Dr Sharma's lesson, everyone was meant to be working on their science projects on their own. But kids were really talking about the game and how they'd step over the ball to fool the keeper when *they* were taking penalties for England.

Dr Sharma must have known she wouldn't get people to stop talking because she pretended not to notice.

She saw me with my hand up. 'This had better not be about penalty kicks.'

She sat at the stool next to me.

'I've got a question. Two questions.'

Dr Sharma raised her eyebrow. 'And?'

I looked down at my lap uncertainly. 'Do you know I had a sister? Danielle?'

Dr Sharma straightened her blouse around her waist. 'I do.'

'Did you teach her?'

Dr Sharma kept straightening. 'What has this got to do with your project?'

'I was just wondering what you knew about her.'

'Very little, I'm afraid. And Fiona, this is no place for soap operas. Science questions only.'

I stared at the edge of the table. I should have known she wouldn't help.

I noticed the outline of the special shape I'd drawn there earlier that year. Before I'd learned the word *swastika*. Before I'd learned it wasn't *my* special shape, after all.

I moved in front of the shape so Dr Sharma didn't see.

'Was that both questions?'

'No. Just one.'

She sighed. 'Is your second question about your project, at least?'

I nodded. 'What does it mean if you say someone's *red-blooded*?'

'Nope. Not science either, Fiona.' She got up from the stool. 'It's a metaphor.'

'That's what I thought.' And now I had to look up the word *metaphor*.

'When someone says *red-blooded*,' Dr Sharma said, 'they're talking about a person being full of life. They eat a lot, that kind of thing.'

I wouldn't exactly call Lewis *full of life*, but he did eat a lot of raspberry laces.

If red-blooded wasn't a science thing, that made it an English thing. A *metaphor* would be something like a *paradox*, something to make conversations more confusing and take longer.

I arrived in the classroom for English later than some of the other kids. Sean nodded at me, but didn't say hello, just looked away again.

What?

I sat down and got out my pencil tin. I rearranged my pens in confusion.

But aren't I the best girl in school now?

Surprisingly, Mr Kellett hardly spoke about the football. He just stood at the front, banging on about the play we were reading.

Finally, he looked up from his book. 'Any questions?'

Loads of hands went up.

'Were you any good at penalties when you played for Alty Town, sir?'

'Are we going to beat Germany five-nil?'

'Questions about Katherine or Petruchio? Or Shakespeare? Even Italy?' Mr Kellett looked round the room. 'Anything related to *The Taming of the Shrew* at all?'

All the hands went down.

I put my hand up. 'Can I ask about something else?'

Mr Kellett closed the book in his hands slowly. He hugged the book to his chest. 'Everyone discuss the play, in your pairs.'

He came over to me.

I put my hand down. 'It's another word question. Something I've been wondering since the weekend.'

Mr Kellett slowly crouched next to me. One of his knees made a crunching sound, like a rustled-up crisp packet. 'Go on.'

'I just wanted to know. What does red-blooded mean?'

He stared at me.

'Mr Kellett?'

The bell rang. And kept ringing.

Mr Kellett sprang up despite his crisp-packet knee. *'Fire drill!'* He grabbed his yellow vest-thing from the back of his chair, the one the colour of a highlighter pen.

And all us kids hurried after him onto the school field, hoping and hoping – some crossing fingers and everything – that it was a real fire this time.

Even better than a fire! *School news, school news, school news!*

It was a bomb threat. *Someone threatened to bomb our school!*

Well, not *exactly* bomb our school. They threatened to bomb the train station nearby, and our school's really close to the track. Someone had called the police and used an IRA codeword – that turned out not to be an IRA codeword after all. Or an old one. Or something.

There were so many rumours.

It wasn't the IRA after all, but angry ex-pupils trying to get their own back. It was that kid who got his face blown off in a science experiment. It was Simon Rutherson, losing it after twenty years of kids shouting *orgasm* up scaffolding.

Either way, there was no bomb.

But you should have seen the teachers! Mrs Vernal kept muttering with the New Head about whether we should regroup in the car park instead, even though that wasn't the instruction when there was a fire drill. Miss Jarvis rushed back and forth like a mad rabbit, telling us to *step back from the railway line, no, further back, please kids, listen to me, kids, it's important this time – PLEASE!* Her face was so red and strained, Dr Sharma put her hand on Miss Jarvis's arm and said *calm down, Carrie. Nothing good comes of getting agitated.*

Carrie. The day of the bomb was getting better and better. *Carrie!*

It wasn't all good though. At one point, the New Head looked up and I met her dark gaze. It was like I was looking at Medusa and her head of hissing snakes. A coldness spread across my neck and my back and it stayed there, tingling and spreading, long after the New Head had turned away.

Mr Kellett wasn't happy either. He stood in his highlighter vest, directing kids, looking more serious than I'd ever seen him. I caught his eye once and he stopped directing kids and looked *really* worried.

But the most worried faces of all were on the poor Year Nine girls who'd been doing gymnastics when the bell rang. Now they were on the field with no skirts on, all standing in just Aertex T-shirts and gym pants – *all* of the class. The fat ones, the skinny ones, the ones whose boobs had grown too quickly, the ones whose hadn't grown quickly enough – all trying to cover themselves up, with only their arms to do it. All the while, everyone – *everyone, the whole school* – made comments on how thick their legs were, or how much their boobs had grown, or not grown, like we were presenters on a nature show, or observing penguins in their pool at the zoo.

At teatime, I sat at the peninsula and practised reading the newspaper.

I turned over pages of the business section, waiting for Mum to notice.

On the next page was a cartoon. A man in a suit with a big red face held a bottle labelled *The Economy.* He was trying to protect the bottle from a hunched-over devil, who was trying to take the stopper out of the bottle.

I stared at the cartoon, waiting for it to be funny.

I turned another page.

'Fiona?' Mum said.

I put the paper down flat on the table.

'Fiona, while you're not doing anything, do you want to help me with laying the table?'

'I *was* doing something. I was reading the business section.' I got down off the stool and opened the cutlery drawer. I put the cutlery on the table in a heap. 'Should I put my paper away?'

Mum looked at the paper open on the peninsula. *City jitters expected to stabilise after chancellor's statement.*

She looked at me for a long minute.

I folded the paper up neatly and started arranging the knives and forks in our places.

Mum eventually went back to stirring her sauce. 'Oh.' She jerked her head at the sideboard. 'You've got some post. What's it about?'

'Could be anything. I get letters all the time.'

I took the letter up to my room to open it.

Dear Miss Larson,

Thank you for your recent application for the position of hairdressing assistant.

We have been overwhelmed with applications and have received an abundance of CVs for the role. After careful consideration, we have decided to go in a different direction. I'm sorry to tell you we won't be offering you an interview at this time.

We will keep your application on file in case any positions come up in the future, so there is no need to reapply.

We wish you the best of luck with your continued job search.

Kind regards,

Katie Guest

Salon Manager

I was getting a bit bored of words now, to be honest. So I wouldn't be looking up *abundance*.

I never wanted to be a hairdresser anyway.

15

Calling someone 'red-blooded' has nothing to do with actual blood.
It's a red herring.
Which has nothing to do with actual herrings.

Fiona Larson, 7E's Blood Project

Twenty-four days to the fair

The next day, I waited for Lewis by the lamppost. I still had my glasses on, after wearing them with my parents all through breakfast.

I watched Lewis walk towards me, his edges much sharper than usual. I was about to take the glasses off when I glanced at 56 George Street.

The house had sharper edges too. As did the man inside.

After a moment, the man raised a hand in a wave.

My stomach swished with cold water.

The man Mum had met at the supermarket – the one she called *strange* – was the man in the window of 56 George Street.

'Lewis,' I grabbed his arm, 'run.'

*

'Why are we running?'

I slowed as we reached the park. 'You know the man in the axeman's house?'

'It's not an axeman's house.' Lewis saw my face. 'Go on.'

'I know who he is and Mum says' – I left a pause – 'he's a strange man. Coincidence?'

Lewis opened his eyes wider. 'Of course it's a coincidence.' But his voice was wobbly at the edges. 'I asked Mum about the axeman and she said Sean's having us on and they'd never found a foot in a flipflop in with the bananas at the Co-op. *Never!*'

'My mum said the same,' I admitted.

'And think about it, Fi. Flipflops slide off easily.' Lewis folded his arms in a big message. 'And there's no way a whole family got killed like that and we don't know. You *can't* believe the axeman story.' He saw my face. 'Surely?'

'Fine, he's not the axeman.'

'Great.'

'He's just a normal man, so we can investigate him for spy practice anyway. Find out *why* he's strange.'

'But he might not like it.'

'He won't find out though.'

'He might be dangerous.'

'*Of course* he might be dangerous, Lewis, that's what *strange* means!'

Lewis looked at his shoes.

I gave a little shiver. 'We have to find something to practise spying on eventually. We could either investigate this strange man, or Danielle's death. Your choice.' I was planning to do both, obviously, but it's always best to ease Lewis into things.

He still wouldn't look at me, so I deliberately crossed his path and stood in front of him.

'We talked about this before.' He looked up. 'And you promised me you wouldn't investigate Danielle.'

I put my hands on my hips. 'It's OK for you. You get to go to the fair.'

Lewis just looked at me.

'What?'

He started hurrying towards school, arms still folded, making sure I knew he was still angry with me. In that position, his body leaned forward and he couldn't pump his arms, making rushing away harder.

I watched him for a moment, hitching my rucksack further onto my shoulder. With a sigh, I ran to catch him up, but he must have heard me. He unfolded his arms and hurried quicker now.

I slowed, deciding not to chase him anymore.

With Lewis, it's often best to give him a chance to calm down before I come at him with my good ideas for another round of trying.

School news!

Liam's sister heard the New Head telling off Mr Carter, the IT teacher, when they thought no one was around.

Turns out Mr Carter's getting the computer room rewired and he signed the form with some builders without checking the cost or dates with the New Head, who says the wiring's *non-essential* and *an extravagance* and *she'd only agreed to it in principle, she hadn't signed off the details.*

And now the rewiring is taking longer than expected and the computer room's going to be closed for building work before the end of this term, not just over summer, as Mr Carter had said.

Which isn't great for me and Lewis, obviously, but that's not important right now.

The rumour is the New Head said Mr Carter *forgot himself.* That she'd been clear she needed to be asked about every money decision in the school, *down to the last paperclip.*

Then the rumour is that the New Head punched him to the floor, and kept kicking Mr Carter as he was curled up in a ball – and that's the one bit everyone talked most about as the day went on, but that's the one bit of the story I don't believe.

Apart from that, in school, there was a lot of talk of sausages. People smelling them everywhere, talking about them a lot. Something to do with England playing Germany soon in the semi-final. I pretended to understand, and laughed when other people did.

And, in rubbish school news, all the girls are into fortune tellers – those folded bits of paper where someone picks a number and the paper tells them what to do, or gives them a prediction.

You have to . . . run round the tennis courts.

The number of kids you'll have is . . . two. Twins. One nice, one evil.

The man you marry will have . . . black hair and a wooden leg.

Being at school comes with all kinds of homework. Now, on top of learning who scored what in the football, if I was ever going to make any new friends, I needed to find out how to fold a stupid fortune teller.

And I *definitely* needed new friends. It wasn't just about getting girl friends for the Waltzers. Lewis had walked off from me that morning, and Sean hadn't been at the lamppost this week. He wouldn't look at me in English, even when we thought the building was on fire. And when I'd tried to talk to him in the playground, he'd walked right past me, like I was invisible.

I tried with Lewis, though. I really did.

I saw him in the corridor between lessons and grabbed his coat as kids pushed past us. 'Why are you cross, Lewis?'

'I can't believe you said you want to investigate Danielle's death again. After I asked you not to.'

'Think about it. We need to investigate because what if she's haunting the fair?' I got bumped to the side by a massive rucksack. 'Do you *want* to go to a haunted fair?'

Lewis hitched his own bag higher onto his shoulder. '*Please* never say anything to Gail and Jonathan about Danielle haunting the fair.'

Gail and Jonathan. Who did he think he was? *A mum?* 'You're being selfish. You get to go to the fair, so you don't care about me!'

A group of Year Eight boys charged down the corridor, chanting. *'Eng-er-land!'*

Lewis moved out of their way. 'I'm not taking any part in this.'

'Eng-er-land! Eng-er-land!'

'You won't help me?' I said. 'When you know how much I want to go?'

'I think it will get you into trouble. And investigating the strange man isn't safe either. Let's find another secret. A better one. A safer secret.'

I made a *pah* sound.

'Or we could do something fun.' Lewis stepped to the side for Miss Gold and her pile of textbooks. 'I could teach you how I do my card tricks and we could practise mnemonics? We could get a tray out and put household objects on them and take turns to—'

I shook my head.

'Or we could make some badges to pin on our school bags? We could give them to people and make it a style thing? Like you're one of a good crowd if you have one of the badges?'

I couldn't believe this. 'LEWIS! Card tricks is bad enough, but you're *twelve*! You don't go around making badges like a little kid at *twelve*!'

His mouth twitched.

'You're so scared about investigating things,' I said. 'Your dad's right, you're not red-blooded. I've never met anyone *less* red-blooded in – my – life.'

The bell rang.

'If I was a boy, I'd be so much better at it than you,' I added. 'Better at making friends, better at football, better at fighting – everything.'

And Lewis walked off.

I couldn't find Lewis all lunchtime. I hurried around school looking for him, jumping over the feet of the bigger kids who lined the benches at the side of the main corridor. But he wasn't sitting in a corridor.

He wasn't in the computer room, either. And Mr Carter, who's normally so nice, looked annoyed when I went there and told me to *please leave, Fiona, the room's off-limits today, I've got stuff to do.*

I sat in the playground, leaning against the science block wall, and ate my lunch. When I finished, I flattened my empty crisp packet. I folded the rectangle, again and again. I tucked in the final edge until the packet was a tiny triangle, no bigger than a 50p.

Forty-five minutes is too long for a school lunchtime. Especially if everywhere you can think of to go is just a whole list of places you don't want to be.

The Worst Things Lewis Harris Has Ever Done

1) Put his name down to do magic tricks in the *Monkford High 'Year Seven Search for A Star!'* assembly
2) Learned about mnemonics and bought a special tea tray to use for memory games
3) Asked for a clarinet for his birthday
4) Let his parents take him to France on holiday (Lewis Harris went to Paris)
5) Kept showing how he could make his nostrils flare
6) Brought in sandwiches made with dinosaur cutters
7) Couldn't sleep for a week after dreaming swans lived under his bed

If that kid doesn't want to be friends with me anymore, that's sweet by me.

16

Friends can be the worst people to tell secrets to.

(paradox)

Twenty-three days to the fair

It had been nearly a whole day since I shouted at Lewis and told him he wasn't red-blooded, and he *still* wasn't waiting for me at the lamppost.

I waited there anyway, looking at the newspaper I'd picked up from the bus shelter bench. The whole of the front page was taken up with a picture of two England players roaring in army helmets. *ACHTUNG! SURRENDER! For you, Fritz, ze Euro '96 Championship is over.*

I folded up the paper and tucked it under my arm. I looked towards 56 George Street.

The red Astra in the driveway had a dent in the back bumper and a *Baby on Board* sticker.

The house had a new *For Sale* sign in the flowerbed. The sign called the house a *desirable three-bedroom property*, with *early viewing recommended*. I waited a bit longer before heading into school.

*

In registration, Kirsty and her friends huddled round their fortune tellers, moving their fingers and thumbs, taking turns to pick a number.

'Number eight,' Olive said.

Kirsty peeled back the paper. 'You will get tonsillitis.'

I watched the girls pick numbers and pull back the paper. It was all about the folds, I decided.

Olive saw me looking and whispered something to the other girls. I heard the words *magazines* and *dirty*.

I shuffled in my seat.

'She's disgusting.'

I shuffled some more.

The girls went back to playing fortune tellers, Kirsty holding out the paper to Olive to choose.

'Number seven.'

Kirsty peeled back the paper again. 'You will go to the fair.'

I sat up straighter.

I zoomed in on Kirsty's piece of paper, my gaze an invisible laser.

When the bell rang, Kirsty hurried out with her friends, leaving the crumpled fortune teller on the desk behind her.

I picked up the fortune teller and put it carefully in my secret pocket.

I took it to maths. I spent the lesson pretending to listen to Mr Adams, but kept my hands under the desk, making the paper move.

I picked number seven, again and again. I opened the paper. I traced Kirsty's words with my thumb. Again and again.

You will go to the fair.

*

At break, I rushed towards the canteen because I knew Lewis would be wanting a snack. A rice crispy cake, to be exact.

I spotted him on the main corridor, right on time. 'Lewis!'

He pretended he hadn't heard.

I chased him.

He ran away.

I puffed after him. He had one part of his shirt spilling out of his trousers, one shoelace undone. He ran lopsidedly because of his schoolbag on one shoulder.

I heard giggling from some of the girls sitting on the benches. 'Look at the *state*.'

And I *still* didn't stop chasing him. 'Lewis!'

Still, undone shoelace and everything, he got away.

School news. And not good, this time.

My time of being magazine queen was *definitely* over.

I was on my own in the main corridor at lunchtime when Sean came up with a bunch of lads from the blue estate, and Liam and Greeney too.

I didn't even care how Sean had managed to get back in with them. I didn't want to know.

'Got any magazines, Fiona?' Liam said. People were still saying it, but in a different way now. Like . . . like it wasn't a good thing anymore.

I shook my head.

'You like porn?'

'I like boys' things.'

Liam narrowed his eyes. 'Like football?

'Love it.'

There was a sudden hush. I turned to see the New Head walking down the corridor, a silver lizard badge on her pale blue cardigan today. In her path, kids picked up rucksacks and scurried out of the way.

The crowd kept parting in front of her, quiet spreading all around. Even *the three sea witches* grabbed their bags and scattered.

After a few seconds delay, when the New Head was out of sight, the chattering in the corridor started up again.

'You love football.' Liam turned to me again. 'Did you watch the Spain game, then?'

'Of course.' I swallowed. 'Did you see McAllister's face when he missed that penalty? *Aaah.*'

Liam and everyone straightened. Eyes flicked into focus. Lions all spotting the same old limping wildebeest.

'That was the Scotland game, of course,' I stammered. 'I meant, how good was Seaman in the Spain game? Those *saves*.'

The others crowded in. Sean stood at the back of the group, hands in pockets. He stared at the floor.

'Aren't you hot in that coat?' Liam flicked a flap. 'Why's the front all bumpy?'

I took a step back. *No.*

Liam threw the flap of my coat open, showing the secret pocket.

He took the spybox out of my coat. 'Matches?' He opened it up. 'Not matches.'

Liam threw the box to Sean. 'What's this?'

Sean licked his lips. 'It's a spying kit. They keep them in their secret pockets. Her and Harris.'

I stared at Sean. *Eight days ago*, I'd told him that. When we were lying on the grass in the park, being friends. *Eight days.*

Sean must have remembered too because he looked at the floor again.

'Girls can spy too,' I muttered. 'There's no rule against it.'

'There's the other one!' someone shouted.

'Hey!' Lewis's voice.

Across the corridor, kids jostled Lewis, opening his coat to get his spy kit out.

I looked away. Watching it happen to Lewis felt so much worse than it happening to me.

Greeney threw my spy box on the floor. 'Spying kits? This is *high* school. Grow up.'

And he kicked my spybox to Liam. Who kicked it back.

And the boys started laughing as they all joined in, trampling over my spybox.

Sean didn't join in. But he didn't move away either.

The bell rang for the next lesson and Greeney gave my box one last kick. Everyone scattered.

In the empty corridor, still ringing with the sound of kids' footsteps, I picked up my broken pieces of spybox from the floor. Carefully, I collected the torn code flaps. I picked up the hollow twigs, now snapped and scattered at the edges of the corridor. I reached for my matchstick-wound pieces of paper, stamped flat.

I looked up to see Lewis, but he looked away. And he didn't get down on the floor to put his spybox back together.

He just turned and walked away, leaving his spybox destroyed and on the floor, in pieces.

17

People often say 'in the blood' when they mean 'in the family'. Blood itself does not hold all the information people think it does.

Fiona Larson, 7E's Blood Project

Twenty-one days to the fair

The next couple of days at school could have been worse.

England lost to Germany that night, which meant I wouldn't have to do football homework for a very long time. It meant everyone at school was miserable too, which was good for me. Being sad is tougher when everyone else is happy.

It was still sunny. And I still had Kirsty's fortune teller. I kept moving the paper flaps and picking number seven. Letting it tell me again and again *you will go to the fair,* like my papery fairy godmother.

And I still had my hundred and twelve pounds. And Lewis would forgive me soon – he always did. I could make a new spybox. You could get paper and matches anywhere.

It wasn't over.

*

And the school news on Friday was particularly good.

A Year Seven kid phoned Childline!

His dad wouldn't let him have a Magnum before tea and Stu Meaker, this kid, had had enough. He actually *called*! He'd threatened and threatened, and this time – well. His dad had pushed him too far.

No one knew what was going to happen. No one had ever *phoned* before. There was so much excitement down the corridors.

'Do they have dogs, and vans? How does it work?'

'He'll go to prison. For life.'

'I just came back from his house and there were police there.'

And Stu Meaker just shrugged. 'Look, I love him, but he deserved it.' And he tried not to look too scared. But he definitely rushed off somewhere, hurrying out of school at the end of the day.

Best of all, when I got home on Friday afternoon, there was an envelope addressed to me on the hallway table.

I took the letter out to the back garden and sat on my old swing to read it.

Dear Ms Larson,

Thank you for your letter, and for your interest in our newspaper.

I'm afraid we can't send old copies of the newspaper to individuals, or disclose the personal details of our staff. However, all copies of the newspaper are archived and can be accessed using the microfiche in the library.

But we thank you for your continued interest in the activities of our newspaper. We are always looking for

new supporters and you can join our team of enthusi-
astic fundraisers by . . .

I read it again. The important bit, not the fundraising bit.

. . . all copies of the newspaper are archived and can be
accessed using the microfiche at the library.

I didn't have a clue what that meant.
But I'd find out.

The day got worse, of course. With *Fiona Larson* luck, things
always do.

I helped myself to some macaroni at the peninsula. 'What
shall we do tonight? Can we rent a film?'

I splatted the spoonful of macaroni onto my plate. Mum
and Dad looked at each other.

Mum adjusted her hairclip. 'Didn't we tell you?'

'We've got our group coming round tonight.' Dad leaned
forward. 'It's our turn to host. Sorry, Fi.'

Our group.

The *Dead Kids Group.*

'Can I come?' I *really* don't know why I said that. Sometimes I just say things I don't mean.

'You can stay in your room or go to Mrs Carpenter's?'
Mum said. 'I'm sure she won't mind.'

'You want me out of the way, so I don't remind them,' I said.
'A live kid like me, making people with dead kids jealous.'

'That's not it.' Mum frowned. 'Not at all. Don't say things
like that, Fi.' She paused. 'And it's not just a group about
people losing children, some people got widowed young.'

'It's not that we don't want you there; it's just adult time.'
Dad leaned forward so I had to look into his eyes. 'Like Date

Night. So do you want to stay in your room or go to Mrs Carpenter's? Or I could call Lewis's mum?'

'I'll stay in my room,' I said, knowing I sounded sulky, but not quite able to stop.

I sat cross-legged on my bed, listening to the music and chatting of the Dead Kids Group downstairs. Way too much laughter and fun when you realise these people became friends only because the vicar got them together after *their kids died.*

Or husbands or wives died – whatever. Either way, someone died young to make them sad. And now it's like, they've known each other so long, they have parties.

I wonder what the dead kids would think, looking down/up from heaven/hell.

I once said something like that to Mum. That the parties sounded like people were having too much fun.

'It's such a relief,' Mum said, 'to be with people who *get it.* Something so big changes your relationship with your friends because they can't understand. It was a lonely time.'

'It doesn't sound lonely now,' I'd said.

With the sound of chatting and laughter downstairs, I sat on my bed with some drawing paper. I cut it carefully into a square, and then folded it, copying the way Kirsty's paper was folded.

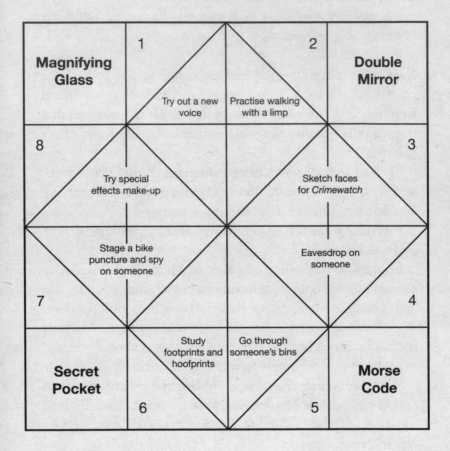

I slotted my fingers and thumbs into my new spy fortune teller. 'What should I do tonight?'

I moved the paper with my fingers and made my choices.

Morse Code. 4. Eavesdrop on someone.

I sighed. I folded the fortune teller into its resting position and placed it onto my bedroom table.

I sat on the landing, tucked behind the top of the stairs so I was invisible. Hoping no one needed to come upstairs to the toilet.

'She was well out of order, saying that,' a man said. '*Well* out of order.'

'And what did you say to that?' a woman in a green skirt said.

'I told her, that's not how I operate.'

'Fair enough,' Green Skirt said. 'I don't like having a female boss myself. They're *so* much harder to work for. Women can be so bitchy.'

'Exactly. And you know me, I'm the kind of person who says things straight.'

I heard footsteps at the base of the staircase. I jumped up and hurried to my room.

When the toilet had flushed, I waited a minute and came out again.

'But she shouldn't have been so bossy. And you know me,' the man was saying, 'I'm the kind of person who hates unfairness.'

There was a pause.

'Shame about the football,' Green Skirt said.

'Yes.'

There was a pause.

'How's Fiona doing now?' Green Skirt said.

I wondered why she was asking the man – *you know me, I'm the kind of man who knows about other people's kids* – but it made more sense when Mum's voice replied, 'Oh. You know.'

I licked my lips.

'A proper handful,' Mum added.

I wondered whether to get angry, but thought – *fair enough.*

'She's started watching *Gardeners' World* and reading the newspaper every day, and I'm not sure what I feel about that. And glasses must be in fashion at school because she wears hers all the time now.'

I pushed my glasses back up my nose.

'She wanders round the house in those glasses like a little skinny owl,' Mum continued. 'Quiet for ages, then piping up with a fact about the constitution of Ukraine.'

I thought about this. Yep. Sounded like me.

I was pleased Mum had noticed.

'Is she still . . . you know?' – Green Skirt had put on a sad voice – *don't put on your sad voice for me, Green Skirt* – 'The stuff at school?'

'She's OK.' Mum sighed. 'Still a bit of a loner. Though she does have one good friend and he's worth his weight in gold. So nice and patient.'

I thought of the last time I'd seen Lewis, running away from me in the corridor. I looked at my feet.

'I worry about her a lot,' Mum said. 'How she drives nice kids away.'

Sometimes, when I'm not around, I want my parents to be thinking about me. And then I find out they *were* thinking about me and I think – *oh.*

'She pushes all the boundaries. She acts out' – *don't tell them about the monkey bars don't tell them about the monkey bars don't tell them about the monkey bars* – 'and she wants to know

146

everything. Always listening at doorways. She never misses a trick.'

Never misses a trick. I felt my chest swell. *Yes.*

'It's not uncommon,' Green Skirt said. 'Dr Ali told me kids who've had traumatic childhoods are often very astute when it comes to—'

'*What?*'

At the tone of Mum's voice, the whole room went quiet. I leaned back against the wall. *Whoa.*

'Gail, I—'

'She hasn't had a traumatic childhood.' Mum's voice was *cold.*

I felt sorry for Green Skirt.

'She wasn't even *here.*' Mum's words were pointier than usual. 'She's had a very happy childhood. We dealt with everything long before she was born.'

'I just meant, it would be hard, having parents who, with the best will in the world, would find having another kid—'

'Are you saying I've messed up my child?'

'Gail. *No.*'

She was, though. Green Skirt was.

'You know I didn't mean anything, Gail, I was just making conversation.'

At the sound of footsteps on the stairs, I scurried back to my room and threw myself onto the bed.

I didn't want to think about what Mum had said, so I picked up my fortune teller and slotted in my fingers and thumbs.

Double Mirror. 2. Practise walking with a limp.

I nodded firmly and stood up. I made my left leg heavy and dragged it after me, deciding maybe I wouldn't eavesdrop again for a while.

*

But I didn't have to try to eavesdrop later. Not when I went to the toilet in the middle of the night.

Downstairs, there was the sound of clinking glasses and fluffing cushions.

'Did you hear *the nerve* of Andrea?'

Mum's voice was so spiky, I paused on the landing.

'It was all I could do not to scream *get out of my house*!'

'Don't sweat it, Gail.'

'Of course I'm not sweating it. It's ridiculous, that's all.'

'Andrea's just one of *those*. She likes to poke and prod till she gets drama.'

'If she does it again, I'm going to poke and prod her right under a moving car.'

I went into the toilet, shutting the door after me. And wondered if maybe Mum didn't have that much fun at the Dead Kids Group after all.

Except – this time it was my fault.

Another one to add to the list.

18

Interesting things can happen in libraries.

(paradox)

Twenty days to the fair

By Saturday morning, I'd done enough spy practising. You couldn't just practise for ever, not unless you wanted to be Lewis.

I ate my cereal opposite my parents at the peninsula. 'Can I go to the library this morning? There's a book I want to borrow.'

Weekends are different from after school – it's not my own free time, and my parents expect to know where I am. I'm not exactly sure why the rules work differently, but they do.

'We can't take you. Your dad's doing the big shop,' Mum said. 'And I'm taking the car to get the oil changed.'

'Can I go on my own?'

Mum and Dad looked at each other.

I mean, the *library*. What kind of trouble did they think I'd get into? The *whole point* of a library is there's nothing to do.

'I'm meeting Lewis. We said we'd meet at ten.'

Mum blinked at me. 'You've already arranged to meet Lewis, but you're just asking me now?'

'It was provisional,' I said. 'We made a provisional appointment.'

Mum and Dad looked at each other. Both laughed.

'You and Lewis. Making *provisional appointments*,' Mum said.

My long words weren't meant to be funny, but it was OK, for once. I was pretty sure that meant I was allowed to go to the library.

And I knew for definite when Dad stood up and said, 'Just make sure you take your inhaler.'

On the way there, I walked past the precinct. Past the boys on skateboards, jumping up, trying to ollie but not doing it very well. Liam was one of the boys, but he didn't look happy. Despite his efforts, he wheels stayed firmly on the ground. He was pretending he couldn't hear the older girls who were standing outside the Co-op, smoking and watching and taking the piss.

I looked at the pile of bikes, to check if Lewis's bike was piled up with all the others. But it wasn't. Of course it wasn't. Mine and Lewis's never were.

I wondered what Lewis was doing this weekend. Whether he was missing me.

I wasn't missing him, of course. Not with my investigations to do.

If anything, I was too busy to think of him at all.

I strode straight up to the friendliest lady on the counter – the white-haired lady wearing the glasses with green sparkly bits.

I put my rucksack onto the counter. 'I want to' – I looked at my letter and read – '*access an old newspaper using the microfiche.*'

I said it like *micro-fitch*.

'Do you now? The micro-*fish*?'

'Yes. I want to *access* the *Monkford and District Advertiser* for July 1982. Please.'

The woman smiled. 'Why?'

Sometimes people think that, because they're an adult and you're a kid, everything's their business. But *a good spy prepares*. 'My mum was in a play once. She said there was a photo of it in the paper.'

The woman smiled. 'How lovely!'

I smiled back.

'Come with me.'

I followed the woman to the back of the library, past the kids' section, with the caterpillar made of letters on the wall. Past the tiny chairs on the open patch of carpet, the boxes of brightly coloured toys. The smell of that area wafted up to me, like it was yesterday.

I flushed.

Thing is, I spent a lot of time on that carpet once, singing rhymes and woofing to stories. The fact I ever did makes me squeeze all my muscles really tight. But when I'm trying to forget something, my head doesn't always do what it's told and—

> *'Lar-ry the pup-py goes*
> *Woof woof woof*
> *Woof woof woof*
> *Woof woof—'*

STOP IT! I screamed at my singing brain. *STOP IT STOP IT STOP IT!*

The woman stopped at a desk in front of a machine. She patted the chair and I sat down.

'What date was it again, darling?'

'July 1982.'

She got a box from a filing cabinet and placed a reel on the machine. She slid the film into a clip and pressed a button.

The reel shot forward and a heading appeared on the screen. *Monkford and District Advertiser.*

I sat up straighter.

The woman peered at the screen, turning a knob. 'What date do you want to start with?'

'The one after the twenty-fourth of July.'

The woman moved the lever. 'You just have to keep scrolling till you find what you need.' The writing on the screen moved down. 'If you want a copy, printing's ten pence a page.'

'Thanks.'

'You move it side to side with this handle.'

'OK.'

'And you can rotate it with this. Do you want me to stay and help?'

'I'll be fine.'

She smiled like I was cute. 'Come and find me if you get stuck. It might be difficult to get the hang of it.'

I smiled and watched the woman walk away, her soft shoes sinking a little into the carpet. I turned to look at the screen.

Monkford and District Advertiser, Friday 30 July, 1982.

Monkford Girls' and Edge Street High schools to merge

I scrolled on to:

Precinct development on track to be completed in Autumn 1984

There was a drawing of our precinct, except it had loads of extra trees and looked really clean. And the names on the shop signs weren't right.

I felt a prickle up my back for no reason. I scrolled further.

Census – Small Area Statistics

Pedestrians Urged Not to Drop Litter as Pigeons in Park Declared Nuisance

I kept scrolling, past pictures of people in roll neck jumpers and thick glasses.

Family Pay Tribute to 'Perfect' Daughter After Fair Tragedy

I took a sudden breath.

A woman browsing nearby shelves looked at me. 'You OK, hon?'

I nodded. 'Fine.'

The woman turned back to the shelves and I looked at the article. Next to it was Danielle's last school picture. The one Mum has on top of the mantelpiece.

FAMILY PAY TRIBUTE TO 'PERFECT' DAUGHTER AFTER FAIR TRAGEDY

By Adrian Sykes

Monkford is mourning local girl, Danielle Larson, who died on Saturday, whilst attending Monkford Fair. The incident is being investigated but her death is not believed to be suspicious.

Father Jonathan Larson said, 'Danielle was the perfect daughter and words cannot express how we feel. She was taken from us too soon and leaves a gap in our lives that will never be filled. She will always be our perfect angel.'

Emergency services were called to Festival Field just after eight p.m. on Saturday 24 July, but Danielle was dead when paramedics arrived.

A memorial service will be held at Dean Road Crematorium on Wednesday 11 August. The family have asked for any donations to be made to the RSPB, of which Danielle was an active member.

'Have you found what you're looking for?'

The woman in the green-speckled glasses stood over me.

I forced myself to smile. 'No. Not yet.'

I watched her walk away. I got my pad and pen from my rucksack and copied out the article, even though it didn't really tell me anything. Except that Danielle was perfect, which I already knew.

I scrolled through the next week's paper, and the one after that, looking for more information. But I couldn't find anything else.

I re-read the article I'd copied out. And realised there was something helpful, after all.

I circled the words.

By Adrian Sykes.

19

If someone's blood type is A positive, they can joke they're a positive influence. If they don't mind their jokes not being funny.

Fiona Larson, 7E's Blood Project

Nineteen days to the fair

On Sunday morning, I knew I should be trying to find out who Adrian Sykes was.

What was stopping me was, I kept imagining him. I pictured a man bigger than Mr Kellett – a man made of too much ham, with a neck wider than Dad's head, and a furious expression.

It was the same face I pictured when I imagined who I'd stolen the magazines from.

So I didn't feel like looking for Adrian Sykes. At least, I did, just not right then. Instead, I got out my fortune teller so I could do some safer spying.

Lewis's words came into my head – a *safer secret* – and I scowled as I slid my fingers and thumbs into the paper.

Lewis Harris didn't know what he was talking about.

I moved the paper with my fingers and mouthed my choices. *Double Mirror. 3.* I opened the tab. *Sketch faces for* Crimewatch.

I folded up the fortune teller and tucked it back in my pocket.

Problem was, I didn't have a suspect for Danielle's death right now. Though there *was* the strange man, I supposed. The strange man, walking the streets with his ponytail, going in supermarkets and standing in windows – being suspicious.

I grabbed a pad and paper and drew him.

I sat back and looked at what I'd done. It wasn't brilliant. If it wasn't for the ponytail, the picture could have been of anyone. He could even have been a girl, till I drew the beard on him.

And – problem was – the supermarket man hadn't had a beard.

I was just thinking this when the doorbell rang and the lights flashed. I heard a girl's voice downstairs – *Selina Baker!*

I threw open my bedroom door. I rushed across the hall-way and down the stairs.

Knowing Selina was there, watching me, made walking down the stairs harder. 'Hi, Selina.' I felt like a baby calf, stumbling around on new hooves.

'Hi, Fiona.' Selina looked from Mum to me, making her long ponytail fly horizontally. Her fringe stuck a little way off her forehead, in gelled lines, and she gave me the kindest, nicest smile I'd ever seen.

I'd been wrong when I thought she was as beautiful as Kelly from Winchester. Selina was *even more* beautiful.

'Hi.' I'd already said that. *Stupid mouth.*

Mum picked up her car keys from the side. 'Fiona, look after Selina for a second while I just have a word with your father.'

I nodded. I turned to Selina and smiled.

She smiled back.

I screamed at myself – *say something!* She was too pretty, that was the problem. 'I need to get a job, Selina. A proper one – a grown-up one. Do you have a job?'

'I do! I work at the stables. I muck out the horses. Best job ever – I love it.'

I tried not to wrinkle my nose. 'Sweet.' I knew what *muck out* meant. And horses' muck must be *massive*.

'They don't pay me for it, but this way I get to spend time with the horses and ride them for free.'

I frowned. *FOR FREE?* 'Sweet,' I said again.

Mum came back then, and that was probably best because I really didn't know what to say to Selina after that.

Girls and horses. I'll never get it.

While Mum was out with Selina, I sat at the peninsula, working on my blood project. I could hear Dad moving beneath me as he cleared out the cellar. He shuffled, he grunted. He muttered an occasional *bollocks* or *arse*.

Dad isn't normally grumpy. But there's something about weekend tasks – the kind of tasks that need cellars and big boxes and tools – that brings out the *moody* in both my parents.

When Mum let herself back in after the lesson, she tossed a newspaper onto the peninsula. 'For you. The business section's at the back.'

She was making a joke but I said, 'Thanks,' like she meant it. I opened the paper up to a random page.

Mum put the kettle on.

I gave a fake sigh. 'Looks like Radovan Karadžić's up to something again. But then, there's talk of him' – I practised the word in my head – '*relinquishing* power.'

'Who?'

'Radovan Karadžić. You know, leader of the Bosnian Serbs.' I closed the paper. 'But I'll look later. I don't like to read too much at once. I like to give the news a chance to sink in.'

I pulled my exercise book towards me and drew a table, concentrating on keeping my ruler straight.

Mum re-clipped her hair back. 'What are you doing now?'

'My blood project.'

'It always makes me shudder when you say it.' Mum pulled up a stool. 'I take it you chose that topic yourself, my little vampire?'

I nodded. I wrote the headings in the first row of boxes: *Me, Mother, Father, Sibling One*. Under *Me*, I wrote *O positive*. 'But I'm writing *about* blood, not *making* blood.' I pushed my ruler to the side. 'What's your blood type?'

'AB, I think.' She tipped her head slightly to the side. 'AB positive.'

Under *Mother* in my table, I wrote *AB positive*.

'What about Dad?'

Mum sat back in her chair. 'I don't remember, darling. You'll have to ask him. Is he still in the cellar? I hope so.'

'How come you don't just *know*?'

'Fi. How is it I disappoint you so often, and in so many ways?' Mum kicked off her shoes and let them fall beneath her stool. 'Most people don't just go around knowing each other's blood types.'

I looked at my chart. 'Can you give blood to me, an O positive?'

'God knows!' Mum went to the sink and filled a glass of water. 'Though I can promise you if any of us need emergency blood, Fiona, there will be doctors to take charge. They won't be looking to us to decide what to do with the needle.' Mum gulped her water and refilled the glass. 'So you're interested in Bosnia now?'

'I've always been interested in Bosnia. Can you go and ask Dad his blood type?'

'Can't you ask him?'

I looked down at the floor. 'He's in the *cellar*,' I said quietly. I never went down there; it was a rule I had. I didn't like not knowing where a spider would spring from and scuttle across the floor.

Mum smiled like I was cute. She pushed herself off the stool. 'I'll go.'

I should point out: I'm not scared of spiders. Being scared of spiders is a girl thing. I just don't like being taken by surprise, that's all.

I heard some conversation beneath me and, a minute later, Mum came back upstairs. 'Dad's A positive. He said to tell you he's *A positive influence*.'

I wasn't sure if that was meant to be a joke, so I let it pass. I wrote *A positive* in the box under *Father*.

I looked at the next box. *Sibling One*. 'And Danielle? What was her blood type?'

Mum's smile stayed there for a second, all relaxed.

And then everything was different. Mum's face. The air of the room.

I realised my mistake. I stared at my exercise book.

'I—' Mum said. 'I—'

I kept staring.

Her words had a waver in them. 'I don't remember.'

I smoothed my page with my hand. 'I don't really need to know. It's not a problem.'

'I'll ask your dad.' She ran down to the cellar again. I could hear Mum's voice now, through the floor, going high-pitched as she fired questions at Dad. 'But how could we *just forget*?'

She ran back up the stairs. 'Your dad doesn't remember either.' She tried to smile, but when she picked up her glass again, her hand was shaking.

'It doesn't matter, it's—'

Mum slammed her glass down. 'NHS records. But where did I put them?' She jabbed both hands into her hair.

'I don't need to fill in anything for Sibling One. I can say I haven't got any siblings, it's fine. It's even true.'

'As long as your dad hasn't thrown the records out.'

Mum threw the cellar door open and ran down the steps. I heard the high up-and-down of voices as Mum took the fizzed-up air from the kitchen down there again.

I turned the page on my blood project and tried to focus on the next topic.

Mum hurried back up the stairs and into the room with a box in her arms. She dumped it onto the peninsula, next to me and my stuff.

I watched her pull files out of the box and scatter them on the table. The box shifted with the movement, scuffing the top page of my textbook.

'If they're not in here' – she pulled out a file marked *Boiler* and dumped it on the file called *Wills* – 'they'll be in the attic.'

I picked up my books. 'I'll finish this upstairs.'

I tucked the newspaper under my arm so she could see me taking it. But she didn't notice.

20

Sometimes, it's good to be a girl.
(paradox)

Eighteen days to the fair
Lewis *still* wasn't there when I got to the lamppost on
Monday morning.

I stood and looked at 56 George Street for a while. The
front lawn was the size of my bedroom and untidy, grass and
higgledy-piggledy bushes all crossed over each other. The
wooden boards on the top half of the house were different
shades of brown, where the paint had faded in patches.

I looked at the *For Sale* sign – *desirable property*, with *early
viewing recommended* – and looked back at the house.

The net curtain in the front window had gone, so I could
see inside the room. I could just make out an old wood-
coloured telly and high-backed sofa, an ugly shade between
green, grey and brown.

When Lewis wasn't there by 8.30, I walked to school.

Tell the truth, I was getting sick of this.

But maybe it was a good thing Lewis was angry at me. If
I was going to be normal, I needed normal friends. If I was
going to be spun on the Waltzers, I needed different friends.

Friends who the boy on the Waltzers would want to push.
There was nothing for it. That meant—
Girls.

Thing is, boys are better than girls. They just are.

And I can say that because I am one. Though I'm not a *proper* girl – not really.

Why I'm Not a Proper Girl

1) I talk back
2) I get angry
3) I throw overarm
4) I'd make a good boss
5) I don't like cleaning or cooking
6) I don't care about stationery*
7) I like camping, not making jam**

apart from Candy's pencil topper. That was a one-off.
**In Monkford, the scouts go camping and the guides make jam. And everybody else is fine with this.*

The best things you can say to a girl end with *like a boy. You throw like a boy. You ride your bike like a boy. You fight like a boy.* If you're a girl, that's all you can hope for. You might still wear make-up and have long hair – you have to, if you want to be with boys when you're older – but you have to pretend that 'looking pretty' stuff just happened, without you doing anything about it.

And in the areas that really matter – like rounders and throwing and knowing the names of the third-division football stadiums – you can't let the boys beat you. Even if that means practising throwing against a wall on your own in the garden, or learning names and places in football annuals in bed with a torch in the dark.

But you mustn't let people know you practise in the dark because then they'd know you cared. You have to make it all look easy and natural, like a boy would.

And if you do what boys do, as well as they do, and make it look easy and natural, then it's like you're not a girl anymore, but somewhere in between. A Girl Plus or a Boy Minus.

I looked round the playground. *How to choose my new friends?*

I hitched my bag on my shoulder and started walking.

The first group I walked past were the worst kind of girls. They sat on the school field, making daisy chains and friendship bracelets. Brushing each other's hair.

Never. Ever.

I passed the sea witches. They normally stood in three equal corners – an equilateral triangle – but the bigger two had just taken a book triumphantly from the third sea witch, who now stood to the side, uncertainly, while the other two flicked through her book. The equilateral triangle had gone isosceles – for now.

Anyway. *Too old, and too mean.* I couldn't risk a flushing.

I passed Martha, the evil one from primary school.

No way no way no way.

I wandered around the school's outside space in big loops, looking at groups to see which one would best fit me.

I noticed the best girls all had their school jumpers round their waists, tied around by the arms, in that way Mum says *stretches the wool*, so I took my jumper off and tied it round my waist.

As I passed one group of girls I heard giggling.

'What does she think she looks like?'

I looked down. I reached for the arms of my jumper. I lifted them up uncertainly and dropped them again.

There needed to be rules for this stuff, like how to wear jumpers round your waist. It needed to be *written down*.

When the bell rang for the end of lunch, I hurried to the maths room.

I had my exercise book out and my protractor set unpacked, and was copying triangles from the board before all the other kids had even arrived.

School news!

That day, Mrs Vernal was wearing a silky cream blouse with black dots. The blouse was so thin it was nearly see-through. You could tell her bra was lacy, because it made the surface of her blouse bobbly.

When Mrs Vernal stretched and the blouse sat close to her skin at the back, you could see everything. You could see her bra straps. You could see where the label hung down at the middle, next to the back fastening.

Everyone noticed. Mrs Vernal walked around our circle in the hall and there was a special energy in the air.

It's things like this, such basic mistakes, that make me wonder whether some teachers ever *went* to school.

Mrs Vernal clapped her hands. 'Get into pairs.'

I walked towards Lewis, but he turned and headed deliberately for Katie Russell.

Everyone was pairing up around me. I moved my weight from one foot to another, waiting.

Eventually, there was no one left alone but me and Jodie Mackintosh.

Jodie Mackintosh?

She had a decent bag and coat. She wasn't too clever or too dumb. She was from the red estate, she was pretty enough, and I'd never heard anyone saying she smelled of food or wet dog.

I took a nervous step towards her.

She smiled and stepped towards me. It wasn't a trap. Either that, or the bad *surprise!* part was coming later.

Mrs Vernal tapped her way round the hall, weaving between pairs. 'Face your partner. Look closely at each other.'

I glanced at Jodie and away again.

Looking at a stranger is harder than you think.

'Pick who's Person One in your pair.'

I pointed to Jodie. She nodded.

'Person One,' Mrs Vernal said. 'Walk around the room, or just go about some normal business. Person Two, watch your partner very carefully and see how they move. I want you to become that person.'

I *really* wished I was doing this with Lewis now. Even though becoming Lewis was pretty much the worst thing that could happen to a kid.

Jodie set off walking, her steps light. I tried to walk like her, bouncing on the balls of my feet, treading carefully. She had long black hair, so long it nearly reached her bum, and rippled as she walked.

I was Jodie for a bit longer, following what she did, sitting down and getting up again, running my hands through my hair, till Mrs Vernal shouted. 'Now swap!'

Nervous now, I crossed my arms over my front.

Jodie crossed her arms over her front.

I started to walk. Knowing Jodie was watching, I moved heavily, like I'd forgotten how my legs worked.

I glanced at her.

Jodie was pretending to be me, walking slowly, but the weird thing was, she didn't make an ugly face or stomp around or anything. She actually walked around pretty normally, like she could have been copying any kid in the room – a kid who was good or bad or anywhere in between.

At the end of class, Jodie and I headed out of the hall together.

Selina Baker was walking down the corridor towards us with a friend, both carrying long tubes of coloured paper. Selina was wearing a short top that showed an inch of skin above the waistband of her leggings.

She saw me and smiled. 'Hi, Fiona!'

'H-hi!' I said.

Selina turned back to her friend and they continued their conversation.

Jodie looked at me, eyes wide. 'You know *Selina Baker*?'

'Kind of.'

'Wow,' Jodie said.

I smiled at her. And wondered if maybe – just maybe – I might be able to make girl friends after all.

But Lewis couldn't avoid me for ever.

We both had swimming club at the leisure centre after school. And, while Lewis could run away in school, and he could swim away in the pool like I was a great white shark, loose in Monkford Baths, he couldn't avoid me in the café bit afterwards. Not if I waited by the vending machines.

Nothing makes Lewis hungry like swimming.

When I got out of the pool, I got dressed quickly without having a shower. I ran to the café bit without tying my shoelaces and made sure I was leaning against the wall when

Lewis got to the café. I rested my arm on top of the snack machine, like I owned it.

He paused when he saw me.

He walked over to the machine.

I knew this kid so well. 'Hi,' I said.

Lewis put coins in the machine. A packet of cheese biscuits uncoiled and fell into the chute. Lewis took the packet and moved to the next vending machine for a cup of blackcurrant squash.

I followed him to a table and sat down opposite. 'I'm sorry I said you weren't red-blooded.'

'Can you stop dripping your hair on my table please.'

I wiped the surface with my sleeve. 'I just wanted to investigate Danielle and I was angry you didn't want to. I didn't mean to be horrible.'

Lewis opened his cheese biscuits and placed the packet on the table – the packet open from the top, not torn down the side for sharing.

'Lewis? I said I'm sorry.'

He ate a biscuit with a room-filling crunch.

'It's just you're the one who's there for all my secrets.' I twisted my dripping hair with both hands, squeezing water onto the carpet. 'I don't tell anyone else my secrets or plans.'

He took another biscuit. 'Your *terrible* plans.'

'My terrible plans. They're not all terrible, some are quite good, but OK.'

Lewis nodded. He put the biscuit in his mouth.

'Can I have one?'

'No.'

I jiggled my knees up and down. 'Can you forgive me?'

'Maybe.' He softened his face. 'On one condition.'

He pulled a string of multicoloured fabric out of his pocket.

'Lewis!' I pushed his handkerchief hand down under the table. 'Not now! *Anyone* could come in.'

He looked at his hand. 'You said *not in school.*'

I glanced around. 'Not *anywhere*, not where anyone can see.' I shook my head. 'Kids from the blue estate might come in. Older kids.'

I glanced up at two women entering the café, wearing supermarket uniforms under their coats.

I gave Lewis a look. *You see?* 'And you don't know *who* they might tell. That could be Greeney and Liam's mums, for all you know.'

'They look way too young to be—'

'You know what I mean. Lewis, magic is for babies. I didn't make the rules. You can show me your tricks when we're in your bedroom, how's that?'

He took a slow sip of blackcurrant.

'This isn't just about me, Lewis. I'm doing this for both of us.'

'But you'll let me show you the trick in my bedroom.'

I rolled my eyes. 'Yes.'

'Can I wear the cape?'

'Do you really think that's a *red-blooded* thing to do?'

Lewis looked up at me. 'I don't know what *red-blooded* means.'

'I don't either.'

But we did, sort of. We both knew if you looked up *the opposite of red-blooded* in a dictionary, it would say *Lewis Harris in a cape doing magic tricks with handkerchiefs.*

Lewis crunched up his cup. 'If you had some hobbies you liked doing, I'd let you show me. You're much better at saying what you don't like doing.'

'That's not true! I like investigating, don't I?'

Lewis looked at the crunched-up cup in his hand.

I needed to get him spy-practising with me. So we could have some fun together, and he would remember we were friends. 'Let's investigate the strange man. Just as spy practice, I promise. We know he's not an axeman, don't we? So it's fine. Harmless.'

He got up to put the empty containers in the bin.

When he came back, I added, 'We'll be careful. And it'll be fun.'

I opened my coat and showed Lewis my secret pocket.

A minute later, he did the same.

We gave each other a secret smile and let our coat flaps fall back.

'We can start investigating him this afternoon.' I reached into my secret pocket and got out my spy fortune teller. 'And this will tell us what to do.'

'Just – only the strange man. Not Danielle's death.'

'OK,' I said. 'I'll listen to you. You're very sensible.'

He frowned.

'Honest.'

He stood up. 'I think I'll get another pack of biscuits, to celebrate.' And I watched him get up and put more money in the vending machine, grateful he'd saved me from having to lie to him too much – which would have been such a shame, when we'd only just made up.

What Might the Strange Man Have Done to Make Mum Call Him Strange?

1. Axeman stuff
2. Paedo stuff
3. Flashing

4. IRA terrorism – Manchester bomb
5. Drink-driving
6. Cut Mum up at a roundabout
7. Went to Danielle's funeral even though he didn't know her, or
8. Went to Danielle's funeral and stopped at M&S on the way back
9. Vandalised Monkford Precinct Christmas display with graffiti that time*
10. Killed Danielle

* 'Jesus is a bellend' and 'Mary and Joseph shagged ↓ these camels'

21

**A good lookout stays cool, calm and collected – ideally,
he has nerves of steel.**
The Junior Spy's Secret Handbook™

Eighteen days to the fair
I stayed crouched behind the parked car opposite 56 George
Street, my heart beating in my ears.

Now? I mouthed.

Lewis fidgeted, all alert, moving his weight from foot to
foot like he was fielding in a game of rounders. We'd agreed
our signals in the leisure centre café but now – an hour later,
now it was actually spy time – Lewis wasn't doing either of the
signals we agreed. He wasn't yawning *or* hooting like an owl.
Instead, he just jiggled by the lamppost, looking wide-eyed.

I strained my neck to make my eyes go as wide as his. *Do
something.*

'Now!' he barked.

Barked. Not *mouthed.* And he still didn't hoot.

Still, I ran.

I ran down the driveway of 56 George Street and towards
the house's black bin. My heart pumped hard as I grabbed
the twigs out of my pocket and arranged them in front of

the bin in a criss-cross shape. Too late, Lewis remembered to owl-hoot, *finally* – his owl sounded sad, more *unhappy pigeon* – and I took the lid off the bin, grabbed my prize, put the lid back on and ran.

Ten minutes later, we sat across from each other on Lewis's bed, the bin bag open between us.

Things in the Strange Man's Bin

1) Fourteen teabags, used
2) A microwave meal carton – chilli con carne, eaten
3) Three takeaway trays with scraps of sauce and noodles. Assume sweet and sour.
4) A bumper tin of value white emulsion paint, empty
5) A third of a bag of potatoes, sprouting
6) Three pairs of curtains with netting, old lady
7) An IKEA receipt for three pairs of curtains, six houseplants and a tap
8) A bottle of WeedBeGone! weedkiller, empty
9) A can of air-freshener in Outdoor Breeze, empty
10) Three family-size packets of Hot 'n' Fiery beef tortillas, empty
11) A two-pence coin, green on one side
12) A cigarette lighter, half full, broken spark
13) A box of twenty Silk Cut, empty

'He buys cigs in twenties.' Lewis nodded thoughtfully. 'That's odd.'

'A lot of adults do.' I tapped one of the packets of Hot 'n' Fiery beef tortillas. 'He got those from Paper Rack in the precinct. Eighty-nine pence.'

'Impressive!' Lewis said. 'How do you know?'

'Because that's where I always got mine. Not lately, though.'

Lewis pressed his lips together in pity – he knew I was avoiding the Paper Rack man.

I looked at our haul again. I moved the teabags so they were more central, to stop so much cold tea seeping onto Lewis's duvet. 'I was hoping to find something Irish. Is any of this stuff Irish?'

Lewis stared at our haul. 'I don't think so. He could still have done the IRA bomb though. He could be a mercenary.'

I shook my head. 'Things aren't always about mercenaries.'

Lewis poked at a carton. 'I suppose bombers eat food too.'

'Good point. And just because there's no bomb stuff here, it doesn't mean the man didn't build the bomb. Just that he didn't put any of the bomb wrappers in this bin.'

There were footsteps on the stairs. Lewis and I locked gazes in panic.

'Lewis?' Lewis's mum's voice was soft. 'Why's this door shut?'

'DON'T COME IN!' Lewis shouted.

I never heard Lewis shout. But I suppose if there's ever one person to make you feel like you're in charge, it's *this old thing, sorry, I'm so stupid* Lewis's mum.

'Why shouldn't I come in?'

'Mu-um!' Lewis made it have an extra syllable. 'I've *told* you!'

She threw the door open. 'And *I've* told *you* that the rules are you keep the door open when Fiona's here.'

'We're not having sex, Mrs Harris,' I said quickly. 'I promise.'

'I can see that, thanks, Fiona.' She sniffed. 'It's chlorine-y in here. You both definitely had showers?'

We both nodded, me furiously, hoping Lewis's mum wouldn't see how tangled my hair was. From not showering.

'Well, I know you kids wouldn't lie to me.'

I gave her a big smile. Mr Kellett would call it *irony* – that Lewis got the trusting mum, when he didn't even need one. When I was the kid who, last Christmas, had to go into school with a *real* temperature of 102, just because of that *one time* with the thermometer and the light bulb.

Mrs Harris looked at the bed. 'Is that a bin bag? What are you keeping in there?'

Lewis looked like he'd forgotten how to speak.

'A school project,' I said. 'It's fine.'

'Is that an *actual* bin bag *from an actual bin*?'

'No,' I said quickly.

'Is that paint? And teabags? On the *duvet*?'

The telly noises from downstairs stopped suddenly.

'Lisa?' Lewis's dad shouted up the stairs. 'What's the boy done now?'

Me and Lewis went still.

So did Mrs Harris. 'He's done nothing.' She lowered her voice. 'Get rid of that, *now*.' She gestured for Lewis to bundle up the stuff and put it under his bed.

Lewis gathered everything up, the paint tin and the air freshener clanking together.

I was about to shove the chilli con carne meal carton into the bin bag, when I saw something papery inside the carton. A shiny flyer, the size of a small envelope. The kind of flyer that comes through the door with the local paper.

And the picture on the flyer looked like—

There was no time to think. I pulled the flyer out of the meal carton and shoved the carton into the plastic bag. I pushed the flyer into my coat pocket, crumpling it in my rush.

Lewis was just pulling the duvet straight when his dad reached the top of the stairs.

He looked from me, to Lewis, to Lewis's mum. 'Everything all right?'

'Everything's fine,' Mrs Harris said.

'It smells like chlorine in here.'

'They've been swimming after school.'

'And paint. Chlorine and paint.'

I jumped up. 'I'd better go.'

I grabbed my bag and hurried out.

I waited until I was out of sight of Lewis's house to slow down and pull the flyer out of my pocket. I unfolded it.

Monkford Fair. Festival Field. Fri 19–Mon 22 July.

There was a smear of chilli sauce over the clown's face.

I turned the flyer over. On the plain side, someone had written messily, in biro:

registrar – death cert
will
account numbers

I stared and stared.

I didn't know the word *registrar*, but the next two words couldn't have stood out more. Not if they'd been written in neon highlighter.

Death cert.

I felt a splatter of rain on my shoulder. Then another on my head. Then another, and another – the droplets splatting down faster now.

I jammed the flyer into my pocket to keep it dry. I pulled up my hood and hurried towards home.

I'd been joking, investigating the strange man. Playing, practising. I'd been messing around when I wrote *killed Danielle* on the list of things the strange man might have done.

I'd been joking – till now.

Death cert.

Certain death.

Words written *on a flyer for the fair.*

I realised the splatters of rain had turned into a full-on shower without me noticing. Heavy rain drops exploded on my coat, like mini-bullets. I started to move, hurrying home.

I turned down George Street just as the shower was finishing. So I slowed at number 56.

The red car was in the drive, a light on inside the house. The criss-crossed twigs in front of the bin were how we left them, undisturbed.

I pulled the flaps of my coat tighter round me and ran the rest of the way home.

22

Sometimes a spy has no choice but to confront his quarry.
The Junior Spy's Secret Handbook™

Seventeen days to the fair
I didn't tell Lewis about the fair flyer on the way to school. We walked past 56 George Street that morning without a peep from me.

Lewis stared at the bins. 'The twigs haven't moved!'

I made myself smile and kept walking. 'Maybe there'll be another bin bag tomorrow.'

It was too nice having him as my friend again. I couldn't ruin it so soon.

School news! Greeney's had a shit haircut!

Really bad as well, like his mum's done it or something.

He swears she didn't. 'I had it done at the place on King Street, the one with the shampoos in the window – British Hairways. And by a barber, not a hairdresser. I can ask him to write a letter to prove it? I'll show you all the letter, that's fine. As if I'd let my mum cut my hair!'

But he would say that, wouldn't he?

His hair's longer on one side of his fringe than the other. Where he used to have two curtains, he now has exactly one curtain, one half-curtain. Which are called *tiers* when you're Mum, making fabric curtains.

I think Greeney should have cut the other side to match, but he obviously decided it was better to have half a shit haircut than a whole shit haircut.

Swings and roundabouts, Dad would say.

Anyway, now every time anyone passes Greeney in the corridor, any kid from any year, they shout *Haircut!* Our corridors get busy between lessons and you can hear when Greeney must be close by, because it's all, '*Haircut!*' '*Haircut!*', '*Haircut!*', '*Haircut!*', like a weird mating call across the school. Though no one would mate with Greeney, not when he looked *that* shit.

Greeney usually hangs around with the blue estate crowd, but I'm guessing he doesn't anymore.

Not for a while.

I didn't trust myself not to spill *death cert* and, besides, I needed time to think. So I told Lewis I didn't have time to hang out after school.

I sat cross-legged on my bed, the Scrabble dictionary and fair flyer on my lap. I stared at the hand-scribbled words.

registrar – death cert
will
account numbers

I looked up the words in the Scrabble dictionary.
Registrar – n – *keeper of official records*
Cert – n – *certainty*

Will – v – *used as an auxillary to form the future tense or to indicate intention, ability or expectation* – n – *strong determination*

I knew another meaning of *will*, from detective books – but Danielle wouldn't have had one. Kids don't have any money to leave.

And then ... *will* could also refer to a person? A person called *Will*?

The doorbell rang and lights flashed. I didn't move, not even when I heard a pretty laugh downstairs. Even Selina Baker couldn't tear me away from *death cert*.

I looked back at the flyer.

It could all be a code, of course. *Hide important information in lists,* that's what *The Junior Spy's Secret Handbook*™ said.

But the whole point of codes was that they were impossible for people to break, without the key.

I pushed the flyer and Scrabble dictionary to one side in frustration.

One of my legs started jumping, on its own. Sending me a message.

Because – seventeen days to the fair. I had to do *something*.

I waited till Selina and Mum had gone out for their lesson and hurried downstairs. Dad was on the sofa, watching a quiz show.

'Fi!' He looked up. 'What do you know?' That was Dad's way of saying *How was your day?*

I pushed *death cert* out of my head and concentrated on what I'd memorised that morning. 'Well, Biljana Plavšić is in charge of the Bosnian Serbs now. Like we expected, Radovan Karadžić has relinquished power.'

Dad's smile faded.

'And Costas Simitis has been elected president of the Panhellenic Socialist Movement of Greece. *And* it's the Russian elections coming up, but I guess you knew that.'

Dad just stared up at me.

'Can I borrow the polaroid camera?'

He kept staring.

'Dad?'

Finally, he took in what I'd said. 'I know you like that camera but the film's so expensive, Fi. I've only just put in a new one. That camera's special occasions only.'

'Lewis has a new packet of film. We can replace yours with it.' Not true, but I could buy film with my money from the car boot sale.

'You promise you have film?'

I nodded.

'And you also have to promise you won't take the camera into school.' Dad got up from the sofa and got the camera from his high cupboard. 'I don't want you getting it confiscated and me having to beg for it back from Dr Sharma. If you break it, you'll have to give up your birthday present to get me another.'

He handed the camera over. Carefully, I cradled it. 'I'll only use it after school, I promise.'

'Oh. And there's one other condition.'

I waited.

'You make a call for me.' Dad smiled and jerked his head at the television. 'That number on the screen? Request an application form. And do me a favour – don't tell your mother.'

I made the call to the quiz show for Dad and gave our details for the application form.

Back upstairs, I sat on my bed, cross-legged, and took the polaroid camera out of its case. I turned the camera over, looking at the curves. I looked through the camera's window, imagining taking a photo.

I hate lying to Dad. But sometimes I have no choice.

This was crossing a line, I knew. Moving from kid's spying to adult spying. Taking secret photos was very different from sketching faces.

But that was fine. I was too old for kid's spying, anyway. No more hoofprints and practising limps. No more of the bits Lewis liked. I needed to focus. And, while I was focusing, I made another decision.

There was a smudge on the camera's window where my eye had been, so I wiped the glass with my sleeve.

No one had taken me seriously applying for any of the adult jobs. The news thing wasn't working, Dad's face downstairs told me that. My parents didn't think I was mature, just weird. *And* it was taking up too much time. It was bad enough having to learn about Bosnia and Greece but, with everything I had going on, I *really* didn't have time for the Russian elections right now.

I zipped the polaroid camera up in its case and placed it carefully into my rucksack.

It was time to get serious. No more kids' spying. No more trying to get my parents to think I was grown up. The key to going to the fair was finding out what happened to Danielle.

Death cert.

And the key to finding out what happened to Danielle was the strange man.

23

A good spy is clever, using red herrings and decoys to mask his true intentions.
The Junior Spy's Secret Handbook™

Sixteen days to the fair

Lewis took a lot of persuading to ring that doorbell at 8.30 that Wednesday morning.

'It's just a bit of fun, Lewis.' I tried to smile, trying not to look as scared as I felt. 'Just fun spying.'

'Of course, I'd help – normally.' Lewis looked at the pavement to avoid my eyes. 'If it wasn't the strange man's house, I wouldn't mind. But you haven't given me time to prepare. That house is the one place. . .'

'It's got to be right now.' I kept my arms folded. 'There are too many people around later, and the sound of that lawn mower will cover the noise of the camera. And it's got to be you. I can't do both jobs.'

Lewis gave a sad nod. He trailed after me.

I positioned myself down the side passage of 56 George Street. I jerked my head at him – *go on*.

Lewis rang the doorbell. We waited.

And waited.

'He's not in,' Lewis whispered, ventriloquist-style.

'Ring it again,' I whispered.

Lewis pressed the button again. Nothing.

He rang the doorbell a third time.

Lewis pulled his hand away and the door opened.

The strange man stood there in just a T-shirt and checked boxer shorts, his hair all messed up round his face.

Lewis went as still as one of those painted men who pretend to be statues in town centres.

The strange man looked down at Lewis. 'Hi.'

Lewis hurried the words out, extra squeaky and fast. '*Dyouneeanyjobsdoin?*'

'Sorry?'

Lewis took a breath and put more space between the words. 'Do you need any jobs doing?'

'Jobs?' The strange man ruffled his hair. He reached behind for a hairband and started tying his hair back. 'What are you on about, mate?'

'Like scouts do. Car washing. Cleaning up leaves.'

'Oh.' The strange man finished tying his hair back. 'OK, I get it. Now you come to mention it, maybe I wouldn't mind some help with a bit of gardening, maybe some—'

I leapt out and took two photos. I darted back into the side passage and let the two pictures spit from the camera into my hand.

'RUN!' Lewis shouted. To *himself*.

I shrank back in the side passage while Lewis legged it. He was up the road and around the corner, heels flying, as fast as I'd ever seen him move.

The man watched him go, reaching behind for a cigarette and lighter. He stood, facing out of the front door, smoking.

I waited until he had gone back in the house before I put the camera back in my bag and zipped it up.

Wafting the two polaroid photos, barely daring to look, I strolled out of the side passage, making my arms and legs extra loose, trying to look like I belonged down there.

At breaktime, Lewis and I stood at the far end of the school field, looking at the photos.

The strange man looked funny in his boxer shorts. In one of the photos, he had his mouth open. In the other, he was mid-blink, leaving his eyes looking drunk. He had curly hairs sprinkled unevenly across his chest and, though he was skinny, he had a rounded lump of tummy just above the waistband of his boxer shorts.

'He's a bit blurry,' Lewis said.

'The pictures are fine.' I snatched the photos back. 'Unless you want to do it again?'

'NO! You're right, they're great.' He scratched his chin furiously. 'Do you think he saw you?'

I felt a cold wind on the warm day.

'No.' I shook my head, hard. 'No, there's no way he could have seen me. I waited till he was back in the house.'

I thought some more.

'I'm positive. He definitely, *definitely* didn't see me.'

School news! It was a bad lunchtime for Craig Parsons, the hardest lad in fifth year.

He'd been on a bench at the side of the corridor, acting big in front of a crowd, showing how to snap a pencil using a karate chop.

Craig had his hand out, ready. 'You have to keep your wrist

straight, see?' He was so busy demonstrating, he didn't see the New Head coming, or the other kids stepping to the side to make room.

The New Head just waited. Craig looked up.

She didn't even have to put her hand out before Craig picked up the pencil and handed it straight over. She walked away, leaving Craig on the bench with nothing to chop, while everyone around, boys and girls, pointed and went '*Aaah!*' and '*Do your karate now, Bruce Lee!*'

Despite Lewis's panic, I'd got the photos I needed, so I worked on my letters in my bedroom that night. Dad was out at the pub and, outside my door, the attic ladder was down. Bumps and shuffling from above told me that Mum was up there, rummaging around.

Dear *Crimewatch*,

There is a strange man who lives in Monkford. I don't know his name but he lives at 56 George Street.

This is a photo of him. His mouth looks funny because he was talking. He didn't know he was having his photo taken.

I think he might be linked to the death of Danielle Larson at Monkford Fair in July 1982.

I thought you could compare the photo with the suspect's description in unsolved cases? Particularly any certain deaths at fairs.

I will keep investigating him and let you know if I find out more.

Thank you,

Fiona Larson

I wrote the same letter to the police, just changing the

section about his mouth to fit the other photo – *his eyes look weird because he's blinking.* I put both letters and photos in envelopes. I was just licking an envelope, thinking Mum and Dad were nearly out of stamps, *again,* when there was a shout from the attic.

'*YES!*'

There was a clanging of someone coming down a ladder too quickly. The floor shook as Mum jumped down.

I shoved my envelopes under my pillow just as she threw my bedroom door open.

'I found it!'

'Found what?'

She beamed at me. 'I *knew* I wouldn't have thrown the NHS records away!' She dusted her hands off. 'They were in the attic, with her old schoolbooks. Danielle was B. B positive.' Mum grinned like she'd found a lost pet.

It took me a minute to realise.

Mum stayed in the doorway, her smile fading a little. 'Go on, then! What are you waiting for?' She made shooing hands. 'Don't you want to write it in your book?'

I slipped off the bed quietly. I got my project book from the bookshelf and filled in *B positive* under *Sibling One* on my chart, next to the others.

Mum nodded. 'Told you I'd find it.'

When I looked up again, she'd gone.

I put my project book away. I got the two letters from under my pillow and put them in my rucksack, ready to post.

I reached for my paper fortune teller and slid my fingers and thumbs between the folds. I moved it, making deliberate choices. Knowing what my future would hold.

Secret Pocket. 7. Stage a bike puncture and spy on someone.

Lewis wouldn't like it. But Lewis had shown that he wasn't a reliable accomplice.

Maybe, this time, Lewis didn't need to know.

24

An effective spy finds a reason to linger near his quarry. He can wait for a bus, or repair a bicycle puncture.
The Junior Spy's Secret Handbook™

Fifteen days to the fair
The most amazing school news!

The teachers have moved the cross-country course this year. The course now does an extra loop round the school field and the back of the sports hall, rather than going down to the railway line and through the fields with long grass, as it used to.

That doesn't sound exciting?

There's a second bit. They've moved the cross-country course this year because of ... *flashers.*

The rumour is that flashers know where us kids run, and there are men in suits and ties, dotted around in bushes, just waiting to flash any kid they can. According to the story, if we ran round the old course, we'd risk seeing some kind of old man, peckers-out, Mexican wave.

I'm not sure it's true. It can't be true. Some facts are too interesting to be true.

*

After managing to keep my plan secret from Lewis all day, I told Dad I was going out for a bike ride after school.

In the garden shed, I pocketed the puncture repair kit and stabbed my bike's back tyre with secateurs. I wheeled the bike to the lamppost on George Street.

I pulled the bike up onto the pavement and lay it down to 'examine' my flat tyre, my best sad face on.

Every so often, I looked up.

The strange man paced across his lounge. I could see him through the front window, talking into a phone.

I did some huffing and puffing. I blew up the tyre with my bike pump. I put my hands on my hips and watched the air hiss back out.

I sat cross-legged in front of my bike.

The strange man came out of the front door, still talking on the phone. He smoked a cigarette.

I tried not to look, but I could still hear his conversation.

'*Thanks, Chris. Yep, I'll do that. Yep. I'm on it.*'

'*Of course. I'll double-check with logistics, but I think we're good to go.*'

I looked up and the man looked quickly away. He jiggled the phone between his hands, like it was too hot to hold.

I tried to remember his conversation so I could add it to a future list of facts. I was just trying to memorise everything he said when I looked up – *right into his eyes.*

'Hi there.' The man stood over me, smiling. 'You got a puncture?'

I tried to breathe. I made myself nod.

He crouched down. 'Let's have a look.' He put his mobile phone on the pavement. I couldn't help staring at it.

He reached for the tyre and pressed it. 'It's a big puncture. Like you've ridden over a hedgehog or something.'

I was about to frown and say *but that would mean loads of tiny punctures, not a big one.*

Then I realised. It was meant to be a joke.

Adult jokes need to be funnier if they want kids to get them straight away. Either way, something about him making such a bad joke made me feel less scared.

He stood up. 'I wonder if there's somewhere round here we could get a puncture repair kit?'

I took the kit out of my pocket and handed it to him.

He smiled. 'Girl guide?'

'No. I don't like jam. I mean, I like eating it rather than making it.'

He opened the kit. He unfolded the instructions to read.

'It says start by *taking the wheel off*.' He waved his hands at the instructions. 'But it doesn't say *how* to take the wheel off.'

He kept reading. For ages.

I shifted the bike's chain to the small cog to make slack, and opened the brake. I pushed back the lever and took out the wheel.

The strange man gave a nervous laugh. 'Right.' He looked at the instructions. 'Point two says *unseat one side of the tyre*. Unseat. What does that even mean, *unseat*? What kind of word is *unseat*?'

He was so weird, in an awkward-rather-than-murdery-paedo way, I forgot to be scared. I used the lever to pull the inner tube out, like Dad had taught me. 'Are you any good at this stuff?'

'Not really. I'm useless. But I'm a grown-up, so probably better than you, right?' He adjusted his ponytail. 'Or not.'

I looked at his mobile phone again. The flip-out bit at the

bottom. The buttons. The yellow of the lettering, telling me the numbers would glow in the dark.

'You like my phone?'

'It's amazing. I've never seen one before.'

'It's really not that great. It's a work phone. If it rings, it means someone wants me to do some work.'

I kept staring at the phone.

'Do you want to hold it?'

I jerked my head up in a panic, but he was definitely just talking about the phone. His trousers were still zipped up.

I looked around. There were other people in the street. It was still daylight.

I took the phone quickly. 'Thanks.'

I felt the weight of it in my hand. I turned it over.

I opened the flip bit and held it to my ear. I said 'hello' into the silence.

'You can make a call,' the man said. 'If you're really quick.'

'No thanks.' I flipped the phone closed. 'My friend Lewis will be having a snack about now. Toast, probably. Peanut butter.'

The man put his phone in his pocket. 'Fair enough.'

He didn't seem to be looking to move, and the instructions were slack in his hand, so I reached down for the puncture repair kit.

'Is Lewis the kid you meet here in the mornings?'

I nodded. I unfolded the piece of sandpaper and started sanding the inner tube.

'Will you tell him to knock back on my door on the way past?' He folded the instructions back up. 'I think I spooked your Lewis, but I would be very interested to take him up on his offer about strimming.'

I nodded. I finished repairing the puncture on my own.

He watched me glue the patch on. 'Looks like I'm here as moral support.'

'Thanks anyway.'

'You're' – he made his voice light – 'Gail's daughter.'

'And you're the man from the supermarket who's come back because his mum died.'

'Yep.' Quickly, he looked at the instructions.

I screwed the lid back on the glue.

'*Seat*, again!' He held the instructions in one hand, batting the back of his other hand against the paper. '*Reseat* this time. What have they got about *seats*?' He turned the instructions over. 'We have to reseat the tyre bead. Any ideas?'

He watched me put the inner tube back in. 'Right. You're pretty good at this stuff, aren't you?'

I didn't tell him I was a girl plus/boy minus. I just smiled.

He helped me stand my bike up. 'I used to work in sales with your mum, a long time ago. Did she mention that?'

'No.'

'Does she still work at the brewery?'

'She's a driving instructor now.'

'Really?' He smiled. 'I can't imagine that.'

I thought about how angry Mum got at roundabouts. 'Nor can I.' I took a breath. 'Did you know my sister too? Danielle?'

'I just knew your mum a bit from work; I didn't know the family.' But he didn't react or look caught out.

I nodded.

He crouched down to pick his phone off the ground. 'My name's Carl.'

'I'm Fiona.' I watched him put his phone in his pocket. 'But everyone calls me Fi.'

'Fi.' He kicked the bike tyre. 'Looks good, that. You did a good job.'

I made myself ask. 'Carl, are you going to the fair this year?'

'Dodgems and donkey derbies?' He smiled. 'I'm forty-five, mate. A bit long in the tooth for hook-a-duck.' He handed me back the instructions. 'I should get back to work. Nice to meet you, Fi.'

He pushed his hands in his pockets roughly and walked away.

His walk reminded me a bit of Lewis when he knows he's being watched, his movements all awkward and spiky.

The Strange Man

1) He's called Carl
2) He has a mobile phone for his job
3) He does work for someone called Chris
4) He used to work with Mum in sales at the brewery
5) He says he didn't know Danielle
6) He wants to talk to Lewis about something called *strimming*
7) He doesn't know how to repair a bike puncture
8) He doesn't know how to follow *basic* written instructions
9) He wasn't that scary up close
10) He says he isn't going to the fair
11) If you didn't know he was a strange man, you'd think he was actually . . . quite nice

Maybe I should have included Lewis in the mission, after all.

If I'd included him, he might not have gone so *parent* about it. Because he stopped playing his computer game the moment I told him that Friday lunchtime. He let his rhino die and span his chair to face me.

'The strange man wants to talk to me about *what?*'

'Strimming.'

'Strimming! Strimming? What the hell is *strimming*? I can't *believe* you did that!'

'It's fine.' I waved a hand. 'Eat your sandwiches, Lewis. *Chill*.'

'A puncture. You really just got a puncture on George Street? And you needed to repair it, right outside his house?'

I nodded.

'Just like it says in *The Junior Spy's Secret Handbook*?'

I swallowed.

'Strimming!'

'I'm sure it's something fine.'

'What was the man like?' Lewis's voice was less squeaky now.

'He was nice, actually. He let me hold his mobile phone.'

'If he was nice to you, that means he's sneaky.'

'It was a really good phone. It had a flip bit at the bottom.'

'And if he's sneaky, we have to be even more careful. Your mum's not a liar. She wouldn't say he was strange if he wasn't.'

'She might not be lying; she might just be wrong.' I really needed to solve Danielle's death, but I wasn't convinced anymore that Carl was *definitely* the murderer. In fact – I was pretty sure now that I'd made a mistake. 'It wouldn't be the first time Mum got something wrong. Remember when she said it didn't matter what rucksack I got? That kids would make friends with me because of *my personality*?' I watched Lewis's rhino on the screen flash dead. '*And* she said everyone would soon forget about me showing my pants at primary school.'

I nudged Lewis's lunchbox towards him, hoping he'd get distracted by his box of raisins.

'He must have seen you taking his picture on Wednesday.'

Lewis left his raisins untouched. 'He suspects you. Otherwise why would he come out to help? Unless he was really good at punctures?'

He waited for an answer.

'He was useless,' I admitted.

'There then.' Lewis sat up straighter. 'He must either have seen you take a photo, or he's a paedo. Those are the only reasons he'd come outside. Which would you prefer?'

'He didn't touch his zip once.' I folded my arms. 'Or ask me to sit on his knee.'

'But paedos don't all act like paedos *all the time*, do they? They have to go to shops and stuff. They can't have their peckers out if they're paying for petrol or sitting in offices.'

'His name's Carl.' I nudged Lewis's box of raisins closer still. 'Carl's not a paedo name.'

Lewis started reaching. He paused. 'What's a paedo name?'

'I don't know. Bill?'

'*Bill?*'

I shrugged. 'Jack?'

Lewis stopped smiling. 'No, Jack's my grandpa. And – hang on, *the man told you his name?*'

'Stop flapping.'

'Did you tell him *your* name?'

I looked down at my lunch box. I put the lid carefully on the top and squeezed it till it clicked.

He gasped. 'Fi-on-a!'

'Fi.'

'Fi! You're *playing with fire*! Don't talk to him again. Promise me you won't.'

I looked down and pretended to brush a bit of dust off my skirt. 'I'm positive I won't talk to him again.'

'Not positive. Promise?'

I took breath. 'Promise.'

The thing is, if you're already really bad, there's not much lower you can go.

But Lewis had scared me. I pretended I needed to speak to Dr Sharma, and went to look at the encyclopaedias in the school library. I needed something better than a Scrabble dictionary to investigate what the writing on the flyer had been on about.

In the library, I got the R edition of the encyclopaedia from the shelf and carried it to one of the big tables in the middle of the room. I put it down with a thud and found the right page.

A **registrar** *is an official keeper of records made in a register. The term may refer to (see specific sections below):*

- *Education*
- *Government records*
- *Medicine . . .*

There were *loads* of sections.

Not all spying is fun.

After what felt like hours, something under *Government Records* caught my attention.

The General Register Office or General Registry Office is the name given to the government agency responsible for recording vital records such as marriages, births and deaths, and items related to property transactions. Marriage, birth and death certificates are issued . . .

I stared. *Death certificates.*

I pulled the crumpled fair flyer out of my pocket.

registrar – death cert
will
account numbers

*Registrar – death cert*IFICATE.

I shoved the encyclopaedia back onto the shelf and crumpled the flyer up in one hand.

I could see it now, as clear as anything. Carl had been on the phone to someone about paperwork. Stuff to do with *his mum* dying, not Danielle. And he jotted down notes on the nearest piece of paper – which happened to be a flyer that had come through the door – a fair flyer. Something that he thought was junk.

That list had nothing to do with certain death. Or the fair. Or Danielle.

Which meant *Carl* had nothing to do with Danielle's death. There was no reason to link them at all.

The bell rang and I picked up my rucksack. I pushed the crumpled flyer into the library bin.

If my investigations had been a game, I would have just bumped back down a long snake. I was nearly back where I'd started.

I had two weeks to go. *Two weeks.* And, now Carl had turned out to be a red herring, I only had one lead. The article on the microfiche at the library. The only clue I had left.

By Adrian Sykes.

25

Sometimes my parents say they've done something for my
benefit but it actually makes my life worse.
(paradox)

Thirteen days to the fair
The next morning, Saturday, I knew Mum was out on lessons. I stood on the stairs, planning to make a dash for the
phonebook while Dad wasn't looking.

Happily, Dad was distracted. His quiz show application
form had arrived, and he was filling it out at the peninsula.

Dad saw me on the stairs. 'Fi, look at this!' He waved me
over. 'What's the capital of Italy, *see*? Twenty grand top prize,
and *these* are the questions!'

I smiled and pulled the kitchen door closed between us. I
grabbed the phonebook and ran upstairs.

I knew I was born unlucky as well as bad. Get this.

There were *twenty-three* A Sykes in the local phonebook,
and *none* of them might be Adrian Sykes the reporter.

I called the first number and a woman answered. 'Five one
two eight three nine.'

I coughed. 'Can I speak to Adrian?'

'Who is this?' The woman sounded like she was eating crisps.

'Fiona Larson.' *I* wanted to be eating crisps.

'Fiona who?'

'Larson. L-A-R-S-O-N.'

Crisp crunch, crisp crunch. 'How old are you?'

'Twelve this month.'

'And you want to speak to *who*?'

'Adrian.' I drummed my pen on my bedside table. 'A-D-R-I-A-N.'

The woman chuckled. 'But there's no Adrian here, pet!' *Crisp crunch.*

I put the phone down and tried the next one.

An old lady answered. '*Hello?*'

'Can I speak to Adrian please?'

'Adrian who?'

How many Adrians did this woman have living with her? 'Adrian *Sykes*.'

'Wrong number. You've got me out of the garden for nothing!'

The dial tone told me she'd hung up, just like that. Rude for an old lady, I thought.

It went on like this. Eleven more wrong numbers. Eleven more people who couldn't hear me properly, or asked me to repeat myself, or talked down to me, like the man who said, in a slow careful voice, 'Can't your mum help you make calls so you get the right number?' – like he couldn't tell the difference between a little kid and someone who was *nearly twelve*.

The fourteenth call took ages.

'What number did you ring?' This woman sounded like she had a cold.

'It doesn't matter because it's not you, is it? Sorry for bothering you.'

'But what number did you ring?'

I checked the phonebook and said the number again.

'That's the right number, but there's no Adrian here.'

I raised my gaze to the ceiling.

It's like, the more time I spend dealing with adults, I'm not sure they're the geniuses we're always told.

'Thanks,' I said.

'Where did you get my number from? I'm wondering if someone's registered it incorrectly in a phonebook and I'm going to start getting lots of calls, or—'

I decided to act like the rude old lady earlier, and hung up. I never usually do that, but this woman *wouldn't stop*.

I dialled the fifteenth number. 'Can I speak to Adrian?'

'I'll just get him.' A friendly female voice. 'Who is it?'

I panicked. 'Fiona. Fiona Larson.'

'Hang on.' There was the clunk of the woman putting the phone down on something. 'Adrian!'

More muffled clunking as the phone was handed over.

'Hello?' A man's voice.

'Adrian Sykes?'

His voice sounded crinkly. 'Speaking.'

'You are a reporter on the *Monkford and District Advertiser*?'

A pause. 'It's been a while. Who is this?'

He didn't sound like a scary wall-of-ham man. 'Fiona Larson.'

'Right. And you are. . .?' He sounded quite nice, actually. Like a nice old grandpa.

'Someone looking for some information. You wrote an article about my sister in 1982 and I found the article on the microfiche at the library.'

'1982!' There was laughter in his voice. 'Well, now.'

I pressed the phone hard against my ear. 'She died. At the fair. And I want to know how she died. Danielle Larson in 1982. She was eleven. Can you tell me?'

When he didn't answer straight away, I added, 'Please?'

There was quiet for a minute.

'You're Fiona, you said?'

Fi. But, 'Yes.'

'How old are you, Fiona?'

'Twelve in August.'

'Do your parents know you're calling?'

'I don't want to bother them,' I said. 'They're busy.'

'Love. Some advice. If you want to know more about your sister's death – and I was very sorry to hear about it, by the way – your mum and dad are the ones to ask.'

'They won't talk about it.'

He didn't say anything.

'And seeing as you're on the phone now, Mr Sykes, and I've already got you up from whatever you were doing . . . it will only take a second. Could you tell me how she died? I definitely won't ask any more questions afterwards.'

The line was quiet. My ear ached where I pressed the phone against my head, and I moved it further away.

That was better.

'Fiona, I couldn't tell you if I wanted to. I wrote a lot of articles for that paper. Thousands. I was a news reporter. And it was a long time ago.'

'But she *died.* You'd remember a girl who died.'

'I'm sorry, love. When you work on a local paper – a lot of people die.'

'But she was *eleven.* People don't die at eleven. You'd re-member *that.*'

He said nothing.

'You *said* she was perfect.' I realised I was pressing the phone hard into my head again. 'You *said* my parents were devastated. You said she was active in the RSPB, and she was dead when the paramedics arrived. Danielle Larson. Blonde hair. Smiley. Tall for an eleven-year-old. Pretty as a picture. You *must* remember! Surely no one else has ever died at the fair?'

He still didn't reply.

'Are you still there?'

'I don't know what to say to you, Fiona.'

'Is there any way you can find out?'

'I retired, love. Five years ago.'

'But do you still know some people at the paper? Do you have your own records or—'

'I'm sorry. I'm going now.'

I switched the phone off. I looked at the address of the number I'd dialled. *23 Chestnut Walk*.

I closed the phonebook and I sat there on my bed, for a very long time. I didn't even hear Dad come up the stairs, till he was in my doorway.

'Come to the shops with me, Fi. Let's go and get something interesting for dinner.'

It was a shame, I decided, that if you wanted to have your secret pocket, you needed to wear a coat.

Because today, the sun had fully *got his hat on*, as the song went – and now everyone was smiley and other people were all *hip hip hooray*-ing in their T-shirts and shorts.

But not me.

The first thing Dad said as we left the house was still, 'Have you got your inhaler?' But we weren't even out of the drive before he followed it with, 'Aren't you hot in that coat?'

Have you got your inhaler? and *Aren't you hot in that coat?* follow me around like *haircut* follows Greeney.

'You never know when you might need a coat,' I said. 'We might bump into some kid from school and they might ask me over for a barbecue. And it gets cold at night.'

We turned down George Street and I tried to imagine something less likely than me bumping into some kid from school and them inviting me over for a barbecue.

I trailed behind Dad when we reached 56 George Street, out of habit. Just to see what he did.

But Dad didn't cross at the postbox, just walked straight in front of Carl's house. He smiled at me as he walked.

I pointed at the postbox. 'I usually cross the road here with Lewis and Sean.'

Dad nodded. 'So I hear. Your mum said there's a story about an axeman killing his brothers and sisters in that house.' His voice was even.

'Just his brothers, I think. No sisters. Or maybe he didn't think to mention the sisters.'

'Do you believe the story?'

'I don't think so. Hardly at all.'

Dad smiled. 'Is your friend Sean the kind of kid who makes things up?'

I nodded. 'He has an awful lot of cousins. Drummers in bands. Racing car drivers.'

'Do you need me to tell you that story about the man with the axe isn't true?'

I shook my head.

Dad and I reached the park and passed the big wasps' nest. I watched the wasps buzz around it in a cloud, circling the nest like moons around a planet.

'You know you mentioned going to a kid's house later for a barbecue? Why do you never invite kids over to ours?'

I would never say it was because of the flashing lights when someone rang the door. 'It's just easier to go to Lewis's.' He looked sad, like he knew anyway, so I added quickly, 'And because I don't really have any friends.'

But then Dad looked sadder still, so I said, 'It's fine.' *Change the subject.* 'Now, I hear Mum used to work in a brewery?'

Dad nodded. 'She worked in sales there. Your mum was good at sales.' His smile faded. 'But it's really unfair for her to expect other people to be as good when they haven't had any formal training. And, as I tried to explain to your mother, not a lot of people *want* ironing board covers.'

It took me a second to realise what we were talking about.

'Anyway, Mum worked in sales at the brewery,' Dad said, 'but she changed jobs when she was pregnant with you. We both made the decision to change jobs at the same time. You know I used to be an aeroplane engineer?'

I frowned. 'It was my fault you stopped being an engineer?'

'No, silly!' He smiled. 'Me and your mum both worked long days and we didn't always see each other that much. My work was over an hour away, and your mum was always on the road, driving all over the country. And we wanted a different life. Something happening, something big, makes you rethink what you want. And when Danielle—'

I held up my hand. 'Right. That.' Always.

'We wanted to be better to each other, and we both wanted to be around more for you, Fi. To be better parents. We wanted to make the most of our time with you, and we don't regret it for a second.'

I looked at the park's second-biggest bush.

A bunch of boys and girls sat on picnic blankets, smoking

and drinking Coke, flicking through magazines. These kids were made differently from the kids from our school. They were shinier, with newer clothes, and the boys talked in a different kind of loud and, I knew – even though they weren't in uniform – they wore blazers and school uniform, even in sixth form.

Chester Road School kids.

I'd once asked Mum if I could go to Chester Road and she laughed like it was the funniest thing ever, and said, 'Yes, fine. And we can get a chauffeur and a butler, too.'

I saw what the kids were doing and my heart stopped.

These Chester Road kids were, right now, sitting in front of our bush – *reading magazines*.

Had I stolen the magazines from *these kids*? Would they look at me and just *know*? Chester Road kids weren't as hard as Monkford High kids – it was just a known fact – but still.

I moved onto the other side of Dad, trying to look casual and un-thief-like. But none of the kids said anything as I walked past. I'm not sure they even noticed me there, at all.

26

A spy cell is only as strong as its weakest member.
The Junior Spy's Secret Handbook™

Eleven days to the fair
The rest of the weekend passed without anything exciting going on. When I waited for Lewis at the lamppost on Monday morning, there was a big truck outside 56 George Street, and a dirty yellow skip in the driveway. Carl was outside in a T-shirt and shorts, talking to a man in grey overalls.

He saw me and waved. I waved back.

Lewis walked up and stared.

I shrugged. 'Just waving to Carl.'

'Hey, kid!' Carl waved both hands now, trying to get our attention. 'Lewis, is it?'

Lewis looked at me in panic. He set off in a rush.

'Come back!' Carl crinkled his face up in confusion. 'Why are you running? I won't bite. I just want to talk to you about some strimming!'

I hurried after Lewis and found him in the park.

'Strimming.' He looked like a wild animal was after him. 'Strimming! *What is strimming?*'

'I'm sure it's nothing bad. He wouldn't shout it in the street, would he?'

'We don't know what he's capable of, Fi! That's the whole point!'

'I've decided Carl might not be a strange man after all. I've got him all wrong. And think about it. If strimming is like flashing, he wouldn't be making a big deal of it. Flashers don't shout *I'm flashing*, do they? They just open their coats and do it.'

'I feel dizzy,' Lewis said. 'And I've got a tummy ache.'

'You've just got scared and ran too soon after breakfast.'

'Do I look right to you?'

I stopped and gave a big sigh. I turned to study him.

His skin was shiny with sweat. He had a fuzzy look in his eyes.

'You look fine,' I said kindly. I pulled on his arm. 'Come on.'

School news. But not good school news.

Turns out Lewis *was* ill.

He threw up in English, all over his copy of *The Taming of The Shrew*, and his mum had to come and pick him up. I'm not in that English class, but I heard Mr Kellett told all the kids to get back, while the rest of the class laughed and pointed and made Jaws music *ner-ner-ner-ner* and Robert Kitson shouted, *Harris is about to blow!*

Which – turned out – he was.

Everyone heard about it. Which meant I hoped Lewis was off ill for a few days, at least. For his own sake.

On the way home, I headed down George Street. It was fine – I felt *way* more relaxed walking past Carl's house now.

The van had gone but, next to the skip, there were boxes

and old household things. A broken lamp. A metal shelf. A frilly tissue box.

Carl came outside carrying a box. His T-shirt had a cartoon with *Duff Beer* on it, even though that's from *The Simpsons*, and *The Simpsons* is a show for kids.

He rested the box on the edge of the skip and started pulling things out.

I crossed the road. 'What are you doing?'

'Getting rid of Mum's stuff.' Carl got a lamp out of the box and placed it on the lid of the skip. 'We're exchanging contracts on the house in a couple of weeks. Hopefully.' He nudged the lamp with his foot. 'Keep or throw away? Would anyone want this?'

The lamp was one of those desk ones with a little hat, on a long bendy stem that folded in on itself. This lamp had a broken bit of stem which made the hat loll to one side, like a rose that needed dead-heading.

'*No one* would want that stuff.'

He looked down at the lamp. He picked it up and put it in the tip after all.

'Your mate, Lewis.' Carl leaned on the skip. 'I don't get that kid. He knocks on my door to offer to help me and then I say *great, thanks* and he just runs off? And now runs off whenever he sees me?'

I pressed my lips together. *What can you do?*

'Now, I've got something for you and I think you're going to like it.' He turned and opened his front door. 'Come in.'

I took a step to follow him, then stopped. A hand of fear squeezed my stomach.

'Sensible girl. Don't go into strangers' houses.' He nodded. 'Wait here.'

I watched him go inside.

He came out, holding his flip-bottomed mobile phone. He gave it to me to hold and I turned it over, admiring it.

Now he had his hands free, I waited for him to pull what he'd got for me out of his pocket.

He didn't move.

I looked up. We stared at each other.

I waited again.

'Aren't you going to say "thank you?"'

I frowned. 'Aren't you going to give me something?'

He nodded at the phone. 'What do you think *that* is?'

I looked at the phone and back at Carl. I still didn't get it.

Thing is, I'd been alive nearly twelve years now, and things like this just don't happen to me.

Carl sighed. 'My work have given me a new contract mobile with a new number, so I don't need this old pay-as-you-go anymore. I was going to throw it away, then I remembered the little girl who looked so interested in my phone while we fixed her puncture. And I thought – *why not make her day?*'

I looked at the phone again.

'It's yours. If you want it.'

I turned the phone over in my hand. I was misunderstanding. Hearing what I wanted to hear, like Mum said I did. Because it sounded a bit like—

'Fi.' Carl shoved his hands in his pockets. 'Don't make this weird. I didn't mean it to be weird.' He took out his hairband and retied his hair. 'I'm not weird, I promise. I'm not . . .' – he gave a high laugh – 'God, no, nothing like that. Oh Jesus, I really wish I hadn't started this. I'm just giving you this because I don't need it and you liked it. But I could just throw it in the skip with the other junk. And you don't owe me anything. It's not a big deal.'

I looked down at the phone.

'There's less than a fiver of time left on it.'

A *phone*.

A real, proper phone.

My phone.

'But if you don't want it—'

'No!' I gripped it tighter. 'Please can I have it?'

Carl nodded. 'That's more like it!'

'It's mine? Really mine?'

He laughed. 'No one else here, is there?'

I looked around, just in case. Like I said, things like this don't just happen to Fiona Larson every day. *Especially* not Fiona Larson.

'I'd suggest phoning your friend to test it out, but you probably don't want to waste your credit.'

I held the phone in both hands.

He scratched his top lip. 'Probably best not to tell your mum and dad it's from me.'

I looked up. 'Why?'

He left a long pause.

'I'm a stranger, aren't I? We don't really know each other. Your parents' – he took out his hairband, retying his hair *again* – 'well. Never mind.'

We stood there in his driveway, both looking at the ground.

'Thank you for the phone. Carl.'

He rolled back on his feet, his hands in his pockets. He rolled forward again. 'No problem, Fi.'

'Do I need to write you a thank-you letter?'

'Definitely not. Careful crossing the road, now. You seem in shock.'

'I am.' I shielded my eyes from the sun and looked up at him. 'Carl, people don't go around giving me presents every day.'

He raised his palms. 'Look, it's not *that* great a present. The screen's scratched and the three button sticks. Sometimes it freezes for no reason and you have to hold down the off button to get it going. Takes ages. Like I said, there's hardly any credit on it. I just thought, rather than throw it away, I'd give it to you.'

I nodded. 'Thank you.'

'Bye for now.'

'Bye.'

I slid the phone into my secret pocket and turned towards home. I tried not to run. I tried to walk like this was just any normal day. Just feeling the outline of my phone, jiggling against my chest as I walked.

I'd been so sad this weekend. And that seemed so long ago now.

Because this – *this* – changed EVERYTHING.

This phone was absolutely, positively, the best thing that had ever happened to me.

27

Lewis doesn't want good things to happen to us.

(paradox)

Eleven days to the fair

I rang Lewis after tea – from the house phone, of course. I wasn't going to waste the credit on my new mobile.

His mum answered. 'He can't come to the phone, lovey. It's nice you're concerned and I'll pass on your regards.'

'I need to talk to Lewis though. Urgently.'

'He's too ill to talk, the poor thing. No one will tease him about being sick, will they? The other kids will be kind?'

I picked up the mobile phone. I tested the weight of it in my hand. 'No, Mrs Harris.' I kept my voice level. '*No one* will tease him at all.'

'I'll tell him you called. I'll tell him you said to get well soon.'

I took the phone downstairs, to where Mum and Dad were on the sofa.

I put the phone back in the cradle. 'Mum. I've got a word question.'

Mum paused. 'A *word question*, hmm.' She turned to look at Dad, then gave me a small smile. 'What do you think, Jonathan? Hypothesis?'

Dad put his finger on his lip, like he was thinking. 'Provisional?'

'Or am I going to be asked again to explain'– she pronounced it carefully – 'an-ti-dis-est-ab-lish-ment-a-r-i-an-ism?'

'Not antidisestablishmentarianism.' I said it more easily than her, but then, adults don't say it as much as kids do. 'I'm sorry if this is a really bad thing to ask about, but I really, *really* need to know.'

Mum and Dad looked at each other.

'Oh God,' Mum said.

'Not *fellatio*, again?' Dad said. 'Please, Fi. Trust us when we said we'd explain that when—'

'Please don't get angry.' I took a breath. 'But what, exactly, is *strimming*?'

At lunchtime the next day, I stood in the playground, near the tennis courts, my mobile phone to my ear. When any kids walked past, I talked like I was having a conversation.

'He said *what*?'

and

'What did she do then?'

I took my phone away from my ear when I saw a teacher because you never know with Lost Property. There's a rumour Dr Sharma wears confiscated earrings to wine bars at the weekends.

I walked up in Sean's direction, but he mustn't have seen the phone because he turned and walked away.

It was fine. Besides, Sean was no good to me now – it was girl friends I needed for the Waltzers.

I walked around the school field and weaved between the groups of girls on the grass. Every so often, I said something into the phone.

'That's so funny!'

'He said he fancies me?'

'No! Things sound so much better at your school than mine!'

I kept this up for the whole of lunchtime.

That night, I took the house phone to my bedroom to ring Lewis again.

'It's so sweet of you to care so much, Fiona, it really is,' Mrs Harris said. 'His temperature's dropped and he's kept some toast down, so he might be back in before the weekend, if you're lucky.'

'Can I speak to him?'

'If you're quick, hon.'

I heard Lewis's mum's footsteps. There was a rustling and a clunk.

'Lewis? Is that you?'

'Hi, Fi.' He sounded so weak and ill. Tiny Tim in *The Muppet Christmas Carol*.

'*LewisI'vegotamobilephone!Lewisanactualmobilephone!*'

It took a while to explain because he didn't believe me. Which was fair, because I didn't believe me either. If you'd told me I'd made the whole thing up, that would have made *loads* more sense, actually.

To Lewis, too. 'He can't have *given* it to you!'

'He definitely did.'

'Is this like when Sean's uncle let him drive a Ferrari that day on the farm?'

'Nothing like that.'

'You haven't stolen it?' A softer voice now. 'Fi. I'll forgive you as long as you don't lie. Have you stolen it?'

'LEWIS!'

'OK, sorry.'

'I promise – he said straight out that it was mine. Quite a few times.'

'Promise or positive?'

'Promise. Actual *promise*.'

I picked up a pen and tapped it against the bedside table. I waited for him to catch up.

'Does the phone work?' Lewis asked.

'I think so, I haven't tried it. Either way, it's still a good thing.'

'I don't like this, Fi. I have a bad feeling.' It's like Lewis doesn't *want* good things to happen to us. 'First strimming, now this. He's *got to be* a paedo.'

'LEWIS! Strimming means he wants you to cut his lawn, because you knocked on his door and offered to do jobs for him, *you absolute fool*. And he's not a paedo, he's never tried to touch me, not even once. *Or* got his pecker out. Not even just the end.'

Lewis went quiet.

'Are you still there?'

'Your mum says he's strange, Fi.'

I shook my head. 'You're missing the point, as always. It doesn't matter that—'

'Why would your mum say he's strange if he wasn't?'

'She probably said *a strange-r*, I didn't tape-record the conversation. And you know what Mum's like, she gets stuff wrong. She blames me for everything, doesn't she? She blames the snails on the step for getting stepped on.'

He didn't answer.

'It's been fourteen years and she *still* mutters about those ladies from work who went to Danielle's funeral in one car and stopped at M and S.'

Lewis still didn't say anything. He was making his point the sneaky way, with silence.

'Look. Carl's a really good man. Really, *really* good. He gave me a mobile phone. That's proof. What more proof do you need?'

'Carl is either really, really kind,' Lewis spoke carefully, like an adult reading a story. 'Jesus-kind. *Or* he's really, really bad. Because no one—'

'That's enough.' Lewis's mum's voice in the background. 'You need your rest. Say goodbye to Fiona.'

'Bye, Fi.'

I put the phone down. I pulled back my pillow and touched the mobile phone. And tried really hard not to think about what Lewis had said.

28

Teachers get more upset about stuff happening to us kids
than we do.
(paradox)

Nine days to the fair

Dear Miss Larson,

Thank you for your letter to *Crimewatch*, dated 3
July 1996.

It is always encouraging to receive correspondence
from our younger viewers, especially those with such
a strong sense of justice.

I'm afraid we do tend to start our investigations
with specific crimes in mind, rather than with a sus-
picious-looking character. And we have no open cases
in our files from fairgrounds – about certain death, or
otherwise. But we revisit unsolved cases regularly and
we have made a note of the information you sent.

I'm sure you understand we can't update members
of the public on case progress, but we do appreciate
your help and encouragement.

Thanks again for writing in.

Yours sincerely,
Aimee Sweetman
Crimewatch Liaison Coordinator

School news! Mr Kellett is moving to Glasgow!

He smiled around as he told us at the end of class. 'You've not driven me away, I promise. And you've got me till the end of the year.'

There were lots of sad looks – more than you'd expect for a teacher. I think some of the boys wanted to cry.

Greeney looked like he'd lost his favourite dog. 'Who's going to teach us football?'

'They'll be getting a replacement. And there's always Mr Corbett in the meantime.'

Grumbles ripped through the room.

'He's a hundred.'

'He's shit.'

'He's never played for Alty Town.'

Mr Kellett stopped me as the class rushed out. 'Fiona. You're friends with Lewis Harris in my other Year Seven class?'

I nodded.

'His mum's asked for some homework to keep him busy while he's off.'

I frowned. The *unfairness* of Mrs Harris.

'But he doesn't have a copy of *The Taming of The Shrew* anymore.'

'He does,' I said, 'he's just got sick all over it.'

'Quite. Well, not *quite,* because I've binned that other one. So Mrs Harris says can you drop this in for him?'

I shook my head slowly.

'You can't drop it in?'

'It's fine, I can do it, I just think it's *really* unfair of Mrs Harris.'

He smiled. 'It's one of the better pieces of homework to do when you're ill, I would have thought? English? Reading a comedy?'

I was about to reply, but he confused me, so it took a second to remember what I meant to tell him. 'You know, if you want to know stuff about what to do in Glasgow, I can ask my grandma. She moved up there.'

'Thanks Fiona, that's very kind.'

'Are you leaving because of the New Head? Is it because she makes you change out of your PE kit?'

He laughed. 'No!' He stopped laughing. 'And she doesn't make me change out of my PE kit, that's not exactly it, she—'

'I just hear quite a lot about the New Head. Miss Jarvis said—'

'I don't know what you think you've heard, Fiona, but you must have got confused. Everyone here likes and respects Mrs Shackleton very much.' Was that a twinkle in his eye? 'All the teachers are very, very happy, and we thoroughly approve of the new way of doing things. We really appreciate having more structure in our lives. It helps us grow.'

I nodded.

'And definitely don't be telling people that's why I'm leaving. My partner has a new job in Glasgow, so that's why I'm leaving. Nothing to do with Mrs Shackleton.'

'What does she do, your partner?'

He scratched his mouth. 'My partner's a doctor.'

'Sweet.' I gave a nod. 'Can I ask you something else?'

'If you're quick.'

'Is it true the cross-country course got changed because of flashers?'

Mr Kellett reached behind him for the teacher's table. He sat back. 'Where did you hear that?'

I shrugged. 'Playground.'

'We don't want anyone to be scared.'

'I'm not scared. Just interested.'

Mr Kellett looked behind me, like he was hoping someone would come and disturb us. 'There are few – very, *very* few – people out there that might cause kids harm, Fiona. And it's our job as teachers to consider risk and do whatever we can to ensure—'

'It's true? It's *actually true*?'

'I thought you said you knew?'

'The course has been moved because of *all the flashers*?'

'Not exactly that, not *all* the flashers, it's more about lighting and the density of the foliage and proximity to—'

'Thanks, Mr Kellett.' I waved *The Taming of The Shrew*. 'I'll take this to Lewis tonight.'

'Fiona.' He leaned forward. 'This must be hard to take in. Do you want to talk about it?'

When Mr Kellett said *Do you want to talk about it?* he said it less hungrily than Mrs Vernal. More like he could take it or leave it. Less like he wanted to have our feelings as a snack.

I shook my head. 'Unless you can tell me any more about the flashers? How many there are? What they wear and stuff? Whether they work in teams or alone?'

He took a moment. He shook his head.

'Thanks, then. See you later.'

At lunchtime, I perched on the low wall near the tennis courts, deliberately close to Jodie Mackintosh, the girl from drama. She stood with her group of three friends, all eating crisps, while I talked into my phone.

When Jodie looked over, I waved.

She waved back.

I kept talking into my phone, glancing up at Jodie and her three friends.

'Bye then!' I put my phone back in my rucksack. I sat back on the wall and looked up at the sun.

I closed my eyes and felt the warmth on my face.

'Fiona!' Jodie waved me over, a friendship bracelet slipping down her arm.

I picked up my rucksack and walked to stand with the group, like this kind of thing happened all the time.

'Hi, Jodie.' I nodded at Jodie's friends, who were also all wearing matching friendship bracelets. 'Most people call me *Fi*, not *Fiona*. My friends at other schools, I mean.'

'Is that phone yours?' Jodie asked. 'Can I have a look?'

'Yep.' I got it out of my secret pocket and handed it to her. 'Be careful. It's valuable.'

Her friends crowded round to look at the phone.

'Wow,' Yasmin said. 'Who gave it to you? Your parents?'

I pushed my hair behind my ears. 'Just a friend.'

'Who do you call with it?' Alison Fisher asked.

'Oh, you know. Just people.'

I've never spoken to Alison Fisher, but she's the one whose mum works as a receptionist at the doctor's. Her mum wears her hair in a scrunchie and calls everyone *duck*.

'Do you call Selina Baker on it?' Jodie turned to the others. 'Fiona knows Selina Baker. I saw them talk in the corridor.'

'I don't call Selina. We're friends, but not phone friends.'

Dean Prince walked past, dribbling a football as he walked. 'All right, Fi.'

'All right, Dean.'

Jodie looked at him and back. 'You know Dean Prince?'

I nodded. Turns out older kids are really nice if you've sold them a porno mag.

'He plays for Port Vale!'

'Yep. Under sixteens.' I sold him *Mayfair*, if I remember right. Gave me twenty-five quid.

Alison narrowed her eyes at me. 'Who do you call on your phone, then? If it's not *your best friends* Selina Baker and Dean Prince?'

'Friends from other schools. My boyfriend.'

Jodie looked at the other girls and back. 'Is your boyfriend at another school, too?'

'I know who he is,' Naomi pulled at her plait. 'I've seen them together. It's Lewis Harris.'

And for some reason – well, actually because I hadn't planned for this conversation, and say what you like about Lewis, but he's actually *real* – for that reason, I nodded.

And the other girls nodded back. They didn't say *Ew, Lewis?* or *Lewis Harris went to Paris,* or anything about how glasses at his house tasted of dishwasher. They didn't even call him *The Sickboy of the Shrew* – probably because there had been a fight on Festival Field since then, *and* a boy had come into school with boiled egg all down his tie, so we'd all moved on.

Jodie handed the phone back.

Alison was still looking at me like I'd made a bad smell. 'Your mum's the one who makes everyone's curtains.'

'Definitely not. That's someone else's mum. Your mum's the one who works at the doctor's?'

She looked at her feet. 'No. Fisher's a common name.'

'Got to go.' My lies were twisting up in my tummy like hot cartoon vines. 'I said I'd call Lewis before maths.'

I put my phone to my ear and hurried into the school building.

I reached the computer room and shut the door behind me. I sat completely still. I didn't play a game. I didn't even switch on a computer.

Well.

Everything had changed. *Everything*.

I looked at my phone. I put it in my secret pocket and patted it gently.

Now. I just needed to break the girlfriend news to Lewis. And break it to him in the right way, and make him realise it was OK – before he ruined everything and made us *both* look stupid.

How to Make Friends (According to Mum)

1) Remember beggars can't be choosers
2) Let it happen naturally, don't force it
3) Don't try to impress people with objects
4) Ask people about themselves
5) Don't try to fit in
6) Don't show off
7) Don't draw attention to yourself
8) Just be yourself

Mum didn't have a clue.

29

Some friends aren't very friendly.
(paradox)

Nine days to the fair
Lewis called me that night. 'Mum says you're allowed to come round with my homework.'

'Are you still infectious?'

'No.'

'Then I'll be there in ten minutes.'

I grabbed the letter I'd got back from *Crimewatch* and headed off to Lewis's house.

Mrs Harris let me in. 'Aren't you hot in that coat?'

'No. I hope he's feeling better.' I passed the photo on the wall of Lewis with a wand and a cape. 'I should have brought him some grapes or something.'

Mrs Harris smiled. 'You don't need to do that.'

'I do because . . . well, Lewis is my boyfriend now.' I needed to practise saying it. 'Can you wait for him to tell you first, though, in case he minds that I've ruined the surprise?'

Mrs Harris stared at me. 'Boyfriend?'

Mr Harris looked up from his paper.

I beamed. 'It's official. From today.'

'Does he know that?' Mrs Harris asked.

'He will do in a minute, don't worry.'

'Good lad!' Mr Harris looked to Mrs Harris, smiling, and back at me. 'And with a temperature and everything!'

Mrs Harris frowned at him.

Mr Harris chuckled. 'A chip off the old block.'

'Geoff, stop it.' She turned to me. 'Leave that bedroom door open.'

Lewis's dad turned a page. 'Don't do anything I wouldn't do.'

I held up my bag of schoolbooks. 'We've got a lot to talk about.'

I scampered up the stairs to Lewis's room.

I knocked and walked into a waft of *ill*.

I wrinkled my nose and decided not to shut the door. 'It smells of Grandma's soup in here.'

Lewis didn't get out of bed. 'Hi.' He still had that Muppet Tiny Tim voice.

I stayed at the other side of the room. 'Have you been sick again?'

'I'm nearly better. I haven't been sick all day.' He waved at the washing-up bowl. 'That's just in case.'

His hair looked greasy and stuck to his forehead. He was wearing Spiderman pyjamas. A book called *The Twenty Greatest Magic Tricks* sat on his bedside table next to his favourite stuffed raccoon.

I know beggars can't be choosers. Mum's right about *some* stuff. But, just for a second, I thought maybe I should have picked a better boyfriend.

'It's true it was flashers, why they moved the cross-country course. Can you believe it?' I pushed the door wider open to let the smell of Grandma's soup out into the landing. 'Now, I've got something to tell you and you've got to promise not to get cross.'

He didn't say anything.

I sat on the end of his bed. 'Lewis? You promise?'

'I'm thinking.'

'You don't need to be thinking. Just go ahead and promise, so I can get on and tell you.'

He folded his arms. 'I'm thinking about the past. How things have turned out when you've said things like that.'

'This is different.' I shifted closer. 'At first, you might not understand how what I'm telling you is brilliant. You might need me to explain it so you get it properly. Just remember that.'

I waited.

He lifted his head.

I made my voice light. 'It's a funny story and definitely an accident' – I looked past him, out of the window – 'but people think you're my boyfriend.'

I took one look at his face and went back to looking out of the window.

'*Which* people?'

'Jodie and Naomi and Alison Fisher and Yasmin. You know, my group. My group of girls.' I looked around his eyes. Not actually at his eyes, that was too hard, just in the centre, at the top of his nose. 'And, thing is, now everyone else thinks you're my boyfriend, too.' I shook my head. 'I know gossip gets around quick, but *still*. People were staring at me.' I looked from his left temple to his right temple. 'In a good way. No one tried to trip me up when I walked past the benches in the corridors. They took their legs *in* when I walked past.'

'What did they say to you? Tell me exactly.'

I looked away. 'Nothing.'

Do you do tongues?

Has he touched your bra?

Have you spanked his monkey?

'People think we're too mature to make fun of now. Honestly, Lewis, it's brilliant. We should have thought of this ages ago.'

'What did people say?'

'Nothing. Nothing much. I just sat there smiling and said "that's my business" and "get your own boyfriend if you're so interested". And people *listened*. It's like I've got a superpower.' I glanced at him. 'Like *we've* got a superpower. Lewis!' I leaned forward. 'You might even become friends with the lads from the blue estate! Especially if I tell people I let you put your hand up my top. And everyone's forgotten all about you being sick in English.'

Lewis just sat there. 'No one said anything bad?'

'Of course not.' Lewis *would* have to ruin this. He wouldn't want to know Liam said *Harris must have got ill because you gave him crabs.*

'We can break up soon,' I said, 'but not straight away, or it'll look fake.'

Lewis adjusted his pillows so he was higher up the bed. 'And why are we doing this again?'

'So people think someone would want to go out with us.'

'Am I going to have to kiss you?'

'No. Just get our stories straight about what stuff we've done. I thought that might be good for both of us?'

'Or it'll make things worse.'

'We *deserve* to be more popular, Lewis. Think about it. Who made the rules that you and me are on the bottom rung? We're the *best ones*.'

I tried not to look at his magic book or stuffed raccoon.

'I'm not kissing you. You're like my sister.'

I turned to stare out of the window for a long time. 'I wish I *was* your real sister. *My* real sister's a ghost.'

I kept looking out of the window. I waited.

I glanced back. 'Why aren't you saying something?'

'I'm cross you're trying to catalyst me.'

My face went hot. 'I wouldn't have to catalyst you, if you could just be mature and accept you've got a girlfriend now.'

Lewis looked down at his duvet. He stroked it.

'And this is your first girlfriend present.' I took the fresh copy of *The Taming of The Shrew* out of my bag and put it on the bed. 'Though, get this, Kellett called it a *comedy*.'

Lewis furrowed his brow. 'A *comedy*?'

'And look.' I got the phone out of my secret pocket and laid it on the duvet.

He picked the phone up.

'Isn't it beautiful?'

He stared at it for a moment. 'It's *too* good, that's the problem. Things like this don't happen to you, Fi. You know in a cartoon, when someone finds treasure and it's actually cursed?'

I snatched the phone away. 'Why won't you just be happy for me?'

'If you're so happy, why do you look scared?'

I stared at him. Why did he have to say that? I *wasn't* scared, but – now, because he said the word and made me think about it – my chest was going all cold. 'I'm not scared.'

'This could be something really *bad*. This isn't funny.'

I tried to ignore the chill creeping further down my body.

'No one would give you a mobile for no reason. *No one*.'

I looked at the carpet.

'You are scared, aren't you?'

'No. I was for a little bit though. I did think for a while when I was investigating Danielle, maybe Carl was the one who killed her at the fair and that's why my mum doesn't like him, but—'

At Lewis's reddening face, I stopped. I started to panic. 'I mean—'

His face went redder still. 'YOU PROMISED!' No more Tiny Tim. 'You *promised* you were going to stop looking into Danielle dying. You *promised*. WHY WILL YOU NEVER LISTEN TO ME?'

I grabbed the phone from Lewis and put it in my rucksack. He'd never sounded less Muppet-y.

'Go away and leave me alone!'

'Lewis?' Mrs Harris's voice came up the stairs. 'Are you shouting?'

'Shouting?' I said. 'He's braying like a donkey.' I looked him up and down. 'A *sweaty* donkey. I'll leave you to calm down. Bye, Lewis.' I picked up my bag and ran down the stairs.

With all Lewis's *braying*, I'd forgotten to show him my letter from *Crimewatch*. I'd do it next time.

Fortunately, Lewis is too nice. He *is* like Muppet Tiny Tim. Because however bad I am, whatever I've done, he always, *always* forgives me in the end.

30

Sometimes, the police don't want to solve crimes.

(paradox)

Eight days to the fair

When I checked the doormat the next morning, there was a letter for me in the pile.

Mum came downstairs in her dressing gown as I was squirrelling it away. 'What's that?'

'Nothing.'

'You're getting a lot of post.' She tied the belt of her dressing gown tighter. 'Why?'

I dumped the letters for her and Dad on the side. 'Blood project stuff.' I ran upstairs before she could ask anymore.

In my room, I opened the letter. My polaroid photo of Carl fell out.

Dear Miss Larson,

We have received your letter dated Wednesday 3 July 1996. It is not clear whether you intended the letter to be a prank.

If you have real concerns, please raise them with your parent or guardian. Unless your concerns are about a parent or guardian, in which case please raise them with a trusted adult.

If your letter was intended as a prank, please note the police are very busy protecting lives. We will not follow up on this occasion, but you would be wise to remember there is a criminal offence called Wasting Police Time.

I enclose the photograph you sent, which we will not be keeping on file.

Stay safe,

Cheshire Police

I pulled the bin from under my dressing table and dropped in Carl's sent-back photo. I didn't need it anymore. Not now he wasn't a suspect.

As I pushed the bin back, I tried not to notice the special shape – the bad Nazi shape – that I'd carved into the leg of the dressing table. I looked away and glanced under my bed.

There was a lot of junk under there. I should have remembered to look there before the car boot sale. Along with the dust, there was an old keyring with a bear on it. I spotted a hairband I thought I'd lost, and an old duckling jigsaw.

And I remembered. That was where Mum kept Danielle's Box of Special Things. Under her bed.

I'd forgotten that box completely.

I didn't have time to look before school. But soon.

And now I finally had a new lead. One that didn't involve knocking on the door of the house belonging to Adrian Sykes.

*

School news!

All the Year Nine and above girls got a free parcel in a special one-off class.

Rape alarms!

Attack alarms the teachers call them, but we know what they're really called. Everyone was using them at break – boys trying to steal them from girls' bags, hoiking them out by the strap. Kids going up behind other kids and pulling the pin out right next to their ears. Some kids made it into a game, setting traps for each other like Grandmother's Footsteps, seeing who could get the closest before the alarm went off.

I asked Dr Sharma why we Year Sevens didn't get a parcel and she just looked at the ceiling. 'Year Nine and above, Fiona.'

'On the day of the Tampax, Year Sevens got the free parcel, too.'

'Attack alarms are not toys.'

'I know they're not toys, that's why I want one.'

Dr Sharma made a *pff* air-noise with her mouth. 'Even with this one, Fiona? *Even with this one*, you don't want to be left out?'

At lunchtime, I walked with my mobile phone through the playground, to find Jodie and Naomi and Yasmin and Alison Fisher. I mean – my friends.

I spotted them in their usual place by the tennis courts, and walked up to them quickly before I got unbrave. 'Hi.'

Jodie stepped to the side to make space in the circle. 'Hi!'

The others kept eating their crisps. They weren't as smiley, but they didn't tell me to go away or call me *pants girl* either. So that was something.

'Is Lewis still not back in school?' Jodie asked.

'No. But I went to see him last night and he's getting better.'

Alison swallowed her mouthful of crisps. 'Is it true you gave him crabs?'

'Ha ha. Of course not.'

'Everyone said you two shag in a bush in the park,' Jasmine said.

'That's not true,' I said quickly, 'and we've never been anywhere near that bush.'

'How was Lewis?' Naomi asked.

'OK.' I scratched my nose. 'He didn't look as fit as usual. But then, he was in pyjamas, with a washing-up bowl by his bed.'

Jodie laughed. 'What pyjamas?'

I paused. 'Tottenham ones. He's really into football and his cousins live near the ground, that's why he never goes to games up here.'

'Heads up!'

A football bounced past me.

Sean chased after it. He stopped when he saw me, letting one of the other boys get the ball instead. 'All right, Fi!'

I blinked. It was the first time he'd spoken to me for weeks. 'All right, Sean.'

'I hear you've got a mobile now?'

I got it out of my secret pocket. I showed it to him.

He whistled. 'Sweet. See you in the computer room later? One last game of Rhino Rampage? The room's closed for rewiring after today.'

I shrugged. 'OK.'

He nodded. He put a hand through his hair and ran back to join the game.

Jodie looked between Sean and me. 'You're friends with Sean Anderton?'

'A bit.' I didn't add *when he wants to be.*

The girls looked at each other and giggled.

'Alison likes him,' Jodie said.

I frowned. 'Really?' *Sean?* He wasn't even one of the good ones.

'I like him sometimes. Not always.' Alison was blushing. 'Is it true he's had trials for Stoke City?'

'Yep.' Obviously, not true. 'But he's a Port Vale fan so he's turned them down.' I'm a better friend to Sean than he is to me.

'Can I look at your phone again?' Alison said.

'Of course.' I gave it to her.

She turned it over in her hand. Not so sneery now.

I licked my lips. 'Alison, do they have records of dead people at the doctor's? About how they died?'

Bam. The sneer was back. 'Why are you asking me?'

'Because your mum works there.'

'I *told* you, *she doesn't*, there are lots of Fishers. A *whole page* of them in Monkford and they can't all be my mum, can they?'

'Fair enough.' Alison Fisher's mum *definitely* works at the doctor's.

Jodie folded her crisp packet in half and put it in her bag. 'Who do you normally stand with at lunchtimes, Fi?'

'I'm normally with Lewis. Sometimes Sean.'

'No girls?' This Alison was a pain. 'Groups are meant to be all boys or all girls.'

I shrugged. 'Thing is, my girl friends all go to Radcliffe High. Mum sent me to this school so we didn't get into too much trouble together.'

Alison dabbed in her packet for the last bits of crisp. 'That's one slutty school. I keep hearing how the fit girls from there are always having sex with boys from here.'

'My friends aren't, though,' I said. 'The only person they know from here is me. So there's no point asking any of the boys who my friends are. In case you were thinking of asking. They just won't know, so there's no point.'

I put my phone back in my secret pocket. I started inching out my fortune teller. 'Do you girls like spying?'

Alison was quick. 'No.'

I pushed the fortune teller back down. 'Me, neither.'

'Fi.' Jodie looked at Alison and the others. 'If you want, you can stand with us at lunchtimes now? We always meet at this spot.'

I hitched my rucksack further onto my shoulder. 'I probably will, then. There's quite a lot of space here.' I ran my hand along the top of the wall. 'It's a good bit of wall.'

'We always eat the same crisps as each other,' Jodie said. 'It's tomato ketchup flavour on a Thursday. It's ready salted tomorrow, then prawn cocktail on Monday. Salt and vinegar on Tuesday and pickled onion on Wednesday.'

'I can do that.'

I put my hands on my hips and looked around me, at the view from *my* spot in the playground. From here, I could see the tennis courts. The school building. The school field.

It was *perfect*.

'So that's agreed.' I kept my hands on my hips and looked at Alison. 'Now. Next time the ball comes in this direction, do you want me to say how great you are in front of Sean?'

<u>To Go to the Fair I Need:</u>

1) ~~Money for the rides~~ √
2) ~~Girl friends, so the famous boy will push me on the Waltzers~~ √
3) Mum and Dad to let me go

31

A spy knows when it's time to go off-duty.
The Junior Spy's Secret Handbook™

Eight days to the fair
After school, my group walked together out of the school gates, heading for Naomi's house.

Mum was there, leaning against her *Gail Larson Driving Instructor* car at the entrance roundabout, and *even that* didn't dent my day.

'Back in a sec.' I dropped my rucksack and hurried over. I nodded at the Year Twelve girl in the passenger seat, who was changing out of DMs into thin-soled Nan shoes.

I looked at Mum. 'Just going to Naomi's house. With my girl friends.'

'Girl friends?'

I pointed. 'Jodie and Yasmin and Naomi and Alison Fisher.'

'Really?' Mum's face brightened. 'Then – have fun!'

I ran back towards the girls. I passed Mr Kellett, getting into the passenger seat of a car. The driver had the visor pulled down. It was Mr Kellett's friend from the shopping centre.

I thought about this for a minute as I headed back to the girls.

'And *then* Kellett said *Taming of The Shrew* was a *comedy*.' Naomi turned to me. 'What did your mum say, Fi? You look like you're thinking.'

'Nothing important. But I *was* thinking.' I picked up my rucksack. 'I was thinking, our group should get cookies one time. You know, those big soft ones they sell in shopping centres. We should get a whole bag each and eat them together at break.'

They all nodded, so I was pleased I said it out loud. We all walked on to Naomi's house, chattering together about cookies the whole time, and I had a warm feeling in my belly that I'd made it happen.

Turns out Naomi's house was one of the massive ones on the hill out of town. One of the houses set back from the road, not joined with a group of others, like normal houses. Naomi's house was just there, alone, behind gates.

The four of us stood awkwardly in the tiny bathroom attached to Naomi's bedroom. We squeezed in tight, as we looked at the sink and the shower and the Little Madam Make-up Set.

'It's on sweet,' Naomi said.

'It *is* on sweet.' It made sense, like *on fire*. I pointed at the half-toilet thing next to the main toilet. 'What's that?'

'A beeday,' Naomi said.

I shrugged in a question.

'It's not mine,' Naomi said. 'It was here when we came.'

We all squeezed out of Naomi's personal bathroom, and I looked at the little white cabinets, all matching and lining the bedroom, with no gaps. It was like the cabinets were born with the house, rather than added later.

Mum would *definitely* want to know how often this family went on holiday.

Naomi showed us all her CDs and toys and board games – and I mean *all*, I had a real *Candy's house* feeling. At the sight of a perfect orange pencil-topper on Naomi's dressing table, my gaze locked on like a laser.

I shoved my hands in my skirt pockets, just in case.

It's only stationery, I told myself.

I don't even *like* stationery.

Don't steal it don't steal it don't steal it don't—

I didn't. Which was a massive relief.

When Naomi had finished showing us her room, she took us through to her sister's room, which was even better. Same cabinets, but with so many extra eyeshadows. And every *Now* CD set from number 7.

I whistled.

'She's Year Ten,' Naomi said.

I spotted a photo card for East Cheshire College on the side. I picked it up. 'Your sister has *fake ID!*'

Naomi nodded. 'She knows someone who gets them done for a fiver. There's a machine that makes the plastic right at his Saturday job at the warehouse.'

I looked at the date of birth – 14.12.79. Naomi's sister was sixteen. Fake-sixteen.

I studied the card. I wouldn't say they'd got the plastic *right*. You could see the girl in the picture had shoulder-length dark hair, but the picture was bad, and the licence was all bobbly where the plastic hadn't stuck perfectly. It was almost like—

I felt a surge of something. *Yes.*

'Let's go out.' I waved the card. 'With this.'

Alison Fisher frowned. 'Why?'

'Hi, ladies!' Naomi's mum came into the room, not looking like a *mum* mum. She wore high heels in her own house and had make-up all over, an extra layer on her face, like a TV presenter. Not quite Kelly from Winchester, but more like her than normal mums.

She stopped smiling. 'What are you doing in Elizabeth's room?'

'Nothing,' Naomi said.

'Do nothing in your own room.' And, just like that, she was a normal mum. 'And you girls need to be gone before supper. You know the rules, Naomi, we eat on the dot of seven thirty.'

'We eat tea at six,' I said.

'Then you'll need to be home by six.' She gave a smile that was suddenly too kind. 'Fiona, isn't it?'

'Yes.' I looked away so I didn't see the head-tilt. It's always weird how adults know my name.

Naomi's mum left the room and I turned to the others.

'I'm going to borrow this.' I held up the college ID. 'Just for tonight.' I turned to Naomi. 'Please tell your sister I'll definitely give it back tomorrow. And I'm going to have a surprise tomorrow. Just you wait.'

And Naomi didn't say *no* – she didn't say anything – just led us back to her room. For the rest of the afternoon we recorded our voices introducing songs on her fancy stereo, being DJs. The whole time, I held onto that ID, feeling something bubbling up from my belly – a laugh that really wanted to come out, like a burp after too much Coke. That feeling when you know it's coming, and it's coming soon, but you don't know when it's going to happen, or how loud it's going to be when it does.

*

Outside Paper Rack, I took off my jumper and tie. I put them on the grass next to the pile of bikes.

I walked into the newsagent's, concentrating. *Fourteenth of the twelfth, seventy-nine. Fourteenth of the twelfth, seventy-nine.*

I took a deep breath as the door chimed.

The bald man looked at me. 'You.'

I slapped twenty pence on the counter with a ping. *Fourteenth of the twelfth, seventy-nine.* 'One single please.'

'You're how old?'

'Sixteen, sir.' *Fourteenth of the twelfth, seventy-nine.*

'*You're* sixteen.'

I nodded. 'Fourteenth of the twelfth, seventy-nine.'

'You're what – four foot six?'

'I'm a hundred and thirty-five centimetres. I was born small.' I shrugged. 'My sister was loads taller, I got unlucky.' I got out the ID and placed it on the counter. 'Here.'

The man didn't reach down. He moved his eyes to look at the ID, *surveillance-style.*

'I know you sell singles,' I said, 'because I've seen you sell them to other kids.' I paused. 'And by *other kids*, I mean *other sixteen-year-olds*.'

The man didn't even look, just handed me a cigarette from the packet.

I know I said finding the magazines was the best day of my life. And then I said it was the day of the phone. Both times, I was wrong.

It was *this*. Because this time, I'd done it *myself*.

I'd got *served*.

Everything was going my way. And, that evening, I even got the opportunity to look at the Box of Special Things.

Mum had gone out for a driving lesson after tea. I'd made

a phone call for Dad, to get him another application form. I'd even answered the sifting question for him– *'A baby deer? It's a fawn.'* Dad read my lips and gave me a thumbs-up, while I wondered what kind of person this quiz show was screening out, exactly.

Everyone knows a baby deer is a fawn. *Everyone.*

And now Dad was downstairs washing up and I could hear the water sloshing round, telling me it was safe. I'd get a *one-minute* warning when I heard the⁻ chugging as Dad pulled the plug out.

So I got on my hands and knees and kneeled on the carpet in Mum and Dad's room.

I looked under the bed.

Ugh.

Balls of hair-and-something lay around in lumps, like fur sheared from an animal. I had to get past a piece of toenail, a sock, and a piece of exercise equipment that looked like a butterfly's wings.

It was fine. I knew by then, that whatever the films show, spying isn't all private planes and casinos, and girls in silky dresses who look beautiful dead.

I moved a box of tissues. I pushed past an open shoebox of dusty standing-up books, glancing at the spines. *Dealing with Grief. Losing a Child. The Fundamentals of Male Infertility. Learning to Trust Again. When the Second Baby is Difficult.*

I felt myself flush, though I realised I wasn't in a position to mind. After all, the second baby – me – *was* difficult. But when I pulled the book out, it turned out to be about getting pregnant.

The encyclopaedias and novels went on the shelves in the lounge, and these were the sad books, kept in the dark.

I reached for Mum's Box of Special Things and dragged

it out. I took off the lid, trying to ignore the feeling of tiny creepy crawlies marching up my neck. Because it felt like being in Danielle's bedroom again.

On the top of the box was *Baby's Special Book,* with a picture of baby's footprints.

I flicked through the book but stopped at a see-through envelope, holding a curl of hair. I realised what I was looking at. *The baby hair of a dead girl.*

I snapped that book shut.

I put the baby book and scrapbook to one side, and looked at objects in the box.

There was a thin silver necklace, still in its plastic packet. The faded writing on the packet said *Christening Gift.*

There was a smooth stone from a beach, swirled with layers of different blue-greys.

There was a hand-painted mug with *Dani* painted in massive, little kid letters – a mug that any self-respecting kid would have thrown away when she turned eight.

And that was all. That was what Mum thought *special* enough to keep for fourteen years.

I wondered what she'd keep for me.

I reached for Danielle's scrapbook and opened it to a random page.

In a cutting from a newspaper, a fat-cheeked Danielle stood round a patch of soil with some friends. Each kid held a too-big garden spade, with one foot on the metal bit. They all wore corduroy trousers that went wide at the bottom. *Local children dig garden for charity.*

And there were the creepy crawlies on my neck again. Marching faster. Marching too fast now.

I shut the book and put it back in the box with everything else. I shoved it under the bed.

I scrambled to my room and got the cigarette out of my secret pocket.

I laid the cigarette on the bed and stared at it, trying to make myself excited again. Trying to remember that I was having the best time ever. Trying to remember that – only a few hours ago, I'd got served.

Trying – trying *really hard* – to forget there had ever been another kid who lived in this house. Another kid, who dug gardens for charity, and who was easy to have around, and did things for other people, and who always did everything better than me.

32

Sometimes when you're at your nicest, people think you're
being mean.
(paradox)

Seven days to the fair
Next day, at the lamppost, Lewis was back.

He was quiet on the way to school, but I didn't realise at
first. I had *so much* to tell him.

'I've got the grill lighter to light it with.' I patted the side of
my bag. 'We'll smoke it in our bush. And whenever anyone
asks what age I started smoking, I can say *eleven*.' I put my
hand on his arm. 'Though twelve's *nearly* as good.'

I glanced at Lewis. He had his hands in his pockets.

'Do you want to see my letters from the police? And
Crimewatch? I got *an actual letter* from *Crimewatch*.'

He shook his head. A really small shake.

'People say we shag in the bush, you know. But they're
babies. If they had a boyfriend of their own, they won't have
time to be making up—'

'You are going to come to the computer room at lunch?'
Lewis asked suddenly. 'I need to talk to you.'

'The computer room's shut from today though. For

rewiring. Also, I have a group now, and you have to stand with your group during lunch. That's how it works.'

'And I just have to eat my sandwiches on my own?'

I held up my hands. 'I didn't make the rules, Lewis. What do you need to talk about? We can talk now?'

He shoved his hands further in his pocket so his shoulders hunched and walked ahead, into the building.

School news!

In RE, Greeney's brother called Miss Jarvis *Mum*.

Before this, Greeney's brother was one of the best lads in Year Nine, pretty high up in the blue estate boys. He won't be anymore.

In fact, he'll probably have to move schools, if he knows what's best for him.

Those kids who call a teacher *Mum* – well. Things are never the same again.

And it's not good for Greeney either, coming so soon after his bad haircut. The school holidays are due to start in two weeks, but I bet they can't come soon enough for Greeney.

I showed the girls my prize in the playground at lunchtime, holding the cigarette up in the middle of our circle. 'Next time I'll get us one each.'

No one looked as excited as I'd expected. They just carried on eating their crisps.

I looked around the playground uncertainly. In all the excitement, I'd got the days wrong. I'd packed salt and vinegar, not ready salted.

'Are you allowed to smoke with your asthma?' Alison Fisher asked.

I should really stop thinking of her as Alison *Fisher*, I decided. Now she's one of my best friends.

'Alison. *None* of us are *allowed* to smoke. Remember?'

I noticed Naomi glance at Alison and back. 'I heard Dr Sharma say to make sure you have your inhaler on the trip to the science museum.'

'I don't really need the inhaler.' I shrugged. 'I only carry it because my mum freaks about my health. The doctor says it's up to me whether to carry it – she can tell I'm mature enough to decide.'

'You only carry it because your mum freaks about your health. . .' Alison looked at Naomi. The two had stopped eating.

Attack. 'What does your mum say, Alison? She's the doctor's receptionist.'

'No, she's—'

I put my hand up, as if to shade my eyes. 'Is that Sean? Want me to see if I can get him to come over?'

'Let me get this straight.' Alison folded the top of her crisp packet over. 'You don't really need an inhaler, but the doctor gave you it anyway, just to please your mum.'

I nodded.

Alison looked at Naomi and back at me. 'And the doctor said you don't need to bother taking your inhaler if you don't *feel like it.*'

I pulled my rucksack further onto my shoulder. 'Thing is, the inhaler isn't about me.' I left a gap. 'My sister *died*, you know. My big sister.' I left a longer gap. 'And when that happens, your parents get extra careful. So I let them fuss because it makes them feel better. And the doctor feels sorry for Mum and Dad, so she gave me an inhaler.'

The girls left a pause after my catalyst.

'Do you get asthma a lot?' Jodie asked.

'Hardly ever.' I held up the cigarette one last time and put it back in my pocket. 'Anyway, I'm going to smoke it after school with Lewis.'

Jodie pointed. 'There's Lewis now.'

Lewis walked through the playground, his coat completely done up – top button and everything – on the twelfth of July.

I raised my hand to wave. He turned and walked the other way.

'Are you *definitely* going out with Lewis Harris?' Yasmin asked.

'Definitely.' I hurried after him. 'I'll just check he's OK.'

But when I reached the school building, he'd gone.

I made Lewis sit next to me in drama. I chased him round the room with my chair, and it was like musical chairs, trying to make sure I was in the right place next to him when Mrs Vernal quieted the class down.

It worked.

The first exercise was something about expressing inner rage, but I wasn't listening properly. I was watching Lewis, who looked far away. As Mrs Vernal said, 'In your pairs, begin!', I could see his eyes going all watery.

I turned my chair to face his. 'You OK?'

'Something awful's happened.'

I glanced around but it was safe. For now, Mrs Vernal was supervising other kids' inner rage. 'What?'

'Dad's moved out. For good, Mum says.'

I felt something fill my throat. *No.*

'After you went that night, they shouted at each other. Then Mum made him go.'

His eyes were getting wetter.

I pulled his arm, hard. 'Not here! Never here. Stop that *right now.*'

'Very good inner rage!' Mrs Vernal stood over us, looking at Lewis's face. 'Very internalised!'

She looked closer, at the wetness of Lewis's eyes. Her own eyes gleamed.

I pulled Lewis round so she couldn't see his face. 'He's a good actor.'

Mrs Vernal stood looking at us for a second. She walked away.

'We should find our inner rage.' Lewis was staring at his shoes. 'We haven't got long.'

I glanced around to check no one was looking. 'Do you mean it? You think your dad's gone for good?'

'He's never left the house before. Mum sat me and my brother down and gave us a long talk about how they weren't good for each other. And it was after you said I was your boyfriend. Mum hated how happy Dad was. So it's your fault.'

'Lewis, hang on.' I sat up straighter. 'It can't be *my* fault!'

'Back to the circle!' Mrs Vernal called out.

I sat down and Lewis hurried quickly to a chair on the other side of the room. I shook my head at him, though he wasn't looking. I edged my chair nearer to Jodie's.

'Now.' Mrs Vernal sat down, her legs wide in her floaty trousers, like a man on the train who doesn't want anyone to sit next to him. 'In twos, I want you to discuss what you want to be when you grow up.'

Jodie and I moved our chairs to face each other.

'This really isn't drama,' I whispered.

'She said it's self-development when I asked,' Jodie said. 'She said it's an important part of drama.'

'I don't know what that is but it definitely isn't drama.'

Jodie glanced up at Mrs Vernal, walking by. 'So, what *do* you want to be?'

I thought. 'A farmer maybe. But I wouldn't be good at the early starts. Postman?'

'Early starts again.'

'I could work in sales for the brewery, like Mum did. Or be an aeroplane engineer, like Dad was?'

'I thought your mum was a driving instructor. I thought it was *Gail Larson, Driving Instructor.*'

'She used to work in sales though.' I pictured Monkford main street. 'Hairdresser – no. Newsagent – no.' I thought some more. 'I could work at the fair? Be the person who takes the money and starts the rides?'

Behind me, I heard a little laugh.

I flinched.

'Fiona! Can't you think bigger?' Mrs Vernal talked in a voice loud enough for the room. 'Newsagent? Taking money on the fair? Whoever taught you kids to think so small?' She shook her head. 'Do none of you want to travel the world in an orchestra? Or cure cancer? Imagine that! We're talking about living *dreams.* You can do *anything.*'

Me and Jodie looked at each other.

'I want to cure cancer now,' Jodie said.

I looked up at Mrs Vernal. 'I did say aeroplane engineer earlier, Miss, but you didn't hear me.'

She smiled at me kindly. 'And *why* did you say aeroplane engineer?'

I looked down. 'My dad was one.'

Mrs Vernal gave another little laugh. She moved on.

'Lewis,' I heard her say, 'what about you? I bet you've got big dreams.'

There was something about Mrs Vernal asking Lewis in front of people that made me freeze. *No.*

'I could be a train driver.'

I relaxed a little bit.

'You *could*. What else?'

'I could be a driving instructor.'

'But a creative boy like you, Lewis, can't you think of something else? You could be a dancer or a singer? An artist? A dress designer?'

There were titters round the room.

'You didn't see the horse he drew in art last week, Miss.' I jumped up. 'Two massive back legs and two spindly ones at the front. That horse wouldn't be able to *walk*, let alone canter. *No way* Lewis is an artist.'

Mrs Vernal stopped smiling. 'Fiona. *Enough.*'

Lewis stared at me. He looked back up at Mrs Vernal. 'I want to be a *train driver*.'

Mrs Vernal sighed. 'Where are all the actors and astronauts?' She looked around the room. 'Does *nobody* want to be an astronaut?'

'How about being a teacher?' I asked. 'Is that the job you always wanted?'

Mrs Vernal licked her lips.

The room was silent.

'Fiona, I will be telling Dr Sharma you've been incredibly nasty. And I will tell your parents, at Parents' Evening.'

I slumped back in my chair. *Nasty? How?*

I looked at Lewis, who was staring into space.

I hoped he – *at least* – would realise I'd been trying to help.

*

At the end of the lesson, we all started picking up bags and coats. I hurried over, but Mrs Vernal got to Lewis first.

'Can you stay behind?' she said.

I squeezed his arm. 'I'll be outside.'

I left in the crush of thirty kids, all trying to get through the doorway in one bunch. I waited for Lewis at the round-about outside school, kids flooding past me, knocking my rucksack.

The flood slowed to a trickle. No rucksack-knocking anymore, the pavement different now it was quiet. It was like that bit in *The Lion King*, when the wildebeest stampede turned to nothing.

Dr Sharma walked past, sunglasses on. 'I thought you usu-ally couldn't get out of here fast enough, Fiona?'

'I'm waiting for Lewis. Mrs Vernal made him join her for one of her special chats.'

'Special chats?'

'The ones when she tells us why we should be sad.'

Dr Sharma laughed, then stopped instantly. 'Don't be rude about your teachers.'

'I wasn't being rude!'

But she'd gone.

I waited for ages, but Lewis didn't come out past the roundabout.

I realised he must have gone a different way out of school for once, so I sat waiting for him in the second-biggest bush in the park, cigarette and grill lighter laid out in front of me.

I waited for an hour. But Lewis never came.

33

Dead people can be more interesting than live ones.
                    (paradox)

Seven days to the fair

I still didn't want to go home so soon – not on the day before Danielle's birthday. I needed to make the home part of the day as short as possible.

And Danielle's birthday being tomorrow meant it was only a week to the fair.

I needed to focus on my spying. I'd got nowhere with the Box of Special Things and I had no leads anymore. Except Adrian Sykes' address, and I was still working myself up to go there because – well. The thought was terrifying.

Carl wasn't even a lead anymore. Still, I found myself slowing as I walked past his house, spying on him partly out of habit. Partly because I needed to kill time before going home.

Mainly, because he was all I had.

I stood at the lamppost and put up the hood of my anorak as a disguise. And I got lucky because it started raining.

I stared through the rain at the house and waited. Carl's car was there, with its *Baby on Board* sticker and the picture of the blue buggy on the back windscreen. There was a car I didn't recognise parked next to it on the drive.

The rain got louder on the hood of my anorak. I tugged it further up.

'You OK there, hon?' A lady walked past with an Alsatian on a metal lead. 'You lost something?'

'I'm waiting for someone.'

The front door opened. Carefully, trying not to move too much, I hunched my hood further up.

Carl showed a man and a woman out. 'Just come back any time. Any questions at all.'

They shook hands and the couple got in the car. Carl gave the roof a tap goodbye – 'Adios!' – and turned to walk back in.

He saw me. 'What are you doing there in the rain, Fiona?'

'It's not raining anymore!' I shouted back. 'Not much, anyway.'

He beckoned me with a finger and I walked over.

'Those were the *excellent* people who are buying this house. Hopefully. They're getting a builder round, so keep your fingers crossed we still exchange contracts next week. They've had a couple of surveys fall through already. They've got a lot of questions about damp and termites. I was well out of my depth, though I know this is a newish house so they shouldn't have issues with—'

I stared at him.

Carl rubbed the back of his head. 'But you don't care about all that.'

We stood there for a second, Carl rocking on his heels.

'Why do you have a "baby on board" sticker when you don't have a baby?'

Carl looked at the sticker. 'Ah, but I *do* have a baby. He lives with his mother. I suppose I still live there too, kind of.'

He reached up with both hands and adjusted his ponytail. 'I'm not sure. We both had busy jobs and it was fine till the baby came along. That's partly why I've done the house sale direct, give her some space so she has some time to see sense and—'

He stopped.

Carl had a lot more extra words for a kid than most people do. Most people don't think it's worth telling a kid anything except instructions.

He swallowed. 'Anyway, I don't live with her. Well, I do and I don't. Anyway, how's the phone?'

'It's perfect.'

He smiled. 'Have you called anyone yet?'

I shook my head.

'Brilliant.'

He was so smiley, it made me take a step back.

He peered at me. 'What's up?'

I looked at my shoes.

'Spit it out.' Carl smiled. 'Lies are always worse than the truth. At least – that's what my wife says. Ex-wife. No – wife. It's just complicated because—'

One week to the fair – I needed to hurry this up. 'My friend Lewis thinks you want to flash me.'

There was a splashing noise. A car drove through a puddle.

Carl didn't move out of the way. Some of the puddle splashed up his jeans.

He *still* didn't move. 'What?' He gave an awkward bark, like a laugh made of fear. '*Flash* you? NO! *God!* It would never cross my mind!' He paused. 'But I'm hearing myself, and the more I *say* I'm not going to flash you, the more that sounds like something someone *like that* would say, and I'd never, NEVER—'

He kept going a bit longer.

Thing was, I believed him. Flashers didn't talk about damp course, and termites, and excellent people, and girlfriends who might be ex-girlfriends and *it's complicated*. If flashers talked to you at all, it was about puppies. Usually they just stood, in silence, macs open, peckers out.

'You promise?' I said.

'The fact you'd even ask. . .' Carl crouched, so I was the taller one, looking down at him. 'Fiona, I'm a normal guy. I'm a parent. And I don't go around . . . you know.' He bounced on the balls of his feet. 'I like kids, but in the right way. Why does Lewis think I might be . . . one of *those*?'

'Well.' I scratched an itch on my cheek. 'At first, it was because you wanted him to do strimming.'

Carl wrinkled his forehead. 'But only because he knocked on my door and offered to—'

'And then you acted interested in what I had to say. When I'm a *kid*.'

'But I was just making conversation.'

'And *then* you gave me the phone.'

'Right.' He stood up again. 'OK.' He turned away. 'Shit.'

The rain was getting heavier. I pulled my hood further up.

'I think, maybe' – he ran his hand through his hair – 'giving you that phone was a mistake.'

I pulled my coat flaps tighter. *No.*

'I'd forgotten how small towns work. Which is why I moved away. Have you got the phone with you?'

I pulled my coat tighter still. 'No.'

'I should take it back. Please go and get it for me.'

'You can't give a present and then take it away! That's not how presents work!'

'But if it makes you think I'm a—' He shuddered. 'Jesus.'

'I don't think you're a flasher.' He flinched every time I said it. 'It was *Lewis* who said you were a flasher. Lewis is a worrier and he gets everything wrong. Causes me *all sorts* of problems.'

Carl rubbed the bit between his nose and his top lip.

'Come and sit on the step, out of the rain.' He indicated the front step, under the little porch.

I took a step towards the road. 'Here's fine.'

'I thought you said you knew I wasn't . . . *one of those*.'

He made his voice softer. 'Fi?'

'I've got to go.' I rushed down the drive.

'This isn't right. I've done nothing wrong. *Nothing*.' He raised his voice after me as I hurried away. 'I promise you, Fiona. You don't understand. I'm actually a *really* nice man!'

I had to go home in the end. Sometimes, you have no choice.

I tried my best to make conversation with Mum and Dad over our Friday takeaway, as we ate burgers at the peninsula.

I didn't make a great start. 'It's rainy for July.'

Neither responded.

'Do you want to know the science behind why people say blood is thicker than water?'

Dad nodded, like I'd said a fact, not a question.

I sighed. Time to bring out the big guns. 'Mrs Vernal called me nasty today. She's going to tell you at Parents' Evening.'

They both looked up.

'Nasty?' Mum focused her eyes. 'Nasty, how?'

'She made us discuss what we wanted to be when we grow up.' *Ha! I won. Kind of.* 'She said there are other jobs apart from the ones you can see. Asked why we talked about being driving instructors and farmers and why none of us wanted to be astronauts or actors. She said our dreams were small.'

Mum looked at Dad. 'Hmm.'

'And then I asked if she'd always wanted to be a teacher.'

'And?' Mum said.

'And that's it. Hand on heart. *Is that the job you always wanted?* And she called me *nasty* for that.'

Mum nodded. 'OK.' She stared at her burger. Like she wasn't sure how it had got there or what she was meant to do with it.

Dad looked out of the window. He didn't tell me off, either.

Which meant it had started.

I forced a long chip into my mouth, letting it break in the middle so I could get it all in.

It wasn't the actual day till tomorrow, but that didn't matter. The air in the house had changed.

Danielle's birthday had started.

34

Sometimes the kindest thing is not to try to be kind at all.
(paradox)

Six days to the fair

When I woke up the next morning, I remembered straight away. The air was heavy on my duvet. *Danielle's birthday.*

I shuffled down to the kitchen, where Mum sat at the peninsula, wearing her smart coat. The one made of a dark, thick fabric, with neat tucks and folds like a carefully wrapped present.

'Hi.' I reached past the bunch of wrapped flowers and got the cereal box out of the cupboard.

Gerberas, those ones are called. If flowers ever committed crimes, I could pick these out of a police line-up. '*Flower, flower, flower – GERBERA!*'

I'm not into flowers, obviously. I just know the name of this one.

Mum spoke, finally. 'Gerberas were Danielle's favourite flower.'

I didn't say *I know because you always tell me*. I got a spoon out of the drawer. 'Do you know what my favourite flower is?'

I wasn't sure Mum heard me, but she looked up. 'You don't have a favourite because you don't like flowers.'

'Correct. But if I did have a favourite flower, it would be a foxglove. Or deadly nightshade. Something to make poison with.'

Grandma once bought me *The Young Person's Guide to Flowers*. I read it to be polite.

Anyway, Mum nodded, like I'd said something really interesting. Just nothing interesting enough to need an answer.

Grandma's train from Glasgow didn't arrive till the afternoon, so she couldn't babysit while Mum and Dad were at the grave. I spent the morning with Mrs Carpenter, the old lady next door, which meant no spying time.

Well, hardly any spying time.

'Danielle?' Mrs Carpenter stretched her feet out. Her chair tipped back and a foot support appeared. 'Don't know anything about her, I'm afraid. There's only been you next door, while I've lived here.'

'Oh.'

'Only moved in ten years ago. You were just a baby yourself.' Mrs Carpenter patted her lap. Snowy, her Papillon, jumped up and settled down. 'I'd forgotten you ever had a sister, till your mum asked me to look after you today.'

I kind of liked her for that.

So that bit of the day wasn't too bad. Mrs Carpenter made a big fuss of me. She let me watch Saturday cartoons and I ate a whole pack of fig rolls. I stroked Snowy and took him round the garden on his lead, and I remembered not to ask about Mr Carpenter, or his brother's wife who was welcome to him.

So even though I didn't get any spying done, I actually had quite a nice morning.

I was reading a magazine in my bedroom after lunch when the doorbell rang and the lights flashed.

I rushed to the door and pulled it open with a grin. *Grandma!*

Not Grandma.

A man and a woman outside, the woman carrying something all wrapped up in blankets. A baby or a Yorkshire Terrier, maybe.

The woman with the baby/terrier waved at me. 'Hi, Fiona.'

Annette was once Danielle's school friend, and the man with the hairy hands was her husband, Mike.

'Hi.' I walked them into the lounge. 'I'll go and make the tea.'

If I make the tea, it moves it along, and then this whole thing is over quicker.

I took the mugs of tea on a tray into the lounge. Dad was tidying up the shed, so he could show Mike something. *Something so they don't all have to be in the same room with all this loud quiet*, I decided.

The other three sat round, looking like they were waiting for an ammonium nitrate bomb to go off.

Annette beamed. 'Now that *is* service. Fiona's a credit to you, Gail.'

Mum didn't say anything. I put sugar in my tea, just to see if she noticed, but she didn't.

Annette bounced her baby on her knee. 'Do you want a hold?'

Mum nodded and they both stood up.

I stirred my tea loudly, banging the spoon against the mug.

'Hello, little one.' Mum took the baby from Annette and smiled softly. 'Aren't you a princess?'

The baby gripped Mum's finger. Mum looked like she was about to cry.

I looked down at my cup of tea and stirred it again. *I knew it.*

Annette put her arms round Mum and the baby. 'I'm so sorry, Gail. I shouldn't have brought her.'

'She's lovely,' Mum put her hand over her mouth. 'It's just—'

'I know.' Annette rubbed Mum's back. 'I know.'

I took a sip of my tea, all thick with sugar, and put my cup down. *Ew.*

Mum handed the baby back to Annette. ''Scuse me a minute.' She ran upstairs and shut the bathroom door.

I stretched my arms in a fake yawn. 'So, Annette, that night when Danielle died...'

She looked so shocked, I stopped talking.

I cleared my throat. 'So, that night at the fair—'

The toilet flushed. Mum hurried down the stairs. 'That's better.'

Annette gave a quick glance at me.

Mum sat down like nothing had happened. 'Danielle wanted four babies. *Four.* Can you believe it?'

The others smiled.

Eleven-year-olds must have been different in 1982.

'She said she was having two girls and two boys, and she was going to call them Benny, Bjorn, Agnetta and Anna-Frid.'

I glared at Mum. Even *Danielle* wouldn't want her mates

knowing she'd said *that*. She *especially* wouldn't want her mates knowing that *now* – now her mates had cars and coffee breath and husbands with hairy hands.

'We *really* liked ABBA, didn't we?' Annette said, smiling.

Mum smiled. 'Do you still like ABBA?'

'Oh.' Annette glanced at Mike and back. 'Of course. I mean – I'm mainly into indie now. But everyone likes ABBA, right?'

Mum looked wobbly round the mouth.

Annette turned to me. 'And who's your favourite band, Fiona?'

I shrugged.

'She's more into world events.' Mum tried to smile at me. 'Bosnia and Serbia. The elections in Russia and Greece.'

'Right. Wow.' Annette gave a little cough. 'I wouldn't even know where to start!'

I took another sip of too-sweet tea.

Dad came back into the room. 'Want me to show you that box of tools, Mike? Let the girls chat?'

Mike left the room as quick as he could.

I stood up. 'I'm going to go and make a fortune teller.'

I headed into the kitchen to take up an eavesdropping position, while Annette's voice travelled through the hatch from the lounge. 'She's smart.'

'Smarter than me. And her father,' Mum said. 'I don't know where she gets it from. Russian elections!'

'She's got spirit, too.'

I was thinking maybe Annette wasn't *so* bad, but then she said:

'Like Danielle.'

A whole ten seconds.

I got a piece of paper out of my bag. I hadn't been lying

about making a fortune teller – the girls didn't like my spy one, so I needed to make another.

I cut the paper into a square with the kitchen scissors and put them back in the drawer.

'Mike doesn't get it when I want to talk about her,' Annette said. 'Says it was half my life ago and I should try to get over it.'

'You know what other people say if I talk about Danielle? They talk about *distractions*. They talk about *closure*.'

I copied the folds of my old fortune teller. Next to the clean white paper, the folds of the old spy paper looked loose and grey.

'Closure!' Mum put on a little girl voice. '*Is it better now? Has enough time passed? Have you forgotten and moved on?*'

'They're trying to help,' Annette said. 'People can't imagine it, even if they want to.'

It was easier to do the folding, second time round. I'd make a *superpower* fortune teller. Because even girls want superpowers, right?

Even girls. They *must* do.

'They even had *Jonathan* talking about closure sometimes,' Mum said. '*People grieve differently*, that's what the counsellor said. But then, Jonathan was the one who wouldn't stop sleeping in Danielle's bed. When I hated him. But that was so long ago. It doesn't seem real now. And I can't bear to even think about my own moment of madness.'

I unfolded my new fortune teller and pushed the paper straight with my fist. I'd heard it all before, so I didn't let it upset me like it used to. *Yeah, yeah* – being sad made Mum and Dad go crazy and they argued a lot, but they were fine now. They changed jobs and spent more time together and had their date nights. They hardly ever argued now. Except about whose turn it was to do the DIY – and about me, of course, sometimes. But that was *my* fault. That was nothing about them.

I looked at my fresh fortune teller. I started writing in the fortunes.

You will be bitten by a bat and able to hear through walls.

'Everyone knows the pressure you were under,' Annette said.

You will be bitten by a chameleon and be able to camouflage.

'Not much fun being the town gossip.' Mum's voice was faraway in my head. 'But those people who talked about distraction – they were right, in a way. It switched my brain off for a while, however unreal it all seems now. But I was just opting out. From real life.'

You will be bitten by an eagle and be able to fly.

'You did what you had to. It was so long ago.'

You will be bitten by a cheetah and be able to run fast.

Mum sniffed. 'Over twelve years ago and I still feel guilty. And so I should.'

The word *guilty* made me stop writing. Had Mum killed Danielle *herself*? Not *murder*, of course – but an accident? Is that why they didn't want to tell me, so I didn't think Mum was a murderer? I'd heard Mum say before, on bad days, that Danielle's death was her fault – but I just thought she said it so others went, 'No, it's not your fault, not at all.' Like when we kids learned to say *My drawing is so rubbish, yours is so much better,* so other kids said back, *No, your picture is so much better than mine!*

'Beating yourself up doesn't change anything. And life takes strange turns. One good thing came out of it, didn't it?'

'Exactly! *The* best thing, for all of us! So we can't regret it for a second.'

This was why listening made no sense sometimes. Especially half listening. Because this definitely couldn't be about Danielle anymore.

I shook my head and focused on my fortune teller. It was *hard*, thinking of new animals. *You will be bitten by a dolphin and be able to walk on water.*

'I'm so pleased you get it,' Mum said. 'If you'd told me back then – *you know who you're going to talk to about the complex emotional side? Annette Desai. You know, Danielle's little friend with the side ponytail. The one who thinks she's going to marry Shakin' Stevens.*'

They both laughed.

I was running out of animals. *You will be bitten by a bat – a different bat – and be able to sleep upside down.*

'So, how's Mike?' Mum said in a new, sunny voice. 'How's the factory?'

I finished off my fortune teller – *you will be bitten by an ant and be able to fit in a matchbox* – and heard *way* too much about Mike and the factory. About collective bargaining and shift breaks. About union reps and ballots and shop stewards – stuff that wouldn't have made sense even if I'd *tried* to listen.

I folded up my fortune teller. I tested it with my fingers and thumbs, checking it worked. I slid it into my secret pocket.

Annette comes to the house on Danielle's birthday every year, even though she always makes Mum cry. And one day, when Mum's not there, I'm going to tell her it would be kinder to Mum if she didn't come at all.

'I hate it, Grandma,' I said into her neck.

We sat together on my bed that night while Grandma rubbed my back.

'I know, lovey.' Grandma pulled back. 'But your mum and dad need to do this. Every other day of the year is about you. This is just the one day about Danielle.'

'Wrong, Grandma. *Every* day is about Danielle.'

'Everything your parents do, they do for you.'

'I don't want to argue, Grandma, but you're not actually here.'

'No?' She gave a sad smile. 'I'm sorry to hear it feels like that. But what about me, then?' She gave me a big smile now so I could see her corner teeth, the ones that are a bit vampire-y. 'Don't you think, to me, everything's all about you?'

'But you live in Scotland!'

She stretched her feet out. I looked at the plastic jewels of her flipflops. Beneath her toenails' orange varnish, ridges stood up, like lines in a map. 'But don't you realise I'm thinking about you all the time when I'm in Scotland?' She showed her vampire teeth again, though *no one* is less vampire-y than Grandma. 'When I'm on the bus. When I'm raking the leaves. Who do you think I'm thinking about then, hey? The prime minister? Batman?'

She tickled me and I squirmed away.

'Didn't you like Danielle, then?'

She sniffed. 'I loved Danielle. But she's not here, and you are. And you're what matters now.'

I raised my head hopefully. 'Can I come and live with you?'

Grandma gave another sniff. 'You wouldn't want to, not really.'

'You could clear out your ironing room and put an airbed down.'

She gave a sad smile.

'You could still use the room for ironing. Just as long as

you knocked before you went in. And put the ironing board away after.'

'Ah, lovey.' Grandma shook her head. 'This is just one day, Danielle's birthday.'

I watched her, watching me, and I felt a bubbling up inside. I didn't know what to call it, this bubbling, it was just *there* on days like this. And then I thought about how unfair things were, and the feeling bubbled more.

And then the bubbling made me think bad things. Like – how if Danielle wasn't dead, I'd still want her to be dead because of how she ruins things.

And then I felt even more bubbling, for knowing that's a bad thought. And then I wanted to scream, as loud as I could, so I couldn't hear the thoughts in my head anymore.

I raised my head a little. 'Am I bad, Grandma?'

She laughed. 'No! No, you're perfect.'

I gripped the corner of the duvet and looked up. *How did Danielle die, Grandma?*

But she was smiling at me so softly, I just couldn't ask.

She stood up. 'I'm going to check on your mum.' She gave her friendly-vampire smile. 'You're all right now, darling?'

I smiled. 'I'm all right.'

I watched her walk out and stopped smiling. I pinched my leg, hard, until it hurt. I did it again, harder, and kept doing it, till the bubbling calmed down.

It was good I hadn't asked. I wasn't going to ask.

I couldn't let Grandma find out that, deep down, I was bad. Right the way through to my blood.

I couldn't show her that. Not when she was the only person who'd ever liked me too much to notice.

35

Even if people know you're the bad one, they still act
surprised when you prove it.
(paradox)

Five days to the fair
When I woke up the next day, I made a decision.

I *had* to ask Grandma.

I didn't want to, but I had to. I had no choice, if I was going
to get to the fair.

I got dressed as slowly as I could, trying to put it off. I
found Grandma in the kitchen, wearing Dad's apron, stirring
a big pot on the cooker. The room smelled like fields and
sludge.

'Morning, little one,' Grandma said without looking round.
'Your dad said I must ask what you think about the trial of
some war criminals?'

I pulled myself up onto a stool. 'Where're Mum and Dad?'

'They went to buy painting stuff. They're going to do some
decorating.'

'They won't do any decorating. They'll just buy more stuff
and leave it in the garage.'

'I'm making soup.' Grandma tapped the wooden spoon on

the side of the pan and put it back on the chopping board. 'Tell your mother she'll need to put some milk in when she reheats it. And some parsley from the garden. It always tastes better with a bit of parsley.'

'I don't think we have parsley.' I took a deep breath. 'Grandma. What happened the night Danielle died? No one's ever told me.'

Grandma didn't turn around. Had she even heard?

I swallowed. 'Were Mum and Dad with her? At the fair?'

Grandma bent over. She concentrated on the cooker's temperature dial. 'Why are you asking, darling?'

'I don't want to ask Mum and Dad. I just keep thinking about Danielle. About how it feels to die.'

Grandma put her wooden spoon down.

'And I don't want to think she was on her own when it happened.'

Grandma put one hand to her chest and rubbed herself softly.

I tried to look in her eyes, but couldn't. 'Was she on her own?' I whispered.

Grandma lowered herself onto a peninsula stool, more carefully than usual. 'She wasn't alone. She went to the fair with her friends.'

'With Annette?'

'And others. Annette's dad was there too. Danielle was very loved, don't you worry.' Grandma stared at her lap. 'It's hard for me to talk about. I don't want to talk about this.'

Don't ask any more. 'But when she died—'

'It's so thoughtful of you to care about other people.' Grandma brushed her hand across the surface, pushing crumbs into a neat pile at the side. 'You're a good girl, Fiona.

The most precious thing in the world.' She kept brushing. 'You know that?'

I started to cry. We both knew that wasn't true.

'Come here.'

I let her hug me, my eyes and nose burning with tears. So much feeling bubbled up – in my chest, my throat. I shrugged out of Grandma's hug and ran into the garden.

'Fiona!'

But I couldn't let her look at me.

I ran into the garden shed with the spiders and the earwigs. I slammed the door, and locked myself in with the key.

Half an hour later, Grandma was still trying to coax me out of the shed.

And now there was whispering outside. Mum and Dad were back from the shops.

I *definitely* wasn't coming out now.

'Fiona.' Grandma's voice was soft. 'What's all this commotion for, darling? My train goes at one – I can't stay an extra night because I'm on the till at the charity shop tomorrow. Surely you want to say goodbye?'

I hugged my legs tighter to my chest.

'Goodbye, then. I love you, darling.'

'FIONA LARSON, GET OUT HERE AND SAY GOODBYE TO YOUR GRANDMA! NOW!'

If I wasn't coming out for Grandma, there was *no way* I was coming out for Mum.

'Right, well. Your father's staying in the house,' Grandma said, 'while your mum drives me to the station. I hope you feel better soon. I'm sorry we didn't get to say goodbye. I love you so much, darling.'

*

It might be hard to understand for someone who's not bad themselves.

But when someone says they love you and you know you've been bad, it hurts. And you have to do something to make the hurt stop.

After I heard the car start up and leave, and I was sure Dad was back in the house, I got the big saw off the hook in the shed. I held the saw with both hands and looked at it, feeling its weight.

I headed out of the shed and towards the swing.

It took longer than you'd think.

The metal handle cut into my hands. I had to keep putting the saw down to take a rest. My arms burned everywhere – my elbows, my fingers, my underarms. I had to lean on the saw, pushing it down to get through the wood. My T-shirt stuck to my back in the sunshine. My fringe stuck to my face.

Eventually, the wood broke in two.

I put the saw back on its hook in the shed. I shut the door, but didn't lock it. I sat down, cross-legged, and waited.

I bit my thumbnail at the side. I bit too far down, so it bled.

I tensed at the sound of the car in the drive.

'Where is she?' Mum's voice. 'She'd better be out of that shed.'

I took a deep breath and stared at the door. At the padlock, hanging down and open, where I'd left it.

'What the—'

I bit my other thumbnail and tore a piece off with my teeth. Pain rushed in.

I looked at the blood pooling at the bottom of my nail,

overflowing the white half-moon at the base. White blood cells. Platelets. Plasma.

'FIONA LARSON!'

One big pool of O positive.

Mum threw the shed door open. She stood there, shaking.

I stayed cross-legged on the shed floor. I stared at a dusty rake.

'Please tell me you haven't destroyed the swing. *The swing*. And that you haven't been playing with *a saw*.'

I stared at the rake. The plastic was rubbing away at the handle, leaving green bits that bobbled and peeled.

She pulled on my arm. 'Get up!'

I tried to pull my arm back, but she was too strong. She lifted me to my feet and half dragged me outside, my feet skittering along.

Pieces of hair fell out of her clip and into her face.

'Look at it!'

We both looked at the swing. At the metal frame. At the seat, which hung in two pieces from the chains, the two chunks of wood turning slowly.

She shook my arm. 'Look what you've done!'

I looked down at the grass.

'Your grandma says I should try to understand that you find Danielle's birthday hard, but she didn't see *this*, did she?' Mum still hadn't clipped her hair back, so it all hung in her face. 'No other kids go around sawing up swings, do they? Who else does this? *No one*.'

I looked at my thumb. *O positive. Plasma. Platelets.*

'Look at it. How does that make you feel?'

She put her hand on my head and turned it. I looked at the two bits of wood dangling from the chains.

'Say something.'

'No.' I ran away and upstairs. I slammed my door and sat on the bed.

I waited for Mum to stomp after me, but she didn't. I heard raised voices downstairs. Even though Mum and Dad must be furious with me, they had room to be angry with each other.

I looked at the blood on my thumbnail.

I pulled the notepad by the bed closer. I tipped my thumb onto the pad, dripping blood onto the paper.

I put my first finger into the blood and pressed hard, making a bloody red fingerprint, like on the front of a detective book.

I stared at it. At my bad blood.

I took a magnifying glass and looked at the fingerprint. The lines whirled and circled.

I heard footsteps heading upstairs. Slow and heavy. Dad's.

He opened my bedroom door. 'Hi.'

'Hi.'

He stayed in the doorway. 'We're very upset down there.'

'Mum's angry, not upset.'

'No.' He sighed. 'No, she's not. It might sound like it, but she's not.'

'She said she was furious.'

'Only because she's very upset.'

I looked down at my bloody fingerprint. At the platelets and plasma. The O positive.

'I think you'd better avoid your mother for the rest of the night.' Dad looked at the piece of paper and back. 'Is that part of your blood project?'

I looked down at the fingerprint. 'Yes.'

'Is it your blood?'

I gave a small nod.

I felt the mattress move beneath me as he sat on the bed. 'Where did you get that blood from, Fiona?'

I turned my hand so he could see my thumb.

'Christ! Did you do that with the saw?'

'I did it with my teeth. On purpose.'

'Don't move.'

He hurried out of the room and came back with a box of plasters and cotton wool.

He sat next to me and wiped my thumb with wet cotton wool. I winced as it stung, but I deserved it.

Dad pressed a fresh piece of cotton wool against my thumb. He held it there. 'Why did you ask Grandma about how Danielle died? Why did you try to upset her?'

'I wasn't trying to upset her. No one ever tells me anything.'

He took the cotton wool away from my hand and peeled back a plaster. 'And you must never play with tools.'

I watched him stick the plaster round my thumb.

'I know that.'

'Do you?' He pressed the plaster hard into my skin. 'Because you picked up that saw happily enough.'

'But I didn't use the electric saw. Just the still one.'

'FIONA!' Dad let go of my hand. 'I don't want you to *ever* even *think* about the electric saw.' He rubbed his hands through his hair. Strands stood up like he'd been rubbing a balloon. 'I'm going to have to lock the shed and hide the key now, you know? Christ, Fiona, what do you do to us?'

I didn't say anything.

'Do your friends do things like this? Does Lewis torture his parents this way?'

I put my blood-printed finger in my mouth and sucked it. My finger tasted of an old penny.

Dad made his voice softer. 'Never do that again. Promise me now.'

'I'm positive I won't play with tools like that again.'

'Take your hand out of your mouth so I can see and say it again. *And promise* me. Promise me or I tell you, Fiona – you're never leaving this room for the rest of your life.'

In the end, I promised. I stayed in my room until after tea-time, when I heard the phone ring and the overhead light flashed.

Mum answered the phone. 'Hello?'

I opened the door so I could listen.

Mum spoke again. 'That's good, Mum. No delays?'

I crept onto the landing.

'Thanks for calling. Tell Kenneth I said hi.'

I scooped my skirt underneath me. I sat at the top of the stairs, just out of sight, my back to the wall.

'No, I didn't,' Mum said. 'I was going to speak to her about why she asked but then . . . something happened. You don't want to know. But I handled it badly, of course I did, and—'

Mum sighed. 'Not *awful* awful.'

I put the end of my thumb in my mouth.

'She sawed the swing in half.'

I sucked the plaster.

'*Sawed* it.'

'I don't know how else to put it. *Sawed* it. With an actual saw . . . No, the wooden seat, not the metal bit. Who do you think she is, world's strongest man? I don't know *how*, exactly. She's got arms like spaghetti.'

I wrapped my arms round my body.

'*Is* it, though?' Mum's voice went higher. 'I feel like *every* age is a difficult age. When do the difficult ages end? How did you manage with me? But I was so much easier.'

I hugged myself tighter.

'Mum.' My mum's voice hardened. 'That was *forty years ago* and you know I paid the ice-cream van man back.'

At that, I raised my head.

Mum sighed. 'I know the point you're making; I just don't know what I'm meant to do. I'm not as good at this as you. I try *so hard*.'

There was a long silence while Grandma talked. I imagined what she was saying. *It's not your fault. Fiona was just born bad.*

'I just think – I'm really bad at this,' Mum said finally.

I felt myself frown.

'Jonathan can stay calm but I just can't. Maybe I was never up to doing this again. Maybe I shouldn't have ever thought I could do this, after everything.'

I looked at the plaster round my thumbnail.

Sometimes, I wish I didn't have spy skills after all.

I tiptoed into the bedroom and shut the door quietly, so I didn't have to hear Mum say she wished she hadn't had me.

<u>Bad Scar Things I've Done</u>
<u>New 1996 Summer Term Update – Part 2</u>

1) Looked up Danielle's death in the library and phoned Adrian Sykes
2) Took the polaroid camera to school when Dad told me not to
3) Accepted a present from a stranger Mum told me to stay away from
4) Went through Carl's bins
5) Lied to everyone about having friends in another school
6) Lied to everyone about Lewis being my boyfriend
7) Used fake ID to buy a cigarette
8) Asked Annette how Danielle died
9) Asked Grandma how Danielle died. Even though she asked me not to
10) Sawed up the swing
11) Didn't say goodbye to Grandma

I told you I was the bad one.

36

Many great spies end up working alone.
The Junior Spy's Secret Handbook™

Four days till the fair
I didn't speak to anyone before school the next morning. As I reached the bottom of the stairs, Mum came out of the kitchen, rearranging the clip in her hair.

We both looked quickly away.

I don't think Mum knows what to say when things like this happen, either.

Mum crouched in front of the Cupboard of Office Things and opened it. 'It's sunny out there,' she said into the cupboard.

And before she could say any more to the cupboard about the weather, I picked up my rucksack and hurried out of the door.

Lewis wasn't at the lamppost.

I'd made Mum so cross she was pretending I was invisible and talking into cupboards. And I'd made Lewis so cross that he preferred to have *no* friends than be friends with me.

It was fine. It was all fine.

I had new friends now.

*

But at break, I couldn't find the other girls. I looked and looked, but knew it must be one of those games where I didn't understand the rules, and I'd ruin the game if I asked.

So I stood there in our normal spot anyway, watching the boys play football.

Lewis was playing. I watched him chase after the ball and kick it to Sean. He didn't do too badly, actually.

I tried to catch his eye, but he didn't look over. Even though the only reason he was allowed to play football with the good kids now – with his wrong coat and rucksack, when he wasn't very good – was because of me.

I finally found my girl group on the far side of the tennis courts.

I walked over. 'Hiya.' I got out my blood project. 'Check this out. Actual blood.'

I got to the right crispy page of my project book and held it open in front of me, like a flasher with his mac.

The girls all jerked their faces back.

I frowned. 'It's my blood so it's fine. No one died or anything.'

Yasmine shook her head while looking at Alison Fisher. 'Why aren't you doing photosynthesis, like everyone else?'

I shoved my project book into my rucksack. I thought desperately.

'I've also made a fortune teller.' I got it out of my secret pocket and slid my fingers and thumbs in.

The girls looked at the four labels.

'*Cape, Boots, Mask, Cuffs,*' Jodie read.

'It's about superpowers.' I looked at the paper. 'That's *cape* as in *a superhero's cape. Definitely* not a magician's cape.'

Naomi looked at the others. 'We don't like superpowers.'

'Don't like superpowers?' I dropped the fortune teller against my leg. 'How does that even *work*?'

But the bell rang for the next lesson, so no one even answered.

School news was the worst yet. The very worst.

In RE, the school secretary knocked on the door. 'Can Fiona Larson please come to Mrs Shackleton's office.'

There was a ripple of interest round the room.

What's she done?

Who's she shown her pants to now?

Miss Jarvis looked at the school secretary in a question.

With a tiny movement of her mouth, the school secretary made an *eek* face.

Miss Jarvis looked at me with *actual sadness*. 'Take care, Fiona.' She waved me off with a pitying smile, like she was sending me to the guillotine.

I packed up my pencil tin and books, and hurried down the corridor with the school secretary. My legs felt like they were dragging behind my body, and it wasn't as easy to walk as usual. Everything about me trembled.

We turned the corner into the staff corridor and I dropped my pencil tin. My stuff scattered everywhere.

I crouched down, picking up pens and pencils. The school secretary crouched to help.

I reached under a big metal radiator to get to my protractor. I had to reach through a trailing clump of ruched-up spiderweb to get it, letting the clump flap against my hands. I didn't even shiver. I barely noticed the webbing – not now. Not now I'd been called into the New Head's office.

I stood up, cradling my equipment in my arms. The school

secretary handed me some stuff she'd picked up – a pen, a rubber and a pencil sharpener. She looked at my hands and I could tell she noticed they were shaking. She was about to say something, but then didn't.

We kept walking. Down the staff corridor, where I wasn't normally allowed to go. The place where—

Too soon, we stopped outside the New Head's office.

'You can go in,' the secretary said.

I looked up at her, my legs trembling even more. *Please!*

But she just opened the door.

I stepped inside. I had no choice.

The New Head, Mrs Shackleton, looked up from behind the big headmaster's desk. She stared at me like I'd deliberately kicked her best cat.

She wasn't alone.

Dr Sharma was there, in the chair next to her. And Mrs Vernal, standing behind the desk.

Both looked at me with that same *cat-kicker!* expression.

And I still didn't know. I'm that stupid – *Fiona Larson is so, so stupid* – that I still didn't get it.

Until I saw it, finally, just *there*. On the New Head's desk. The ruffled-up copy of *Mayfair*.

37

If you're afraid, you say your 'blood runs cold'. It is the release of the body's 'fight or flight' hormones causing a chain reaction that leads to the vasoconstriction of arterioles that causes this unpleasant sensation.

Fiona Larson, 7E's Blood Project

Four days to the fair

'Sit,' the New Head said.

I don't know how I got my legs moving, but I got into that chair somehow.

The New Head looked from me to *Mayfair* and back. 'Look familiar?'

I shook my head.

'A boy in Year Nine told Mrs Vernal you sold it to him.'

'I've never seen it before. Look, whatever Dean Prince says—'

The three teachers twitched into focus. Birds of prey, spotting a mouse.

I added in a rush, 'Or any other Year Nine boy.'

The New Head stared. 'How do you know we got this magazine from Dean Prince?'

'It's just . . . he's said to me before . . .' I kicked the table leg.

'Because he was the kid who bought the *Mayfair* one.'

The teachers looked at each other.

'Bought the *Mayfair* one?' the New Head repeated.

Dr Sharma looked from the New Head to me. 'There were others?'

Damn it, Fiona! I nodded.

'Were all the magazines ...' Dr Sharma closed her eyes and put her finger and thumb to her eyelids. '... well, I'll just say it.' Dr Sharma took her hand away. She opened her eyes. 'Porn?'

'One had films in it. Only the others were porn. And I didn't sell them here. I sold them at the car boot sale. I never brought them into school.'

Mrs Vernal folded her arms. 'This is utterly shocking.'

Dr Sharma held up a finger. She kept her gaze on me. 'Where did you get the magazines?'

'I found them.'

'Just shocking. As if—'

Dr Sharma interrupted Mrs Vernal. 'Did you find them in your *father's* things?' Dr Sharma's lip went up at the edge at *father's*.

'No. He wouldn't like these magazines.' I hoped it was true. I *hated* these magazines now. Kelly from Winchester and *everything*.

'You don't have to defend him,' Dr Sharma said. 'He's not a pupil here.'

I shook my head. 'I found them in the park.'

Mrs Vernal looked at the New Head. 'This is serious. You've been extremely clear with the rules, Mrs Shackleton, you've set your stall out about sanctions, and—'

'Let's discuss this without Fiona here.' Dr Sharma's voice was calm. 'There's a complicated history, from before your time.'

I lifted my head a tiny bit. Was Dr Sharma using my catalyst?

But I saw her face and put my head straight back down.

The lunchtime bell rang.

'We will talk now, alone, Fiona,' the New Head said. 'Sit on the bench outside and we will call you back in shortly.'

I took a seat outside the room. I crossed my feet and tucked them under the bench, trying to make myself as small as possible.

Sanctions.

Sanctions meant *suspended.* Or *expelled.*

I imagined Mum's face as she got the call from the school. Dad's face as she explained to him what I'd done.

I was so scared, I couldn't even cry.

Even if I wasn't expelled– *me! Expelled! What would I do? Where would I go?* – this was *it*. It was over.

There was no way I'd be allowed to go to the fair.

I waited a bit longer. Through the open window, in the playground, a kid shouted 'Haircut!' Then a chorus started. *Haircut! Haircut!*

It couldn't still be about Greeney. But I didn't even have the energy to wonder who'd got a haircut now.

I jiggled my legs.

The teachers had told me to stay on the bench, but there was no way I was staying outside that office. My jiggling legs were telling me something.

I got up. Still too scared to cry – but so scared that I couldn't just sit there either.

Trying not to think what I was doing, I grabbed my ruck-sack and rushed down the staff corridor.

*

I hurried round the playground, my fear making it hard to focus – still, looking everywhere. Finally, I found my girl group at the far end of the field.

I took a minute, trying to calm down, hoping my face wasn't too red. They wouldn't want to hear what had happened. Alison had called my magazines *disgusting*.

I ran up to the group. 'Hi! I couldn't find you, you were miles away.' I pulled out the cigarette again. 'Da da!' I tried to make myself breathe normally. 'Me and Lewis didn't smoke it in the end. Let's go to the park and have it together now.'

The girls looked at each other.

'It's lunchtime,' Naomi said.

'But we could go anyway! The gates aren't locked.' I patted my rucksack. '*And* I remembered the grill lighter.'

The group widened their eyes at each other, like what I was saying was incredible.

I licked my lips. 'Jodie?'

She twizzled her friendship bracelet round her arm. She looked at her feet.

I grabbed my empty wrist. I'd forgotten to make a bracelet, *and* I'd forgotten my crisps.

'I'll tell her.' Alison turned to me. 'We've got some sad news. We've realised we're not the right size anymore. We're too big.'

'Are we going on diets? If we have to. I thought we'd wait till at least Year Eight, but . . .'

Jodie stayed looking at the ground.

'Bless,' Alison said. 'We've realised *this group's* too big now.'

A thud in my chest. This must be how it felt to get shot, for the second time. *Bang.* Falling to the floor. Just getting up again then – *bang*.

'Four is a good number. Five just feels too many.' Alison shrugged. *Can't be helped.*

She nodded at Naomi. *Continue.*

'We're starting a new group from scratch,' Naomi said. 'Me and Alison.'

I should have just walked away and pretended I didn't understand. But my heart was going too fast to think properly. And sometimes I can be *really really fucking stupid fucking stupid Fiona.*

I made a show of checking my fingernails. 'Who's in the new group?'

'It was just me and Alison originally. But then some others asked to join.'

I looked at Yasmin. I looked at Jodie.

Both looked at the grass.

I took my mobile out of my secret pocket with shaking hands.

Alison looked at it. 'Your mobile phone isn't going to get you back in the group.'

I swallowed. 'I'm going to phone a friend.'

'Selina Baker? Dean Prince?'

Even then, I narrowed my eyes. 'Definitely not Dean Prince.'

'One of the other sixth-formers? The kid who's definitely your boyfriend, *Lewis Harris went to Paris?*'

I took a shaky breath. 'I'm going to talk to one of my friends from Radcliffe High. Unless,' I turned to Yasmin and Jodie. 'You could be in two groups? Three's enough for a group, isn't it?'

'My mum says three's a crowd,' Yasmin said into her feet.

'We could start a new group. Get some other people. Better people. Maybe some boys?'

Naomi and Alison snorted.

'It doesn't work like that. I'm really sorry.' Jodie turned to me. 'You can't have boys in a group.'

I nodded. I did know that, really, but I was desperate.

'It's this sort of thing' – I knew Jodie was trying to be nice – 'that made Alison and Naomi start a new group. They say you don't understand.'

I took a deep breath. I put my phone to my ear.

Alison glanced at Yasmin. 'Don't you need to actually make a call first?'

I turned to leave. I hated Alison. *No – not Alison. Alison Fisher.*

'Sorry,' Jodie and Yasmin said, at the same time.

'We can still be friends in drama,' Jodie added. 'And in non-group situations.'

'OK.' I strode away.

I ran up to where Lewis was playing football. I tugged his sleeve.

'Lewis.' I tried not to cry. 'Shall we do some spying practice? Do you want to see my letter from *Crimewatch*?'

'What?' He shook me off and turned his back on me. 'Leave me alone.'

'Or the police?' I started crying now as I reached for him again. 'Because I also got a letter from—'

'Fiona. Get away from me. You're not a spy.' He shrugged me off again. 'This isn't real. No one cares whether you can do a seal crawl, or a feline crawl, or a flat feline crawl. No one cares if you can read hoofprints, or if you've got a secret pocket.' He was using his dad's meanest voice. 'Give it up.' He even had a look of his dad now. 'And leave me alone. I'm not messing. Just leave me alone – for ever.'

*

I hurried out of the school field and towards the park.

I just sat there, in the second-biggest bush, until it was time for the bell for afternoon classes.

I rested my head on my knees and cried.

Eventually, I lifted my head. The bell would definitely have gone by now.

The New Head would have found I wasn't outside the office anymore. And afternoon lessons would have long started.

I'd been scared of being expelled, half an hour ago. It had been a possibility. And now – just by being *Fiona* – I'd made things so much worse.

Now I'd *definitely* be expelled.

I had cried so much I was shaking again. I felt cold, despite the patches of sunshine, dappling through the branches and leaves above.

My brain was full. Full of words, all shouting how stupid I was. About how much trouble I was in.

I wouldn't be allowed to go to the fair.

I *had* to go to the fair.

I looked at the wasps' nest. From this distance, the wasps circled round it like specks. I remembered the kids playing *chicken* with the wasps – putting their hands near the nest, and pulling them away.

I imagined doing that for a second, how it would make everything change.

I had to do something. Something to get me to the fair. Something, anything, that could make all this OK.

I pushed myself up from the grass. I brushed the twigs off my skirt.

*

I hurried to Chestnut Walk and stood outside number 23. I made myself knock.

An old woman answered. She had an apron on, the curly writing saying, *Kiss the cook and bring her wine.*

'Is Adrian in?' I made myself taller. 'Adrian Sykes.'

The woman frowned. 'Yes.'

'Can you go and get him please?'

'Shouldn't you be in school?'

'I just want to speak to Adrian,' I said, and – *don't do it don't do it* – started crying again.

Ten minutes later I sat, shaking, with a glass of orange juice, on a squishy old sofa draped in blankets, inside 23 Chestnut Walk.

I took a sip. The glass tasted of orange juice and dishwasher, like in Lewis's house.

At the thought of Lewis, I sobbed more.

The two strangers sat facing me.

The man – Adrian – looked at the woman and back. 'Please tell me your parents' names. We need to call them.'

He was a lot smaller than I was expecting. Nothing like the man in my head. Not scary at all. Which made me cry even more.

'They'll be worried.' He glanced at his wife. 'They might already know you're not in school.'

I shook my head. 'I need to know about my sister.' My words came with extra burbles at their edges. 'The one who died at the fair. The one you wrote about in the paper.'

Adrian looked helplessly at his wife.

His wife took her apron off. 'What's your sister's name?'

Adrian frowned. 'Christine, I don't think . . .'

The woman shook her head at him. She folded her apron

and placed it on the sideboard. She looked back at me.

'Her name's Danielle. Danielle Larson.' I turned to Adrian. 'The girl from the fair in 1982. Active in the RSPB, dead when the paramedics arrived. Blonde hair. Smiley. Tall for an eleven-year-old. Pretty as a picture. Dug gardens for charity.' I glanced up at Adrian. 'You might not know that though. I found that out from the Box of Special Things.'

'And what was her address?' the lady – Christine Sykes – said gently.

'Fourteen Archer's Way, Monkford.'

'Is that where you live, too?'

I nodded.

The two glanced at each other. Mrs Sykes got up. 'I'm just going to refill the kettle.'

She went to a drawer behind the sofa.

I turned back to Adrian. 'Do I call you Adrian? Or Mr Sykes?'

I glanced at Mrs Sykes, who left the room with something in her arms. I heard an electrical chirrup and the sound of the backdoor opening and closing.

'Adrian is fine.' He stretched out his feet. 'You know – I've lived round here a long time. Sixty years. Can you believe that? It's changed a lot.'

I took a sip of dishwasher orange juice. 'The precinct must have got built since you moved here. There were just fields there before.'

He smiled. 'I'd forgotten there was a time before the precinct. Well, now.'

'And the schools merged. There used to be three schools around Monkford, and now there's two.'

'Wow! You know a lot for a little one.'

'I got it from your paper. From the microfiche.'

His smile faded.

'Did you know my sister?'

'Ah. I'm pretty sure I didn't know her. I'm just trying to think. 1982, you say?'

'July 1982. Happened on the twenty-fourth of July. The newspaper was on the thirtieth of July.'

There was another electronic chirrup from the kitchen. Mrs Sykes came back in. 'Do you want more orange juice, Fiona?'

'I'm fine.'

'Grand. I'll just finish off the tea.' She looked at Mr Sykes and the two had a mini-conversation with their eyes.

'Adrian, my sister—'

'I'm just thinking,' he said. 'Leave it with me.'

Mrs Sykes came back into the room with two mugs. She placed one in front of Mr Sykes and sat down. 'What did you do in school today, love? Before you came here to find us?'

I shuddered.

'OK, you don't want to talk about that,' she said quickly. 'That's fine.'

Adrian got up. 'While I'm thinking – it takes me a long time to think these days – I'm halfway through a jigsaw.' He showed me the big board on the dining-room table, on it a half-finished jigsaw of spaniel puppies in a basket. 'I could do with some keen young eyes. Want to help me, while I can try to think what I remember about your sister?'

I sat with Adrian at the dining-room table for a while, doing the jigsaw while he tried to remember. I put in at least fifteen pieces while Adrian congratulated me, because – Adrian was right – I *did* have keen young eyes.

And the jigsaw even helped a little with the churning feeling in my stomach.

The doorbell rang. Adrian and Mrs Sykes looked at each other.

Mrs Sykes got up. 'That must be the postman.'

I froze for a second, hoping it wasn't my dad. But no – he couldn't know I was here. And then I heard voices and relaxed, thinking it must be a lady postman and – *no!*

Mum burst into the room, the fabric belt of her dress undone and flying behind her.

38

A good spy knows when he's been cornered.
The Junior Spy's Secret Handbook™

Four days to the fair
Mum rushed straight to me. 'What's this all about, darling?'

I just cried, my shoulders heaving.

'Thank you *so* much,' Mum said to Adrian. She threw her keys on the carpet and crouched next to me. 'Fi, you can't just leave school in the day. However upset you are.' She looked up at Adrian. 'I'm so, so sorry. She looked down at me. 'What's happened?'

Mrs Sykes made a nice smile. 'She's had a falling out with some friends, I think.'

The worry flew off Mum's face. I watched it harden. 'That's *not* a reason to leave school.' She closed her eyes and pressed her thumb and forefinger to her eyes, like Dr Sharma had an hour before. This is what I did to adults now. Made them press on their eyes and make this face. 'You can't just leave when you want. You can't just *do* these things.'

I put my arm over my face and pushed my eyes into my sleeve.

'I'm so sorry – Christine, you said?' Mum said.

'Yes.' Mrs Sykes patted Mum's arm. 'It's been no bother. We had little ones once.'

Mum stood up from her crouching position. 'But I'm sure you're busy enough, Christine. Thank you for calling me. And for looking after her.' She picked her keys up from the table. 'Come on, Fiona. We're going home.'

We drove home in silence. Nearly silence, anyway. I was gulping and snuffling.

'Do you want this?' Mum's voice was soft as she held out my old Eeyore blanket.

I shook my head. That blanket should have been thrown out – *ages* ago. Why she kept it in the boot of the car, I didn't know.

Mum put the blanket on the back seat.

And that was it for our conversation on the journey.

At home, Mum pulled a stool out from the peninsula and waited for me to sit on it.

I sat down, my legs shivery.

'I've spoken to the school. We're to go in and see Dr Sharma together, after registration in the morning.' She pulled out another stool. She got on the stool and shuffled it forward, so our knees were touching. She nudged me with her knee. 'What's going on, hey?'

I looked down at the grey of my school skirt and the blobs of tears on it. 'I want to wait for Dad.'

'Dad's working. Why did you leave school? Why did you think it was OK to go to that house?'

I looked up. 'Didn't they tell you?'

I could tell she was trying to keep her face soft. It made her look weird.

'I want to hear it from you.'

'I thought if I found out what happened to Danielle at the fair, I could prove the same thing wouldn't happen to me.'

Mum closed her eyes. 'This is about the fair. This is all about the fair.'

'I thought I could prove I'd learned Danielle's lesson, then you'd have to let me go.' My voice was so small and wet-sounding, like a baby's. 'So I did some spying.'

'*That bloody spying book!* And I begged you not to ask what happened at the fair!'

After all the soft talking, Mum's sudden shouting made me tense.

'Sorry.' She looked down at my school skirt and stroked it straight. 'Fi, there's nothing you could find out that would make it OK to go to the fair. Nothing. Your sister died there. Don't you understand what that means?'

I shook my head.

She took a deep, noisy breath through her nose. 'I can't think about this now. I can't think about you spying about your sister's death. It makes me too angry.'

I flinched.

'We will talk about this properly another time.' She was trying her best to sound calm. 'But explain to me the other bits. Why today? Why did you decide it was all right to leave school and go there today?'

I looked down. Even if she did really want to know, where could I even start? It was like one of those puzzles where there are lots of different threads, all tangled up, and you have to follow the right thread through the mess and not get distracted to get free.

And I was pretty sure, this time, there was no right thread to get free.

'Lewis doesn't want to be my friend, no matter how much I make him.'

Mum stroked my knee. 'He puts up with a lot.'

'He thinks I'm the reason his dad's left home.'

'Well, that's just ridiculous.' She paused. 'Geoff's left home?'

'Lewis says his mum and dad rowed because I said Lewis was my boyfriend.'

Mum stopped stroking.

'It's not even true, I just made it up. But Lewis's dad was happy, though he's never liked me *and* he calls me *girlie*. And Lewis's mum was upset he was happy. So, Lewis blames me.' I took a breath. 'And my other friends have started a new group.'

'Is Geoff coming back?'

'I don't know, Mum.'

Mum nodded. 'OK. So, there's a new group.' Mum straightened my skirt pleats again. 'Can you join this new group?'

I scratched one fingernail with another so I didn't have to look in her eyes. 'The whole point of the new group is it's the same as the old group.' My voice was so quiet now. 'Just without me in it.'

'Oh.' Mum smoothed the pleats some more. 'I remember how hard this stuff can be.'

'I've got nowhere to go at lunchtime. And they said I can't be in the group even though I've got a ph—'

I stopped myself. *Not that thread.*

I had no friends, no fair, I was going to get expelled from school.

That phone was all I had.

'A ph—?' Mum prompted.

I licked my lips. 'A ph-riendship with Jodie.'

'Could Jodie start a new group with you?'

'She's got a group. You can't be in two groups at once, it doesn't work like that.'

'And if I spoke to Jodie's mum?'

'*NO!*' I jumped up. 'You said you remember being a kid and then you say things like *that*! You don't remember *at all*!'

'OK, OK,' Mum put her hands up, palms out. 'I'm just thinking aloud.'

'Speak to Jodie's mum!' I shook my head.

'It will get better.' Mum stroked my knee. 'But you still can't leave school in the daytime, however hard it gets. Can't you go to the computer room at lunchtime anyway? Even without Lewis?'

'The computer room's closed. They're putting extra wires in for something. It's going to be closed till the end of term.'

'But, still. Fiona, you can't just leave school in the daytime. It's a criminal offence.'

I waved a hand.

'Fiona. People go to prison for criminal offences.'

I finally stopped crying. 'I won't go to prison for missing school.'

Mum sighed. 'This was all so much easier when you were five.'

I shuffled forward so my knees were touching Mum's again.

Mum's voice was gentle. 'It's going to be OK, you know.'

I wiped my noise, sliming a trail up my shirt sleeve.

We sat there in silence, knees touching. With my feet bent beneath me, my knee looked hard, like a fist. A fist, with tiny hairs on top.

'Before we finish.' Mum took both my hands in hers. 'Have you told me everything about school?'

Mayfair.

I shook my head.

'I think it's best you tell me everything today. In one go. One day. And I won't get angry.'

I kept shaking my head. Though I'd need to find a way to tell her before the morning, I realised. Because – Dr Sharma. *The New Head.*

That thought made me cry again. *So hard.*

'Fiona?'

I stared at the carpet. 'I sold some – magazines. Porn mags. I found them in the park. I sold them to older boys at school. That's how I made so much money at the car boot sale.'

I risked looking up. I looked straight back down again.

'The teachers know. Dr Sharma. Mrs Vernal,' I whispered. 'The – *New Head.*'

Mum said nothing for ages.

'This is a lot to take in.'

I nodded.

'When I said I wouldn't get angry, I didn't realise that you'd be telling me something like this.'

We sat in silence for quite a bit longer.

Mum took another deep nose-breath. 'Now – can't believe I'm asking this – but is there anything else? Apart from the bunking school, the spying, the investigating your sister's death, the selling pornos from your father's car boot?' Mum squeezed my hand until I looked into her eyes. 'Because we need to get everything out, lady. If you tell me now, I'll forgive you anything. I think. I'll really try.'

I looked at my feet again.

'Fiona?'

'You won't get cross?'

'Fiona?'

I reached for my coat. I opened it up, and she saw my pocket.

She sat up straighter. 'Is that Eileen's curtain fabric? The one that ended up being too short and I had to buy again?'

I opened my secret pocket and got out the cigarette.

Mum's chest rose. 'What the—'

I put it on the table. 'I bought it using fake ID. Someone else's. Not mine.'

'BUT YOU'VE GOT ASTHMA!'

She'd said she wouldn't shout, but I couldn't blame her. Because she didn't know I was going to tell her *that*, did she? Mum's always been really funny about health stuff.

She pressed her lips together.

'Where are the rest?'

'I only bought a single.'

'But . . .' She stopped. 'Not important. Why?'

'I thought my friends would like me if I helped them grow up.' I wiped one eye with my sleeve. 'But they don't.'

Mum's eyebrows moved a little towards each other. 'It's not grown up to smoke.'

I wiped my other eye. 'Course it is.'

'It isn't, and you can't just bring things to people to make them be your friends.'

I pressed my knees more tightly into hers.

'You weren't *really* going to smoke it?' She frowned. 'You couldn't have been, not with your asthma. You wouldn't be that *stupid*. Besides, you had nothing to light it with.'

I looked at her. At how she didn't look angry now, just tired.

I reached in my rucksack. I got out the grill lighter and placed it on the table.

'But *you promised*!' Mum's voice was uneven as she tried not to shout. 'You promised you wouldn't take risks with your health! You're our *only one*!'

'But that's not my fault, is it?' I leaned forward. 'You should have had extra kids if you were that worried.'

'WE COULDN'T HAVE MORE KIDS, FIONA. Don't you realise that? That's why Danielle was an only one in the first place. You were a miracle. A special, wonderful, unexpected' – she sounded *so* angry – 'miracle.'

You can say *miracle* like *bowl of shit*. In case you're wondering.

I saw my coat was open, showing my secret pocket. *No!*

I gripped my coat closed immediately. I edged it towards me.

Mum looked at the coat and back at my face.

'Fiona.' Her voice was hard. A warning. 'What else is in there, please?'

I hugged the coat.

'If there's anything – anything   you've not told me, and you don't tell me right now, while you've got the chance and I'm being so patient and nice, so help me, Fiona, I don't know what I'll—'

I unhugged the coat and opened the secret pocket.

I pulled out the mobile phone and placed it on the table. Mum stared at it.

I rushed the words out. 'I didn't steal it.'

She raised her gaze. She looked so old.

'This time, it's true. Someone gave it to me.'

'Like the time Candy gave you her favourite pen topper?'

I looked down. 'No,' I whispered. 'Not like that.'

'But why would anyone give you a *mobile phone*? If you knew what was going through my head right now—'

'I didn't steal it! And I didn't ask for it, either! He just gave it to me.'

'*He?* Why do you do this?' Mum rubbed her eyes with her fists. 'All the *lying*! No one would ever give you—'

'*Carl* did!' I jumped off the stool. 'I didn't ask for the phone, Carl just gave it to me!'

Mum went still.

'*Carl!*' The room's air had gone weird but I was too angry to stop. 'You lie to me *all the time*. You said Carl's a strange man but he's not and this proves it. He's never flashed me, he's never got it out to show me – not even just the end – and he even helped me with my fake puncture. Carl's kind, and this proves it, because he gave me a *mobile phone!*'

I grabbed my phone and ran upstairs.

I slammed my bedroom door and sat behind it. I listened. There was no sound of keys, no opening door sounds from downstairs. Just silence.

I got under my duvet and arranged it over me so no tiny bit of body was peeking out. Trying – trying as hard as I could – to make myself safe.

Half an hour later, I was still under the duvet cover, body completely covered, sweaty from my breath bouncing back onto my face. I heard the scratch and clink of Dad's key in the front door.

I heard him go into the kitchen. The up and down of voices.

Mum would tell him right away, of course. They had a *united front* when it came to me. Whatever the row was about, it always ended two against one. In our family isosceles triangle, it was always me on my own at the pointy end.

I pushed back the duvet. I sat up on my bed and waited.

The kitchen door opened.

'Going to the pub for a quick one, Fi!' Dad shouted up the stairs. 'Mum says not to disturb you doing your homework. See you when I'm back!'

I heard the front door go.

A minute later, Mum came into my bedroom, carrying a hammer and a hand towel.

I put the duvet over my head again.

She shut the door behind her. 'Give me the phone.'

No! I jumped out of the bed.

She held out her non-hammer hand. 'The phone.'

I widened my eyes. 'Mum! No!'

'Give me the phone *now*.'

I scrambled across the room till I was on top of my coat, protecting it with my body.

'Don't make me peel you off.' Mum's jaw was hard. 'You must never accept gifts from strangers. *Never*.'

'No! No please!' My voice went up to a squeak. 'I'm *sorry*! He helped me fix a puncture!'

'He's never fixed a puncture in his life. He's a *parasite*. And I can't let you keep that phone.'

'I'll never speak to strangers again. Just let me keep the phone. It's the only thing I have. It's the only way I can make friends. *Please!*'

Mum put the hammer and hand towel on the dressing table.

I pressed my back up against my coat. 'I won't even use the phone, I promise, I'll just hold it. I've never even used it anyway. Mum!'

She wrestled me away from the coat.

'I just hold it and pretend to talk to people! That's all I do!'

She opened the secret pocket, batting away my grasping hands. She took out the phone and placed it on the towel on my dressing table. She picked up the hammer.

She threw her non-hammer arm out in a barrier. 'Stand back.'

I screamed.

Mum lifted the hammer and smashed the screen. She did it again. And again.

The phone screen cracked. Bits of plastic flaked off, then keys and metal. Bits of green from inside the phone now.

I kept screaming. Mum kept swinging. The clip fell out of her hair and onto the carpet. Hair flew in front of her face as she hammered.

The phone skittered across the table, bouncing into the mirror. Mum mis-hit, dinging a yellow semicircle into the white wood of the dressing table.

Mum stopped hitting. She dropped her hammer against her thigh. She was panting. Bits of hair stuck to her red face.

I looked where she was looking. At the broken plastic and twisted metal on the towel.

She dropped the hammer onto the bed. She took a step back.

I ran over to the dressing table. I picked up the towel gently at the corners, holding the pieces of phone in a hammock.

Mum didn't stop me.

I carried the towel hammock back to my bed and placed it on my lap. I cradled it all.

Mum reached towards me. I cringed to the side, but she just reached past me and picked the hammer up off the bed.

She saw me flinch. 'Fi, don't. I'd never—'

She held the hammer against her thigh. She turned and left the room.

I lay folded over so I was covering my broken phone, protecting it too late.

I cried into my skirt, mouth open, my body folded over. I stayed there for a long time.

39

**People talk about something being 'too rich for my blood',
but they are more often talking about taking some kind of
risk, rather than making a comment about a haematological
disorder.**

Fiona Larson, 7E's Blood Project

Four days to the fair

I lifted myself up. I'd left a dark mess on the pleats of my
skirt. A circle of snot and tears.

I'd been sad and scared.

But now, as I stared at the dark circle, I stopped crying.
Another feeling was building in me. I was crunching my jaws
so tightly together, I'd made my cheeks hurt.

How could she do this to me?

I jumped up.

It wasn't even my stuff she destroyed. It was Carl's.

She couldn't just *do* things like that to other adults, could
she? She wasn't allowed.

*Let him see me like this. Let him see what she's done. I'm going
to knock for him, then I'm going to show him my broken phone,
then. . .*

I folded my arms, imagining banging on that door.

Imagining Carl's face as I told him. *Your mum did what? That's terrible. Poor you, Fiona. Mums aren't meant to do things like that. I'll go round and give her a piece of my mind, right now.*

The thought of Mum getting told off calmed me down a little. Just enough so I could control my movements and be quieter.

With baby steps, I headed down the stairs and listened at the kitchen door. I heard Mum moving around. I stayed silent.

After a few minutes. I heard the back door open. The clink of bottles and cans – Mum taking the bin bag into the garden.

And I hurried out of the front door, out of there.

I didn't go straight to Carl's. I needed to be calmer, so I could explain properly. I needed to let off steam.

I walked loops of the park, trying to stop shaking. Past the second-biggest bush. Past the tennis courts. Past the wasps' nest. I walked like one of those old people who walk for exercise, arms pumping, my legs moving as fast as they would go.

But the shaking in my body wouldn't stop. It was like there were little explosions everywhere. *Pow, pow, pow.*

I sat on a bench and rubbed my hands up my arms, my skin pricking up in goose pimples. My thoughts were going too fast now. I was feeling *everything*.

And, suddenly, my anger turned off like a tap. A few drips left, then nothing.

Because I realised. This was nobody's fault but mine.

I'd done this. I'd done this to *myself.*

Lewis was right. I'd never been a good enough friend to him. He kept trying, and I let him down.

I was bad. *Really* bad. Everyone knew it. My family did. My teachers did. The girls did. Lewis did.

It was all my fault.

I deserved punishment.

I looked up. I imagined the satellites and planets, all held up by nothing, all hurtling towards me.

I looked over at the park's biggest bush. The one with the wasps' nest.

I walked over slowly, feeling empty, like I wasn't really there. Like I, the real Fiona, was somewhere at a distance, watching this Fiona walk.

I put my hand to the floor and lowered myself down onto my knees, a metre away from the moving sea of wasps. I watched the crawling lump of black and yellow bodies, antennae twitching.

Because I didn't deserve to feel OK.

I leaned closer.

The buzzing from the nest was soft, a radio that wasn't properly tuned in.

I watched the wasps crawl over the nest. Their tiny wings fluttered against their pointy bodies.

My head was full. Full of thoughts I didn't want. But if I pushed on this nest, right now, something would change.

I raised my finger.

I watched my finger to see what it did. I watched it move towards the nest.

I got into a high kneel and shuffled closer.

A wasp jumped off the nest and onto my finger. Another wasp jumped onto my shoulder.

One wasp landed on my cheek. I put my hand to my cheek and – *owowow!* – there was a flash, inside my head.

And my finger went on fire.

I pulled my hand away. I stumbled backwards.

And it worked.

Like I'd wanted – like I *think* I wanted – wasps followed.

I opened the back gate and ran dizzily through the garden. I staggered over the grass towards rockery.

Mum saw me through the kitchen window.

I made a shape as best I could with fat lips. 'Wasps.'

Mum put her hands to her mouth. A second later, she ran out with her car keys.

My skin hurt so much it buzzed. But the journey to the hospital was silent.

Mum had wrapped me in the Eeyore blanket. Everywhere the blanket touched, my skin sizzled.

I turned my head to look at Mum. She was driving, tears streaking the make-up on her cheeks.

I turned my head back to look ahead, so I didn't have to look at her face.

'Shit.' In the hospital car park, Mum fumbled in her purse. 'Shit, shit, shit.'

She shoved at the purse in her lap. Coins tinkled out, into the footwell.

Mum strained furiously against her seatbelt, like it had kidnapped her. She banged her hand on the steering wheel and closed her eyes.

After a minute, Mum opened the car door. 'They can ticket us. Let's go.'

Mum signed us in at A+E in her loudest voice. *'Of course I understand there's a triage process but just look at her! That's all the triage you need!'*

We sat in the waiting room, on hard chairs nailed to the floor. I felt Mum's thigh pressing into mine.

I stared straight ahead, my Eeyore blanket round my shoulders, while people moved around us with clipboards and walking sticks.

The pain wasn't a sheet covering my whole body anymore. I could focus on the different bits that hurt. My lip. My eyebrow. My cheek. My hands and arms.

I tried to test my lip by biting it, but it didn't feel like my lip anymore. It felt too big between my teeth, and numb. Like it wasn't part of me at all.

Mum didn't look at me. 'How are you feeling?'

'A bit better.'

'Do you need me to adjust your blanket?'

'No.'

A nurse came out. 'Mr Chapman.'

An elderly man got up and followed her to a room.

Mum watched. 'One sec.'

She strode over to the woman on the counter again. There were a few low urgent words, and Mum slumped back in the chair next to me.

I held myself as still as possible until, eventually, we were called in.

Mum had said earlier that I was *a miracle*.

I wondered whether I was *a miracle* now.

In the car on the way back, Mum was quiet.

'I'm feeling a bit better,' I said. 'So that's good.'

Mum flipped on the indicator.

'That doctor said it was fine,' I added.

'The doctor did *not* say it was fine. She said you had significant localised reactions.' She pulled into a junction jerkily, swerving to miss the kerb. 'Is there any way it could have been an accident?'

She glanced at me.

I shook my head.

She looked back at the road.

'You killed my phone,' I said.

'Christ!' Mum banged her hand on the steering wheel. 'I had to.'

'You wanted to.'

Mum gave a tight laugh. 'OK, I wanted to.' She gripped the wheel harder. 'You *don't understand*.'

I felt a stab of pain where my seat belt touched my arm. I changed position.

'That phone had to go.' If Mum kept flipping the indicator this hard, she'd break it. 'I believe you now, that the man gave it to you. But it still had to go.'

I pulled my Eeyore blanket further round me. I lowered my head till a bit of unstung face was touching it.

'Strange men don't give little girls presents for no reason.' Mum indicated again – *flick-flick, flick-flick*. 'Bad men like little girls, Fiona. I'm sorry, but it's true. I will never be angry if a man approaches you. But you have to tell me.'

She turned to face me.

'You do look *a little bit* angry.'

Mum flicked the indicator hard again. 'Well, I'm not.'

I let my chin rest on my arms. 'You're going to break that lever, you're so angry.'

'I'm angry *at the situation*.'

Mum pulled the car into the drive. She switched off the car.

She twisted round to face me. 'Your dad will be really upset about these wasp stings. Even more upset than I am, and I'm

very upset' – she saw my face – 'yes, *upset*, not angry, *UPSET*.'
She took a breath. 'Christ, Fiona! Your dad *must not find out*
about that man and the phone. That will be hard for him to
hear, and he's no need to know. You hear me? Nod your head.'

I nodded.

Mum nodded back. 'Good.'

In the kitchen, Dad jumped up from his stool. His voice was
all breath. 'Fi-*ona*!'

He held both hands behind his head and stared, like a
footballer who'd missed a penalty.

'Please don't hug me.'

'Your cheek! Your lip.'

Mum gave me a lying-eye smile. 'Don't worry, they're fine.'
She glanced at Dad. 'She's been stung by wasps. I'll explain.
We've been to hospital. Fiona's looking loads better already.'

'Not *Ff-iona*.' My fat lip made my *f*s longer and watery.
'Ff-i.'

Dad let his hands fall back by his sides. 'Yes.' He gave a big
smile. 'You look fine, Fi. If your mum hadn't said you'd been
stung by wasps, I could hardly tell.'

I lay in bed, with Mum and Dad taking turns to check on me
every few minutes.

If I'd accepted every cup of tea and orange juice I'd been
offered that evening, I reckon I could have drowned.

And I didn't hear *all* the conversations that were going
on downstairs. I wasn't in the mood for spying. But some
conversations were too loud to ignore.

'I just don't understand!' Dad's voice.

'What's not to understand?'

'Our eleven-year-old daughter was selling *porn*?'

I pulled my Eeyore blanket tighter.

'She found them, OK? She *found* them. She wasn't exactly selling porn.'

'How can you be OK about this? She was profiting from the sex industry.'

'Come on, Jonathan, you're not Victorian. She's not exactly Hugh bloody Hefner.'

'Are you trying to play this down? Saying it's OK?'

'Of *course* it's not OK! And how did you not notice? If she was selling them at the car boot sale, right under your eyes? *How did you not notice?*'

The door slammed shut. I pulled my Eeyore blanket tighter still.

Just before bedtime, Dad came into my room carrying a piece of paper. 'I'm very cross with you. But we're not going to talk about it today.'

'Ff-ank you.'

'Are you doing OK?'

I nodded.

'You feel sick?'

I shook my head.

'You look nearly mended. Just tiny bumps now.'

'I've got a mirror in here, Dad.'

He nodded. 'Right. Of course. Sorry.' He sat on my bed. 'Now, this might interest you. The Hague have issued arrest warrants for – hang on, I've written down the names' – he unfolded his piece of paper – 'Radovan Karadžić and Ratko Mladić.' He looked up. 'How about that, hey?'

I smiled as much as I could with my fat lip.

'I'll leave it here.' Dad went to put the paper on the dressing table. He stopped and frowned. 'What's happened here?'

He ran a hand across the table, where Mum had dinged it with the hammer. 'Why's the table damaged?'

Don't tell your father about the phone.

Dad looked up, still waiting for answer.

'I dropped a book or something.'

Dad kept examining the table. 'I'm not going to tell you off today, but you need to be more careful with your things.'

I nodded.

'You've carved the leg too – oh, *Fiona!*' Dad looked closer. 'Is that a swastika?'

'Not exactly.' *This day!* 'Let me explain.'

Half an hour later, Mum stormed into the room. 'This has been quite the day of developments, Fiona. First, you're peddling erotica.' She crouched to look at the dressing table. 'And swastikas now?'

'It wasn't a swastika, it was my special symbol I invented. Made of *F for Fiona*-s.' I paused. 'It's not my special symbol anymore.'

Mum stood up. 'The money you made. With the magazines. How much?'

I swallowed. 'A hundred and twelve pounds.'

Without her having to ask, I pulled off my Eeyore blanket and shuffled off the bed. I opened my jewellery box and the ballerina turned. The plink-plonk music played.

Maybe, if I was really good now. . .?

No. Just – no.

I handed Mum my fair money. I didn't even keep any back because I was being good now. It was too late, but still.

And Mum just took my fair money – all of it – and walked out of the room.

To Go to the Fair I Need:

1) ~~Money for the rides~~ √
2) ~~Girl friends, so the famous boy will push me on the Waltzers~~ √
3) Mum and Dad to let me go
4) Money for the rides (again)
5) Friends again. But any friends now. Any friends at all.

40

When you get what you wish for – you might wish you'd
never got it.
(paradox)

Two days to the fair
My parents kept me off school on Tuesday.

On Wednesday morning, I sat on a stool at Dr Sharma's
high desk at the front of the lab.

Mum sat next to me, her legs crossed beneath her in a
knee-length skirt. She looked smarter than usual and was
wearing the jacket she wore for funerals, which wasn't a good
sign, I decided.

The bell rang for the start of morning lessons. None of us
moved.

Dr Sharma looked me over. Not rushing, just taking in
every red, bumpy sting.

Out of the corner of my eye, I could see my own cheek.

Finally, Dr Sharma spoke. 'Proud of yourself?'

I shook my head.

She leaned forward. 'Are you sure?'

I inched closer to Mum, though knew I'd get no protection.
Mum and me might be sitting on the same side of the table,

but we were in another isosceles triangle with Dr Sharma – and I was *definitely* all alone at the pointy end.

Now I'd stopped hurting, I was feeling a bit stupid. I mean – *wasps?*

'I should make clear' – Dr Sharma made a show of putting a lid on her fountain pen – 'that if you break school rules, then deliberately injure yourself, that does not mean we will forget. I suppose what I'm saying, Fiona' – she put the pen down – 'is we were not born yesterday.'

I nodded.

'We grown-ups can think many things at once. We can feel sorry for you about your face – whilst also feeling irritated you did it deliberately – whilst *also* remembering that you were in a lot of trouble. Firstly, about the magazines.'

Dr Sharma's pen rolled slowly across the table. She gave it a light tap.

'And then by leaving school in the daytime. Without telling anyone.'

I shifted in my stool.

'*And* you brought cigarettes into school.'

I veered round to glare at Mum.

At the look on Mum's face, I shrank. *Pointy end, remember. You're always at the pointy end.*

'*One* cigarette,' I mumbled. 'And I only brought it in to show people. I wasn't going to smoke it in school.'

'Oh.' Dr Sharma gave a wave of her hand. 'That makes it OK.'

There was a shout outside. Something hit the lab window.

Dr Sharma glanced over. She lifted herself up and replaced herself in her seat. 'Now. What was I saying?'

'You were explaining to Fiona,' Mum said, in an echo of Dr Sharma's brisk voice, 'that children are not allowed cigarettes and porn. And that cigarettes and porn are not allowed at school.'

'Ah, yes.' Dr Sharma turned to me. 'Had those facts escaped you, Fiona?'

'No,' I whispered.

There was a long silence.

'Now,' Dr Sharma stared at me, 'the magazines.'

I looked at my feet.

'This is *school*. You may get exposed to that stuff at home—'

Mum sat up. 'Hey, now.'

'—and we teachers can't control what you see there,' Dr Sharma continued.

Mum sat up even straighter. 'You've misunderstood, Dr Sharma.'

Dr Sharma glanced over. 'Are you sure?'

'Of course.' Mum sat back. 'I mean, I'll ask Jonathan again, but—'

'I found them in the park!' I looked from one to the other. 'Honestly. It wasn't meant to be anything bad. It was just Finders Keepers.'

Dr Sharma linked her fingers. 'Mrs Vernal thinks it was no accident it was you who brought the porn into school. She thinks you're a troublemaker.'

Mum made a sound under her breath. A Mum-growl.

Dr Sharma turned to her.

'Sorry.' Mum waved a hand. 'It's just – that new drama teacher. She says Fiona should use her feelings about losing a sister to get better at drama. You know Mrs Vernal's trying to get them to want to be astronauts and actors rather farmers and driving instructors? The more I hear about that teacher, well' – Mum glanced at me – 'I'm just saying she seems confused. About how the world works.'

Dr Sharma gave a small cough. 'Mrs Vernal worked closely with the New Head at their old school. She is a valued new member of staff and very welcome. Her progressive and new-fangled suggestions are a breath of fresh air.'

'Of course.'

The two looked at each other for a long moment.

'Now,' Mum sat forward, 'are you going to suspend Fiona? You've got to do what you've got to do, of course, but I'm sure there's lots of paperwork. And it's difficult this end with work – I'm not begging exactly, though maybe I am a little bit, because—'

'I have put the case forward to Mrs Shackleton,' Dr Sharma said, 'that I don't think either suspension or exclusion are the right choices here.'

I tried to work out whether I was happy about that. I was, I supposed. But I couldn't trust myself to know what I felt about anything anymore. After all, I was the kid who, on Monday, *chose to get stung by wasps.*

But Mum was definitely happy. 'Oh!' She slumped back. 'Thank you.'

Dr Sharma stared at me. 'Your mum explained on the phone about your difficult day on Monday. She said you fell out with your friends.'

I felt myself flush.

'We all have bad days,' Dr Sharma said. 'I had one on Monday, too. That does not mean I ran away from school and into a bunch of wasps, in the hope everyone would see my swollen face and feel sorry for me.'

'I didn't want people to feel sorry for me.'

'Why, then?' Dr Sharma glanced at Mum and back. 'Did you want to hurt yourself?'

I shrugged. I was honestly the wrong person to ask about

all this – I didn't have a *clue* why I did the Fiona-y stuff.

'You've done three things.' Dr Sharma held three fingers up. 'You've sold porn and left school. You have also got yourself stung by wasps, which, I think you'd agree, is not a positive thing, and not to be recommended.'

She waited. I nodded.

'And the cigarette.' *Whose side was Mum on?*

But she hadn't mentioned the spying and Danielle. Mum wanted to keep the punishment for that all to herself.

And she hadn't mentioned the mobile phone, I noticed. That phone didn't exist.

'*Four* things. And those four things,' Dr Sharma said, 'are clearly bad. But you – Fiona Larson – are *not* bad. Bad *things*, not bad *person*. Can you see the difference?'

I shrugged again.

They glanced at each other.

Dr Sharma sighed.

'Fiona is far from forgiven.' Mum adjusted her jacket. 'But do you think you could speak to the friends?'

Dr Sharma looked at Mum for a moment, then to me. 'Fiona? Do you want me to speak to your friends?'

I shook my head.

'Thought not.'

'It's lunchtimes,' I whispered. 'They're the worst. The computer room's shut and there's nowhere I can go.'

Dr Sharma nodded. 'You can sit here in my lab, if you want. You can watch my fridge for me. Make sure no chancers come looking for my animal hearts.'

I nodded, though there was *no way* I was coming to Dr Sharma's lab at lunchtime.

'All the colours and shapes!' Dr Sharma peered at my face, like I was behind glass in a museum. 'Does it hurt?'

'A little bit.'

'You ever going to walk into a wasps' nest again?'

'No.'

'Then I think we've all learned a lesson here.' Dr Sharma stood up. 'Get to class, Fiona. I will tell Mrs Shackleton we've had a full discussion and say it's my recommendation that this is the end of the matter. And if Mr Kellett asks why you're late, tell him to speak to me.'

I slipped out of the room and left Mum with Dr Sharma.

I walked the empty corridors to my English class and knocked on the door.

'Sorry I'm late.' I walked to my table and sat down. 'Dr Sharma says it's her fault.'

Sean glanced at me and quickly away. It was like we'd never met.

Then, the whispering started.

'Oh my God. What is that?'

'She looks like a monster.'

'What's wrong with her lip?'

Mr Kellett stared at me. 'Quiet, everyone.'

'It was just wasps. Just normal, everyday, park wasps.' I got my books out of my bag. 'I'm fine. So, let's all please just get on with the lesson and please, *please*, no one look at me.'

School news!

Was about my face. Obviously.

I held my head high as I walked down the corridor at lunchtime, whispers following.

'It's the elephant man.'

'So ugly.'

'If I looked like that I'd top myself.'

I walked those corridors looking straight ahead. Trying not

to see kids at the side of me, reacting to my face. I pretended to myself the sides of my eyes didn't work, imagining I was in blinkers, like one of Selina Baker's horses.

In the distance, down the corridor, I saw the New Head in the distance, carrying a tray with frilly plates and a teapot and saucers.

I abandoned my blinkers plan and darted into the classroom to my left. I knelt behind the door, so no one could see me through the glass window. I only stood up again when one of my legs went dead, a few minutes later, and I was pretty sure the New Head must have gone.

I headed outside and went to find Lewis playing football because – well. It seemed wrong all the other kids had seen my face and Lewis hadn't.

Lewis looked so normal as he waited to be passed the ball, his hands on his hips. Not that it mattered if he was normal or not anymore. I'd take him as my friend any day. Cape, magic tricks – the lot.

I coughed. 'Lewis.'

He turned slowly. He looked at me.

I waited.

'Wasps?'

I nodded.

'The big bush in the park?'

I nodded again.

He shrugged.

'My finger. I pushed the nest with it.'

Lewis didn't react.

'Mum was furious I left school at lunchtime.'

'Why did you leave school?

'To find the newspaper man who wrote about Danielle's

322

death. And Mum destroyed my phone, Lewis! Can you believe that?'

'You're still investigating Danielle.' He didn't even sound
angry – just tired. 'Even though I begged you not to. Even
though you *promised* me.'

I looked at my feet. I could feel him looking at me, making
his face all *disappointed parent*, and felt my cheeks going red.
My skin started prickling, in waves. It was nothing to do
with wasp stings, this time. I was going red and prickly, from
the inside out.

The feeling of letting down Lewis was worse than the
wasps.

I stood there, prickling. 'I'm going to listen to you from
now on.' I spoke into my shoes. 'You know better than me.
You know better than me about everything.'

'I would *certainly* never run into a wasps' nest.'

'Exactly. I should listen to you more. And I will, from now
on.'

I waited. I looked up.

'You're too hard to be friends with, Fi.'

I nodded. I scuffed one of my shoes into the other.

'But you're not going to stop investigating, are you? So you
really want to know about Danielle?'

I looked up. The prickling stopped. 'What?'

There was a long pause.

'What do you mean, Lewis?'

Lewis shoved his hands in his pockets. 'Asthma.'

I waited. 'Asthma?'

'Your sister died at the fair, but not because of the fair. She
died of asthma.'

I stared at him.

'I've always known. Mum told me ages ago.' He looked

right in my eyes. 'Your parents didn't tell you because they don't want you scared you're gonna die.'

A tennis ball bounced off the wall next to me, but I didn't move.

Asthma.

Asthma, asthma, asthma. I said the word over and over in my head. So it made sense, and then it didn't. And then it did again.

You can die of asthma?

Despite the sun beating down, I pulled my coat flaps closer round me. 'I'm going to die.'

'You're not going to die.'

'But I've got asthma, Lewis.'

'Yours is nowhere near as bad. Danielle's was a really dangerous kind and it was a completely different situation, and I know that because Mum promised me. But I always made sure you had your inhaler with you.' He didn't even sound angry. 'And now you know everything, you don't need to investigate anymore, do you?' Lewis turned away. 'And you can finally leave me alone.'

I stumbled away and round the school field, through the corridors, bumping into people, half blind from my own thoughts.

Asthma.

I tried the computer-room door. Locked.

I turned towards the main block.

People don't die *of asthma. They just get a tight chest and use inhalers to get better.*

I reached the library, but it was shut. The sign said *Closed for Stocktake.*

I banged on the door anyway. 'I want to look up asthma!'

No answer.

I headed back outside.

You can die of asthma.

I *could die of asthma.*

And Lewis knew, all along.

I did another loop of the tennis courts. I saw my group of girls, back standing in their old place, eating their pickled onion crisps. Their new group looked so much like the old group – it was like I'd never been there at all.

Asthma.

I walked round daisy-chainers and football players. I walked round kids sitting on jumpers, kids with fortune tellers. I walked around kids bouncing tennis balls and kids standing in groups that were just the right size.

After I'd gone everywhere else in school a person could possibly go, there was only one place left.

I took a big breath and knocked on the door. I opened it.

Dr Sharma sat at her desk, hunched over a pile of exercise books, writing with a red pen. She wore Princess Leia headphones, the wire connected to something in her drawer.

She pulled one headphone speaker slightly away from her ear. 'Make sure you don't get crumbs on the desk.'

She let the headphone speaker spring back. She continued marking.

I headed for my usual stool. I sat there for a moment, listening to the kids screeching and laughing outside.

I slid my lunch box from my bag and opened it.

I set my pickled onion crisps to one side. I didn't even *like* pickled onion.

I took one last look at Dr Sharma, and picked up a sandwich and started to eat.

41

People don't always like being told they're in the right.

(paradox)

Two days to the fair

After school, I looked into the mirror in the lounge, arranging my scarf around my face. Trying to make it hang in a way that made me look OK.

Mum and Dad were both home. Both just sitting there, on the sofa. Both off work, on a weekday. Because of me.

I didn't want to think about that. 'Can I go and see Lewis?'

Dad was eating toast and jam. He swallowed as Mum said, 'Absolutely not.'

'Just to apologise? He hates me.'

'He doesn't hate you.'

'He definitely does.'

Dad put his half-eaten toast down. 'You know it can't possibly be your fault Geoff left home. Not everything's about you, sweetheart.'

'It is my fault. A little bit.'

I brought my pack of French playing cards out of my bag. Lewis had always loved them. 'I was going to take him these.

They say *D* for *Duchess* instead of *Q* for *Queen*.' I waited. 'Am I allowed to go to his house?'

Dad glanced at Mum. 'You're going straight there?'

I nodded.

'And straight back?'

I nodded.

'And definitely not visiting any wasps' nests on the way?'

'I won't be doing that again,' I said quietly.

I knocked at Lewis's door.

Mrs Harris opened it and blinked. 'Oh! I'd heard, but I never believed they'd be *that* bad.'

I pulled the scarf higher up my cheeks.

Mrs Harris stared. 'A scarf's not going to cut it, you need a balaclava to hide those, hon. And it's Geoff's afternoon. Lewis is off playing mini-golf with his dad.'

I held up the pack of cards. 'I brought him a present. They say *D* for *Duchess* instead of *Q* for *Queen*. They'd be good for,' I made my lips say it, 'magic tricks.'

'That's thoughtful.' Mrs Harris stepped back and held the door open. 'Why don't you come in?'

Mrs Harris eyed my face from the other side of the table.

She picked up her mug. 'How come the wasps didn't mind their own business?'

'I pushed on their nest. With my finger.'

'Ah.' She took a sip of tea. 'That'd do it.'

I wobbled my glass of blackcurrant accidentally. Some purple jumped out of the glass. 'Sorry.'

'No bother.' Mrs Harris tore off a piece of kitchen roll to dab the spill. She moved a pile of letters out of the way. The top one said *Mr Geoffrey Harris*.

'I meant to hand those to Lewis to give his father this afternoon. I forgot.' Mrs Harris started ripping the kitchen roll absentmindedly. 'You kids won't make fun of Lewis, will you? For his parents splitting up?'

I frowned. 'Never.'

'Are you sure?'

'Of course. It will make him better, if anything.'

'Better?' Mrs Harris was leaving paper confetti all over the table. She didn't seem to notice. 'Better, how?'

'A lot of the best kids don't live with both parents,' I said. 'And now he'll get a new rucksack and pencil case whenever he wants.'

'No, he won't.'

'That's what happens, though.'

Mrs Harris picked up her cup jerkily. 'That *definitely* won't be happening.'

'And Lewis will be pleased his dad moved out in the end. He didn't like the way Mr Harris spoke to you. The way he acted like you weren't as clever as him.'

Mrs Harris slammed her cup down on the table. She put both hands over her face.

'Mrs Harris?' I said carefully.

She gave a kind of yowl.

I looked at my lap uncertainly. 'I just don't think he is cleverer than you.'

'Oh God,' Mrs Harris moaned, her hands still over her face. 'I'm so humiliated.'

'You were *definitely* better at TV quizzes.' I wasn't sure what she wanted to hear. 'That time when he said a baby horse was a *pony*. When he said it was a *herd* of camels and you were wrong because *it can't be a caravan, caravans have wheels, Lisa.*' I shook my head. '*You* should have been the one telling *him* what to do.'

'*No one* should be telling anyone else what to do!' Mrs Harris pulled her hands away. 'Maybe Lewis would be your friend again if you didn't tell him what to do all the time. Have you thought about that?'

I looked down.

'Sorry,' she said.

'He told me, today, that my sister died of asthma.'

'Oh.' She was about to take a sip of her tea, but stopped. 'Then your mother's going to wring my neck.'

'It's good he told me. Because I thought she'd been got by a paedo. Or murdered. Or both.'

'Christ.' Mrs Harris shook her head at her cup. 'It was definitely asthma.'

'Lewis said Danielle's asthma was worse than mine. But was it? And how do I know without asking my parents?'

'Please don't ask your parents.'

'Am I going to die?'

'No.'

'Then how do they know her asthma was worse?'

There was a long silence.

'If your mother ever finds out I said this, please explain the circumstances.'

I nodded. It seemed *everyone* was afraid of my mum.

'I gather Danielle had lots of attacks before that one.' Mrs Harris put her drink down. 'Bad ones.'

'Am I going to—'

'No. And Lewis said you've barely needed your inhaler in all the time he's known you.'

I thought about this. It was true. I'd usually only take a puff to make a point, or for something to do.

'From what I've learned,' Mrs Harris said, 'because I've never actually asked your parents, *obviously* – your sister had a chest infection. It was a humid day. And something to do with pollen. All the bad stuff just came together for her.'

'I can ask my parents.'

'*Please* don't ask your parents.'

'So it wasn't the fair that killed her.' My voice was breathy.

'It *happened* at the fair. It's the *one place* that really upsets them,' Mrs Harris said. 'So why would they ever want to go?'

I thought about this.

'And you wouldn't want to upset your parents by asking again, I'm sure.'

I swallowed. Mrs Harris had a higher opinion of me than I did.

But maybe she was right. After all I'd done, there was no way I could ask about the fair again now.

Mrs Harris got up. 'I need to get on with making tea.'

I stood up too. 'Can you give Lewis the pack of cards and say he can show me magic tricks with them? As long as we're on our own. Tell him I'll be nicer from now.'

'It's hard to change.' Mrs Harris gave me a *look*. 'Personalities get set early on.'

'You think I can't be nicer?'

She picked up her mug and my glass and placed them in the sink. 'You can't just *say* you're going to change. Fine words butter no parsnips.'

'Parsnips?'

'But I don't think your personality's set,' she gave me another *look*. 'Not if you don't want it to be.'

*

While I walked home, I thought about what Mrs Harris had said about personalities setting.

Maybe that meant I wasn't completely bad. My personality couldn't be completely set. The old Fiona wouldn't have given Lewis my best pack of cards.

But then, old-me Fiona had never poked at a nest full of wasps for no reason. So if my personality was just setting, I hoped it didn't set *exactly* this week.

At bedtime, in my pyjamas, I sat on my bed reading the leaflet.

The phone rang and I heard the up-and-down of Mum talking to someone.

I kept on reading.

Do not use:
- *If you are allergic to salbutamol or the other ingredients of this medicine (listed in section 4)*
- *If you unexpectedly go into early labour or threatened abortion*

Warnings and precautions
Talk to your doctor, nurse or pharmacist before using if you have any of the following:
- *Any diseases affecting the heart or blood vessels*
- *Any infection in your lungs*
- *Overactivity of the thyroid gland*
- *Low levels of potassium in your blood*
- *Diabetes*

Dad stood in the doorway, a sheet of sandpaper in one hand. 'Can I come in?'

I put the leaflet down. 'Yes, please.'

Dad put the sandpaper down on the bed. 'You're reading your inhaler leaflet?'

I nodded.

He sighed. 'Mrs Harris has just phoned. We know she told you about Danielle's asthma.'

'Don't tell her off.'

'We won't tell her off.'

'At least I know Danielle wasn't murdered now.'

'Dear God.' There was a hiss of breath outside the room. '*Murdered*.'

Dad saw my face and frowned. 'What?'

'Mum's listening outside the door. And making snake sounds.'

'She is?' Dad turned to face the door. 'Didn't we agree you'd leave us to it, Gail?'

Through the gap at the side of the door, I saw a flash of blue. I heard Mum's footsteps go down the stairs and into the kitchen.

'Has she gone?'

I nodded.

'We didn't tell you because we didn't want you to worry. Are you worried?'

'Mrs Harris said my asthma's not as bad.'

'*Nowhere near* as bad.'

'How do you know, though?'

'Danielle had lots of other attacks. We had to go to hospital a lot. It was terrifying.' Dad stared at the worn knees of his jeans. 'But we didn't want to stop her doing fun things. We wanted her to have a normal life.'

I squeezed his hand.

'She was a kid. It felt like the right decision.' Dad kept

staring at his jeans. 'We didn't want you to be scared and we don't like talking about this.'

'Because you want to talk about Danielle's life, not her death.'

Dad smiled. 'You're a good girl, really.'

I wondered whether Danielle got *you're a good girl*, or *you're a good girl, really.*

I looked at the sandpaper on the bed. 'What's that for?'

'To get rid of the swastika,' Dad said. 'Your dad's about to do some DIY. Unless you *want* a Nazi symbol on your dressing table for ever?'

I shook my head.

He smiled. 'That's a relief.' He knelt down on the carpet and looked at the carving. 'What did you do this with anyway? Kitchen scissors?'

'Compass.'

He touched the carving. 'It's all blue.'

'I coloured it with a biro.'

'Course you did.'

Dad put the sandpaper to the dressing-table leg and started scratching. Dust puffed into the air.

After a minute or two, he sat back on his heels. Where he'd sanded, the wood was a lighter colour.

Dad looked up hopefully.

'It looks awful,' I said.

'We can stain it later.' Dad picked up the bin. 'Here, get this bin out of the way so your dad can get a better angle.'

He glanced in the bin as he passed it over. Suddenly, he stopped. He pulled the bin closer and reached inside.

I waited, but he didn't seem to be passing me the bin anymore.

I let my hand drop. 'I'm just going to read for a bit.' I got under the covers. 'I'll definitely clean my teeth before I switch the light out.'

I made myself comfy. I rearranged my pillows, punching them, getting them fluffed up right.

Dad was still there, on his knees, the bin in front of him. Not moving.

'Dad!' I waved my hand in his eyeline so he looked up. 'You don't need to do more sanding tonight. I can hardly see the bad *F*s now, anyway.'

He nodded and stood up. He had the bin in his hand – Dad always empties my bin for me, though not usually at night. I realised I'd thrown Carl's photo in there, but that was fine – I didn't need his picture anymore.

I reached for my book. 'Goodnight.'

I turned back to check he'd seen me speak, but Dad and the bin had gone. There was just the whoosh of wood across carpet and the click of the latch, as Dad shut my bedroom door behind him.

42

Bad blood isn't a real thing. Type B isn't good and type O isn't bad. You can't tell if someone's good and bad from their blood.

Fiona Larson, 7E's Blood Project

One day to the fair

The sandpaper was still on the floor when I got up the next morning. I shook my head. *Dad.* I couldn't even put it in the bin because Dad had forgotten to bring that back, too.

When I opened my bedroom door, Mum was on the phone. 'Just tonight after school, till just after seven.' Mum spoke quietly. 'I'd really appreciate it, Lisa. I've got to work till seven and Jonathan . . . Jonathan's away. For a few days.'

I frowned.

'Well – you get it. You of all people,' Mum said. 'I'm sure things will be fine, it's just complicated.'

She was talking so quietly that I was struggling to hear.

'I wouldn't ask if I wasn't super-stuck,' Mum whispered. 'I'll find a longer-term solution after tonight.' There was a pause. 'What, tonight? No, I'd completely forgotten, what with everything. Thanks so much, Lisa. I owe you.'

A moment later, Mum stood in my bedroom doorway.

'You're to go home with Lewis after school today.'

'Lewis is angry with me, though.'

Mum made a swatting motion, like there was a fly in front of her face. 'It's not up to Lewis, it's up to his mother. I'll pick you up from there before Parents' Evening tonight.'

Parents' Evening. How had I forgotten that?

But then – *fair-phone-Adrian-cigarette-porn-wasps-New Head*. That's how.

Either way, Mum hadn't remembered either. And she didn't sound happy about it.

'Why am I meant to go to Lewis's after school? Where's Dad?'

'He's gone to a conference.'

'He should have told me. When he was doing the swastika last night.'

'Yes.' Mum turned to go downstairs. 'Yes, he probably should.'

It was only mid-July, but our flash of summer was over already. The rain poured down that morning, drumming hard on my coat hood as I half ran into school.

I passed Carl, who was carrying several shirts on hangers. He hunched over to keep the shirts dry before putting them in his car.

'Carl!' I shouted.

He didn't hear me over the rain. He went straight back into his house, leaving his car boot up.

I kept walking. It was probably better to tell him about Mum and the phone some other time anyway. Some time when it wasn't raining so hard.

And I couldn't be late for school today. Not when I was in too much trouble already.

*

School news!

They found *a turd* in the corridor behind the science labs! A human turd!

It was definitely human because animals can't get in the school without people noticing. And the turd was *massive*. Like someone had been saving it up.

All day, kids who hadn't seen it had been trying to describe the size and shape. By the afternoon, it was the biggest, curliest turd that had ever been known.

The kids noticed before the teachers did so, all morning, kids kept appearing at classroom doorways, saying each other needed to be called out of lessons because *I've got an urgent message from his mum.*

Everyone says The New Head was furious because the turd was so big she thought it might be one of the teachers'. But she calmed down now she's been told this happened last year too.

I'd forgotten it happened last year. Sometimes, there are just too many school things to remember, and you can end up remembering the wrong ones.

Anyway, the turd was the talk of the school today. It was the new *Greeney's haircut*. It was the new *Fiona's wasp-face*.

I was pretty grateful to that turd actually.

'And it was *so* curly, Dr Sharma. Like a brown Mr Whippy.'

'I said you could sit here at lunchtime, Fiona.' Dr Sharma didn't even look up from her marking. 'I didn't say you could talk to me.'

Dr Sharma glanced at my face and sighed. She closed the exercise book. 'Come on, then. While you're here, show me this blood project you've been working on.'

'Dr Sharma! It's *lunchtime*!'

Dr Sharma patted the chair at her side.

I slid my blood project book out of my bag and walked up to her marking table.

Dr Sharma let the book fall open, at the page with all the bits of bloody paper.

'That's *my* blood.' I slid into the chair next to her. 'So it's fine.'

Dr Sharma hunched her eyebrows together. 'You cut yourself, Fiona? On purpose?'

'Who would cut themselves on purpose? No, I was showing you what O positive looked like. I took the opportunity when I made lots of blood with my teeth. But it was by accident.' I glanced at her. 'I didn't do it with the saw.'

Her eyebrows moved up now. 'The saw?'

'But I didn't do it with the saw,' I repeated patiently.

She just stared at the page for a moment. 'So much blood. So unnecessary.'

She turned the page, to my family blood chart.

'See?' I tapped my table. 'O positive. We've got all the different letters in my family. Mum's AB, Dad's A, Danielle was a B. But we're all positive. Dad said he's *A positive influence.*'

Dr Sharma kept looking at the page. She put her forefinger and thumb to her mouth. She pulled her bottom lip forward a millimetre.

'Exactly,' I said. 'I didn't think it was very funny either.'

There was a scream of excitement from the playground outside.

Dr Sharma took her hand away from her mouth. 'Right.' She snapped the book shut. 'I'm delighted to say you've done some good work on this project.' She held the book to her chest, arms folded over it. 'But I'm going to keep hold of this because it's actually unsanitary.'

'The blood won't spill, it's dry.'

Dr Sharma opened her top drawer and threw the book in. I saw confiscated earrings, a penknife, a Walkman. That drawer was a treasure chest. 'Dr Sharma—'

'That reminds me. You keep asking about your sister.' She slammed the drawer shut. 'What did you want to know? I taught her briefly.'

I blinked. 'You taught Danielle?'

She nodded.

'What was she like?'

'Oh, you know.' Dr Sharma leaned on her elbows. 'Like a kid.'

'What does that mean?'

'Fiona.' She gave a kind smile. 'I'm afraid none of you are that different. You all merge' – she wafted a hand – 'into one.'

'But you can't have forgotten *Danielle*. She was perfect and special.'

'I think I would have remembered if I'd ever taught a perfect kid, don't you?' Dr Sharma chuckled. 'Perfect kids. *Honestly*. What are you like?'

'But wasn't she as pretty as a picture?'

Dr Sharma raised her gaze. 'Fiona, I don't know what you think goes on in teachers' heads, but we just want to get through the day and get on with our lives. I do remember Danielle a little. Not because she was perfect, but because she died. She was polite and she did her work without a fuss.' She studied me. 'She wasn't a troublemaker. Making dramas didn't run in the family.'

'Please don't say that to Mum at Parents' Evening.'

'I think your mother knows. I got that sense when I called her in *just yesterday*.'

'Go on,' I said quickly. 'Tell me more about Danielle.'

'There's nothing else to say. She concentrated in class. She didn't cause trouble. But special?' Dr Sharma sniffed. 'She was no more or less special than any other kid I've ever taught.'

I slumped back in my chair.

'Why do you look so shocked?'

I licked my lips. 'Are you just saying that to make me happy?'

'Why *on earth* would I want to make you happy?'

There was a thud. A ball outside, hitting the wall of the lab.

'Dr Sharma, can you tell from the blood type who's good and who's bad? Is O blood the bad kind and—'

'*No!*' Dr Sharma's shout filled the room.

I stopped.

'You've just done a *whole project* on blood. I thought you'd actually learned something. Then you come out with this nonsense. Am I wasting my time? I am, aren't I?'

I wasn't sure if she wanted me to say *yes* or *no*.

She folded her arms. 'Blood just ferries oxygen round the body. That's all.'

'It fights diseases, too.'

She waved a hand. 'Yes, yes.'

'And carries oxygen and nutrients. It carries hormones—'

'Well done, Fiona.'

'And heat. It carries heat too.'

'Yes, enough, you know a lot about blood.'

'I only ask about blood types because . . . I'm wondering if I'm bad, right down. Down to my blood.'

'*Fiona!*' Dr Sharma shook her head like I was stupid. 'Blood doesn't tell you whether you're good or you're bad.

In fact – this will really blow your mind, get ready for this –
there's no such thing as good or bad.'

'O isn't bad blood?'

'What would that even mean?'

'And B blood isn't good?'

'Stop talking. I don't ever want to hear you speak of blood
types, ever again.'

I shuffled in my chair.

She walked over and opened the door. 'If I ever hear you
talking about blood types like horoscopes, I will be furious.
That reflects on me, you know? On my professional skills.
On *my teaching.*'

I picked up my school bag and stood up. I looked at her
drawer.

She looked where I was looking. 'Your project book's
confiscated.'

'Will I get it back?'

'No.'

I did a few loops of the school field for the rest of lunchtime,
and headed into my geography class.

Halfway through, the school secretary knocked on the
door. 'Is Fiona Larson in here?'

She looked around the class and spotted me. The shaky-
legged girl she'd help pick up pens and pencils in the corridor,
two days ago. The one she'd taken to the slaughter.

Not *slaughter.* You get what I mean.

'Your mum rang. She says you're to go straight home today,
after all.' The secretary glanced at her note. 'Your grandma
will be there.'

I was so relieved it was only that, I barely noticed all the
ooh, grandma! noises.

But the secretary kept looking at me. 'Also, Mrs Shackleton said to say, you must go to see her tonight. Introduce her to your parents. At Parents' Evening.'

The *ooh grandma!*s stopped.

The secretary smiled at me – like she hadn't just dropped a bomb in my lap – and left the room.

I tried my best to have a lovely time with Grandma after school. She said it was a *surprise holiday*, and that *surprise holidays are the best holidays*, and she made a big fuss of me and we baked a coconut cake while we waited for Mum to get home from work.

But, still. I couldn't forget.

The New Head.

Parents' Evening.

43

Parents' Evening is the one time kids don't comment – or
seem to notice – that you have parents.

(paradox)

One day to the fair
It's like a whole-school ceasefire. It's like when those World
War One soldiers stopped shooting and played football on
Christmas Day.

For most kids, anyway. As long as no one's mum wears
a top that's too low-cut, or calls their kid *Mr Tickles* or *my
special little man* or something. Then it's different rules again.
For that kid, the ceasefire's definitely off.

The tables in the school hall were laid out like a grim res-
taurant and I went up to table after table with Mum and
Grandma, while teachers talked about me like I wasn't even
there.

I'd got those appointments in a deliberate order, leaving
Mrs Vernal and Dr Sharma till last. Hoping the world would
end before we got there.

But the world didn't end. And, too quickly, it was time.
We sat in the waiting area in front of Mrs Vernal's desk –

and I *still* hadn't introduced Mum to the New Head.

This, I decided, was going to be worse than the wasps.

'That's the teacher?' Mum's gaze narrowed a millimetre at Mrs Vernal. 'The one who said you should use your feelings about Danielle to get better at drama?'

I tugged on her sleeve. 'Mum, please don't . . .'

Lewis walked past with his mum and dad.

'That Mr Kellett's got his head screwed on,' Mr Harris was talking to another parent, smiling, making conversation like he was playing World's Best Dad in a sitcom.

Mrs Harris saw us all. 'Hi, Larsons!'

On seeing my mum, Lewis quickly rushed round to the other side of Mr and Mrs Harris.

'Jonathan's still at a conference,' Mum said.

'Whereas Geoff's actually *here*.' Mrs Harris looked dazed. 'And asking loads of questions too. He never came to Parents' Evening when we were together. Though,' she scratched the side of her mouth, 'he *is* mainly asking about PE.' She nudged Lewis. 'It's polite to say hello, you know.'

Lewis stayed behind his mum. 'Hi.'

Mum sighed. 'Lewis, I know you told Fiona about the asthma.'

Silence.

'I'm not cross,' Mum added.

'OK,' Lewis said, still behind his mum. 'I just like standing here.'

'*Fiona Larson!*' Mrs Vernal beckoned us with a finger.

Mrs Vernal sat opposite Mum, me and Grandma, a brochure titled *Drama Brings Out Life!* on the table between us.

Mrs Vernal gave a smile that was polite on the surface, something else underneath. She left one of her special pauses.

Grandma smiled back – a proper smile, like the world was a sunny place and she had all day.

Mum folded her arms.

Mrs Vernal continued with her special pause.

Mum sighed. She shifted in her seat.

'I'm afraid to tell you, Fiona can be disruptive.'

Mum nodded. 'Tell me about it.'

'She doesn't always follow instructions.'

Mum picked up the brochure and started flicking through. 'You should have been there for primary school.'

'And the magazines—'

She kept flicking. 'We've spoken to Dr Sharma and it's been dealt with. My daughter's not exactly Hugh Hefner.' Mum turned another page of the booklet.

Mrs Vernal pressed her lips together. 'Fiona seems to have trouble integrating.'

'She does.' Mum kept flicking. 'Is that everything?'

'Well—'

'Now.' Mum threw her brochure down. 'I hear you've been telling them to become astronauts.'

Mrs Vernal gave a little laugh. 'I've just tried to help them lift their horizons.'

'You don't think they should work in farms and florists.'

'It's about opportunities. Don't we all want better for our children than we have for ourselves?'

'I just don't think it's *helpful* to be telling eleven-year-olds to expect to go into space. And please never, ever again tell my daughter to use her feelings about having a dead sister to get better at drama.' Mum stood up. 'Don't want to be late for Dr Sharma. Thank you very much for your time, Mrs Vernal.'

Grandma beamed, like Mrs Vernal had given her a present. Over-smiling, to make up for Mum.

We took a seat in Dr Sharma's waiting area. Mum stared straight ahead.

She smiled at another parent. 'Disruptive,' she muttered.

The points of the Isosceles triangle were moving quickly tonight.

I looked around for a catalyst.

'See that family, Mum?' I nodded at Naomi and her mum. 'They live in one of those massive houses on the hill. Naomi's room is massive and she has little cabinets that are stuck to the wall, like they came with the house. She has her own bathroom.'

Mum frowned. 'On sweet?'

'*Very* on sweet. It even has an extra half-toilet. And they call tea *supper* and they have it at half-seven. Sometimes eight.'

Mum looked at Naomi and her family with interest. 'I bet they do.'

'Fiona Larson!' Dr Sharma shouted.

I noticed Dr Sharma had got changed since school earlier – at least, she was wearing a special scarf. Like Mrs Vernal did.

Like Mum's funeral jacket, this felt like another bad sign.

But Mum was much nicer this time.

'Thing is, Dr Sharma,' Mum leaned forward on the table. 'She's not *exactly* Hugh Hefner.'

Dr Sharma held up a palm. 'I have no intention of discussing that tonight. I'm sure you've had a conversation with her father now.'

'They weren't his magazines.'

'I notice he's not here.'

'He's at a conference.' Mum sat up straighter. 'Nothing to

do with the magazines, don't read anything into him not—'

'The obvious aside, Fiona's done some good work for me.' Dr Sharma looked at me. 'She did a great blood project. The enthusiasm was dripping from the page.'

'I've heard her talk about that a lot,' Mum said. 'A little ghoulish, but whatever.' She turned to me. 'Can we see the final project?'

'The problem was, that book was a health hazard,' Dr Sharma said. 'It had so much human blood in it.'

Mum looked at me.

'The day with the saw,' I explained.

Grandma's smile wavered.

'And I don't think you would have felt it necessary to keep the project, Mrs Larson, if you'd seen it.' Dr Sharma crossed her arms. 'I can describe it to you, if you like. Along with all the pages of Fiona's actual blood, there was information about haemoglobin and clotting.' Dr Sharma looked across the room. 'A lot about how blood transports nutrients around the body. And a table of all the blood types in the family, which I had no interest in lingering on.' Dr Sharma smiled at someone walking past. 'But apart from all the good work, the main takeaway was that the book was full of actual human blood.' She looked back at Mum. 'I decided it was so unsanitary, I put the project in the incinerator.'

Mum looked down. 'Thank you.' She cleared her throat. 'I mean – thank you, Dr Sharma. I really appreciate it.'

Dr Sharma gave a brisk nod. 'Anytime. But, in case Fiona's forgotten, before you go . . .'

Dr Sharma looked up and waved.

I looked up.

At the New Head, *who was heading over.*

I jumped up. 'Mum, Grandma, this is Mrs Shackleton.'

Mum stood up, looking faraway.

I tugged her sleeve. 'Mum.'

'Hi! Sorry.' Mum put her best smile on for the New Head. 'Thank you for your leniency with Fiona. I can assure you she is extremely sorry. She understands how severe her punishment will be if she does – well, anything. Expect perfect behaviour from now on.'

I looked at my feet. I shuffled them a little.

The New Head smiled back. *Smiled*, like a normal person. 'Dr Sharma says it's out of character. And said that she will keep a close eye on the situation.'

Mum coughed. 'Thank you.'

'Father's not here?'

'He's at a conference.'

'Ah.'

'No, not like that. He's really at a conference.'

The New Head smiled again. 'Well, it was nice to meet you anyway.'

And Mum smiled back.

And that was all. I was *free*.

I shook my head as we walked away. Mum was nice, the New Head was nicer. *That really wasn't how I thought it would go.*

Mum glanced backwards and I followed her gaze. The New Head had walked over to Mrs Vernal. The two were talking, and looking over.

Mum stopped smiling.

I put my hand on her arm. *Don't.*

Grandma put her hand on Mum's other arm.

'I really wish Dad was here,' I said.

'So do I,' Mum said. She got her car keys out of her bag, not taking her eyes off the New Head and Mrs Vernal. 'I've never wanted him to lipread more.'

44

Trying to forget something makes you remember it more.
(paradox)

Zero days to the fair

I wasn't quite as cross with Mum when I got up early and rang the doorbell for Carl the next morning.

After all, Mum had defended me to Mrs Vernal. She had got Grandma to come down for a surprise holiday. She hadn't said anything bad to the New Head, and even told her I would behave in future – which I had mixed feelings about, actually, because that wasn't always in my control, was it?

But Mum was trying. I could tell she was trying. She was being really quiet round the house, but that was OK. Quiet was better than shouting.

So I wasn't quite as angry anymore – but, still. I was planning to tell Carl what she'd done anyway, just so he knew. In case he heard I didn't have a phone anymore, and thought I had been careless and hadn't looked after it properly.

But when I rang Carl's doorbell, there was no answer. And his car wasn't in the drive.

He must be up and out already.

Even though he never really did look like an early riser.

*

I tried not to do it. But with all my free time before school, I went the long way, to look at Festival Field.

As I walked through the village, Monkford looked different. Barer. People were bringing in their hanging baskets and their gnomes, moving their window boxes inside. The fair was coming, bringing visitors from nearby towns. And Monkford people clearly believe visitors from nearby towns steal hanging baskets.

Eventually, I reached festival field and walked up to the fence. I held the metal in front of my face, my hands like claws.

The field was *full*.

Trucks with pictures of clowns were parked up all around, mud tracks behind them on the grass. People in woolly hats unpacked the rides – talking and laughing, unboxing and clipping sections into place, like the fair was a LEGO set.

A group of men stood around smoking, but none of these men could be the Waltzer boy. Too old. Too ugly.

A smoking man adjusted his beanie. 'Anyone tested the chemical toilets?'

I turned to listen to another conversation.

'Will you be there in Hull?' another smoking man said.

But I didn't hear the answer.

Slowly, I pushed myself away from the fence.

I wasn't going to the fair now. I'd accepted that. But even knowing it wasn't for me, knowing how much it hurt, to stand there and stare – I still couldn't quite pull myself away.

I stared at the field for a long time.

*

School news!

Stu Meakin, he of the Childline dad, heard Miss Jarvis call Mr Kellett *Kev* at Parents' Evening! Mr Kellett's got a first name, and we know it, and it's *Kev!*

Poor Mr Kellett. He can't move in school without someone shouting *Kev! Kev, Kev, Kev!*

And *Kevin Kellett* – were his parents *mad?*

Also, Sean heard Liam's dad say *she can teach me history anytime* about Miss Gold. And now all the boys have decided that Miss Gold is fit.

It's changed everything. The boys can barely speak in her classes now – they look away when she asks questions and go red when she's talking to them. There's lots of talk of boys with books over their laps in her class, but I don't know if that's true. Besides, I don't mean this nastily – I like Miss Gold – but she's no Kelly from Winchester.

Despite the good school news, the day was generally awful – as it's always going to be when people are getting excited about something amazing you can't do.

'As soon as I get off the dodgems I'm going to run round and get right back on.'

'I've heard our Year Nine are gonna have a fight with Radcliffe High Year Nine by the doughnut shed.'

'Dad says he'll pay for the rides so I've got enough in my money box for four hotdogs.'

It didn't matter that Mum and Grandma were extra nice to me when I got home. It didn't matter that Grandma had made fairy cakes and we had a takeaway. It didn't matter that my face was healing a little, with the bumps going down.

Just because you want to forget something, it doesn't mean you can actually make yourself forget.

And sometimes – even if you don't want to – the more you want to forget, the more you find you're making yourself remember.

And though I promised myself I wouldn't do the Rapunzel thing, when I went to bed that night, I found myself opening my bedroom window and leaning out anyway. Taking in the bright lights reflecting off the garages over the road. The screams and the fast music. The sharp onion smell.

I breathed it in. I breathed it all in.

The fair had started.

45

The people who love you most can keep the most secrets
from you.
(paradox)

Minus one days to the fair
I got the letter the next morning.

Dear Fi,

By the time you get this, your Parents' Evening will be over. I'm sure you had good reports from all your teachers and I'm so sorry I didn't get to hear them. I went to a conference, then Uncle Jim had an emergency and he needed me to come over and help.

I'm sorry I left without talking to you. At the times we're not dealing with his emergency, I'm having a lovely catch up with Uncle Jim. We've been talking about the antics we got up to at school when we were your age, and we've been lounging on sofas in his attic, drinking beer. His children have left home now, so Jim's converted Nick's bedroom into a space just for him and his records. It's like a palace up there. You'd love it.

It's times like this I am really sad we can't talk on the phone.
See you soon.
Loads of love,
Dad x

I folded the letter and slid it back into the envelope.

Dad had never been gone for more than a couple of days before.

A conference, and he hadn't said goodbye.

A conference – then straight to Uncle Jim's for an emergency?

I traced Dad's writing on the envelope. Something wasn't right.

I felt something big, like a plum, in my throat.

Mum was working, so I found Grandma was on her knees at the rockery by the front door, weeding. She liked *making herself useful*. She always said *it doesn't suit me, being a guest*. Along with *it's dangerous to lean back on your chair* and *you need to leave that tea towel to air, darling, or it'll go musty*.

'Grandma. Has Dad left us?'

Grandma wiped her forehead with her hand. 'What's that, darling?'

'Has Dad moved out?'

She took her time. 'Of course not.'

'Where is he, then?'

Grandma gave a little laugh. 'Are you the Spanish Inquisition? Am I going to get the rack?'

I shook my head. I can tell when people are lying to me.

'Shall I ask Mum?'

'No! Honestly, darling, he's at a conference.'

Something was going on. And they weren't going to tell me.

I crept about the house all weekend, trying to listen to Mum and Grandma, putting the radio on in my bedroom to pretend I was in there.

On Sunday morning, Grandma came out of the spare room with an armful of washing. She stopped when she saw me on the landing carpet, peeking through the crack.

'Fiona!' She put a hand to her heart. 'You'll be the death of me, darling. You nearly gave me a heart attack.'

She chuckled to herself and walked on, still carrying the pile of clothes.

On Sunday night – *bingo*.

Mum and Grandma were washing up together while I crouched outside, underneath the window. I had my radio on in my bedroom as a decoy.

'Can we talk? Where are those little ears?' Grandma said.

'Upstairs,' Mum said. 'Be careful, though.'

'Have you heard from . . . you know?' Grandma kept her voice low. 'Has he been in touch?'

He. Dad.

'No,' Mum said. 'I hope he got the message when I spoke to him. He acts like he's the good guy – but he can't exactly pretend to be the good guy with Fiona's best interests at heart anymore, can he?'

I moved from a crouch to a sit. But Dad *was* a good guy. Of course he had my best interests at heart.

'What was I *ever* thinking of, Mum?'

'That doesn't matter now. The important thing is, is he staying away?' Grandma asked.

I frowned. *Grandma!*

'I think so,' Mum said. 'I don't think he meant to start anything. He just – didn't think.'

Something was big in my throat. I couldn't breathe properly.

'But you're still not going to tell her.'

'Don't look at me like that,' Mum said. 'I am going to tell her one day. Just not yet.'

I looked at my shoes uncertainly.

'He's completely irresponsible,' Mum continued. 'A sob story about a marriage gone wrong and, what? He thinks he can come back and mess things up for everyone, walk back in, just walk into Fiona's life like there's been a *vacancy*, and—'

'Mum, please!' I jumped up and ran into the kitchen. 'Don't say your marriage has gone wrong. Of course Dad can come back!'

Mum stared at me, frozen in her washing-up gloves. The soap suds from the plate she was holding dripped into the sink.

Grandma looked afraid. Like it was a brown bear that had rushed through that back door.

'*Please* let Dad come back. He can't live somewhere else, he's not like Lewis's dad. This is where he belongs!'

The plate slipped from Mum's hand, into the washing-up water.

'I don't care what Dad's done.' I felt my eyes wetting. 'Just let him come back. *Please!*'

Grandma put her hand on Mum's arm.

'WHY ARE YOU LISTENING AT WINDOWS?' Mum screamed.

'BECAUSE YOU NEVER TELL ME ANYTHING!' I screamed back.

'Gail. It's OK.' Grandma squeezed Mum's arm. 'Calm down, Gail. Think about it.' Grandma rubbed Mum's arm in quick hard strokes. 'It's OK, don't say anymore. Just *think*, darling.'

Mum closed her eyes. Still in her washing-up gloves, she

put one thumb and forefinger on her closed eyelids.

Grandma took a step forward. 'Your dad is just taking a few days to himself. That's all.'

'Fiona.' Mum opened her eyes. 'Your dad and I have had a row. Married people argue all the time. Your dad will come back and everything will be OK.' She reached for my hand.

I squeezed her fingers through the wet rubber of the washing-up glove. 'You promise?'

'I promise, Fiona.' Mum squeezed my hand so hard it hurt. 'Dad will come back, then you'll stop listening at doorways to things you don't understand, and then I promise, *promise*, everything will be OK. And go and get me your spy book. *Now*. Because, Mum,' she turned sharply to Grandma, 'that's the final straw. She's left the radio on upstairs while she's listening, out there, and *where do you think she got that idea?* I'm binning that book. I still can't believe you actually bought it, for a *child – what were you thinking of?*'

46

I know more about the fair than people who actually went.
(paradox)

Minus three days to the fair
School news! Was about the fair. Obviously.
   I tried to avoid hearing about it.
   It was *everywhere* on Monday morning.

<u>The Fair This Year</u>

1) There aren't as many *dodgem* cars as last year
2) It's *actually impossible* to get a basketball through any
   of the oval hoops
3) No one knows where the ghost train has gone
4) The amazing boy still works on the Waltzers
5) The field is mushy and turning into mud soup
6) The hotdog buns are *too* warm and crispy
7) There are still a few turquoise owls, but it's mainly pink
   panthers. Though they're not properly pink, they're
   orangey. Pink(ish) panthers.
8) The rides aren't as much fun in the rain, the droplets
   hammer on your face like bullets

9) The fair finishes tonight
10) It sounds amazing

I was crossing the playground at lunchtime, trying to find somewhere to go, when I heard, 'Wait! Fi!'

I turned to see Sean running after me.

'There's a rumour going around that you've split up with Lewis.'

'Is there?' I shrugged. 'OK.'

Sean shoved his hands in his pockets. 'I didn't tell anyone it was never true in the first place.'

'You keep our secrets now? Makes a change.'

He licked his lips. 'It was good for Lewis. You can tell, the lads are letting him play football now. Even though he's shit.' He fell into step next to me. 'But I was just wondering.' He coughed. 'Seeing as Lewis isn't speaking to you and doesn't seem that grateful.'

I slowed.

'Would you mind being *my* pretend girlfriend instead?' Sean couldn't look me in the eye. 'And it would be *really* good' – a blush crept up his neck – 'if you'd let me tell the lads I've touched your bra.'

More school news!

In between all the *(cough) Kev!*-s, in Mr Kellett's class, we found out he's not the only teacher leaving school at the end of the year. The New Head is leaving, too!

Mr Kellett looked scared when he saw our surprised faces. 'Has no one told you?'

'*You* have now, sir!' Greeney said cheerfully.

'Oh, God.' Mr Kellett sat back on his desk. 'Maybe I'm not meant to have told you. I'm sure everyone knows.'

He ran a hand through his hair. 'They *must* do.'

'Is this why Miss Jarvis is saying *hello* and *what a lovely day it is* and smiling at us all in the corridors?' Greeney said.

'Of course not.' He paused. 'And I'm sure she isn't acting any different.'

'She definitely is,' someone said quietly.

'Has the New Head been sacked?' Katie Russell asked.

'No! She's very ambitious, this was only a stopgap for her. She's moving on up, to a school with better prospects.' Mr Kellett paused. 'Though this school has great prospects, of course. And, before you ask, I've not been sacked either. Like I said, my partner's got a new job in Glasgow.'

'No one would sack you, sir.'

Greeney realised what he'd said and went red. He did an extra loud cough and *'Kevin Kellett!'* to make up for it.

'Everyone's leaving,' Zara said. 'Mademoiselle Brun left too.'

'She was a student teacher, she just went to a different rotation.'

Mademoiselle Brun! I sat back. I hadn't thought about her in ages.

I wondered if she still wanted to be a teacher, after all. Or whether the food fight had put her off.

'So don't be losing any sleep this summer, kids.' Mr Kellett opened his copy of *The Taming of the Shrew.* 'I'm sure there will still be enough teachers left to educate you all.'

I waited till the other kids had gone before I went up to Mr Kellett.

'Fiona.' Mr Kellett sat on the edge of the teacher's desk. 'Good to see your face is healing.'

'Is Mrs Vernal leaving?' I asked hopefully. 'She's friends with the New Head.'

He smiled. 'No. No, it doesn't work like that.'

'Dr Sharma?'

He shook his head again. 'The rest of the teachers will still be here in September.'

I squidged my mouth to the side. 'Oh. OK.'

He smiled politely. 'Is there something else?'

'I wanted to ask you a word thing again, if that's OK? Seeing as you were so helpful last time.' I zipped *The Taming of The Shrew* into my rucksack and took a breath. 'Mr Kellett, who is *Hugh Hefner*?'

On the walk home, I thought about what Mr Kellett told me, imagining how it would feel to live in my dressing gown in a house with loads of girls like Kelly from Winchester.

I let myself in and stopped.

Dad was at the peninsula with Mum, mugs of tea in front of them.

I dropped my rucksack and rushed over to hug him. I pressed my cheek to his chest.

I felt his arms, tight around me, and his heart, beating quickly. He smelt of a different deodorant than usual – of washing-up liquid mixed with the sea.

I looked up so he could see my lips. 'Are you back?'

'I am.' He smiled. 'I'm so sorry I missed your Parents' Evening.'

'It's not like Lewis's dad?'

'It's not like that at all.'

'Your father and I have been talking.' Mum picked up her mug. 'Everything is OK now.'

Dad nodded. 'Promise.'

'Has Grandma gone?'

Mum gave a half-smile. 'Your grandma's gone to Keep Fit at the leisure centre. She's going to stay around tonight, so the two of you can say goodbye.'

'And,' Dad picked up a big book from the side, 'I bought you this.'

He handed the book to me. It was *heavy*.

A Comprehensive History of the Balkans by P.T.R. Cavendish. I stared at it. 'Thanks.'

'Come on.' Dad stood up. 'Let's go for a walk, Fi, just you and me.'

We walked through the park, past the second-biggest bush.

Dad slowed, looking at the tennis courts.

I tugged on his sleeve. 'You always stare at the tennis courts when we come to the park.'

'Do I?'

'That's where you taught Danielle to serve. She had a strong forehand, but you especially helped her with her backhand. And making sure she used the whole of the court.'

Dad looked at the ground. 'We talk about her too much.'

'Yes. But it's OK.' I don't know why I said that.

We walked through the park and the fields, then down by the brook.

Dad sat by a silver birch tree, legs sticking out. 'Sit with me.'

I did.

'Your face is looking better. You haven't disturbed any more wasps while I've been away?'

'No,' I said quietly.

'How about bees' nests? Lions? Sharks?'

I shook my head. I scratched a piece of the silver birch's skin and peeled it down. The strip narrowed to nothing and jumped into a spiral, like a ribbon curled with scissors.

'I had to go away.' I could feel Dad watching me. 'And it was nothing to do with you.'

I concentrated on my peeling. 'Did you really go to Uncle Jim's?'

'I did, for one night. But I spent most of the time at a hotel. I was cross with your mum.'

'What did she do?'

'She was worried about something and she didn't tell me.'

'Was it about me being given . . . a something?' I'd worked it out. It took me a while.

Dad nodded. 'She thought I'd be upset about a strange man giving you a phone, so she didn't tell me. Which really hurt me. Me and your mother shouldn't have secrets. We promised ourselves a long time ago that we'd never have secrets again.'

'Does the strange man know I don't have the phone anymore?'

Dad paused. 'Yes. I went to see him, to explain that he shouldn't be giving little girls presents. And he understood.'

'What's strange about Carl, Dad?'

'Nothing, he's just a stranger, that's all.' Dad made a funny half-smile. 'That's the whole point – he's absolutely no one.'

I picked up all the peelings from the ground and rested them on one palm. 'Who was in the wrong, then? You or Mum?'

'I said we're OK now, Fiona.'

I made my voice quieter. 'Mum told everyone you were at a conference.'

'Sometimes you don't have to tell people everything.'

'Like you and Mum didn't tell me about Danielle's asthma.'

Dad sighed. 'We're your parents, Fi. It's our job to work out what to tell you when.'

I shook my head and kept peeling.

'Did you want to know Father Christmas didn't exist when you were three?'

I stopped peeling instantly and clenched *everything*. The fact I *ever* believed those icing sugar footsteps were made by a herd of reindeer trotting through our lounge made me want to run, just *run*, as fast as I could – just to get away from the thought of *stupid young stupid STUPID Fiona*.

'But you've told me everything now,' I said. 'And you won't ever lie to me again.'

Dad looked across the field. 'Something's hovering. Is it a kestrel?'

I nearly looked. 'Promise me, Dad.'

Dad crossed one leg over the other. 'Are you a grown-up, Fiona? Do you pay for your own food and clothes? Do you drive a car and vote for a government and go to work and earn money?'

'You know I don't.' My voice was tiny.

'Do you remember when you wanted to stay up and watch that film about the clown? And we said you wouldn't like it, so you pretended to go to bed, but watched it in our bedroom instead?'

I flushed. I concentrated on peeling. 'No.'

'Do you remember you had to sleep in our bed for weeks? That you kept picturing that scary clown and the blood in the bathroom?'

I stopped peeling for a second. 'Please never tell anyone from school.'

'We made the decision long ago, that we would tell you about Danielle's asthma when you were thirteen, and not before.'

I looked down at the peelings in the lap of my school skirt. 'But I'm nearly twelve and I'm fine. You were wrong.'

Dad leaned further back on his hands, not taking his eyes off me. 'We made a judgement.'

'What age will I know everything?'

Dad laughed. 'I'm fifty-two. I still don't know everything.'

'Dad.'

He looked at me and sighed. 'You know pretty much all there is to know. The *Comprehensive History of the Balkans* has got nothing on you. But eighteen's a good age, isn't it?'

Eighteen. Would I ever, *really*, be eighteen? That was older than even Selina Baker. That was Kelly from Winchester age.

I'd be so tall at eighteen. I'd have had a massive growth spurt and overtaken everyone. I'd wear a bra every day. I'd wear shoes with heels and no straps. I'd have long straight hair that I could flick behind my shoulders, like Kelly's. I'd drive everywhere – but in a car like a boy's, without stuffed toys in the hatchback. I'd drive past lads in the street, poking my cigarette out of the window to flick ash while they watched.

Dad was still talking.

'Say that again,' I said. 'I wasn't listening.'

'I said, if there was anything we were keeping from you, we'd tell you at eighteen. And that's a promise.'

I thought about this. 'But you aren't keeping any secrets from me now?'

Dad gave me a big smile. He pulled me in for a hug.

'You know I'm a good spy. I find out in the end,' I said. 'Always.'

I felt Dad go stiff for a second.

Then he went softer. 'Then it's a good thing,' he said into my shoulder, 'that we don't have any secrets. Isn't it?'

After our walk, Dad let us back into the house.

Mum came into the lounge straight away, smiling at me. 'What did she say?'

'I haven't told her yet.'

I looked from one to the other. 'Haven't told her what yet?'

'Two things.' Dad glanced at Mum and back. 'Your mum and I have been talking . . . a lot. And we think it might be a good time to move house. Get a new house.'

I tried to take this in.

'Still in Monkford,' Dad said.

I *still* tried to take this in. *A new house.*

The words didn't make sense.

'To live in.' Dad frowned. 'Fi?'

I got it. 'A *new* house?'

Dad nodded.

'No promises,' Mum said. 'We're just going to start looking. It's expensive to move, there's estate agent fees and stamp duty. And the prices removals companies charge' – she shook her head – 'are actually *criminal.*'

'Can I have the second-biggest bedroom?'

'We don't know what the house is, so we can't answer that question.' Mum rearranged the clip in her hair. 'Depends on the layout, where the light is, which room has the best view. And it isn't definitely happening yet.'

'But you won't have to save a bedroom for Danielle?'

Dad went to speak, but Mum interrupted him.

'No,' she said. 'We won't have to save a bedroom.'

'You can save her the third-biggest room, if you want.'

Mum was looking sad, so I tried to cheer her up. 'And if we're moving, that means you don't have to paint the hallway anymore, doesn't it?'

'No.' Mum sighed and leaned against the wall. 'I'm afraid, Fiona, this time, it means we *definitely* have to paint the hallway.'

She and Dad made eye contact.

'This weekend,' Mum said.

Dad nodded hard, like nodding would make it happen.

They turned back to me.

Dad coughed. 'So that was the first bit of good news.'

I nodded.

'And,' Dad made his voice bright. 'The other news is that we've taken in what you said. That you really *really* want to go to this fair.'

I held my breath. *No.*

I raised my head slowly to look at him. *It can't be.*

'We've spoken about it' – Dad looked at Mum – 'at length – and your mum and I don't think we can go.'

'But I could go on my own?' I said hopefully.

Mum gave a faint smile. 'Your grandma's going to take you. After tea, when she's back from Keep Fit.'

'I'm going to the fair?' I shrieked.

'Though please don't tell us about it afterwards. It has very bad memories for us.' Mum rubbed her upper arms. 'I'm sorry, love.'

'I won't tell you anything. However good it is. I'll just keep it quiet.'

Dad gave a little smile. 'I'm not sure you'll manage.'

'And I haven't got any money.'

'We'll sort that. As long as you promise not to come back with a goldfish,' Mum said. 'Tell your grandma I said that.

Remind her if you start hooking ducks and she gets one of her ideas. *Massive stuffed toys* – fine. *Living things* – not fine.' Mum took a breath. 'Tell her, Fiona, and I'll tell her too, because there's *no way*' – Mum folded her arms, furious with Grandma in advance – 'that I am going out at ten on a Monday night to buy a bloody fish tank.'

47

Sometimes I get so happy it makes me sad.
(paradox)

Minus three days to the fair
I always knew what I was going to wear if I ever got to go to the fair, so I didn't need time to decide. I ran upstairs and got straight into my best jeans and denim jacket.

I took my trainers into the bathroom and cleaned them with wet toilet roll.

I put the front of my hair into a knot and put my dolphin chain round my neck. I smeared raspberry lip balm on and pressed my lips together. I slipped the pot into my pocket.

I came back downstairs casually and sat in the lounge, where Mum, Dad and Grandma were watching the weather.

My family glanced at me and smiled at each other. And no one said anything.

It was still light when Grandma and I walked to the fair.

We passed a woman, hand-in-hand with a toddler. The toddler was carrying one of last year's turquoise owls rather than a pinkish panther, but I supposed the kid was too young to know any better.

'Do you want me to come onto the rides with you?' Grandma asked. 'Or would you prefer I just watch?'

'Maybe just watch? Sorry.' The boy wouldn't push my car on the Waltzers if that car had an old lady inside. Even if the old lady was as great as my grandma, it just wouldn't happen.

The whooping and music got louder as we got closer to festival field. The sweet and sour mix of bitter onions and candyfloss filled the air.

A man shouted through a tinny speaker. *'Place your bets! Donkey derby is ready to go!'*

Grandma grinned. 'You're holding your breath. Try to breathe, darling. It's more fun if you breathe.'

I concentrated. *In and out. In and out.* My chest felt wrong, like it had Lewis sitting on it.

We turned the corner, onto the main road. I reached for Grandma's hand.

Across the road, festival field – the place of slippy leaves and dog mess, the place I'd practised cartwheels, where older kids practised drinking – was *transformed.*

Hundreds of people moved around behind the barriers. A big wheel carried cars into the sky, its shape outlined in white lights. A hut called *Games Shack* glowed with lights, all zigzagging and changing colour.

I took a step forward.

Grandma squeezed my hand. 'Careful. The road.'

The music was so loud now, it made my heart throb. Underneath the song, 'Blooded Face' by Knives of Pain, there was a continuous whirr, like someone was hoovering the field with a giant vacuum cleaner.

We crossed the road and slipped between the barriers. The floating onion and candyfloss smell was stronger still.

Just – *magical.* It was all magical.

We walked through all the people, past the hook-a-duck tent and the shooting range. Selina Baker passed by, carrying a pinkish panther. It was so neon bright it was almost orange, with skinny arms that whipped and dangled.

And even though I'm too old for stuffed toys, she was *Selina Baker*. 'Can we get a pink panther, Grandma? Mum only mentioned not getting a goldfish, she didn't say anything about a panther.'

'Only if we can find one to buy,' Grandma said. 'The games are all rigged.'

'Grandma!'

I looked closer at one pinkish panther, hanging sadly next to its friends in the front of the 'test your strength' stall, in what looked like a mass panther crucifixion. On closer look, the kids at school were right. The panther was too orange to be *the* pink panther. And the snout was too long.

Still. There was no way I was leaving tonight without one.

In front of the stall, a huge dad, his arms criss-crossed with sticking-out veins like ropes, raised a hammer and smashed it down on the metal button.

The red marker on the thermometer went a third of the way up, past *featherlight* to *weedy*.

'See?' Grandma grinned at me. 'Rigged.'

I frowned. 'It can't be. Not *the fair*.'

Grandma waved in the direction of the claw machines. 'Ever seen anyone win on one of those?'

I blinked. 'No, Grandma. I've never been to the fair. Haven't you been listening? That's the point of me.'

I looked up at the cars of the big wheel. I stilled.

Grandma looked at me softly. 'Breathe, darling.'

That made me think of Danielle. Of Danielle, at the fair, not breathing.

I looked at Grandma. She couldn't have realised what she'd said, so I tried to smile.

But I looked around me, at all the people. Wondering. When *Danielle* happened, did the Waltzers stop? Did the hot dog turning machine keep going, or did someone switch it off? Were people still going on rides all around Danielle, while she was on the grass? When the ambulance came?

I shivered a little.

You have a different kind of asthma.

There was a chant of kids behind me – *'fight, fight, fight'*. I turned to look, and—

Lewis.

Not fighting, obviously. Just watching. He stood with his hands in his pockets, hitching up the bottom of his fake leather jacket so you could see a skirt of yellow football shirt.

I swallowed and walked up to him. 'I like your Tottenham shirt.'

'My dad got it for me.'

'I guessed that.'

Lewis glanced at Grandma and back. 'You were allowed to come in the end, then.'

I nodded. I looked up at Lewis's mum. 'Hi, Mrs Harris.'

'Hi, Fiona.' Mrs Harris was eating candyfloss, though candyfloss is for kids. 'Why don't you two go on a ride? Me and Helen' – she waved a hand at Grandma – 'can go and buy a very expensive coffee.'

Lewis looked at his feet.

'Lewis.' I'd never heard Mrs Harris's voice so *harsh*. 'You don't want to keep going on rides with me. I'm your *mother*, for God's sake.'

'We'll still be able to see you, mind,' Grandma said, 'so don't be putting any of your parents' hard-earned cash in that claw machine, Fiona. I will negotiate a good price for a panther later.'

They walked away. A kid I knew from primary school walked past, mouth open wide as he jammed a hot dog in, but Lewis and I didn't say hello. This kid was the year below, still at primary school. *And* he had tomato ketchup and onion trails down his T-shirt.

I turned to Lewis. 'Shall we do the Waltzers? Maybe?'

'Waltzers sounds good.'

We walked past two Year Eight kids, kissing under the tree. They kissed hard, lots of bobbling head movement going on.

Twelve other kids, separated into boys and girls, stood nearby. Still, and silently watching.

'I know they're Year Eight and amazing,' I said. 'But I just think it would look better if the boys and girls stood together.'

'Other people aren't as good as we are.' Lewis smiled. 'I think the boys like me more now, you know.'

'I knew it! It's because of the girlfriend thing. Honestly, Lewis, I did you a favour.'

'It's not because of you. It's because of *me*. My mum says you should be yourself and then everyone will like you.'

I gave that the biggest eye roll. 'Lewis—'

'Don't say my mum's stupid again.'

'I don't want to, do I? I *like* your mum. But then she goes around saying stuff like that. Look!' I pointed. 'Sea witches!'

I pointed to the three girls who had been mean to me in the toilets that time. But now, they looked scared, the two smaller ones hanging back. The main sea witch was getting picked on by an *even bigger* sea witch. A Queen Ursula.

I shook my head. 'The circle of life.'

I looked down. At nearly twelve, I *really* needed to stop saying things from Disney cartoons.

We reached the Waltzers queue. The cars were spinning so fast you couldn't see the people's faces. A boy in a baseball cap skipped across the platforms, spinning the cars faster. *The boy with the money pouch* that I'd heard so much about.

He stood tall suddenly and looked out at the queue, feet apart, keeping his balance on the moving platform. A disco ball threw colours across his face, over his cheekbones and eyebrows. The way he stood over us, the colours bouncing off him – he was lit up like a hero.

And I got it.

I could barely look at him, he was so perfect.

We shuffled forward in the queue, 'Blooded Face' playing again.

The reaper will take you, take everyone you love
And we are all alone at the last.

It was now my favourite song, and it was going to be my favourite song for ever.

'I'm not saying you're my girlfriend anymore,' Lewis folded his arms. 'I don't want people thinking I'm a fake.'

'Fine.' I glanced at him. 'Except do you still say you support Tottenham?'

'That's different,' Lewis said quickly.

'I know, course it is,' I said, even faster.

'And *Spurs*,' he said. 'I have to call them *Spurs*.'

'Spurs,' I said. 'Right.'

'I'm so unlucky though.' He kicked out at the barrier. 'Spurs are playing Stoke away in a testimonial next week. Dad's made Mum change our Saturdays so we can go. The ticket's an early birthday present, and I've got to go and watch the game instead of going to my cousin's party. And it's a swimming party. *And* he's getting one of those big floating things.'

Lewis looked so sad, I couldn't help laughing.

And then he started laughing, too.

And we just stood there in the queue, pushing each other, our eyes watering, like it was the funniest thing we'd ever heard. I couldn't catch my breath, and nor could Lewis, because he started hiccupping – and then he looked like he was in actual hiccupping pain, and it got funnier still. And even *Lewis* found it funny as he went all Tiny Tim again, and his hiccup turned into a croak. And it wasn't even *that* funny. It was just that we were friends again.

Lewis made a sign for me to hit him on the back, eyes streaming. Still smiling.

'Hi, Fiona!' Selina Baker walked past, grinning. 'Enjoying the fair?'

Instantly, Lewis stopped croaking.

I beamed at her. 'It's amazing!' My smile faded a little. As well as the pinkish panther in her arms, she now had one of last year's turquoise owls with her. *Didn't she know?*

She waved her pinkish panther's paw at me. '*I'm so pweased you're enjoying the fwair, Fwi-ow-na.*' Selina moved the panther's mouth along with the words.

My smile faded completely now.

Lewis and I looked at each other.

'*My name's Mwister Pink,*' she continued. '*Like in the film.*'

She lifted her owl's wing. I realised it was about to be the owl's turn to speak.

I shook my head.

She lowered the toys.

If I was the best girl in school, I'd definitely be better at it than *this*.

'I've been meaning to say, Fiona. You were asking about

my job? There are some jobs going in the stables now, if you want me to put a word in?'

'No thanks. Selina, this is my friend, Lewis.'

She grinned. 'Hi, Lewis.'

When Lewis couldn't say anything, she smiled at him and walked away.

He hit my arm with the back of his hand. '*Selina Baker* said my name!' He paused. 'It would have been better if she hadn't done the panther baby talk, but still. What's that about a stables?'

'Girl's job. Cleaning up horse muck. *Unpaid*. At *seventeen*.'

Lewis shook his head.

We moved forward in the queue. I saw Jodie outside the Sweet Shack with her group of girls. Their sugar dummies glowed red under the lights.

Jodie saw me and handed her dummy to Naomi. She ran over.

'I *told* them you were friends with Selina Baker!' Jodie looked from me to Lewis. 'Are you two back together?'

Lewis found his voice. 'Definitely not.'

'We're just good friends,' I said.

She nodded. 'I didn't think you'd be cheating on Sean Anderton. Look,' Jodie glanced back, 'Alison's thinking we might need to make the group bigger again soon. She thinks it might be better for ice-skating and stuff. Though she fancies Sean, so it could be weird.'

'I'll dump him, then,' I said.

'Really?'

I shrugged. 'Why not?'

'Sweet.' Jodie scratched her cheek. 'Though Alison *was* thinking of fancying Clark now. He'll get his brother's paper round when his brother starts work at the petrol station.'

I nodded. 'I'll dump Sean anyway, though. Just in case.'

'You're getting much better at girl stuff.' Jodie looked at the queue. 'Is there room for me in your Waltzer car?'

We nodded. Jodie crouched under the barrier and got in the queue with us, just as the boy with the money pouch came over to lift the barrier.

We scrambled into the car and pulled the metal bar down over us.

We all handed the boy our pound coins. It went quiet, for a second. Then that song started again. 'Blooded Face'.

I felt the vibration start under my feet. I looked beyond to the big wheel and all the lights and the people.

And I knew, right then, that this was about to be the best time I would ever have.

I held my breath as I felt the car start to move. I sat up straighter, grabbed the metal bar, and waited for the boy to spin us.

He didn't spin us. Of *course* he didn't.

I could blame Lewis for being a boy. But it probably wasn't *all* Lewis's fault. The car the boy span instead had four girls in it – all sixth-formers, in black eye make-up and purplish lipstick. They were grown-up height, with long brown legs in cut-off denim shorts, and tops so low you could see the rise of their boobs under long necklaces.

And I didn't really have time to mind about the spinning. My head was too busy trying to stop jerking as it was.

As the ride slowed to a stop, the boy with the money pouch helped the older girls out of their car. Taking their hands, like they were old ladies or something.

'Maybe he'll push us next year,' Jodie said. 'We might have boobs by then.'

I looked at the older girls, smiling and chatting with him. And I knew I wasn't going to look like those girls next year. Or the year after that. Or even the year after *that*.

'Maybe.' I turned to Jodie. 'But we can definitely wear more make-up.'

It was late when I got home that night but, still, I dug through the songs I'd recorded off the radio till I found 'Blooded Face'. I played it in my bedroom, over and over.

*We will all die, and decay into dust
And no one will care about my blooded face.*

I sat in my pyjamas on my bed, my knees to my chest. I hugged my pinkish panther, breathing in the vinegary smell of the fur. I threw one skinny panther arm over my shoulder and cried and cried into its neck.

Mum came rushing into my room. 'What's wrong?'

I didn't answer. I couldn't.

Mum approached the bed. 'Shush, Fi.' She held me. 'It's OK. It's all OK.'

I kept sobbing, harder and harder.

Mum stroked my hair. 'I wouldn't have let you go to the fair if I'd known it would make you this upset.'

'It's not the fair's fault,' I said between shudders. 'And I'm not upset.'

Mum just kept stroking my hair.

Dad came in. 'Hey now, love.' He sat on the bed. 'This'll distract you. They've just said on the telly Radovan Karadžić's resigned. He's been indicted for war crimes.' Dad scratched his cheek. '*Indicted* means – well, I don't know exactly what *indicted* means. It's like arrested, I think. Bad, anyway.'

I pressed my face into the sodden fur and cried more.

It was over. The fair was all over.

The best thing in my life. *Over.*

I would never, *ever* be this happy again.

Mum and Dad didn't tell me to go to sleep. And Dad didn't talk any more about Radovan Karadžić. They just let me sob into the panther, letting all the tears stream out.

And I just cried and cried, not even knowing why I was crying. Just listening to 'Blooded Face' and smelling my panther and sobbing till it hurt. Sometimes gasping, sometimes spluttering. Knowing nothing I ever did – no moment in time – would ever be that perfect again.

48

Not all presents are good.

(paradox)

Three hundred and sixty-one days to the fair
'Fi!' Dad shouted up the stairs the next morning. 'It's nearly eight o'clock!'

Then Dad was in my room – I don't know how long later – pulling my duvet off me.

'You can't be late on your last day of term!' He dumped the duvet on the floor. 'Now where do you want this? You left it downstairs.'

He gestured with a book. A big book. *A Comprehensive History of the Balkans* by P.T.R. Cavendish.

I pointed to the spot on the bookshelf next to Grandma's long-legged owl, in what was becoming The Corner of Wrong Presents. 'There's fine.'

I really needed to start doing and saying stuff, I decided, that I actually liked. No more football. No more Balkans. Definitely no more wasps.

'And look!' Dad waved a letter at me. 'The best news! How clever is your old dad?'

Dear Mr Larson,

Thank you for your application for Quiz Bounce, the fastest finger first game with all the bells and whistles!

We are delighted to tell you that you have made it through our initial sift, and we would like to invite you to a live audition on 1 August at . . .

I licked my lips. 'That's great.' I tried to sound like I meant it. 'Well done.'

Dad nodded happily and folded his letter. 'I'm going to write and accept straight away. You can come to the audition, if you like.'

'Thanks.'

'And now, you have to say goodbye to your grandma because she's going home today.'

'I'm so tired.'

'Was it worth it, though?' Dad asked.

The Waltzers, the lights, the pinkish panther.

'It was worth it.'

Dad hurried out of the room, and I got dressed quickly in the same jeans and T-shirt as last night. My best clothes, for 'out of school uniform' day on the last day of term.

A moment later, I heard a drawer slam. 'Bloody hell, Gail, again! Where are all the effing stamps, *again*?'

I said goodbye to Grandma in the lounge.

'Thank you for taking me yesterday.' I glanced at Mum and Dad and lowered my voice. 'To . . . you know.'

Grandma kissed my cheek. 'It was a pleasure.'

'My spies tell me you and Lewis went on the Waltzers together,' Mum said.

I looked up at her. 'Do you think that means he's forgiven me?'

'I expect so.'

'Do you think that means he'll be waiting for me to walk to school?'

Mum made a wafting motion with her hands. 'Maybe go there and find out?'

I grabbed my bag and my pinkish panther and ran to the lamppost.

I checked my watch. 8.20. Still loads of time for Lewis to arrive.

I looked at the house over the road.

Carl's car wasn't there. The house was dark, all the curtains drawn. Now I thought about it, his car hadn't been on the drive for a while. A bit of white leaflet had been peeking out of the letterbox for a few days, from where the postman hadn't put it all the way through. The estate agent's sign on the front lawn had an extra red banner across it. *Sold.*

I waited some more. I checked my watch. 8.26.

A few doors down, a woman was putting her window boxes and hanging baskets back outside, now it was just Monkford people in Monkford again.

I stared down the road. Still no sign of Lewis.

I looked at my watch. 8.28.

I took one last look down the road.

At 8.30 I put my bag on my shoulder and, with heavy feet, turned towards school.

In that morning's lesson, Dr Sharma didn't put an end-of-term video on like the other teachers. She wanted to punish us with learning, right up to the end, so she made us give presentations about our science projects. All the while she was telling us, kids piped up.

'*Did you* scarf *down your breakfast, Dr Sharma?*'

'*Are you* shawl *you want us to read out our science projects?*'
Cough. '*Scarf!*'

Dr Sharma had been walking away for this last one. She turned slowly on the spot.

The Cough, '*Scarf!*'-er, Liam, gulped.

'Why are you saying *scarf* to me, Liam?'

Liam looked from left to right, desperate.

'I'm waiting.'

He swallowed again.

'Shall I help you out? Is it because I wore a scarf at Parents' Evening? When I don't normally wear one?'

He was perfectly still. Then he gave a little nod.

She nodded too. 'And that's funny . . . how?'

He found his voice. 'I can't explain.'

'But it's definitely funny?'

'I'm not sure . . . I don't think it is anymore.'

'No?' Dr Sharma said. 'Have I ruined it? Well, that's a shame.' She turned to the class. 'Next project presentation.' She looked at her register. 'Amy Barton. You're up.'

'She's not in. She's got a sick gran.'

'A sick gran?' Dr Sharma shook her head. 'Poor effort. I will make a note to ask Amy's parents in September what date they went on holiday.' She looked back at her register. 'Mark Cutter.'

Mark stood up and went to the front. He coughed. 'Now. What *is* photosynthesis?'

Other kids went up to the front of the class, one by one.

Turned out pretty much *all* the other kids had done their projects on photosynthesis.

Dr Sharma sat at the front, marking other classes' exercise books.

I tried not to think about Lewis because it made a lump come in my throat. I wrote a list instead.

Things at the Fair That Weren't Quite as Good as I Thought They'd Be

1) The donkeys on the donkey derby wobble
2) The hotdog buns *are* too warm and crispy
3) The sugar dummies cost two whole pounds
4) The toys are really bad. The stitching's going on my pink panther's shoulder. And it smells of vinegar. And if I hold it for too long it makes my skirt stick to my legs.
5) The dodgems hurt your neck when someone drives into you
6) If you *go* on the Waltzers three times in a row, you feel sick. And not *good* sick. *Bad* sick.
7) The Waltzer boy isn't *that* great, and he looks pretty old, close up
8) Under the onions and candyfloss, the field smells of toilet
9) The mud ruined my best trainers

I'm *definitely* still going next year.

I closed my book of lists as Andrew Lane walked back to his desk.

Dr Sharma looked up. 'Fiona Larson!'

I went to stand at the front. I placed my hands together, like the vicar did in church.

'I did my project on blood.' My arms felt weird, like I had too many. 'I did loads of good stuff, but you'll have to take my word for it. I can't show you my project book because Dr Sharma stole it.'

There was a ripple of interest round the lab.

'I *said*, the book was unsanitary.' Dr Sharma leaned onto her elbows. 'Fiona decided to make hers a practical project. She put a substantial amount of her own blood in there.'

Someone muttered, *'Freak.'*

I fidgeted. 'It wasn't what it sounds like. And I made the blood with my teeth, not the saw.'

'Not the saw.' Dr Sharma drew a tick with a flourish. 'Still not going to ask *why not the saw.'*

'There are lots of different types of blood,' I said to the class. 'And you have white blood cells and red blood cells. And plasma. But mainly, I've learned that blood doesn't matter that much.'

Dr Sharma looked up. 'Doesn't matter that much?'

'I mean, blood groups don't make much difference – unless you're having an operation, they don't matter. Blood just ferries oxygen round the body. There are no good and or bad blood groups.'

Dr Sharma nodded. 'No horoscopes.'

'No horoscopes. Blood groups only . . .' I stopped. Something made me stop, and I tried to work out what it was. The thought was fluttering round my brain now, like a moth, and before I could catch it—

'Yes, yes.' Dr Sharma looked up sharply. 'And what is plasma, Fiona?'

I sighed. I'd been having a science thought; she should have been happy. 'Plasma is a light-yellow liquid. It carries water, salt and enzymes. It—'

Dr Sharma kept nodding, and made me go on for ages. Even though she hadn't asked anyone else any questions.

'Great. Good project, well done. Sit down.' She looked at her book. 'Michael Green.'

Greeney got up and I walked back to my seat.

'Now.' Greeney rocked forward on his feet. 'What *is* chlorophyll?'

At lunchtime I headed onto the school field. I walked a big loop, feeling the sun on my face. Being on my own was OK.

I would make friends with a girl group next year. I'd do it properly. I could learn to be different these summer holidays – learn to be someone else. I'd get a denim jacket in exactly the right shade of blue. I'd get a new rucksack for my birthday. I'd start drinking my milk skimmed and stop eating lunch. I'd—

A shout from faraway. 'Fi!'

I looked round.

Lewis sat, legs crossed, in the middle of the field, on a spread-out blanket. The blanket was loaded with some kind of picnic. Plates of cake and sausage rolls. A cool box. Some lumpy bits covered with a tea towel.

He pointed at the empty plate on his blanket. 'For you!'

I ran over. 'What's going on?'

'I asked Mr Kellett if I could bring a picnic in for the last day of school, and he said it was fine as long as I gave money to charity. Mum drove me in.'

'That's why you weren't at the lamppost this morning? I thought you were still cross with me!'

'What?' Lewis laughed. 'We made up last night, didn't we? And I couldn't exactly carry all this stuff in on my own.'

My throat was full. Too much feeling.

'You're going to sit down?'

I nodded.

I took my seat on the picnic blanket, tucking my feet underneath me. I didn't even notice the other kids crowding round us at first. Then, when I did notice, I tried not to.

Lewis opened the cool box. 'Lilt?' He handed me a can. 'Thanks.'

I looked up, at the crowds gathering round us. Quickly, I stared down at my can.

'Help yourself to cake and stuff.' Lewis opened the cool box again and pulled out an ice-cream lolly. 'Mini-milk?'

I took it. 'Don't mind if I do.'

Lewis opened his can. He took a sip. 'Aaah!'

He put his can on the blanket beside him, and got his sunglasses out of his rucksack.

Sunglasses on, he laid his head back and closed his eyes. 'This is the life.'

I unwrapped my lolly and nodded.

'Hi, Lewis.'

There were murmurs in the crowd.

Lewis looked at me and back. *'Selina Baker!'* His voice was a squeak.

'This looks fun!' Selina nodded to my lolly. 'You got any more of those?'

Lewis coughed. 'Strawberry or chocolate?'

Selina smiled. 'Chocolate.'

'May I?' And then Selina sank down and *sat cross-legged on the picnic blanket.*

And then *her friend Rachel did the same.*

Lewis handed them both lollies, as the crowds gathered and whispered. Around Lewis Harris and his weird picnic.

'I told you Fi Larson was friends with Selina Baker.' Jodie's voice.

'I got a pinkish panther at the fair. Like yours, Selina.' I looked at the picnic blanket. 'Though this one definitely doesn't talk.'

She smiled and bit into her lolly. 'Cool! So, are you two a couple?'

We both *pah*-ed.

'Just good friends,' Lewis said.

'That's so great.' Selina stretched her legs out. 'It's nice you're so comfortable with the opposite sex in Year Seven. I definitely wasn't that mature at your age.'

Rachel caught her eye. 'I'm not sure some of the boys we know are that mature *now*.'

The crowd was getting bigger. It felt like *the whole school* was watching. And, for once, that was a good thing.

Lewis picked up a plate and offered Selina some chocolate cake.

'Thanks, Lewis.' Selina took a slice – I didn't ask why she wasn't on a diet. She turned to Rachel. 'This is lovely, isn't it?'

Rachel took a slice of cake. 'Heaven. Maybe you'll start a new school trend with this, Lewis? This can be a Monkford High last-day-of-term ritual now, and *you* started it!'

Lewis looked at me, mouth open with joy.

And maybe, because everything was a bit too perfect, I should have been on my guard. Because we were sitting there, with the best sixth-form girls, and everyone was looking at us, and Lewis was so pleased with himself that—

'Selina,' Lewis pulled some fabric out of the cool box, 'tell me, what do you think when you hear the word *mnemonic*?'

'Lewis!' I jumped up, eyes wide. 'NO!'

I was too late.

Lewis was standing up now. Face flushed with pride, he whipped the tea towel off the lumpy bits on the picnic blanket. Under the tea towel, a tray was loaded with items – a notepad, a candlestick, a thimble, and a hundred other awful Lewis-y guessing things.

There was a ripple in the crowd.

I couldn't even look.

'Oh my God, is that a cape?'

My heart was – hurting.

'You know what?' Selina got up. 'I'd better...' She pointed into the distance. 'Rach?'

'Yeah.' Rachel got up too. 'Thanks for the food.'

I watched them walk away.

Jodie shrugged. She mouthed *see you soon,* and headed back to her group.

The noises of the crowd were different now.

'Who brings in a picnic blanket? To school?'

'Trust Magic man.'

Cough. *'Lewis Harris went to Paris.'*

Cough. *'Gail Larson, Driving Instructor.'*

The crowd started moving away.

Lewis turned to me, tea towel drooping from one hand. His cape drooped from the other.

'Well, you ruined that,' I said. 'I hope you're proud of yourself.'

He put the cape and tea towel slowly into the cool box.

He clipped it shut and started smiling again, just a little. He sat back on the blanket. I closed my eyes, feeling the warmth on my face.

'This is nice,' he said.

I nodded. As long as I kept my eyes closed, I couldn't see anyone looking at us.

'Can I show *you* my memory game, Fi?'

I opened one eye and looked at the tea tray. At the thermometer. The box of matches. The special roleplay-game dice.

I glanced at the kids on the field, some still glancing over.

I *really* hoped everyone would have forgotten this by September.

'OK.' I turned to face him. 'But you can't wear the cape. And *please*, Lewis,' I glanced around, 'please, *please* be quick.'

49

**People say blood is thicker than water because blood is a
non-Newtonian fluid. This means it has flow properties that
depend on conditions. Blood becomes less viscous under
pressure so it can flow in narrow capillaries.**
So does ketchup.
And this is why filmmakers use ketchup for blood.

Fiona Larson, 7E's Blood Project

Still three hundred and sixty-one days to the fair
Afternoon school news!

Miss Gold joined Miss Jarvis's GCSE class for the last RE
class of the year. The two teachers put out a special Jewish
Shabbat meal.

They sang hymns and lit candles and had blessings over
bread, then had stew and salads. No cake or anything. It was
meant to be a treat for the kids, but it didn't sound *that* great.

But it wasn't like Mademoiselle Brun's pâté-falling-down-
the-Eiffel-Tower food fight. This time, *loads* of teachers were
there, and they made sure they got there ten minutes early.

When the kids arrived, there were teachers all standing
around like bouncers, like the RE room was a prison cafe-
teria. The teachers all had arms folded and hard faces, glaring

at the kids, and no one dared throw as much as a crumb of bread.

And the other bit of school news happened in the last class of the year.

Like Dr Sharma, Mr Kellett didn't put on an end-of-term video. Instead, he made us read out 'What I'm Doing This Summer', the kind of thing I'd really hoped we'd left behind when we left primary school.

The other kids talked about holidays to France, and caravan parks in the Lake District, and cousins who could drive. Naomi even talked about a trip to Disneyworld in Florida.

When it was my turn, I talked about the trip to the hotel in Wales, and going to the American diner for my birthday.

I saved the best for last. '*And* we're moving house. I'm going to get the second-biggest bedroom.'

There were nods of respect at that.

'Not definitely, but probably. Mum says it depends on the layout and the light and stuff. But we won't have to save a room for a dead girl anymore.' At the awkward faces, I waved a hand. 'Sorry. Didn't mean to use my catalyst.'

After I said my bit, a few more kids went up, talking about trips to Benidorm and Crete. About grandmas in Cornwall and caravans in the Peak District.

Mr Kellett sat on his teacher's desk, listening.

When everyone had finished, he said, 'That all sounds excellent.' He picked up his pad. 'Now, my turn. What I'm Doing This Summer.'

(Cough) 'Kev!'

(Cough) 'Kevin Kellett!'

He smiled and bent his head to read. 'This summer, I'm moving house, and will be setting up a new home in Glasgow.'

He paused. 'I'm really sad to leave this school, but my partner's got a job at a teaching hospital there. He's a consultant in cardiology. I'm excited about the move, though I'm sure the kids in my new school won't be as much fun as you lot. But I'm hoping I'll get less stick about Leeds United.'

He looked up and smiled.

No one smiled back.

We must have misheard.

'Your partner's a consultant?' Greeney said carefully.

Mr Kellett made eye contact with Greeney. 'Yes. David's a consultant in cardiology.'

A pause. A ripple round the room. *David!*

But only a few kids said it. The rest of us just stared.

'But you teach *football*, sir.' Liam explained Mr Kellett to himself. 'You support *Leeds*. You were semi-pro.'

'I'm well aware of that, Liam.' Mr Kellett's voice was clipped, but he smiled kindly.

And then Mr Kellett looked down at his pad and read some more about his summer, about how he was going to walk up a mountain in the Lake District, like the massive thing hadn't just happened.

There were no more *(cough)* '*Kev!*'s after that.

I waited after class. 'Mr Kellett—'

'Fiona. It's that time again, is it? Who are you going to ask about now?' He gave a patient smile. 'Larry Flynt?'

'I just wanted to say, *well played*, sir.' I nodded in respect. 'You hid it well.'

'No.' He sat up straighter. 'No, Fiona, that's not what happened here. I didn't hide—'

There was a cough from the doorway.

'We meet again, Fiona.' The school secretary nodded at me.

No.

'Mrs Shackleton and Dr Sharma need to see you.'

No, no, no.

Behind the school secretary, Lewis's face appeared in the corridor, his eyes wide with panic.

'I'll wait for you,' he said.

My legs had gone wobbly. 'You don't have to.'

'I'll help Mum put the picnic stuff in the car and then I'll wait for you.'

'Hurry up, Fiona.' The school secretary stood back from the doorway to let me through. 'Term's over. No time for being Romeo and Juliet.'

I turned back to Mr Kellett. 'Bye, sir.'

'Bye, Fiona. I hope, whatever they want with you, it's not *too* bad.'

I left the room.

With one last, scared glance at Lewis, I followed the school secretary down the corridor. Past kids, screeching through the hallways, throwing pens. Swapping phone numbers. Tearing their shirts off, writing on each other's in biro.

The school secretary pretended not to notice. 'Fiona, I hope I won't be meeting you like this quite so much next year.'

'I hope so too,' I whispered.

She waved me straight into the New Head's office.

I knocked anyway to slow things down.

'Enter!'

I took a breath, and made myself go in.

On the other side of the big desk, the New Head and Dr Sharma were waiting.

But, this time, there was nowhere for me to sit. The chair opposite was full. As full as a chair could be – if the kid in it was trying to make himself really small.

A Year Nine kid. *Chin Rash Skittle Breath.*

On the table between them – *Razzle.*

I looked up at the New Head and Dr Sharma. 'I'm not exactly Hugh Hefner.'

The New Head indicated the magazine. 'Jordan said he bought this from you at the car boot sale.'

I swallowed.

'*Did* he get it from you?'

They looked serious, but the teachers weren't shouting, just asking. And it hit me.

I'd already been in trouble for this. I was *safe.*

I was about to say *I don't grass,* but Chin Rash Skittle Breath looked at me and shrugged.

I turned back to the teachers. 'He bought it from me at the car boot sale.'

'Thanks, Fiona.' The New Head didn't sound thankful. 'You can go.'

I hurried out of the room, my legs working better by the second.

Lewis rushed up to me. 'Was it OK?'

'They had *Razzle.* But it was Chin Rash Skittle Breath they wanted, not me.'

Lewis nodded.

'Thanks for waiting.'

'Of course.'

'Would you have waited for me if you'd had to go in?'

'No way.'

'Fair enough.'

We walked through the empty school corridors. The noise of kids outside sounded faint and far away now.

At the computer room, we stopped and read the sign on the door.

Reopens in autumn term, when the school will be freshly con-nected to the World Wide Web!

'That's what they're calling the new wiring,' Lewis said.

I shrugged. 'They try to make things sound more exciting than they are. Don't get your hopes up, Lewis.'

'Wait!' Sean scurried up to us. 'Some of the blue estate lads took my PE kit. Mum would have battered me, but I found it in the end. In the big bins outside the canteen. I washed the gunk off, it's good as new.'

His voice was so loud in the quiet corridor.

'It's like we've got the run of the place.' Sean looked around. 'We *will* run the place next year, of course. When we're Year Eight. Those little Year Sevens won't know what's hit them. And we'll be thirteen, finally. We'll have paper rounds and everything.'

I kicked a drinks can. *Thirteen!* The can skittered away and down the stairs.

I hadn't even caught up with twelve yet.

'Are you two coming out for my birthday in August?' I said.

Sean nodded. 'Your boyfriend has to come out for your birthday.'

'Oh Sean, I forgot. You're dumped.'

'Did I get to touch your bra first?'

'You did.'

'And I can still come out for your birthday?'

'Yep. And you can come to the house, too.' I paused. 'Though I should tell you, the lights flash when the doorbell goes because my dad's hearing-impaired. Deaf.' I folded my arms. 'He's too good at reading faces, so don't bother trying to lie to him, and he can lipread when everyone's swearing in the football – even in other languages. As long as it's German.'

'Really?' Sean's face was all bright. 'Why didn't you tell us *that* when Euro '96 was on?'

I shrugged.

'We'll be watching the Olympics round at yours, then, this summer, Fi?'

'No way.'

On the way home, I made the boys go the long way around, past festival field. The three of us walked slowly up to the metal fence. We stood in silence.

The field was empty.

Not *quite* empty. Abandoned drinks cans glinted in the sun. In the distance, a grey-haired woman threw a ball for an energetic border collie.

But there were no trucks. No crowds, no lights. No throbbing music. No big wheel or Waltzers, or men in beanie hats.

No fair.

I let all the air puff out of my body. 'But it was *just here!*'

In the centre of the field – where the rides and crowds had been busiest – there was no green to see, only mud. Round the edges, the grass had been flattened, or churned up with tyre tracks. Just a few green untouched patches remained, showing what the field had been like before.

Lewis gave me a small smile. 'The fair will be back.'

I felt something brush past my leg. A plastic popcorn wrapper. 'Not for ages though.'

I watched the wrapper flutter and spin, over the road, under a car. I looked back at the field.

'Come on.' Lewis pulled lightly at my rucksack strap. 'It won't come back any quicker just for staring.'

We turned to walk home. The sky was changing, I noticed. Darkening.

'My dad told me something that will cheer you up, Fi,' Sean said.

Lewis and I looked at each other.

'Go on,' I said carefully.

'My dad told me there's a place in the East, by the sea, where all the fairs from all of Europe all join up, every October.'

We turned the corner into George Street.

'One big fair in every direction, as far as the eye can see,' Sean said. 'Loads of dodgems, big wheels. Waltzers and popcorn stands everywhere you look.'

Lewis raised his eyebrow. 'A magical place. In the *East*. By the *sea*,' he repeated.

We shook heads at each other, smiling.

'No, not like that! I promise! This time it's *actually true*!'

Lewis leaned on the postbox. 'What's this magical place in the East by the sea called?'

Sean stood up straighter. 'It's *real* and it's called *Hull*!'

'Hull?' Lewis's voice was scornful. 'What kind of place—'

I put my hand on his sleeve. 'Hull.' I remembered the fair workers talking. *Will you be there in Hull?*

Hull. The place in the East, by the sea.

'Lewis.' I clung tightly onto his sleeve. 'We're going to Hull.'

'You can't listen to *Sean*, Fi. He talks rubbish! He said an axeman lived *there*, remember?' Lewis jerked his thumb. 'Flipflops, in with the bananas, ring a bell?'

I looked over at the house.

There were two new cars in the drive now, Carl's car nowhere to be seen. A tower of empty cardboard boxes sat next to the front door. There were lights on in several rooms, and two kids' bikes were propped up under the front-room window.

Sean looked at the house. 'The axeman thing was a joke though. Surely you can take a joke?'

I noticed the sky felt blacker still as we all crossed the road.

I shivered. I mouthed the word to myself. *Hull.*

A woman came out of the front door of Carl's house wearing slippers, a black bag in her hand. Through the open door, I heard the sound of a Hoover going.

It started to rain. One drip, on its own, then three. Then – all at once – *whoosh.*

Too late, Lewis, Sean and I all pulled up our anorak hoods.

The boys each held up a hand in *goodbye,* and rushed off in the direction of their houses.

I took one last look at 56 George Street, staring for a second, but my face got so splattered, I couldn't look for long.

I hitched my rucksack further up my shoulder and tugged my hood forward. Hard bullets of rain drummed the top of my head as I started to move, then jogged faster still, until I was sprinting around the corner of George Street with my arms and legs flying, running at full pelt towards the safety of home.

CREDITS

Caroline Hulse and Orion Fiction would like to thank everyone at Orion who worked on the publication of *All the Fun of the Fair* in the UK. Special thanks to Ava Fouracre Gildersleve.

Editorial
Emad Akhtar
Lucy Frederick
Celia Killen

Copy editor
Clare Wallis

Proof reader
Marian Reid

Contracts
Anne Goddard
Paul Bulos
Jake Alderson

Production
Ruth Sharvell

Design
Debbie Holmes
Joanna Ridley
Nick May

Editorial Management
Charlie Panayiotou
Jane Hughes
Alice Davis

Finance
Jasdip Nandra
Afeera Ahmed
Elizabeth Beaumont
Sue Baker

Marketing
Helena Fouracre

If you loved *All the Fun Of The Fair*, don't miss Caroline Hulse's hilarious and heartwarming debut novel . . .

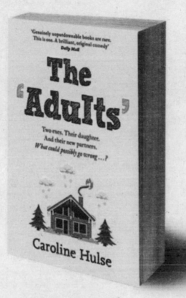

Two exes. Their daughter.

And their new partners.

What could possibly go wrong ...?

'Funny, dry and beautifully observed. Highly recommended for anyone whose perfect Christmases never quite go according to plan!'

Gill Sims, author of *Why Mummy Drinks*

Another achingly funny, uncomfortably relatable novel from Caroline Hulse . . .

Stella and George are getting divorced.

But first, Stella's mum is throwing a murder mystery party.

All Stella and George have to do is make it through the day without their break-up being discovered – though it will soon turn out that having secrets runs in the family . . .

'Part Fleabag, part Agatha Christie, Like A House On Fire *is everything I love in a book . . . I was hooked from page one.'*

Josie Silver, bestselling author of
One Day in December